LISA HELEN GRAY

LANDON

A NEXT GENERATION CARTER BROTHER NOVEL
BOOK THREE

FAMILY TREE

(AGES ARE SUBJECTED TO CHANGE THROUGHOUT BOOKS)

Maverick & Teagan

- Faith engaged to Beau

-Lily

-Mark

-Aiden

Mason & Denny

-Hope

-Ciara

-Ashton

Malik & Harlow

-Maddison (Twin 1)

-Maddox (Twin 2)

-Trent

Max & Lake

-Landon (M) (Triplet 1)

-Hayden (F) (Triplet 2)

-Liam (M) (Triplet 3)

Myles & Kayla

-Charlotte

-Jacob

Evan (Denny's brother) & Kennedy

-Imogen

-Joshua

LANDON

ONE

PAISLEY

TODAY HAD BEEN A TRYING DAY. Not only had I woken up with high glucose levels, my vision blurry, and feeling tired and worn out, but the Family of the Year competition had taken place at Noah's park.

The family day, organised by the town's council and other organisations, could have been a day to take my mind off my illness. However, my brothers used the potentially fun-filled day to compete with the Carter family, making the whole event stressful.

Personally, I think their rivalry is a load of crock. If they got their heads out of their arses for five minutes, they'd see they have a lot in common.

Smothering female members of their families, being one.

Wyatt, one of my eldest brothers, snaps at the nurse to be careful. I sigh, giving the nurse an apologetic look.

"Don't give her those sorry eyes. She nearly took my eye out," he growls at me.

Today didn't end up well for anybody. Bailey, a sweet girl I had met at Family of the Year, who was dating Aiden Carter, was badly beaten. Four girls had kept me from helping her—not that I would have been much help. With my glucose levels rising, I'd needed my insulin, so I was already feeling weak when the girls cornered us.

Now, Bailey is upstairs, heading into surgery. Seven of my brothers are in the waiting room, in possession of evidence that will send the girls away for a very long time.

I clutch my stomach, still feeling sick over the bits I heard them talking about when they thought I was out of earshot.

Wyatt, my only brother not in the waiting room, is being treated for a watermelon incident. He had been part of a competition to see who could put the most elastic bands on their watermelon before it exploded. A group of women on the side-lines—according to Ashton—distracted him, so he missed his chance to duck before it exploded, and bits of the melon and its seeds got into his eyes. They were inflamed, red, and looked irritated.

"You don't need to be so rude," I whisper-hiss, glancing at the nurse briefly. Her shoulders shake with silent laughter. Not that I blame her. Wyatt has been a grouch since he walked in, hating the fact they wouldn't let him come with me until they treated his eye.

"Whatever. This shit stings. Is it done?" he asks the nurse sharply.

"Won't be long," she tells him softly, amusement in her tone.

I smile inwardly. I like her. Anyone who doesn't take crap from my brothers, I like. They tend to intimidate everyone around them.

Placing a hand on his shoulder, I nudge him, forcing him to glance away from the nurse's behind. "I came to see if you were heading home or going upstairs to waiting room and joining the rest of them."

I don't dare tell him I'm leaving because then he'd feel inclined to come with me. And I need a breather. They've been smothering me far too much lately, and I just want some freedom. They don't think I can take care of myself, and I admit, there have been times in the past when I've forgotten to check my levels or take my insulin. But none of it was ever intentional. I genuinely lost track of time. But with my brothers, you'd think I did it on purpose and, therefore, needed to be put on suicide watch—so to speak.

They took over the role of guardian when our dad died in a boating accident. He had left for a stag weekend with his long-time friend, Larry. The fishing trip took a turn for the worse, and only one out of eight men survived that day.

Our mum was a little lost for the first few years after he died, so my eldest brother, Jaxon, raised me. I had only been ten at the time and was struggling to cope with the loss; so, they stepped up. I'll always be grateful to them for it. I loved my dad, was a complete daddy's girl.

When my mum got better, their protective instincts didn't lessen any. They just got worse as I grew older and began to develop.

"I'm going to head up. Did you want to grab something to eat before we do?" he asks, rubbing my arm.

"I already ate and all my tests are perfect. I was fine not long after having my injection," I tell him.

"Reid said he had to give you a higher dosage," he tells me, something I already know.

"I don't want to talk about this," I tell him grumpily.

He grins, then hisses when the nurse runs a cotton swab along the bottom of his eye.

I inwardly smile. I shouldn't enjoy it, but it's bringing me satisfaction to see him act like a baby.

"I'm gonna head upstairs. Those Carter's are unpredictable. It will be worse if they're grieving."

I scoff. "She's not dead, Wyatt. And don't you always say they're predictable and that's why they can never beat you?"

He watches me for a moment, reading me. "If I didn't know any better, I'd say you were sticking up for them. You know we don't like them."

"Doesn't mean I have to dislike them," I argue, feeling myself getting worked up.

"Which one do you like?" he asks sharply, trying to sit up.

I roll my eyes and push him back down on the bed. "Just let the nurse do her job. I just came by to tell you I'm leaving."

He relaxes back into the bed. "Good. That means you won't be around them. Are the twins going with you?"

My youngest siblings are both mentally challenging. They have such high IQ's, their teachers didn't know what to do with them when they were at school. They also can't sit still, always needing something to do—mostly getting into trouble since living like normal people bores them to death.

My shoulders slump. I should have brought them with me. Knowing the twins, they'll impersonate doctors and treat someone, or worse, try to operate on each other.

It wouldn't be the first time they've wandered off and caused mayhem at a hospital. They've had plenty of chances to get imaginative with the amount of times I've spent inside one.

"No. My taxi will be here soon. Mum is waiting for me," I explain. The taxi isn't booked, but if I tell him that, he'll wait with me, and I just want to go home.

"You can't go alone," he starts to refuse.

"I love that you care, but I just want to get back. And you're right, it was getting pretty heated upstairs before I left," I half lie. It had started to get heated upstairs, but there were people there who had it under control.

My body warms as I think of Landon Carter. He and my brothers got into it upstairs, but it soon calmed down.

Before Wyatt can answer, I lean down and kiss his cheek. "See you at home," I call over my shoulder, waving.

"Paisley, wait!" he yells, but the nurse shoves him back down on the bed. "Paisley?"

I ignore his calls and skip down the hall with a satisfied smile on my face.

My mind wanders back to Landon Carter, the guy who had been my crush for so many years it was a joke. After years of watching, of being envious of his ex-girlfriend, my crush turned into love.

My heart races a mile a minute whenever I see him, and my stomach flutters with butterflies. He's all I ever think about.

His silent treatment towards outsiders—and by outsiders, I mean anyone who isn't his family—is legendary. He can scare grown men into running away with just his stare and silence. But to me, his silence is deafening. When I look at him, I see anguish and pain. I see a guy who's inwardly screaming for someone to help him.

He had always been quiet, kept to himself. But after his girlfriend died, he changed. There's a solid wall of rage behind those beautiful chocolate eyes, and so much pain it can choke you.

There have been times I've seen them dim, all of them whenever he's been with his cousin, Charlotte Carter. The bubbly woman can bring light to anyone's darkness. Her soul shines bright upon the world.

Still, I get jealous. My crush on Landon has been my secret. Not even my best friend, Adam, knows, and we share everything.

Sometimes it feels like Landon sees me, too. Other times, he looks right through me. But in those moments he does see me, I feel so many emotions I become dizzy with them and end up making a fool out of myself. It's why I keep mostly quiet around him, happy to just observe the fine specimen he is.

Walking outside, the sun is beginning to set. I need to ring a taxi. If we didn't live in the middle of nowhere, I would walk. But the farm is at least a fifteen-minute drive.

Looking down at my phone, I'm about to call for a taxi when a cloud of smoke blows into my face.

I cough, waving the smoke out of my eyes, and gasp at who I come face to face with.

"Landon," I greet, my voice raspy. I'm surprised to see him smoking. I didn't think any of his family did.

His dark eyes run over me with appraisal, making a shiver run down my spine. With just that one look, he could ask for anything he wanted from me and I'd happily give it to him.

I swallow past the lump in my throat. He has a round face with high cheekbones, a shadow of hair on his jaw, and the most amazing lips I've ever laid eyes on. They're plump, the lower slightly fuller than the top.

His biceps bulge against the short-sleeved, black T-shirt he's wearing, and I know underneath he has washboard abs. I've seen this guy play sports with no shirt on. I've even seen him down at the lagoon in just his swimming trunks. His body is hard all over.

"Paisley," he drawls, glancing behind me. Surprise flickers across his expression before he wipes it. "No entourage with you?"

"I'm not always with my brothers, you know," I fire back.

He grins. "What has you out here? Were you looking for me?"

God, his voice is sexy, deep, lazy… I shake myself out of it.

"No. I'm heading home. Just about to call a taxi."

"You won't get one at this time. It's a Saturday night." I grumble a curse under my breath. I don't want to go back upstairs to my brothers. I just want to go home. "Come on. I'll give you a lift."

He wraps his meaty hand around my bicep and pulls me towards the carpark. Once the shock of him touching me wears off, I pull my arm back. "I didn't agree to that."

He stops, turning to give me a pointed stare. "Did you want to go run back to your brothers and ask for a lift home?"

I narrow my eyes. He's goading me. *Why?* I can't figure that out. This is the most I've ever heard him talk. And I've known him most of my life.

"Just show me where your car is," I mutter, giving in.

And the only reason I'm giving in is because it's Landon. If not to spend the fifteen minutes alone with him, then to stare at him whilst he drives.

He leads me over to a black BMW. I'm not at all surprised by the colour. For some reason, it suits him.

I hadn't expected him to open the door for me, so when he does, I begin to swoon. I can feel my cheeks heating and quickly duck into the car before he sees. For once, I want Landon to see the real me. Not the naïve girl who blushes and runs when she's spoken to.

I rub my hands up and down my arms. The air has gotten cooler and goose-bumps rise on my arms. I shouldn't have worn a dress but it's one of my favourites. It doesn't make me feel confined like my jeans and tops do. Not that I'd give up my jeans, hell to the no. But sometimes, I just like wearing comfortable clothes.

"You cold?" he asks, no emotion in his expression.

"I'll be fine. It's not too far away."

He grunts, reaching into the back and pulling out a hoodie. He passes it over to me, not even glancing at me once as he continues to start the car.

I pull the hoodie over my head, sniffing in his scent as I do—a woodsy, spicy smell. I love it.

Not wanting him to know I'm being creepy by sniffing his jumper, I push my head and arms through and pull it down my body.

It swamps me.

I try to take sneaky glances at him, but he must feel my gaze because he turns towards me with a knowing smirk.

"I'm surprised your brothers let you leave. Don't they have a tracker on you?" he muses.

I roll my eyes. "You aren't any less protective of the females in your family," I point out.

He grunts, not denying or admitting it. "Are you going to let them rule your life forever?"

I shift in my seat so I'm facing him. "Look, I get you have this rival thing going on with my brothers, but don't pretend to think you know them. You don't."

He gives me a sideways glance, his eyebrow raised. "Is that right? Your brothers don't let you have a life. Hell, you even work for them. Isn't there anything *you* want to do? Aren't you bored of being good little Paisley? Don't you want to let your hair down, just once?"

Not liking his tone, I grip the door handle. "Stop the car."

His grin turns into a snarl. "You don't like me pointing out the truth?"

"No, what I don't like is you thinking you know me." It hurts to hear he sees me as a boring, submissive girl and not as the woman I am. Yeah, I might not have an extremely interesting life, but I'm still a person.

He pulls the car over to the side of the road. Thankfully, it's a deserted one that rarely gets any traffic down it. I don't even care that I'm still feeling a little weak and tired. Walking the five minutes back home will be worth getting away from him.

He shuts the car off before glancing in my direction, leaning into my space. My breath hitches and I suck on my bottom lip.

He tucks a strand of hair behind my ear, and my eyes close briefly. "Paisley, I'm not insulting you."

"Yes, you are. I know I'm boring, Landon. I know I'm nothing like the other girls who hang on your arm," I tell him, hating the times I've seen them all over him. "But I'm still a person."

Come to think of it, I don't think I've ever seen him kiss a girl other than his ex-girlfriend. It doesn't mean he hasn't slept with them though.

His gaze bores into me. "Thank fuck. I can't be around them for more than two minutes. You, Paisley Hayes, are different."

My cheeks heat at his comment, but I choose to ignore it and instead tease him, hoping it will deflect is compliment. "Two minutes? You don't last long, then."

Lust and the dark promise of something naughty passes across his expression. "Trust me, I last a lot longer than two minutes," he rasps, running his finger lightly across my jaw. "But I don't fuck virgins."

I blink, wondering if I heard him right. "I'm not a virgin," I blurt out.

How did this conversation do a full one-eighty?

His jaw tightens, and his eyes narrow into slits. "Who the fuck touched you?"

Ignoring the anger in his tone, I pat him on his chest, even though I'm a wreck inside. I've longed for this moment; to have him look at me as more than an annoying insect or passing over me all together. This isn't something I'm going to pass up.

I want him. I always have.

"Adam, my best friend. When we were in school, I wanted to know what it felt like, and he wanted to know if he was gay," I explain, ignoring the hardening around his eyes. "After the third time, we concluded he was gay, and that sex isn't everything." I shrug like it's no big deal. And it isn't. I didn't lose my virginity to some random stranger or someone who would leave my life in the future. I had sex with my best friend.

My brothers suffocated me to the point I was scared I'd be a thirty-year-old virgin. So Adam and I made a pact, and after, we never spoke of it again. Another motivation behind my pact with Adam was I knew the only person I truly wanted to be with didn't want me. He had a girlfriend who he so obviously loved and adored, to the point I knew he would never look at another girl, let alone me, and want a relationship of any kind.

After, well, I had come to terms with the fact he would never look twice at a girl like me. It was a mixture of things. Firstly, was because after his girlfriend died, he became more withdrawn from everyone around him. I noticed girls would try to get his attention, and he'd never give it. And those girls were drop-dead-gorgeous. Then there was me. I was a Hayes. I wore tatty clothes because I was forever helping Mum on the farm, and I wasn't social. I was content with that.

"You've never fucked a *man*," he states, leaning closer. The seatbelt unclipping and loosening at my waist makes me inwardly jump, but I daren't show him a reaction.

"What are you doing?" I ask, trying to keep the nerves out of my voice.

He rakes his eyes all over my face, a small smirk lifting his lips. "I want you. One time. No promises—no forever. Just tonight."

"What?" I gasp out, wondering, once again, if I heard him right.

"I know you want me, too," he says, his voice low and full of sex.

I clench my thighs together and lift my chin up at him. "I may have had a crush on you in school, Landon, but I don't have one now. It might come as a surprise to your ego, but not every girl will spread her legs for you."

I'm lying. He knows it; I know it. But he seems to like the challenge—if his expression is anything to go by.

He leans in closer, his hand snaking around my waist to pull me closer to him. My breath hitches as I rest my hands on his bulging biceps.

"You're wet; I can smell your arousal from here," he says, then brings his nose to my jaw, making his way to my ear. Need builds inside me, and I drop my head against his shoulder, turning to liquid at his words.

"W-what?" I whisper weakly, needing the relief so badly.

A squeal escapes my lips when he lifts me from my seat and over onto his lap. He leans down, his face pressing against my breasts, and then we're moving. The chair slides back, giving me more room to straddle him, and my dress hitches higher up my thighs. When the seat is as far back as it will go, I press down on him. I moan, becoming delirious as I feel his hardness pressing against me.

He feels big.

"Tell me you want me, Paisley. I won't touch you until you do," he rasps out.

All my feelings for him build up in that moment and explode. I throw myself at him, grabbing his face and bringing his lips to mine. Our teeth and tongues clash together, but I don't let it stop me, kissing him with urgency.

Moaning, I roll my hips down onto his lap. He growls, his hands running up my thighs, under his hoodie. He lifts my dress until it's bunched around my waist, and if he pulls back, he'll see the red underwear I put on this morning.

"Fuck, you make me hard," he grunts, his fingers teasing the edge of my knickers.

His thumb brushes over my clit, and my hips buck as I throw my head back. The contact is already becoming too much, and then I hear the ripping sound of him tearing my knickers from my body, and I swear I have a mini orgasm.

"I can smell you," he growls into my ear, kissing my neck. His thumb rubs torturously over my clit while his other hand snakes up my stomach and to my chest, kneading my breast through my bra. I whimper, needing more.

Feeling brave, I run my fingers down his chest to the button of his jeans. The second I touch his hard, ripped stomach, he groans, shoving my hands out of the way and freeing himself from his jeans.

"I'm sorry, but I can't wait any longer. I need to be inside you," he rasps out harshly.

Nerves flitter through me, but I lean up on my knees, waiting for him to line himself up at my opening. His hands grip my hips, and in one fluid movement, he pulls me down onto his hardness. I cry out, feeling full, his hardness stretching me. There's a slight burn, but I wouldn't trade this moment for anything.

When I tried this position with Adam, it felt awkward, and I hated how vulnerable and exposed I felt. At least lying on my back, lights off with the covers over us, I felt kind of protected in a way—covered.

This, with Landon, is completely different. I still feel exposed, but in a sexy way. This time my vulnerability isn't derived from being embarrassed or uncomfortable, it's from knowing this is a one-time thing. Yet despite knowing this, I still feel comfortable in my own skin right now. Confident, even.

The first time Adam and I had sex, it hurt like hell, and all I could do was cry. It's why we agreed to try it the second time; to see if it got better.

It didn't.

This kind of pain is something I could get used to, something I could crave.

The third time we had sex was experimental; to make sure we hadn't done anything wrong the first two times. It was something we were able to do because we're such close friends. We can openly communicate honestly, even about sex. Well, except Landon. I just didn't want Adam telling me everything I already knew: that I wasn't good enough to catch the eye of the likes of Landon Carter.

Landon glances up at me, and the heat behind his eyes has my stomach fluttering. He cups my face, bringing my lips down to his. I begin to move my hips, needing to chase the pleasure he's promising. His hand on my hip helps guide me, moving me up and down as his tongue swirls against mine.

I move until only the tip of him is left inside me and pause, before grinding down on him hard. A guttural groan escapes his luscious lips. I still for a moment, hoping I didn't do something wrong, but when I open my eyes, his expression is filled with pleasure, and a wave of power and need overwhelms me.

Emboldened, I move again, Landon's ever strengthening grip helping me glide effortlessly up and down on his hardness. Every time he hits a spot deep inside me, I feel something coiling tighter, a wildness bursting to be free.

Sweat beads at the back of my neck, the flutters in my stomach building and building. I bring my mouth to his again, our lips barely touching as I move harder and faster on top of him, going deeper each time. Puffs of air come out in small gasps as out lips mash together, not really kissing, but not separated either.

"Oh God," I cry out, gripping his shoulders.

He begins to meet my thrusts, his movements jerky within the confines of the small space.

"Fuck, I'm going to come soon," he whispers harshly against my lips.

Wetness pools between my legs at his words. I know I'm about to come; I can feel it building, and I ride him harder, needing that release like my life depends on it.

His tongue runs up the side of my neck before he lightly bites down, and my core tightens. Wave after wave of pleasure crashes into me, causing me to cry out with ecstasy.

Landon's head snaps up at the feel of my core tightening around him. His eyes darken, and his thrusts become frantic. I'm still riding out the aftershocks of my orgasm when he shoves his face into my neck, growling out his own release. His body shudders against mine, his thrusts slow and lazy.

I just had sex with Landon Carter.

Landon fucking Carter.

And it was so good I could write about it. If I was a writer, that is. I practically purr inside when I rest my head against his.

"That was… That was… Wow," I breathe out, smiling against his temple. I lean back and reach for his lips, needing that touch. It's something I always regretted with Adam. We didn't love each other on a romantic level, so we didn't cuddle or kiss afterwards.

His kisses me back, his tongue strokes lazy, now taking his time.

He rests his palm against my arm, gliding it up until he reaches the nape of my neck. I pull back, watching as an intense look passes over his expression, like he's lost in some sort of deep thought.

"Landon," I whisper, feeling myself responding to his touch once again.

He jumps, tensing beneath me. When his gaze meets mine, lust and desire are no longer present. Instead, he looks lost.

"Get off me. I can't do this," he rasps out, pushing me back. The steering wheel digs into my back, and I wince.

"What's wrong?" I ask, trying to get my leg out from under me. It's stuck, wedged between the door and his large thigh.

"Get off me!"

Clearly not moving quick enough, he grips my hips and shoves me over to the other seat. I grip the headrest as a lump forms in the back of my throat.

"Landon?" I whisper, hurriedly pulling my dress down. He finishes tucking himself in before gripping the steering wheel until his knuckles turn white.

I reach for him but his harsh voice has me pausing. "Don't touch me. I need you to get out, Paisley."

"What did I do wrong? Talk to me," I plead, my eyes watering.

The dead expression that settles over his features has me feeling like something is crushing my chest. "I said get the fuck out of my car. Go! Go, Paisley. It was just a quick shag in the front seat of a car. What did you expect? Roses and chocolates?"

I reach for my bag, tears streaming down my face as I swallow past the lump in my throat and look at him pleadingly, wanting him to tell me everything is okay. "Landon, please… talk to me."

His face turns red, and the veins in his arms, neck and temples pulse. "I said get out, Paisley! Get out!"

Jumping at the harshness in his tone, I hurriedly pull the door handle. My fingers slip and I cry out, trying again.

I fumble to get out of the car, nearly falling on my face. I hiccup, turning once more to Landon, hoping he can see how much he's hurting me. Yet he's not even looking at me, instead staring straight ahead, his jaw hard.

He drives off, leaving the door to slam shut on its own, and I'm left watching his taillights disappear into the distance, feeling deflated and so confused.

I straighten out my dress, more tears falling when I realise my knickers are still in his car.

He left me.

I sink to my knees as a wave of dizziness overwhelms me, a sob rumbling up my throat. I clutch my chest, feeling dirty and cheap.

He left me.

As I wait for the tears to subside, a wave of anger hits me. He never promised me tomorrow; he didn't promise anything, made it clear he couldn't. But to disregard me with such disrespect is something else entirely. I don't deserve to be treated like that. He's left me on the side of the road, with no knickers on and no answers for his behaviour.

He isn't who I thought he was.

I should have listened to my brothers when they told me the Carter's were players, that they only break girls' hearts.

The pulsing of my blood rushing through my veins subsides as I get up from the floor. I'm not one for pity parties, and I'm not one for feeling worthless. I don't have time for it in my schedule.

I'm certainly not going to let Landon Carter turn me into one of those girls. Yeah, it will hurt for a while, but I'll push forward, like I always do.

With that in mind, I begin my walk home, pretending my heart isn't breaking.

That I'm not still madly in love with Landon Carter—even more so now I know what it feels like to be with him.

TWO

LANDON

THE CROWD ROARS WITH VICTORY as I step out of the circle after winning my third fight of the night. Blood, sweat, dirt and mould contaminate the air around me as I walk through the crowd to the locker room of the old, run-down gym.

When Benny texted me where the fight would be tonight, I was grateful. I needed the release only fighting can give me right now.

The old gym isn't my favourite place to fight. Larkhill has that down since it's out in the open and makes the fight a little tougher when the ground is uneven. But tonight, it's chucking it down with rain, so I'm grateful they moved it here. Since my cousin had his baby a few months ago, he's been on at us not to bring colds or anything around her. And as I've spent a lot of time with her, I don't want to be the reason she becomes ill.

The hinges on the locker room's door squeak as I shove through them, the sound echoing down the halls.

Heading over to my bag stowed under the bench, I grab some fresh tape. The bench creaks under my weight when I take a seat, making me tense.

Fucker better not break on me.

"Hey, man," Benny calls out.

I look up, giving him a chin lift. Benny is the one who helps keep The Circle—an underground fighting ring—going. He's not the brains behind the whole organisation—no one believes that for a minute—but he's who everyone goes to. He's a middle man. He's a bit slow, but an alright guy.

"Listen, man, you're one of my best fighters. You bring in a lot of money and the best crowd. Now, I'm not complaining here, but you've been taking on more fights the past couple of weeks." I stare directly into his eyes, giving him a dry look.

He shifts, uncomfortable at my silence. "Look, just tell me your head is in this. I don't need any dead guys bringing shit to my doorstep."

I inwardly roll my eyes at his dramatics. "I'm good, Benny. Always am."

He snorts. "Yeah, you're right. But you've been off lately, more aggressive. You nearly took that guy's head off. And the next guy ain't a walk in the park. He's one of Rocco's new fighters, meant to be fucking quick on his feet."

"Benny, what is it you actually want?"

His grin spreads across his face, making him look goofy. "A blonde with double-Ds and a big motherfucking house with some maids."

I roll my eyes. "Not what I meant."

"I know. But didn't think you'd appreciate me asking if you were okay. I thought you would have got the hint by now."

I grunt, concentrating on taking the tape off, my knuckles swollen and a little stiff. "I'm good."

He nods. "I'll be back in five to tape your hands. No one with you tonight?"

I shake my head. "Busy."

He doesn't say anything else as he leaves me alone, which is what everyone has learned to do. I'm not really big on talking, and anyone other than my family piss me off, except Drew from the gym. He usually comes with me, especially since he found out about the fights. He's tried to get me to quit, just like everyone else, but I need the peace fighting brings me, the calmness.

Benny is right about one thing though: I've been taking on four, five fights a night, when normally it's one or two at the most.

It's Paisley fucking Hayes. She got under my skin. For weeks she's been all I can think about. She's always stood out to me—I'd never deny that—but this time it's different. It's like I can smell her, taste her, even feel her.

She made me forget; forget about the anger, the rage and grief inside me. Despite how ridiculous it sounds, since losing Freya, I've wanted to make the world hurt the way I hurt. I've wanted to punish myself for not being there for her that night. But mostly, I've been angry at myself for not going to my uncle, to anyone, and telling them what I knew. But Freya had been stubborn and wouldn't have forgiven me if I did.

Then, nine weeks ago, Paisley walked out of the hospital and I wanted her. I hadn't planned on fucking her. It's just… whenever she's around, everything settles. It doesn't go, not completely, but I can control my pain.

Fucking her had felt like a mistake, like I had cheated and failed Freya. Because in that moment, all I felt was Paisley. All I wanted was her; to hold her, to talk to her, to listen to her. I wanted it all.

And I wanted her, *again.*

It scared me, and I freaked out on her. I'll never forget the look on her face when I snapped at her, like I had just crushed her entire world.

After Freya's death, I wasn't intimate with anyone but my hand, until the need became too great and I sought out a willing woman to scratch the itch. They were faceless women, just someone I used, who used me in return.

Until Paisley. She was all I could see.

I've been wanting to see her, to apologise, but with her brothers, it's hard to get to her, and I won't be able to hold back if one of them says something. We come to blows pretty much every time we see each other.

I'm a patient man, biding my time until the time is right. She won't be waiting much longer. I don't give a fuck if her brothers find out, and they will find out eventually; it's a small town. She didn't deserve the way I treated her.

The door creaking open has me looking up. I groan when the four goons walk in like they've got missiles up their arses, their arms shaped like they're carrying twenty shopping bags for their mum. Their intimidation skills need a lot of fucking work. They're laughable.

I dismiss them, grabbing a water bottle from my bag.

"You know why we're here," Blaze, the only one with common sense in the group, says.

I take a swig before glancing up, raising my eyebrow at him.

Of course I know why they're here. They've been hassling me all week to fix the fight, to lose.

Will I fuck though.

"Fuck off!"

Terry snickers, brushing back his greasy hair. "Yeah, it ain't gonna work like that. Our boss gets what he wants, and what he wants is his prime fighter to win this fight. He's got a lot of money riding on it."

His boss, Rocco, goes through fighters like I go through underwear. He thinks if he picks up street kids willing to make a couple of hundred quid, he'll get to keep the profits and have a fighter he can easily manipulate and control. None of them have the training, the cred, or even a gift for any kind of fighting. They get into scraps. The Circle is for the big boys.

"Then tell him to get a prime fighter," I snap.

Rocket, who constantly looks like he's constipated, steps forward, trying to act all big and intimidating. He's five-four at the most. I tower over him.

"Rocco will pay you 10K. It's our last offer and our last warning, Carter."

I give him a droll look. "Am I supposed to be scared?"

"Yeah, you are," Flash says, and I inwardly snicker at his name. Whoever gave these dicks their nicknames were either playing a cruel joke or are truly dumb. The guy is so skinny a gust of wind could blow him over.

"I'm shaking."

"What do you love the most, Landon?" Blaze drawls in a deadly voice. Blaze is the biggest out of the group. He acts like their leader, but really, he's just another puppet on strings and couldn't lead a band.

I stand up, the bench protesting, and take a step forward. Flash and Rocket try to take a sly step back, but I see it and inwardly smirk.

Fuckers should be scared.

"I'm going to say this once, and once only. You do not want to fuck with me."

Blaze smirks, thinking he has something over me. I can see it in his eyes. "Ah. Fix the game and we'll leave everyone you love alone. It's as simple as that. You don't... well, we plan to make it hurt."

He barely blinks before I have my hand around his throat, walking him backwards until his back slams against the door.

His friends try to help, but I turn with a murderous expression. "Fucking try it and I'll rip your fucking throats out."

"Let him go. You don't want to do this," Flash says, a hitch in his voice.

"I warned you, dickhead," I growl, ignoring Flash and bringing my face closer to Blaze, then wincing, leaning back. *The guy needs to brush his fucking teeth.* "My family can handle themselves. You don't want to fuck with them, either. You should see what happens when people try. Now, I'm gonna ask you one more fucking time to leave. Will you do that?"

I tighten my grip and his face begins to redden, his veins bulging.

"Is everything okay in here?" Benny asks.

I stare dead into Blaze's eyes. "It is. Blaze here was just leaving, weren't you?" I ask, digging my fingers in harder.

He nods, and I let him go. He falls to his knees, coughing. His friends rush to help him up, but he shoves them away and pushes himself to his feet. As he reaches the door, he turns, and the anger that shines back at me has mine standing at attention.

War.

He wants a fight, bring it.

"There won't be any more chances. Don't forget what I said," he says.

I go for him, ready to end him, when Benny steps in front of me, letting them walk freely out of the door.

"You know who that is?"

I look down at him, shrugging. "Who cares."

He grimaces. "Look, we might not be friends, but you're a good kid.

Rocco's men might act like they can't tie their shoelaces, but I've heard stories about what they do to people. If I were you, I'd save myself the hassle and do whatever they want me to do."

I raise my eyebrow. "Even fix a fight?"

His eyes narrow dangerously. "No. I'll fucking sort it," he growls. "Let's tape these fucking hands so you can go out there and beat the fuck out of him. And I'll make it clear that if anything happens to you, there will be serious consequences. People might be scared of Rocco, but he has nothing on my boss. He'd snap him like a twig."

My lips twitch at that. "Come on, then. I've got dinner to get back to."

He chuckles. "All right, let's do this."

THE FOG HORN blares as I bounce on my feet, shaking out my limbs. I'm ready to annihilate him, whoever *he* is.

Even freezing, I only wear my navy-blue shorts that end just above the knee. They're less restricting and give the opponent nothing to grab onto. I learned that lesson when some fucker tried to strangle me with my own damn tee.

Benny walks past me, grabbing a mic from the table. He thrusts his fist into the air and screams into the mic as he disappears into the crowd. I shake my head.

"Welcome to The Circle, fuckers. As usual, stay the fuck away from the fighters, don't get involved unless you want your face rearranged, and lastly, if I see any bets exchanged once fighters are announced, you'll be exiled from the fights.

"Now, are you fucking ready?"

The crowd roars, stomping their feet on the concrete floor.

"More blood will be spilt tonight," he yells into the mic, making the screaming begin again.

I stretch out my arms, waiting for the dickhead to announce me.

"First up tonight, we have a new fighter. He's got himself a reputation amongst the streets and is known for his famous choke hold.

"Welcome The Destructor!"

There's a mix of booing and cheering as I click my neck from side to side, waiting to be called.

"The next contender doesn't need an introduction, but I'll give the mean fucker one anyway. With no defeats on his belt, I give you Demolition Man!"

I roll my eyes at the fucking nickname he gave me and step forward. The volume of the cheers explodes in my ears as I make my way into the circle, surrounded by the crowd.

My eyes land on the guy I'm fighting, inwardly scoffing when he removes his zip-up hoodie and begins bouncing and swinging his arms back and forth.

"All right, ladies, if you don't know the rules, learn them quick. No fucking weapons, and if you fall out of the circle, you're fucked and it's an instant lose.

"May the best fucker win!"

With that, a girl, clad in barely there shorts and a crop top flashing the lower globes of her boobs, rings a bell.

I stop bouncing and take a defensive stance.

I eye my opponent, sizing him up. He's a skinny motherfucker, covered in tattoos and piercings, but that means shit when it comes to fighting. Even skinny, he could pack a punch. But he might be one of those who thinks if he looks the part, people will back off.

He's got dyed blond hair, the left side shaved with patterns through it. A scar runs down his cheek and over his lip, enchasing the snarl he gives me.

I wink, taking him aback, and begin to circle him. Blood pumps through my veins, adrenaline coursing through my body.

I'm going to enjoy knocking this fucker out. He looks cocky, *too cocky*, as we stare directly at each other. Predators assessing their prey.

I take a step back when I see his knee twitch—a tell he's going to attack. And I'm right. He charges at me, kicking out with his left leg. Dodging him, I move to the side, grabbing his foot and throwing him off balance.

He comes at me again, and we both move this time, not holding back or pussy-footing around each other.

No time to dance. He wants this as much as I do.

Fists connect with my body, but unlike most fighters, I welcome the pain. It makes me stronger, more determined to hit back twice as hard. I feed off it.

I close my eyes as I block his attempt to grab me around the neck in one of his supposedly famous chokeholds and let the anger simmer up inside me.

I think of Freya, of how I couldn't save her, and like a cloud of smoke, another part of me is opened; a darker part, and I let it free.

He rams his elbow into my back, hoping to loosen my hold around his waist. Lifting my head, I keep punching him, anywhere I can reach, and never let up. Unlike him, who's tiring easily, I won't.

The crowd disappears, so do their chants. All I see is him. I can feel blood trickling down my face from the last blow and growl.

Enough is enough.

I wasn't lying when I told Benny I had dinner to get to. Charlotte is waiting for me with a meal and a movie.

I need to end this. No more playing.

Ramming my knee into his stomach a little harder than I intended to, I hear the air get sucked out of his lungs. He staggers backwards and I pounce, hitting his bloodied face over and over until he falls to his knees. At first, he tries to evade my fists, to dance out of the way, but he isn't a match for me.

I step forward, landing one more punch to his face. Blood sprays all over my chest, and I grimace. This is the only part I hate; being covered in someone else's blood.

His eyes roll to the back of his head as he sways on his knees.

"He's going to go," Benny booms over the speaker.

The crowd begin to scream my victory as he falls face first onto the concrete. I wince, knowing that had to have hurt.

The fight had to have lasted fifteen minutes at the most; longer than most of mine have ever lasted. He'd definitely be worth fighting again.

I step back, ignoring everyone trying to congratulate me, and push my way through the sea of people.

Benny, knowing my routine, meets me outside the locker room like clockwork. "Bro, that was fucking awesome. I'll be in touch with your payment," he tells me.

I hate being paid on the night because most of the time I head back to Charlotte's. I don't want her finding it when she hangs my jacket. So Benny will seek me out in the week to give me the cash.

Giving him a chin lift, I make my way into the locker room, where I grab my hoodie off the bench and pull it over my head. I grimace, a little sore and bruised in places.

The crowd seems louder tonight, thicker, so I move to the back of the changing room where there's a broken window and slip through it.

Out in the alley, I breathe in the fresh air, no longer smelling the coppery scent of blood—well, not as strongly as I did inside.

The rain splatters on my face and I welcome it, moving around the corner and into another alley, the one that leads out onto the street. The streetlight ahead flickers on and off, giving the night an eerie feeling.

I come to a stop, drop my bag, and move into a defensive stance when a figure steps out from behind a bin. People have tried to corner me after a fight before, pissed off they've lost, so this isn't the first time I've had to be quick to act.

"Landon?"

"What the fuck are you doing here?" I growl, looking around for danger. She doesn't belong in a place like this. Nowhere fucking near it.

I regret snapping at her as I watch her flinch and see pain flash across her face.

"I'm sorry. I shouldn't have come here," she whispers, her voice filled with anguish.

Fuck!

She turns to leave, and I pick my bag up from the ground and take a step forward. Once I reach her, I grab her arm, stopping her. "Wait."

Goose-bumps rise on my arm at skin touching skin. She isn't even wearing a jacket; just her usual summer dress. Raking my gaze down her body, I inwardly groan at the sight of her tits bulging out of the top, wanting to feel them in the palms of my hands. "I didn't mean to snap at you. You shouldn't be anywhere near a place like this, Paisley."

There are men in there who wouldn't think twice about taking her against her will. Some of the men in there might be rich, but they're scum and make their money selling drugs to kids and whatever else they are into.

"I didn't know how else to talk to you. I didn't want to turn up at your work."

I rub the back of my neck, looking around the alley once again. "Look, I'm sorry about what happened," I start, shifting. Talking isn't something I'm good at. I never know the right thing to say in situations like this.

She holds her hand up, stopping me. "This is kind of about that night, but I'm not here to beg you to change your mind about relationships. I knew your stance before we... you know," she says, her eyes bulging. She shivers, running her hands up and down her arms. She's completely soaked.

"How long have you been out in the rain?" I ask, reaching for the edge of my hoodie, intending to give it to her.

"No, don't. I'm fine. I haven't been out here long."

"How did you know I was here?" I ask accusingly. I didn't peg her for a stalker.

She looks uncomfortable, looking nervously behind her. "My best friend's brother is always talking about these fights. It's how I knew you'd be here tonight. Look, I just need to say what I have to say, then I'll go and leave you alone. Okay?"

Not understanding where this is going, I nod. "Um, yeah, okay."

A noise behind us, coming from around the corner, distracts me, and I still, listening.

"He was meant to come out that window," Blaze snaps, and I freeze.

"Maybe we got the wrong window," Flash yells to be heard over the rain.

My eyes widen in horror when I turn back to Paisley, who looks up at me with doe eyes. "Yeah, so I'm—"

"Paisley, you need to hide," I hiss, pushing her back towards the bins.

"W-what?"

THREE

PAISLEY

HAVE YOU EVER WATCHED ONE OF those adverts where the bloke tips water over his head and chest? It's made to look sexy, when in reality, they just look like an idiot for tipping water over themselves while trying to pull off a sensual expression. Landon, however, rocks the wet look. Like seriously fucking rocks it.

His dark hair sticks to his face and eyelids. Droplets of rain drip from his bottom lip, and my eyes are drawn to them as I envision licking them off.

I clench my thighs together and take a deep breath, trying to concentrate on what I came here to say. I didn't stand out in the rain, waiting for him for the past twenty minutes, to say nothing.

When his attention turns back to me, a mixture of emotions pass over his face, making me tense. He looks scared, worried and angry.

Maybe he's getting impatient with me just standing here, not speaking.

Just blurt it out. Tell him, Paisley.

"Yeah, so I'm—" I start, but then he moves towards me quickly, grabbing my biceps in a tight grip. I wince at the pain, knowing it will bruise.

"Paisley, you need to hide," he hisses sharply, pushing me to the floor.

"W-what?"

My bag drops beside me as he kneels down in front of me, grabbing my face. I shiver, scared and confused. I don't understand what the hell is going on or why he's acting this way.

"Let's look around. He can't have gone far," I hear a deep voice yell from somewhere close.

I look up, fearful of what is happening. He's hiding me from whoever that man is.

"W-what is going on?" I ask, my voice shaking.

His grip on my face softens a touch, but the determination in his expression doesn't waver. "Listen to me. I don't have time to explain, but whatever happens, whatever they do, do not come out from this spot. They will know I'm hiding you and will do a lot worse to you than they'll ever do to me. Do you understand?"

My entire body quivers, my bottom lip beginning to tremble. "No! What's going on? I'm scared, Landon."

He inhales, dropping his forehead to mine briefly. "Promise me, Paisley. Promise me you won't move from here, no matter what."

I grip his biceps, not wanting him to go. A sinking feeling in my gut has me clutching my stomach. "Stay here with me."

"I can't risk them finding you. Now promise. Quick!"

I nod at the urgency in his voice. "I will. I promise."

Satisfied, he kisses my head, drops his bag in front of me, and moves out into the alley.

I shuffle forward, peeking out from behind the bin, and my chest tightens when I see four men carrying weapons. They notice Landon, and the biggest one grins.

"Well, look who it fucking is."

Landon scoffs, his stance portraying him as unaffected. "You were looking for me, so let's not play games," he snaps, then I watch as he scans them, a snarl lifting his lips. "Ah, weapons. Should have known you pussies would need them. Couldn't take me on by yourselves?"

"We've seen you fight. Do we look stupid?" another voice in the group asks.

Landon crosses his arms over his chest, giving them a dry look. "Do you really need me to answer that, because yes, yes you do look fucking stupid."

"There's four of us," the first voice states.

Blinking rain out of my face, I reach behind me for my bag and grab my phone.

"And you think that makes you hard? Well, it doesn't. It makes you look fucking weak. Come on, Blaze, fight me one on one."

Someone scoffs, but I don't look up. Instead, I try to unlock my phone, my hands shaking, making it hard. This is going to go bad. I can sense it. My stomach cramps painfully.

A cry nearly has me dropping my phone. When I look back up and out into the alley, the smallest man of the group charges at Landon with a bat.

A small squeal escapes my lips, and I watch as Landon's body visibly tenses. He must have heard me. I place my free hand over my mouth to stop any sound coming out. It's hard, because all I want to do is cry out for them to stop.

Landon keeps his focus solely on the guys.

This is happening. It's really happening. And it won't end well. I quickly shove myself back against the wall and dial nine-nine-nine, having finally steadied my nerves long enough to unlock my phone.

Oh my God, I won't be able to speak; the men will hear me.

Tears fall down my cheeks as I leave the call connected, hoping they'll hear what is happening.

I sneak back out a little in time to see Landon dodge the bat. Landon swings out with his fist, punching the next guy in the jaw. The guy staggers back, and before Landon can recover from the attack, the men begin to descend, each looking deadly in a different way.

My eyes catch on the one who spoke before—Blaze, I think Landon called him—and his gaze is murderous.

Landon squares off with them, and my pulse begins to race faster as I watch with a trembling jaw. A serious look settles over his face, like he wants the fight, and it scares me. There's a need for violence there, and the thought unsettles me, making me feel nauseous.

Blaze and his friends swing their bats, and a feeling of foreboding hits me. They aren't posturing, acting this way as a scare tactic. They are really going to hit him with them.

Not knowing whether the police are listening in on my phone, I shuffle back, grabbing Landon's bag as quietly as possible, shivering from the cold. My prayers that I'll find his phone inside are answered when I see it laying on top of a towel. I grab it, grateful it's not password protected, and type out a text to Adam, explaining to him where I am and to call the police. Immediately, the phone begins to buzz in my hand, Adam's number flashing across the screen, so I shove it into my bra to hide the light.

Grunts and low moans have me peeking back out. Landon is raining punches to who I assume is the leader's side, whilst trying to block hits from the other three. I knew he fought a lot. Some of the rumours around town about his fighting skills were too believable not to be true. Plus, I have eight brothers who I've heard rave on about Landon fighting. Not that they'd ever admit that publicly.

Whenever I saw him, he also had new bruises, so that should have been a big indication the rumours were true.

He definitely knows what he's doing as he lands an uppercut on one guy's jaw whilst kicking another, knocking him to the other side of the dustbin I'm hiding behind.

I flinch, holding my breath so he doesn't see or hear me.

My heart stills when Landon yells as a bat connects with his back.

I grimace, my breathing escalating when they begin pounding on him, and in my mind, I feel like they're hitting me, flinching at every blow they land on him. "Please, someone hurry," I whisper.

Time loses all meaning as I watch Landon fight for his life. I see the blood dripping down his face, his tiring body, his movements becoming sluggish, his chest rising and falling as he struggles for breath.

Frantically, I look around for a weapon, something to help him. I may have promised to stay hidden, but that was before I knew how bad it was going to get. I can't sit back and watch them kill him.

I growl in frustration when I find nothing.

Please hurry.

I quickly check my phone and see the call is still connected to the police. "Please, help me," I whisper as quietly as I can.

When I look back up, it's quiet, and my promise to stay hidden goes out of the window.

"No!" I scream as Blaze pulls the knife out of Landon's stomach. All four startle and glance at me as I run out from my spot.

I desperately race for Landon, but before I can reach him, Blaze thrusts the knife into Landon's side and leans forward to whisper something in his ear, and I come to a sudden stop.

Landon's gaze finds mine, and a cloudy haze settles over everything. Sweat, rain, and blood coats him, his eyes flashing with a mixture of fear and horror.

Blaze steps back, dropping Landon. I fall to the ground with him, the sound of the knife leaving his body bringing bile to the back of my throat, before crawling forward to be by his side.

I raise my hand in the air as I survey the four men who are standing too close and place the other on Landon's chest to make sure he's still breathing.

"Stop!"

A slimy-looking guy steps forward, grinning. "Well, well, well. Who do we have here?"

"Leave me alone. I've phoned the police. They're on their way!" I yell in screechy voice.

The smallest of the four shares a look with his friends, before turning back to me, tilting his head.

"Yeah, I don't believe you," he says, and the sinister sound in his voice has me in flight mode.

"We can't have witnesses, sweetheart," Blaze says, and raises the knife in his hand.

"Wait. Let's have some fun with her," another one says.

My breath hitches. I'd rather be stabbed… Anything but that.

"No!" Blaze growls and steps closer.

Police sirens echo in the distance, and I sag with relief.

"Fucking get her!" one of them yells.

My blood races, my hand still in the air. Everything is hazy, moving slow, so I don't see the knife coming down until it's too late. It slices across my arm and warmth trickles down to my elbow.

Frightened that this is over, that my life is over, I close my eyes, ready for what is to come. When nothing does, I see the four guys running down the alley and lights flashing over the surrounding buildings.

"Landon," I cry out, spinning and scraping my knees on the ground. He's covered in blood. Pressing down on the worst of his injuries, I begin to sob. "Please, don't die. Please!"

Wheezing sounds come from his chest, and his eyes begin to flutter open.

"That's it. That's it, Landon, stay awake."

My teeth rattle against each other as I apply more pressure, yet more blood seeps through my fingers. I look around, seeing the light of my phone still by the bin and crawl over, grabbing it and Landon's bag in the process.

"Hello, miss, can you hear me?"

"Hello, my name is Paisley Hayes and my friend has just been badly beaten and stabbed."

I rattle off where I am, just as two police cars come into view. I look up. "I need help! You have to save him. Please," I cry.

"Here, I've got him," an officer says. I look up at his green eyes, seeing truth there, and let him remove my hands so he can take over.

I sit to the side of Landon's head, feeling numb, stroking my fingers through his hair. I know I should reach over for my bag, get my insulin, but my body won't move, too afraid of losing him.

"Where's the ambulance?" he yells to his colleague after assessing the damage.

"Five minutes out."

I sob. "He's going to be okay. He is. He has to be."

"Everything will be okay. The ambulance is on the way. Can you tell me what happened?"

"We were talking, then they came, and he hid me. They just kept hitting him. With bats… and then they stabbed him. Twice. They really stabbed him."

"Okay, just take a deep breath in and exhale slowly," he says calmly.

"You take a deep breath in," I snap, pulling my knees to my chest, my entire body shaking.

"You need to calm down, otherwise you're going to pass out."

"I'm fine. I'm fine. Just help him," I plead. I'll pass out anyway if I don't get my insulin, but I'm not moving until I know he's okay.

Two more officers walk down the alley, shaking their heads at their colleagues, but I ignore them when my phone begins to vibrate in my pocket.

Not my phone. *Landon's.*

I pull his phone out, and through blurry vision, I see Charlotte's name and message.

CHARLOTTE: Where are you? You're late again and you promised me you'd help me find a new pet.

A growing lump forms in the back of my throat as I swipe the message away and scroll through his contacts. I find 'Mum' and hit call.

"Hi, baby," a soft, feminine voice greets.

A gasp of air escapes my lips, more tears clouding my vision. How do I tell his mum he might die?

"Landon, are you there or have you butt dialled me again?"

"Mrs Carter?" I say, my voice hitching.

She pauses, and I hear shuffling. "Um, who is this?"

"It's Landon. It's bad," I tell her and sob. The officer who joined us not long ago kneels beside me, taking the phone off me.

"Hello, this is PC Diggs," he starts, before walking back towards the police car and out of hearing range.

Another officer wraps a blanket around me. "Let's get you inside the car. The ambulance is here."

I look up, noticing the ambulance at the end of the alley. "I don't want to leave him," I whisper.

Paramedics rush down the alley and the world begins to spin, before I feel myself falling.

I WAKE UP feeling groggy, my throat dry and sore. I clutch my head as I sit up. Scanning the room, everything comes flooding back to me, and I rub the ache in my chest.

Landon.

A pretty nurse with mousy-blonde hair walks into the room, a cheery smile on her face. "You're awake. That's great. I'm Laura, your nurse," she greets. "How are you feeling?"

I shake my head, still feeling foggy. "I'm fine," I tell her, looking around the sterile room. "How did I get here?"

"You collapsed when your insulin level got dangerously low. It's still not quite where we want it to be, so we need to keep you in a little longer," she explains, before concern creases her brow. "The police found your bag, so we know you had your insulin on your person when you collapsed. You know how important your insulin is, Paisley. You must take it, especially when you feel the symptoms of hyperglycaemia."

"I know," I say. "I was going to, but then everything happened…" My throat closes, leaving me unable to finish my sentence.

"It's ok, Paisley," the nurse says, placing a hand on my shoulder. She clears her throat and steps back. "I cleaned you up when you came in, and bandaged your arm, but I still need to glue it."

My arm?

I look down in a daze, noticing a white bandage wrapped around it, blood seeping through.

"The guy I was brought in with… Have you heard anything?"

Her expression saddens as she checks the drip and monitors beside me. "I'm sorry. I haven't. It was a stabbing, right?"

I nod absently. "Yeah."

"I'll just go and get what I need to glue your arm. We called the emergency number in your phone. I think your dad is on his way?"

I tilt my head. "My dad's dead."

She looks taken aback. "U-um, okay. I'll just go get that ready."

Whatever.

Needing to know if Landon is okay, I rip off the bandage in my panicked state, not knowing what I'm really doing. The tubes come out next, and I wince at the sting it leaves in its wake.

My knees knock together when I stand, the hospital gown falling to my calves. I stumble out of the room. Laura is standing at the nurse's station, talking to someone else.

"They took him straight up to ICU. It's bad. The doctors don't think he'll make it," I hear the other nurse tell her.

"It's such a shame."

Ducking my head, I quickly make my way out of the emergency ward and into the hallway, where I scan the signs for directions to the ICU.

When I reach the floor Landon is on, my stomach contracts and flutters. All I can hear is people sobbing. The most gut-wrenching cry echoes down the corridor, one only a mother could make. It tears at my heart.

"No!" I hear when they come into view. I watch with my heart in my throat as Hayden rushes over to her brother, Liam, clinging to him.

"What happened?" a deep, panicked voice yells from inside the room they're standing outside.

The tension in the ward is palpable, and I see the Carters' despair; eyes flooded with tears, jaws clenched, cheeks flushed, fists clenched.

And it's as if their fear and pain permeate my skin. I stagger backwards on shaky feet. I heave, fighting to breathe as my throat clogs with grief.

This can't be happening. This is everybody's nightmare; losing a loved one too young.

"He's coding. We're losing him," another deep voice shouts from within the room, this one calm and controlled.

As one, the Carter's turn back to the room they're all standing outside. My eyes are drawn to Charlotte, who has turned away, her face tucked into her father's neck. She must hear something I don't, because the next thing I know, she's fighting her father's hold and running into the room.

"You'd better wake up, Landon. Wake up!" Charlotte screams.

I take another step back, shaking my head. This can't be real. It can't be. I clutch at my stomach, tears streaming down my face.

I look away when they carry Charlotte out kicking and screaming.

"No," I cry, feeling my knees lock. I want to look away, to hide my face from the world, but I can't. Liam and Hayden, Landon's triplet siblings, hold hands, gripping one another so tightly their knuckles turn white.

Pain lances through my lower belly, knocking the breath out of me.

He needs to be okay.

Laura, my nurse, steps into view. I'm confused by her concerned expression and watch as her lips move, but nothing penetrates my ears. Just as I go to speak, I'm distracted by a warm liquid trickling between my legs, and I begin to sway.

Please, no.

Everything around me is a haze as I once again feel myself fall.

———————————

WARM FINGERS RUN through my hair as I wake, and I smile, smelling a familiar floral perfume. My eyelids feel heavy as I force them to lift. Light brown hair with a red tinge and bits of hay sprinkled throughout comes into view. Shadows lay heavy beneath her eyes, worry lines crease her forehead, and she's dressed in her worn, rumpled work clothes.

Mum.

She hums *Mockingbird* under her breath, and I inwardly smile. She has sung that to me since I was a kid. Whenever I was sick or scared, she'd sing that to me until I fell asleep.

Her soft and soothing melody settles over me, almost dreamlike, and I relax into my pillow, feeling like a child again. I'm just about to drift off into a sleep promising tranquil dreams when her voice hitches as she draws in another breath. It's that slight hitch, barely even detectable, that cracks the fragile glass surrounding my mind and brings everything flooding back. Losing Landon. Losing our baby. All of it.

A sob rises in my throat as I shakily reach for her hand resting on the bar beside the bed. "Mum?"

Her head spins towards me, her eyes wide as her shoulders sag with relief. "My goodness. You gave me a fright. Never do that to me again," she scolds, reaching over to give me a hug.

I grip her like my life depends on it, breathing her in. "Mum," I choke out once more. "I lost my baby, didn't I?"

She tenses above me before pulling back. Conflict is written all over her, and I look away. "I'm so sorry, Paisley."

Her hand tightens around mine, but I can't look at her. I lost my baby—mine and Landon's baby. It was why I went to see him tonight; to tell him. As soon as Adam started yapping on about a fight that was going on tonight, I knew Landon would be there. I grabbed my bag and got into a taxi before he could talk me out of it.

It's been two weeks since I found out I was pregnant, and it was actually my mum who had told me. She said she just knew, could see the changes in my body and just knew. I had already told her about Landon, not leaving anything out. She put two and two together and came up with a baby.

At first, I was scared. Who wouldn't be when they find out they're carrying a life inside of them. But then I placed my hand on my stomach and knew I'd love our baby no matter what.

My chest aches as I sob quietly, flinching when I feel Mum running her fingers through my hair once again.

"Baby, you're breaking my heart," she whispers, and I feel her breath on my neck. She wraps her arms around me, resting her head against mine.

"Do they know?" I ask, referring to my brothers.

"Yes. We got here as they were, um… treating you."

I weep harder, clutching her arm across my chest. I feel empty, cheated. It's not fair. Fate give me this precious gift and it was taken away from me before I really had it. I'll never get to hold them, to know if it was a boy or a girl. I will never get to feel them kick inside me or scream when I bring them into the world.

Life hated me. I hated *me*.

FOUR

LIAM

OUTSIDE IS AS GLOOMY AS IT IS IN this hospital; silent, morose, grey. All of us are too scared to go anywhere, even to get a drink. Rain splatters across the carpark, people splashing through puddles as they run to their cars. All of them are mindless to the despair and heartbreak transpiring in this sterile waiting room. I hate them. I hate the woman holding hands with her husband while the orderly pushes him in a wheelchair. I hate the kid leaving with a cast covering his arm. And I hate the couple laughing and joking around with one another.

It's been hours since we've had an update on Landon's condition. I don't know what's worse; the wait or knowing the last thing we'd been told was Landon had no heartbeat and was being rushed to surgery.

Seconds before the room exploded into chaos, my heart constricted, a wave of pain shot through my body, and I just knew. It was like a sixth sense, an awareness, and I knew. I knew he was gone. The machines blared and it felt like my heart had been torn from my body.

Shuffling sounds behind me and I turn to see Aiden still pacing the waiting area filled with our family, baby Sunday in his arms.

His inability to keep still is getting on my nerves, and I have no idea why. It's bad enough I have to listen to my sister's heart breaking as her body convulses with hard sobs. I can feel her pain just as much as I can feel my own.

Charlotte, thankfully, fell asleep from exhaustion not too long ago, but whimpers still escape her, and they're like a punch to my stomach.

My brother was loved—*is* loved.

Aiden pacing the room is just pissing me off. Can't he keep fucking still?

"Will you sit the fuck down? I swear to God, Aiden, she's asleep. You're probably rattling her tiny little brain rocking her about like that."

He startles, and his body goes still. He doesn't bother looking at me, though, instead turning to his mum.

"Put her down in her pushchair," she says softly, clutching Uncle Maverick's hand.

He nods, slowly resting Sunday in the pushchair before huffing and sitting back down next to Bailey, his girlfriend. He drops his head back against the uncomfortable chair, legs spread wide, and scrubs a hand down his tired face.

I scan the room, taking in their expressions, and it feels like I've just had a knife stuck in my gut. They're mourning him.

But he can't be gone. He can't be. I'd know. I'd feel it, like I did before.

"Fuck this. I'm going to find out who fucking did this," I growl, moving towards the door.

In my peripheral vision, I notice Maddox and Maverick stand. Everyone's eyes are on me. Before I get to the door, Aiden stands in front of it, arms crossed over his chest.

"Don't leave yet," he pleads, before his eyes land on my shoulder.

"Move, Aiden, or I'll move you myself. Whoever did this needs to pay."

A hand rests on my shoulder, turning me around. I swallow past the lump in my throat when Uncle Maverick's rugged face stares back at me.

"Aiden is right. You can't go out there right now," he tells me, his voice tense.

"Why?" Dad says gruffly, lifting his head from his hands. His eyes are red with dark circles under them, and his laugh lines are no longer visible. He doesn't look like my dad; just a shell of his former self. My throat tightens further. "I say we fucking can."

Maverick turns away from me and gets up in my dad's face. "Listen—"

Dad's face tightens with anger. "No, you listen. That's my fucking son in there. My fucking boy. We don't even know if he's alive, and you're telling me no? Fuck you!" he says, his voice getting louder and stronger.

"Max," Maverick chokes out, going to rest a hand on Dad's shoulder. Dad shrugs him off, stepping back.

"Since when do we let some fucking scumbag hurt one of us? We've always dealt with little pricks like this," he growls, turning away. His shoulders rise and fall with his heavy breaths for a few moments, before he turns back, tears brimming his eyes.

"You think the police are going to find them? Look around you, Maverick," he says, arms wide. "The entire world is filled with crimes like this, and the guilty are never caught. I'm sorry, but I won't sit by. Someone must have seen something—maybe whoever called the ambulance. I'm going to find whoever hurt my boy and kill them."

Dad collapses back in his chair, and Maverick kneels in front of him, hands on Dad's knees.

"I'm not saying we don't do anything. What I'm saying is we need to be smarter about this. Fuck, we are smarter, Max. We've been through hell and back, and we always pull through. I truly believe Landon will get through this. The kid is made of fucking steel." He pauses, taking a deep breath. "We need to be vigilant. We don't want them to know we're coming, and they will if we go looking for them half crazed. Please, listen to me." He shakes Dad's legs to get his attention. "You'll hate yourself if you fuck this up. We will find them."

"There's nowhere they can run or hide where I won't find them," I tell them, my voice deadly.

The door opens behind me, causing me to jump.

"Landon Carter's family?" a doctor in his late forties wearing blue scrubs asks, his expression unreadable. Mum and Dad stand to my left, Hayden to my right, as the rest of the room stand and wait.

"We're his parents," Mum tells the doctor, her voice strained and filled with emotion. I lean down and take her hand in my left and Hayden's in my right, squeezing them both.

"Is our son okay? Please, just tell us," my dad begs.

The doctor looks at Dad. "I'm Doctor Clancy, your son's doctor. He's still in critical condition but stable for the moment. We will know more in the next twenty-four hours."

Mum's legs buckle beneath her, and Dad catches her, pulling her against his chest. The doctor steers them over to the chairs near the door, where Bailey, Beau and Faith were originally sitting.

"He's a very lucky guy. If he hadn't been brought in when he was, I'm afraid the extent of his injuries, along with the shock, would have been too much for his body to fight."

"Stupid question, but what was wrong? What did you have to do?" Dad asks, gently stroking Mum's head.

"As you know, he suffered two knife wounds to the abdomen. We worried these might prove to be fatal but on examination found no damage to his major organs. He did, however, lose a lot of blood, but we managed to stabilise him after giving him an emergency blood transfusion," he explains, before clearing his throat. "He has broken his fibula and femur. He might need to have surgery again in a few days. We are waiting for the swelling to reduce before taking him in for another X-ray."

"But he'll be okay?" I ask from the side, watching his face for a reaction.

Doctor Clancy's expressions soften. "He's your twin?"

I nod. "We're triplets," I tell him, hugging Hayden to me.

"He's in a medically induced coma right now," he starts, and gasps echo around the room. My heart plummets in my chest. "Landon has what we call blunt head trauma. We don't know what caused the injuries—whether he was hit with a blunt object or fell—but he has some swelling around the brain, and we need to keep him in the coma to control the swelling."

"But he'll wake up?" Mum asks, sitting up. She wipes her nose, staring at the doctor.

"Like I said, it's too soon to tell. He will be closely monitored, and we will update you every step of the way."

"Can we see him?" she asks, her eyes pleading with him.

"He's still in recovery right now, but I will have a nurse come and get you when we've put him into a room. Since it's the middle of the night, we will need to keep visitors to a minimum."

"We aren't leaving him," Dad snaps.

"Under the circumstances, we will let the two of you stay with your son, but I'm afraid everyone else will have to leave," he says, then takes in everyone's angry expressions. "Or you can stay here in the waiting room."

"Thank you," Mum says, pushing her hand out to him. He shakes it before stepping back.

"The other reason I'm here is because the police are outside and need to ask you some questions," Doctor Clancy states. "Are you up to talking to them before you go and see your son?"

"They're here now? After four hours?" Dad growls.

Doctor Clancy takes a small step back at my dad's tone but speaks up. "The girl who was brought in with him was being treated and has only just spoke with them."

"What girl?" Dad and Mum ask, and Uncle Maverick steps forward, his interest piqued. Just like mine. It's very rare Landon sleeps with someone. After losing his girlfriend back in high school, he's never been the same. He's not celibate, but he's no saint either. He usually fucks them, quick and easy, and never sees them again. Ever.

And if I find out this girl had anything to do with his attack, I'll fucking ruin her.

"I can't give out that kind of information. I'm sorry. Would you like me to send them in?"

Dad nods and waits for him to leave before turning to Charlotte, Landon's closest friend. "He has a girlfriend?"

She wipes the tears from her cheeks as she shakes her head. "No. But I told you he's been different lately. He's been withdrawn more. He was supposed to be coming to my house tonight to watch a movie and figure out what pet I should get next," she says, before her face crumbles and she begins to sob. Uncle Myles pulls her to his chest, his face tight with worry.

"It was Paisley," Aiden suddenly says, looking down at the floor distractedly.

"Paisley Hayes?" I ask, wondering if he's taken something. Landon loves to fuck with the Hayes brothers, but he'd never do that.

I think back to the times I've seen him watching her and wonder if Aiden's right.

"I saw her," he admits.

"When?" Maverick asks.

"In the hallway upstairs. Landon had just—he had just…" He shakes his head and looks up. "Anyway, she heard what was happening. She cried out 'no', and then collapsed. I don't think it's a coincidence. She had scrape marks on her knees and hands, and long cut down her arm."

"You think one of her brothers did this?" I growl, stepping towards the door.

"No. She was alone," Aiden says, stepping in front of me. "And I don't think you should go find her."

"Why the fuck not?" Dad says, his voice menacing. He wants blood, just like the rest of us.

Aiden scrubs a hand down his face. "I don't know if what I saw was real or not—everything was a blur up there—but I could have sworn I saw blood."

"You did say she had a cut on her arm," Maverick states.

Aiden looks to his father. "It wasn't coming from there," he whispers, looking back down at the floor.

Oh shit!

The door opens and in walks a nurse and two police officers. I saw them in the hallway earlier, when they were first treating Landon.

"We can take you up to see Landon now," the nurse says gently.

Mum and Dad look to the police, and I know they want answers.

"I'll answer the questions the police have. Go see your son," Maverick tells Dad, patting him on the back.

They nod before turning to me and Hayden. "We will come back and take you to see Landon soon. We'll take turns," Mum offers.

I lean down and kiss her cheek. "We'll be waiting. Maybe explain we're triplets; they might feel for us and let us join you."

She forces a smile. "Hopefully."

Hayden turns in my arms, burying her face in my neck. "He has to be okay."

"He will be," I vow, and as much as I want to hear what the police have to say, I don't think Hayden can take much more. She's strong—she's had to be, growing up with us two as brothers—but deep down, there's a vulnerability inside her, one she rarely lets people see.

Tonight, she's let it all show but still remained lucid and somewhat calm. Hearing what the police have to say might change that, and I know she'll hate it later on.

We sit in the far corner, away from everyone else, and pull two chairs together. I let her lean on me. "Try sleeping for a little while. I'll wake you up once Mum and Dad come back."

"Promise?"

I kiss the top of her head. "Swear it."

She holds out her little finger to me and I chuckle, wrapping my own around hers. "Pinkie swear," she whispers.

"We're too old to keep doing this shit," I tell her, without really meaning it. It's something we've done since we were kids, and not once have one of us broke a pinkie promise. It's weird and immature, but it's us. And I wouldn't change what we have for anything.

"Never!" she mock gasps. "We'll be doing this when we're in an old people's home pushing Aiden and Maddox's wheelchairs into walls."

A light chuckle escapes me as I rest my head on top of hers, both of us leaning on each other.

She clutches my hand tightly, and I close my eyes, praying Landon will be okay.

FIVE

LANDON
FOUR MONTHS LATER

S WEAT POURS DOWN MY BACK AND chest as I push myself harder, punching the bag with full force. Music blares in my ears, and I drown out the rest of the world.

The faces of my attackers flash through my mind, increasing my resolve to get vengeance. The feel of my fist hitting the bag pumps adrenaline through my body, giving me the strength to keep going. My breaths come in heavy pants, but I'm nowhere near finished.

Ever since the day I woke up in the hospital, I've felt different; numb. The doctors kept telling me I was lucky. However, I felt anything but lucky; I felt weak and vulnerable.

I'd lied to the police—to everyone—about who did this to me. The only people who know the truth about that night are Paisley and the four dead men walking. I knew the second I told the police the truth, any chance of getting payback would die. So when they came to take my statement, I lied and said I didn't remember a thing. With my head injury, they believed me. Whether my family did or not, I'm unsure. I've kept my distance, knowing if I do what I plan to and get caught, they won't be held accountable.

And getting revenge is the only thing that has held me together throughout my recovery. It got me through the nights I woke up with night terrors, damp with sweat and throat dry, and helped me cope when my body would throb where healed or still healing injuries were. It was like a wakeup call each night, feeding my need to get even.

I just need to get stronger, faster, smarter. I'm not going to involve my family, even though I know they're still looking for them. They know from Paisley's description that it was four men, but with nothing else to go on, they are looking for a needle in a haystack.

A tap on my shoulder startles me, and I spin around, pulling my fist back. I pause just before I punch my brother in the face.

He watches me with round eyes, his face pale. I pull my earphones out, narrowing my eyes at him.

"Don't fucking sneak up on me," I snap, then glare at Maddox and Hayden behind him.

"You couldn't fucking hear us, and call me vain, but I wasn't standing on the other side of that bag. I'm surprised you haven't taken it off the wall."

I roll my eyes. "What are you doing here? I'm busy."

Hayden looks up from inspecting her nails. "And we're supposed to care? I think you've avoided us long enough."

"I was with you yesterday," I remind her.

She shrugs. "You ignored me pretty much the whole time, and if it wasn't for getting a key cut, you wouldn't have let me in."

I throw my hands up in the air. "Is it too much to ask to be alone?"

Maddox steps forward. "Come on, man. We know you know who battered you and we've kept fucking quiet, because we're on your side. Whatever you're gonna do, we're with you. But you need to stop pushing us the fuck away."

I look away. "I don't know who attacked me."

Hayden scoffs. "You seem to forget we're triplets. We know when you're lying. And I think we've been fucking saint-like in our patience for you to come out with the truth, seeing as you nearly died. Hell, you *did* die. You left us, and you haven't come back. We want our grumpy, challenging brother back. Is *that* too much to ask for?"

Glancing up, I grimace at the fierce expression she's wearing. Her eyes tell a different story, cast downwards, the brightness of their chocolate-coloured depths duller.

"I don't want any of you to get involved. This is my fight," I tell her, softening my gruff voice.

Liam snorts, his face a hard mask of fury. "Are you fucking kidding me? Your fight? Look where fighting got you, Landon. We've been worried sick about you for months. Mum has lost weight, Charlotte is baking more than usual and constantly crying, and Dad is still on a rampage. You need to get your act together. Since when do we do things alone?"

"Never," I admit, guilt hitting me hard. I didn't know about Mum or Charlotte. I don't really notice much of anything lately. After having pins and plates put into my leg to fix the break, I couldn't get around. I lost weight and muscle from my hospital stay, and since I was given the all clear to exercise, I've been training every single day.

When I go for them, I want to be at my strongest, to make sure they can't use one of my injuries against me. It's been slow, but muscle is building back up and I've gained more weight. They will regret ever laying a hand on me and wish they finished me off when they had the chance.

I've been watching them for the past couple of weeks, making sure they don't run. Every time one of them looks over their shoulder, I've made sure they see me—only long enough for them to think they're going crazy.

Their time will come. One by one, leaving Blaze till last.

"Come out with us tonight. We're only going for a few drinks at The Ginn Inn, then going home. Everyone is worried about you, and you know if the roles were reversed, you'd be on our backs like a horny dog," Maddox says, his eyes lit up with hope.

Weighing the decision, I know I have to go. Maybe if I show my face once in a while and try to play nice, then they'll get off my back.

"And no, showing your face won't be enough to get us off your back," Hayden says, not looking up from her phone. "Also, Aiden got a babysitter and has the perfect plan to fuck with the dickheads who attacked you."

I step forward. "I told you I didn't want any of you getting involved." If any of them got hurt like I did, I'd never forgive myself. I was that lost in my own grief over Freya that I didn't really think about the consequences my fighting would bring. Each and every one of them at some point begged me to stop fighting, and I didn't listen. I needed the release it offered me bad enough I thought I was untouchable.

I was wrong.

So very fucking *wrong*.

"Tough shit," she says, looking up from her phone with a wide smile. "It's a great plan until you're ready for whatever you have planned. If you don't like it, tell someone who gives a shit."

"Hayden," I start, but Liam shakes his head, stopping me from saying anything further.

"Don't argue with us. It's as pointless as a white crayon," he says.

"And do you really want to keep hurting Charlotte as much as you have? This isn't you," Maddox reminds me.

And it isn't. Charlotte is my best friend. She had always been fascinating to me, always spouting off random facts, but it was this protective instinct I had for her that brought us as close as we are. Out of our large family, she's the only one with a childlike naivety, and people had taken advantage or made fun of her for it. Over time, I just liked being around her sunny disposition.

Hurting my family isn't something I want to do.

"Fuck's sake," I groan, ripping my gloves off. "Let me take a fucking shower."

They all grin, pleased with their efforts.

In actuality, I've missed them. And I'd be lying to myself if I said I didn't really need their help. Fucking with Blaze and his friends will keep the beast wanting to kill at bay.

For a little while.

"I'M TELLING YA, it will work," Aiden says as I watch him sceptically. His plan has merit, but the chance of it going smoothly with us acting it out doesn't have good odds.

"Aren't you meant to be a dad setting a good example?" Hayden asks him dryly.

Aiden wraps his arm around Bailey and grins. "Yeah, I'm teaching her a valuable lesson: no one fucks with the Carter's."

Hayden shrugs one shoulder. "Can't argue with that."

"We just need to decide who's going with who," Aiden states.

"I'll go with Landon, Maddox and you, Mark and Hayden go together," Liam says, briefly looking at me with a flicker of guilt. "Dad, Myles and Mason are hitting one, and then Maverick and Malik are doing the last."

"You told them?" I snarl, tightening my fists. If Dad knows, Mum will know. My family can't be hurt. I won't let this happen. I want to punch him across the jaw for blabbing his mouth.

More to the point, how long have my parents known?

"Don't worry, they haven't told our mums. They're too scared they'll try to talk them out of it," Liam adds, looking away.

"Dad's more worried Mum will want to come," Hayden tells me, grinning.

I gulp down the rest of my pint, inwardly groaning. I should never have agreed to let them go ahead with this. It's going to go to shit. One of our dads will lose his mind and beat the fuck out them.

"And before you panic, Dad said he can understand you wanting to deal with them by yourself. They can all respect that, so they will have your back when needed but leave you to do the rest," Aiden explains. "They promised to be sly around the mums so they don't get involved."

"Well, thank God for small favours," I reply sourly.

I can't fucking believe they told them, or that they knew more than they let on.

A cold breeze blows through the doorway of The Ginn Inn. Something compels me to lift my head, and when I do, Jaxon, Wyatt, Reid and Paisley walk inside.

My heart stills at the sight of her. She looks tired, her skin pale and sunken. I sit forward in my chair, spreading my legs wide open, waiting for her to see me. Over the past few months, I've been wanting to go to her, to thank her or something. She's been on my mind a lot—also in my nightmares.

I didn't save her—in my nightmares, they hurt her in the worst possible way whilst I'm powerless to do anything.

She's also starred in my dreams, her luscious, delectable body enticing me.

Reid is the first one to notice us, and a grin spreads across his face. "Ah, what's it like to be saved by a girl?" He snickers, scanning me over, like he's looking to see if any of my injuries are still there. They're not. They have long healed.

Jaxon and Wyatt turn around, but my gaze is on Paisley's back. She tenses before slowly turning to face us. We make eye contact for a split second, but then she avoids looking at me, watching everyone else around us.

"What's it like to fight like a girl?" I bite back at Reid, but my gaze keeps flicking back to Paisley, wondering why she won't look at me.

"Fuck you, dickhead," he snaps.

Ignoring him, I watch as Paisley keeps her attention on anyone but me, acting aloof, like we never happened. It bothers me more than I care to admit.

"Can I talk to you for a minute?" I ask, speaking to Paisley.

She turns, but before she can say no—and I can see her refusal on the tip of her tongue by her expression—Jaxon steps forward.

"Yeah, not gonna fucking happen, Landon," he bites out, an accusing look in his eye.

"Why?" I drawl, feigning boredom.

He raises his eyebrows, watching me like I've grown two heads. "Do you seriously have a death wish? You 'ent getting near my sister. I think you've done enough by nearly getting her hurt by those thugs who attacked you. If you want to thank her, consider it done," Jaxon states heatedly.

"I want to talk to her alone. It has fuck all to do with you," I snap, willing her to look at me. But her gaze is on her feet, her entire body tense.

"Landon," Liam warns.

"Paisley?" I call out, and finally, those hazel eyes with dark lashes meet mine. I'm taken aback by the pain shining in them.

What the fuck is going on?

She looks away, tears brimming her eyes, before turning back to me. "I'm glad you're okay," she says, trying to sound unaffected, but I can hear the emotion in her voice, see it in her expression. Her aloofness pisses me off, though, especially when she grabs Jaxon's arm. "Come on, Jaxon."

Fucked off at her reaction, I sit forward, watching her closely. "What, I'm not good enough to even talk to now?"

Her eyes widen in horror, her gaze flicking to her brother briefly. Oh, I hit a nerve; she's actually showing a reaction.

"When have you two talked?" Wyatt asks, more interested in the conversation now.

I smirk. "We're old *friends*."

"Like my sister would be alone with you. She has a brain, unlike the sluts you sleep with," Reid sneers.

Even in fight or flight mode she ignores me. Scanning her body, I lick my lips, pissed at how cold she's acting. I don't even know why I'm letting it bother me.

Because you like her, a voice in the back of my head whispers.

"Didn't seem like that when I fucked her in the front of my car," I snap out, fed up of being treated like I'm a fucking serial killer or some shit.

Pure hatred rolls off her, and I try not to be affected.

Stunned silent for a split second, everyone stares at me in shock. Wyatt turns to his sister, his disgust clear. "You slept with a fucking Carter?"

"Hey, we're fucking awesome in bed," Maddox butts in, earning murderous glares from the three brothers.

"You spread them for *him*?"

"Like butter," I drawl before I can stop myself, wanting to take it back the second it slips free.

Hurt and betrayal is written all over her expression, and I hate myself for making her look that distraught, that vulnerable.

Jaxon audibly swallows, turning slowly to face his sister, his lip curled, a knowing look on his face. "Please tell me this isn't true."

"Please don't," she begs, her eyes filled with fear as she clings to him. "Let's go home."

"Don't?" he spits in her face, before turning his murderous gaze on me. Without warning, he leaps over the table, making a grab for me. I stand, ready to fight back, but Aiden and Maddox step in front. "I'm going to rip you to fucking shreds, Landon."

Mark and the others step in to make sure Wyatt and Reid don't get involved. By the looks on their faces, it won't be long until they kick off either.

"All this time, I've been wondering who it was—who would be so fucking cruel as to do that to her. I should have fucking guessed," Jaxon sneers, before facing Paisley. "You've disappointed me, Paisley. I thought you had more fucking sense than to sleep with a Carter. Dad would have been so disappointed in you."

Hold the fucking door. He did not just say that to her.

Glasses smash and drinks spill as I try to barge through Aiden and Maddox. "Don't fucking speak to her like that. Ever!" I say in a low, menacing tone. I was a dick. I shouldn't have said anything. But the way she was acting… it made me lash out. But this… She doesn't deserve this.

When she turns to leave, a strangled cry leaving her throat, Jaxon grabs her bicep, pulling her towards him. He turns his head slightly to meet my eyes, before straightening to face me fully.

"Let me through," I growl when they keep blocking my path.

Liam turns with a look of disgust. "You've just suffered a fucking head injury and you want to get into another fight? Sit the fuck down."

"Oh, he's looking for more than that. When I'm done with you, you're gonna wish whoever fucked you up finished the job."

"Jaxon," Paisley cries, struggling to get her arm free, tears coursing down her cheeks.

"What is your fucking problem?" I snap, no longer able to look at Paisley, who crumples in on herself.

"My problem is that my sister lost a baby four months ago and has been fucking sick ever since. And to find out the dad was right under our noses the entire time… I should just kick your fucking teeth in for sleeping with my sister, but when I get my hands on you, I'll fucking murder you, and it will be because you left her to mourn the loss by herself," he snarls, taking a step towards me. "I had some respect for you, but this…" He shakes his head. "You're fucking dead."

"What?" I whisper, looking at Paisley now. I feel my blood rushing from my face as I take a step towards her, moving around Aiden, Maddox and the table. I need her to tell me this isn't true. "Paisley?"

Jaxon growls, warning me off. "Don't act all fucking concerned now. You might have been in hospital when it happened, Carter, but you've been out for a while now, and I'd know if you'd been to see her on our property. You just left her."

"Paisley, is this true?" I ask, feeling hollow. And for the first time in years, that anger simmers down, and I feel defeated.

A baby.

She lost our baby.

I treated her like some slut, even though she didn't mean that to me. Not really. I was too afraid of feeling something other than anger, and I hurt someone who didn't deserve it.

I look at Jaxon, swallowing past the lump at the back of my throat. "I didn't know!" I choke out.

Jaxon, looking worn out and tired, drops Paisley's arm. A hiccup, followed by a sob rises from her throat, before she runs out of the pub, the door slamming against the wall behind her.

Jaxon looks away from the door, his expression unreadable. "This isn't over."

"Well, fuck a duck," Maddox blurts out once they've left.

"I have to go," I tell them.

"Wait!" Aiden yells. "You can't go after her just yet. You need to calm down."

"No," I say, frustrated. "I need to know."

"You just embarrassed her in front of everyone, including her overprotective brothers. Going by the look on her face, she didn't want them to know," Hayden snaps, standing in front of me. "For someone who doesn't speak a full sentence, you just said a whole fucking lot, and now she's hurting. Even I'm pissed at you. You've never intentionally been mean to a girl before."

I rub the back of my neck, feeling antsy. "I don't know what came over me. I didn't even mean it," I say, feel hopeless.

Hayden's eyes soften. "Calm down before you go seek her out. And make sure her brothers don't see you."

"Like they'd catch me," I scoff.

"Are you going to calm down?"

Feeling my breathing slow, I nod. I don't like it. I saw how torn up she was; how hurt she was. And it's entirely my fault.

Realisation hits me in the face. The night of my attack… She was coming to tell me—she had to have been.

Oh fuck!

What have I done?

SIX

PAISLEY

I SUCK IN A SHARP BREATH, TEARS still coursing down my cheeks as I slap the front door of our three-story home.

"Boys, is that you?" Mum calls, walking down the hallway from the kitchen, her apron covered in flour. She takes one look at my face and wipes her hands on the dish cloth she's carrying. "Paisley, what is it?"

I shake my head, unable to speak over the lump in my throat. My brothers humiliated me in front of everyone. They told all within hearing range that I had slept with Landon, but worse, they spoke of my baby.

Ever since the day I was told I had lost our baby—who the doctors estimated to be around nine-weeks—I've just felt empty, numb.

My pregnancy was high risk due to my diabetes, but I'd held out hope that everything would be okay. I've been dealing with it one day at a time, but my brothers tore through any progress I'd made when they looked at me with disgust after finding out the baby was Landon's.

Did they mean they wouldn't have loved them because of it?

I wipe at my eyes, angry and mad over how they treated me. I've never missed a day of school unless absolutely necessary, always had good grades, and never got into trouble. But they looked at me like I was a stranger. It was a look I'd never had from them before.

Jaxon has always been protective of me. As his only sister, it was bound to happen, but after Dad died, it became more. He was the man of the house, so to speak. But he's never, not once, shouted at me or scolded me like a juvenile thirteen-year-old.

I'm angry, hurt. They might think it was me who disappointed them, but it was them who disappointed me when they treated me that way.

"Paisley?" Mum asks, hands on my shoulders. She's been my rock since everything happened, helping me come up with the perfect lie as to why I found Landon down that alley.

It wasn't in the best part of town, so Mum had told them I was picking up some spices for her cooking that only the shop on that street sold. Whether they believed the story was their business, but they never questioned why I was there, only why I went to check out the noises I heard coming from down the alley when I was alone.

"Ask your sons," I bite out, furious with them.

Just then, a car door slams shut, followed by two more. Before I can make it two steps up the stairs, Jaxon barges inside.

"Stop right fucking there. You don't get to run to your room, Paisley."

I pause mid-step at the anger in his voice, inhaling through my mouth, then exhaling out my nose, trying to control my breathing as I face their wrath. Their gazes are unforgiving, making me flinch.

"Jaxon, don't speak to your sister like that," Mum scolds.

Jaxon faces her with narrowed eyes. "Did you know who the dad was?"

Mum looks to me before warily watching Jaxon. Her face says it all. "Now, Jaxon, you need to calm down."

He looks at her disbelievingly. "Are you fucking kidding me? You knew and didn't say anything?"

That's enough.

"It's none of your business," I scream, and they all turn to me in shock. I never get angry, ever. "Do I question everyone you sleep with? Do I?"

"Paisley," Jaxon says gently, stepping forward, but I move up a step.

I wipe at my eyes. "No! I don't. I don't get in any of your business," I tell them, making sure to look at each of them. "I don't force girls to stay away from you, I don't treat any of them like shit, and I most certainly don't look at you like something I trod in."

Wyatt, with an impish expression, steps forward. "Paisley, this is Landon."

"And it was Selma last night for you—who, by the way, is a fucking bitch," I snap, and he steps back, surprised by my harsh language. "Did I demand you kick her out when she cornered me in the kitchen and made fun of my outfit? No! Why? Because it's none of my fucking business."

Reid can't even look at me, which makes my stomach turn. I eye Jaxon, waiting for him to say something.

"Why would you be another notch on his bedpost?"

"Who's to say he wasn't mine?" I growl, clenching my clammy hands together.

He rears back, his lip curling. "You were a virgin. You just let him use you."

I throw my hands up in the air. "No, I wasn't!"

"What?" Jaxon bites out.

"Who?" Reid says, piping up now and sounding deadly. "I'll kill him."

I roll my eyes before turning to Jaxon, hurt by his betrayal. "Them, I expected it from, but you… From you I expected better. I didn't think you'd go that length to hurt me. You humiliated me and shared something that was private in front of everyone."

He looks hurt for a second, before he masks it. "If your expectations of me were so high, then why didn't you tell me?"

I shrug. "Because I knew you'd never understand." The disappointment still lingers, and I scoff, shaking my head at him. "I'll never forgive you for what you did tonight. Never. I've never done anything to warrant that kind of behaviour, and quite frankly, I don't deserve your judgement either."

I turn, taking a few steps up the stairs. "Paisley, he's Landon Carter. You've seen how those guys go through girls. You have to understand where I'm coming from."

With my hand on the banister, I look back over my shoulder. "No, I don't. This isn't about the girls that flock to them, this is about your egos. You'd never have spoken to me the way you did, or looked at me like I disgusted you, if it were any other guy. You would have just scared them to death."

"Paisley," he calls out.

When I reach the stop of the first flight of stairs, I look back down, finding them all huddled at the bottom. "Oh, and I quit. Find someone else to run bookings because I no longer want to see you or speak to you."

His lips pinch together, his eyes cast downward. "You don't mean that."

When he looks up, I straighten, remaining calm. "Yes—yes, I do."

With that, I walk to the next lot of stairs, heading for my room, which is located in the attic of the house. It gives me privacy in a house full of guys, but sometimes I wonder if they put me here to keep me locked away, to make it easier to keep an eye on me.

Stepping in my room, I lay down on my bed, sniffling. Midnight, my black cat with coarse fur, jumps up onto my chest, licking my face. I smile, running my fingers through her fur.

"Hey," Mum greets, and I jump, not having heard her come up the stairs. "How you doing?"

"Did they tell you what happened?" I ask, not answering her question.

She sighs, sitting at the edge of my bed. "They said they were rude and outspoken but left out what was said. I think they did it for their safety, not wanting to admit they were in the wrong."

"Mum, it was horrible. You should have seen the way they all gawked at me," I tell her, feeling more tears gather.

"I'm sure they didn't mean anything by it."

I shrug, because we will never know. "He hates me."

"Jaxon? No, he doesn't. I think he just feels helpless and wants to protect you."

I shake my head. "No, not him," I bite out. "Landon. He hates me. The look he gave me when Jaxon blurted out about the baby… He looked devastated, broken."

"It must have been a surprise for him, darlin'. I'm sure he doesn't."

I roll onto my side, taking Midnight with me and tucking her close to my chest. "It doesn't matter anyway. It's not like we were a couple. He didn't want me. Nobody wants me."

"Paisley," Mum chokes out, her voice filled with emotion. "The right guy is out there for you. It's Landon's loss."

I flick my gaze to her. "I just want to be alone."

"Have you checked your levels?"

I inwardly groan, wanting to snap at her. "I did it before I left."

She pats my leg. "Yes, but you're stressed, and you know how your levels get when you are. Let me check them and then you can get some rest."

"No!" I bark out, harsher than intended. "I'll do it in a minute when I go to the toilet. Just leave me alone for a bit, please, Mum. And keep them away from me."

"Okay, okay," she says reluctantly. "Did you really mean you quit?"

"Yes," I whisper, watching her leave, ignoring the pity in her gaze.

Jaxon started the family business as soon as he finished college, and together, we've made it successful. But it's not my dream. It's his and my brothers'.

My dream is next door, currently stalled in its completion.

Since I was young when Dad died, my inheritance has built up in my account, and as soon as I finished school, I made plans on what to spend that money on. The farm is big, but we have less animals here than we used to. With the removal business doing well and Mum getting on a bit, we don't have time to keep on top of the upkeep.

But with a mortgage to pay for, we needed to work. I went to college to get my business degree, just like Jaxon, and when I finished, I sat down and went over all my options. It wasn't until we visited my mum's friend in Wales that it came to me. We stayed in a bed and breakfast near the cliffs, and I fell in love.

When I went to Mum with the proposal of opening one on our land, she was all for it. She even got excited and came up with ideas of her own to help expand the business. One is letting children visit and help feed the animals.

We got the permit to build, so on the left side of our property, as you pull onto our road, we have a huge building with fourteen rooms, a reception with lobby, and a dining room with kitchen.

The builders were on schedule until four months ago, when they arrived for work less and less. I stopped paying them, and after everything that happened, I stopped caring.

Tomorrow is a new day, and I'll begin looking for someone else to finish off the jobs that need doing before booking a decorator to come in and style the place.

Leaving my brothers to run the business feels like a betrayal, but after today, I don't think I'll be able to be around them for a while. God, even thinking about them brings more tears to my eyes.

A while later, there's a knock on my door. I lift my head, narrowing my eyes. "Go away!"

"Um, chick-a-dette, it's me, Adam."

I sit up, eyes wide. Sugar, I forgot to tell him I left the pub. "Come in."

He opens the door, grimacing when his bright blue eyes land on me. Decked out for a night out on the town, he looks out of place. He's wearing burgundy chinos that are far too tight for his skinny legs, and a white T-shirt with a black blazer over it. His dirty blonde hair is gelled into place, something which probably took him hours stood in front of the mirror to do. "I don't even need to ask if it's true. It's written all over your face."

"You heard?"

"Everyone in the pub was talking about it when I got there. The Carter's kicked one guy's arse for talking shit about you."

I cover my face with my hands. "Oh God."

He jumps into bed with me, getting under the covers. "So, when were you going to tell me you lost a baby? Were you even going tell me you were pregnant?"

The hurt in his voice is unmistakeable, and I wince, looking up at him through wet lashes. "I didn't want anyone to know. It's not something you just bring up in conversation."

"I tell you everything," he tells me.

I cringe. "Yeah, a little too much if you ask me. Telling me how it felt the first time you had sex with a lad isn't the same."

He shrugs. "I know, but as your best friend, we're supposed to share these things."

Reaching over, I grab the remote and flick the T.V. on before resting my head on his shoulder.

"Can you forgive me?"

"Yeah—if you put *Grey's Anatomy* on," he says, making me chuckle. I scroll through my Prime account and hit play, letting it carry on from where we last watched.

"How bad was it when you got there?" I whisper, wondering how I'm going to show my face in public again.

He takes my hand, squeezing it. "The Carter's were drunk. I didn't see Landon, but I heard one of them say he went home."

"I think he hates me," I tell him, then continue to fill in the blanks of what happened.

"Your brothers are dickheads, and if they were your parents, I'd tell them to cut the cord. Are you really going to quit?"

"Already have," I tell him. "And as soon as the bed and breakfast is finished and my apartment above it is liveable, I'll move out too."

"They aren't going to like it," he warns.

I shrug a shoulder. "They don't have to. Plus, it's not like I'm going far. It's a five-minute walk to the bed and breakfast."

"You figured out a name yet?"

I chew my bottom lip. "I was going to go with Meadow Inn."

"You not putting your name in it?"

I sigh sadly. "No. We've got Hayes Removals and Hayes Farm; Hayes Inn would just be too much."

"I like it."

I wipe a tear that falls from my eye, the events of the night catching up with me. With my best friend beside me, all I want to do is cry. I've wanted to throttle my brothers so many times, but we've never argued, not even as kids. Having this rift between us, even new, is killing me.

"Come on, don't get upset," Adam soothes, shifting so he can wrap his arm around me.

"I can't help it. It's just so hard to believe this happened."

"I know. Just sleep—"

I elbow him in the ribs, and he grunts. "If you tell me to sleep on it; that things will look better in the morning, I will punch you."

"Why? It works."

"No, it doesn't. I hate that saying—and all of the others you blurt out."

"Hey, don't hate me because I'm awesome," he teases. "And not to sound cocky, but have you looked out your window? The grass *really is* greener on the other side."

I elbow him again, making him laugh. "Shut it."

"Tell you what, why don't I go downstairs and steal a bottle of liqueur."

"I can't drink," I remind him, something he already knows.

He sits up and taps my nose. "Yes, but I can, and if we're going to talk deep, I'll need it."

I giggle, feeling a little lighter. "The deepest conversation you got into was when we were talking about the sale Gucci had."

He sighs wistfully. "Ah, those shoes cost me six hundred quid in the sale."

I shove him. "Go get your drink or no Mc Dreamy for you."

He gets up from the bed, turning to point his finger at me. "You are so cruel."

"Bring up some snacks."

"Hopefully one of your brothers is half naked down there and I can ogle him," he says, winking.

I narrow my eyes and throw a pillow at him. "We hate them, remember," I yell.

He pouts. "You're sucking all the fun out of tonight."

I point to the door. "Go. Snacks. Now!"

He salutes me, grinning. "All right. All right."

SEVEN

LANDON

MY MOUTH TWISTS INTO A GRIMACE as I stand at the backdoor of Charlotte's two-bedroom house.

She's cooking.

Which isn't always a good sign when it comes to her as she cooks when she's happy, when she's sad, or when she has something on her mind. I won't know how bad it is until I get in there, but the thought of eating something she's cooked makes me wish I was back in hospital.

Knocking on the glass loudly so she can hear me over the music blasting from her speakers, I wait. The chances of her hearing me here are better than if I knocked on the front door.

I jump when a face covered in flour and some goo presses against the glass. A flash of sadness fills her eyes before she covers it with a beaming smile.

She opens the door. "Landon, what are you doing here?"

"I came to beg for forgiveness," I tell her, wishing I could pull off the puppy dog look, like Aiden. He's forgiven within seconds.

Bastard.

"What for?" she asks nervously, shifting out of the way.

"You know what for," I state, stepping inside. I inwardly wince at all the baked goods on the kitchen side.

Please don't make me eat.

She looks over her shoulder when she reaches the sink, grabbing a bowl to wash. "No idea what you're talking about," she mumbles, scrubbing furiously.

"Charlotte," I warn.

My eyes scan her body. Hayden and Liam were right: she's lost weight. Her round, curvy figure had always suited her. This thinner frame makes her look ill.

She spins around and bubbles and water splash everywhere. I step back. "You left me," she yells, her eyes rounding when she realises she just had a go at someone. Tears form and I step forward, ready to comfort her. "I'm sorry."

"No, I'm sorry," I declare. "It's not you; it's me. I've been avoiding everyone. Since waking up in the hospital, I've been trying to deal with everything that happened."

She looks at me through watery eyes, shaking her head. "No. You left me before that. You died. I thought I'd never see you again."

Fuck the flour and water. I step forward, pulling her into my arms as a sob rumbles through her chest.

She clings to me, her soapy hands wetting my T-shirt. "It's not like I meant to," I say, feeling a tad uncomfortable.

"So why won't you see me? I've tried bringing you food, treats, but you turn me away or don't answer the door."

Yeah, I'm not about to tell her I didn't want food poisoning when I could barely sit up without being in pain. Imagine what I would have gone through with sickness and diarrhea.

I step back, bending down so we're eye level. "I'm sorry. So fucking sorry. But I'm here now. Can you forgive me?"

She wipes under her eyes. "It depends."

Oh God, I know that look.

"What do you want?"

She bats her eyelashes, smiling and doing a complete one-eighty from the crying woman standing in front of me.

"You have to talk Faith into letting me have a rescue cat."

Fuck!

"Charlotte," I start, but she begins to pout. "She won't let you."

"I swear, I've been watching YouTube videos on how to look after them. It's easy. I promise. And a friend of mine on Facebook said they take care of themselves."

"No, they really don't. You have to feed it, clean its litter tray and all that other bullshit."

She beams brightly at me. "I know," she exclaims excitedly, clapping her hands. "It's going to be so much fun."

"What about another fish?" I try to persuade.

Her nose twitches. "I really want a cat. Will you please talk to Faith?"

Knowing I have a lot to make up for, I reluctantly nod, even if it means I have to take care of the damn thing myself.

She squeals, jumping up and down before kissing me on the cheek. "Thank you. Thank you. Thank you."

I place my hands on her shoulders, stopping the bouncing. "I still think you should get a virtual pet. Did you try that app I downloaded for you?"

She waves me off, moving over to the kitchen counter. "I have this cool one on Facebook, but it's really not the same."

Speaking of. "Why haven't you deleted the account?"

I dread to think of the creepy messages she gets. We've all tried to hack it and delete it ourselves, but her password is solid. None of us can guess it.

"I'm not deleting it. I'm learning new things all the time. And I like reading people's posts—they're fascinating. Like Deborah, she found out her kids' dad was having another baby and totally called him out for not paying child support."

I frown, my eyebrows drawing together. "Who the fuck is Deborah?"

She grins widely, like it's the best thing ever. "I have no idea."

Fuck's sake.

"You don't know her, but you have her on Facebook?"

She nods, like it's no big deal. "Yep. I've met loads of lovely people," she says, then giggles at my horrified expression. "I even get invited to their houses. One lived in Algeria or something."

I'm going to smash her phone and make it look like an accident.

"Charlotte, you can't speak to strangers."

She gives me a dry look. "I know, but the look on your face is priceless."

I rear back. "That's mean."

"So is not telling me about Paisley Hayes."

I wince. I deserved that. "I'm sorry."

"I know. Have you spoken to her?"

I shake my head. "No. It's been four days, but I don't know how to get hold of her."

"I have her on Facebook if you want to message her."

Yeah, that isn't going to happen. I need to see her. I'm still having trouble believing it. It doesn't feel real. "I need to speak to her, face to face."

"Then go see her."

"And have her brothers get in the way again?"

She cocks her hip against the counter. "For someone so clever and level-headed, you can be really dumb. Sneak in. How many times did you do it when you were a teenager?"

I snort. "And end up in one of her brothers' rooms? I think not."

"Well, according to Facebook, her room is in the attic and it's the only room on that floor," she says, shrugging. "She posted a picture of her cat by the window and hash-tagged *tower, attic view* and so on."

"And from that you got that her room is in the attic?"

"Just go. You want to speak to her. What else do you have to lose? And besides, today has been a day of apologies for you."

"What?"

She raises her eyebrow. "You went to your mum's. I take it you apologised to her, too."

"I did, but how did you know?"

She gives me a dry expression. "Facebook."

"You really think I should go?"

"Yes. She probably needs you to. I can't imagine what she's going through," she whispers, wiping a tear that drops from her lashes.

"Fuck it. I might as well. The longer I leave it, the more she'll hate me."

"She couldn't hate you. No one could," she tells me gently.

I roll my eyes. "You really believe that, don't you?"

She beams at me. "Of course. You're my best friend," she replies. "Do you want to take her a plate of cookies?"

I cough to clear my throat. "I don't think I'll be able to sneak in with a plate of cookies. Maybe next time?" I lie.

She nods, leaning up on her toes to kiss my cheek. "Go, before you change your mind." Reaching for the door, her voice stops me. "Landon, try to smile. It might relax her."

Facing her, I force my lips into a smile. "Like this?"

She frowns. "Maybe just be yourself. Love you. And don't forget to talk to Faith."

I groan. "I won't. Promise."

I just reach the door as my phone chimes with a text message. Sliding it out of my back pocket, I glance down at the screen.

MADDOX: MC5 NOW! IT'S ON! PS: REMIND ME NEVER TO PISS OFF YOUR DAD.

LANDON: On way. You can chill with the caps.

MADDOX: AYE, AYE, CAPTAIN.

"See you later," I call out, not telling her where I'm going.

"Good luck."

It's not me who's gonna need it.

STEPPING INSIDE THE room, I'm surprised to find Drew, the only person I can tolerate beyond family, standing with my cousins and brother. Drew, unlike most gym fanatics, isn't beefed up to the point he looks like the nineteen-eighty-one cartoon character, Popeye. He's got muscle, don't get me wrong. His hair is tied back in a man bun, a black gauge in his ear instead of the red he normally wears.

Dad is in the corner with a glass of whiskey, swaying slightly in his chair.

Tonight is not going to end well if my dad is drinking.

Dad turns his head towards the door when it slams shut behind me. He gets up from his stool, nearly tripping over his own feet. I roll my eyes.

"Who the fuck put that there," he growls, loud enough for the room to hear.

I meet him in the middle, giving him a chin lift. "You doing all right, Dad?"

"No. I need you to give me a reason why we can't finish these fuckers once and for all."

I stare at him dead on, not giving away any emotion. "Because I want to hurt them. I've learned from experience that broken bones can heal, Dad. I don't just want to hurt them physically, I want to fucking ruin them."

He looks shocked for a second, before masking it with a sinister grin. "Well alrighty then. That should fucking do it."

"Dad, are you sure you want to get involved in this? I've still not found out about Rocco, the guy they work for. He's some Italian dude who thinks he runs the place."

Dad scoffs. "We've been running this town since we were in nappies. Don't worry about him. Me and your uncles will deal with him personally."

"Dad," I warn, needing to stop this.

He holds his hand up, his eyes narrowing into slits. "No. Don't even bother, Landon. I'm your fucking dad. I'm pissed as fuck you got into this fighting ring business in the first place. If you needed to let off some steam, you could've fucked someone until the cows came home."

Never understood that saying.

"It wasn't frustration, Dad."

"No, I know what it was. You don't think we've been through shit in our life? Your uncle Malik was constantly getting into fights because he held so much anger inside. You should have come to us."

Ah, so that's what this is about. He's upset I didn't have a heart to heart with him. "I know you care. You all do. But it was something I enjoyed, too. I didn't think some low-life thug would set four guys with bats on me."

Dad's eyes harden. It's a side of him I've never seen before. He always made fun out of everything. Liam broke his arm falling out of a tree outside our school after Hayden put all his boxers up there. We were thirteen, and she had just started her period. He announced it to the entire class. It was payback.

Instead of getting angry, he clapped Hayden on the back.

When we got brought back by the police, he didn't get angry; he got even, making us do chores for a week. He even got Hayden to give him a pedicure. And if you had been by dad's feet, you'd understand how that was punishment. He was a gym teacher, always running around in the same pair of sticky trainers.

And although the situation is completely different, something inside of my dad has been missing since the day I woke up. I need to get that back, because he levels me out in a way only he and Charlotte can. By being so goddamn happy all the time.

"Well, it's time to get even, son. When they announced you coded…" He shakes his head, gulping. "I never want to feel like that again, ever. We're in this together now. Nobody fucks with a Carter, let alone my kid." He looks away to gain his composure.

I chuckle. If the situation wasn't so dire, I'd make a joke about how having a beer has made him think he can take on the world. But I don't think he'd get my sense of humour right now.

"It's only going to be small, immature shit at first, Dad. I want to drive them fucking crazy," I warn him, hoping he hasn't got some crazy idea in his head.

He nods but doesn't meet my gaze. I sigh, scrubbing a hand down my weary face.

"Some fucker gonna clue me in on what is happening?"

I want to get to Paisley. For the first time in months, revenge hasn't been in the front of mind. She has.

Maddox steps forward, and his expression doesn't bode well for me. "Ah, your dad and Maverick split us all up."

"What, why?" I ask.

"You, Max and Maddox are going together," Maverick says, but he doesn't sound happy about it. "Just, please, don't fuck around and get caught." He looks at my dad when he says it, and I find it amusing.

"Fuck you, dickhead. I'm not that fucking old," Dad snaps.

"You had a Happy Meal on the way over here because you wanted the toy," Maverick points out.

Chuckles echo around the room, and Dad glares at Maverick. "It was a fucking spy kit. I thought it was fitting, being we were going out on a mission."

"You do know we aren't the special forces, right, Dad?" Liam asks, chuckling.

Max snuffs his nose up at us. "They fucking begged me to go work for them."

"Okay," Liam says slowly, placating him.

Getting annoyed, I snap, "Plan?"

"You're getting the Blaze kid," Maverick informs me, and I grin inwardly, happy I get to fuck with him. He lives in his mum's garage still, and as far as I know, it's just them two.

"Fucking Blaze," Dad mutters.

"Me, Aiden and Liam will get Rocket," Maverick continues, glaring at Dad when he scoffs. "What now?"

Dad bats his eyelashes innocently. "Nothing. Just wondering what his parents were on when they named him."

"I heard it's a nickname," Drew pipes in, and I nod in greeting. He grins, nodding back.

"Ew, please tell me it's not because he goes off like a rocket," Maddox whines, looking utterly disgusted.

Drew chuckles. "The fact your mind went there says it all. But yes, apparently. Not sure if that's true though."

"Drew, Mark and Myles have Flash," Maverick carries on, giving my dad a 'shut up' look. "And Mason, Malik and Hayden have Terry."

"You didn't tell the others?" I ask, relieved.

He shakes his head. "No. The less of us there is, the better."

"Plausible deniability," Dad mutters.

I clap my hands together, taking in everyone's determined expressions. "All right then, let's go."

EIGHT

LANDON

W E PULL UP ONTO THE DARKENED STREET, a few houses down from Blaze's. The area is rough and well known for its people to mind their own business when something kicks off. I'm not even surprised to find this is where that slime lives.

I jump out of the front of Dad's car, ready to head down, when the sound of the boot opening stops me. I turn around to find Maddox looking inside the boot in horror.

"Um, Uncle Max, I'm all for getting revenge and all, but I won't make it in prison. My arse is plump."

What the hell has my dad brought?

I walk over, nearly choking to death when I take in a lung full of air. "Dad," I hiss, taking the chainsaw off him. "What the hell?"

He shrugs, trying to take it back. "What? I scouted the joint earlier today and saw his car is parked under the tree on their drive."

"You were gonna cut a tree down? With that?" Maddox asks doubtfully.

"No, I was going to make it look like extremely bad luck. You don't want him to know you're gunning for him."

Okay, it was better than what we had planned. We were just going to set his car alight, like the others will do with the other cars. Unless the uncles come up with a better plan, which is a high possibility.

"All right. Is Liam sure they are at the pub?" I ask, talking about Dad's high school friend, who he named our Liam after. He's a hacker—a damn good one—and earns a shit load doing hardware security for companies. He also finds shit out for his high paying clients, digging up dirt on whoever they ask for.

Liam pulls out his phone, tapping it a few times before turning the screen to face me. At a round table in some rundown bar, sits Blaze, Flash, Rocket and Terry. I nod and hand Dad back his chainsaw.

Maddox looks horrified, his mouth hanging open as his gaze goes from Dad to me, and back to Dad.

When Dad throws a bag over his shoulder, slamming the boot shut, I step away, heading towards Blaze's house. Maddox jogs to catch up with me and leans down to hiss in my ear, "Do you think giving him a very powerful tool is wise?"

I glance back at Dad, who is scouting the area, and shrug. "What's the worst he could do?"

Maddox rears back like I've lost my mind. "Famous last words."

I frown at the bogie-green car. Although it's a new Ford build, only a year old, it's fucking disgusting. "Um, I think we'd be doing him a favour," I whisper.

"Anyone else have the urge to blow their nose?" Maddox pipes in.

"Where shall we start?" I ask, wondering if we should break in first.

"Dunno," Maddox answers. "What do you think, Uncle Max?"

I look around Maddox, not seeing Dad. "Dad?"

"Will you two stop hammering on like two old ladies and go do what you've got to do," Dad hisses, his voice close.

We look up to where he's perched on a tree branch with wide eyes. Holy fucking shit. *Where did he get that saw from?*

Maddox lifts up the bag resting against the tree and gestures for me to follow him. We walk around the side of the house to where the garage door is located.

Maddox bends down and grabs some shit out of his pocket. "Don't worry, I watched this on YouTube. Should take me a few seconds."

Minutes pass and we're still not inside. Growling, I kick off the wall and twist the handle. It opens, and I glare down at Maddox. "You didn't think to try that first?"

He looks confused. "Why would I? I didn't watch those videos for nothing."

I roll my eyes and step inside. "Fuck!" I hiss out, lifting my hoodie up to cover my mouth and nose. It fucking stinks of weed and shit in here.

"Should have brought extra gloves," Maddox mutters, looking around the room in disgust. The place already looks like it's been done over, but Maddox doesn't even blink as he moves further into the room. The first thing he does is takes a screwdriver to the T.V, digging it into the sides of the screen.

"What the fuck are you doing?"

He glances over his shoulder, giving me a dry look. "We don't want him to know we did this, right? As much as I'd love to stomp all over the fucker, I'd rather it looks okay and have him turn it on before he finds out it's broken. It's the only decent thing in the room, apart from the Xbox One," he says, then, as an afterthought, continues with, "I'll shove some of that yogurt in it after."

"You're nuts," I tell him, even more confused when he turns it so it's upside down. He stands back up, looking proudly at his handiwork before moving on.

I scan the room for the best place to do what we came in here for. The red spray cans rattle in my bag as I pull one out. I step on the bed, cringing when my foot slides in something.

Dirty bastard.

Maddox laughs behind me when I finish. I jump off the bed and step back, admiring my work.

I know what you did.

"Creepy; I like it," Maddox compliments.

I shrug, and I'm about to leave when I notice most of Blaze's furniture is upside down. "Um, Mad, what did you do?" I ask, trying not to laugh.

"Fucker will think he's haunted."

I chuckle, and as I step back towards the door, something poking out from under the bed catches my eye.

Fucker.

I reach down, grabbing the baseball bat, and twist it around in my hand. Blood coats the end of it, and I cringe, thinking back to that night and how every blow felt like my insides were being hit with a sledgehammer.

"Is that…?" Maddox starts, his voice too hoarse to finish.

"Yeah," I bite out, taking it with me.

"Shit, shit, shit, shit," I hear when we step outside.

I rush around the corner to the front of the house, and my eyes widen when I see Dad hanging upside down from the tree, his legs and arms wrapped around it like a pretzel and a panicked look on his expression.

"I've got this!" he calls out, his voice high-pitched. One of his hands lets go of the tree for a second, nearly making him fall.

"What, the tree or the fall you're about to make?" Maddox chuckles, leaning against the garage door to watch the show.

"Just give me a minute," Dad wheezes, hugging the tree tighter.

We watch in amusement as he manages to pull himself upright. He clings to the tree, giving us a relieved smile. "I sawed enough down that it should take me seconds to cut through with the chainsaw. Before the neighbours know what we're doing, we'll be gone."

"Dad," I warn as he turns the chainsaw on, the rev of the engine echoing down the quiet street. I look around, hoping no one comes out and sees us. I don't think he realises the position he's in right now.

"I got this," he says confidently. I open my mouth, ready to yell at him to stop, but it's too late. The chainsaw makes a brattling sound as it cuts through the last few inches, and everything from there happens quickly.

A high-pitched, girly squeal escapes him as the branch breaks off beneath him. He drops the chainsaw and it lands on top of the car, moving seconds before Dad or the tree can land on it. He ends up on his back on top of the car.

The chainsaw rattles, vibrating away from him and the branch he just cut down and towards the window. I cringe at the metal being scraped, the sound grating my teeth together. The second the chainsaw touches the front windshield; the glass shatters and the chainsaw falls into the car.

"Dad, are you okay?" I call out, quickly snapping out of it and moving to the car.

"I'm okay," he groans, lifting his hand up slowly. "I meant to do that."

He slowly sits up, revealing a dent where he had fallen next to the tree. Maddox chuckles.

The neighbour's light switches on, and I groan. "Dad, we have to go," I tell him urgently, rushing over to the car. I don't think anyone will call the cops, not in this area, but I don't want to take any chances.

Dad struggles to get upright, and Maddox grabs my arm, pulling. "Come on, we need to get out of here before the cops come."

Has he lost his mind? "We can't leave him here," I hiss out, shoving his hand off me.

"Why? He'd do the same thing to us," he says matter-of-factly.

"Yeah, I would," Dad wheezes as he rolls off the car roof and onto the ground. Maddox gives me a 'told you so' look.

I wince down at my dad. That had to have hurt.

We help pull him up, and he shakes off dust from his coat. Maddox looks over his shoulder, and when I glance in the same direction, I notice the curtain twitch.

Shit!

"Come on, Uncle Max," Maddox says, pushing him towards the road.

Dad presses his feet into the ground. "Nope," he chokes out, pointing towards the car. "We need to get the chainsaw."

"Uh, no, I think we really need to go," Maddox explains, trying to grab Dad again, but he doesn't budge. "Don't think I won't leave you. You've got to the count of three to get your arse into the car."

"No, we really need to get that chainsaw. It has your company logo on it."

"What?" Maddox whisper-yells, looking close to punching him.

I lean over the window and peer into the car to find the chainsaw vibrating across the seats, tearing them apart.

Well, shit!

"I borrowed it," Dad explains calmly.

"It was locked in the bed of my truck, Uncle Max. Did I mention it was locked?" Maddox growls.

Dad waves him off. "That's not really the issue right now, is it, Maddox. Stop changing the subject and help me get this out of the car."

Groaning, Maddox jumps on the bonnet, leaving two dents. He leans through the window, cursing. Not even seconds later, the sound from the chainsaw is cut off and he's pulling it out of the broken window.

"I'm going to kill you," he tells my dad.

Dad pulls him off the hood of the car. "Stop being a baby. Everything is fine, but we really need to go," he states, before limping away and leaving us standing there dumbfounded.

We rush to catch up, watching as his movements get slower and slower the closer we get to the car.

"I'll drive," I tell him, snatching the keys out of his hand.

He sighs a breath of relief. "Good. Because I think you need to drop me off at the hospital. I think I broke my leg and back."

Maddox chuckles, dispensing the chainsaw back into the boot. I help Dad into the back, trying not to laugh at his pained expression.

"If Uncle Maverick asks about this, I got into a fight with a bloke named Butch, who was built like a house."

"Sure," I say dryly.

"Butch," Maddox repeats, laughing as he gets into the car.

"I mean it, Maddox," Dad warns him.

"What's in it for me?" Maddox asks, leaning around to peer into the backseat.

I pull off, scanning the houses for any signs of someone watching. There aren't any.

"I'll get Lake to make you her apple pie."

"I had a slice Sunday," Maddox states, licking his lips.

I inwardly groan, wishing he wouldn't goad my dad.

"You fucking bastard," Dad gasps. "It was you who ate the last of *my* pie?"

Maddox chuckles. "And it tasted so damn good."

"I'm going to fucking kill you, you pie-thieving bastard. Just let me recover first."

"*You* owe *me*, remember," Maddox taunts, not bothered by Dad's threats. He knows he doesn't really mean them.

"Fuck's sake. How about I won't tell your mum you're blackmailing me?"

"You wouldn't," Maddox calls his bluff.

"I fucking would. I'd been saving myself for that pie all fucking day."

With an annoyed puff, Maddox turns back around in his seat. "Fine! A pie it is. And you'd better not eat it."

"Deal," Dad agrees. "Now, son, please get me to the hospital."

"You did what?" Mum screeches. "You're supposed to be setting a good example for our children."

Aiden, who Maddox had spilled his guts to, hadn't promised to keep his mouth shut, so he blurted it out to Mum as soon as she walked into the room, finding it hilarious.

Dad frowns at her. "I was. I was teaching them not to let people fuck with them."

Mum leans in closer. "You fell from a bloody tree, Max."

"And I'm fine. The nurse said it's not broken and I can go home."

Picking up the ice, Mum looks at his bruised and swollen ankle before slamming the ice back down. "This is ridiculous."

"Ow, woman!" he yells, glaring at her. "Nurse! Nurse!"

A nurse rushes into the room, her eyes wide when she sees us all standing around. "Is everything okay?"

"No!" Dad yells, bright red. "I think my wife just broke my ankle for reals."

Mum takes pity on the nurse. "He loves being dramatic. When can he go home?"

"Go home? I need to be looked after, and you keep abusing me," he says, and to add affect, sniffles.

Mum glares at Dad before turning back to the nurse. "Maybe I should get a doctor," she mumbles, watching Mum closely, like she's waiting for her to attack.

"I'm not a husband beater," Mum sighs, used to this kind of reaction when Dad gets all drama queen.

Dad inhales a deep breath. "It's been tough. I said I liked being spanked *one time*. One time! And now she uses whips, chains… You name it, I've had it."

"Dad," Hayden groans.

"I do not," Mum hisses, her neck and cheeks turning pink. "I don't!"

"I'll go get a doctor," the nurse announces, patting Dad's arm affectionately.

He gives her his best puppy-dog eyes and a pout before wiping his invisible tears away. "Thank you."

"It's my job," she says soothingly.

Her face tightens when she walks past Mum, who is standing open-mouthed.

Mum's lips pinch together when she faces Dad. "I was going to run you a hot bath and order your favourite takeout, but you can forget it."

Dad's expression changes, and he starts begging for forgiveness.

My phone beeps with a text.

CHARLOTTE: How did it go with Paisley? And did you speak to Faith about me getting a cat? I'm going to call her Catnip. You know, Cat-Nip LOL (I mean laugh out loud).

I roll my eyes, fighting the urge to laugh.

LANDON: On my way to Paisley's now. Had to drop Dad off to get his foot X-rayed.

CHARLOTTE: OMG! Is he okay? What happened? I'll bake him a get-well cake right now.

LANDON: He's fine, and everything happened. You know what

Dad's like. He can walk outside and something will happen. I bet he'd love a cake. I'll talk to you later.

CHARLOTTE: Okay. But don't forget to talk to Faith for me. Oh, what about Whispurr? You know, Whisker and purr?

LANDON: Both sound great, but you should wait until Faith gives you a cat.

CHARLOTTE: Yeah. I suppose. Right, good luck and I'll speak to you later.

LANDON: LATER.

Needing to get to Paisley before it gets any later, I step towards Mum and Dad, interrupting their argument.

"I'm off. There's something I need to do."

"See you tomorrow, sweetie," Mum says, leaning up to kiss my cheek. I kiss her back, giving her a brief hug before turning to my dad and slapping him on the shoulder. He winces, narrowing his eyes at me.

"Fucker."

"Feel better and speak to you tomorrow."

No one follows me when I leave the hospital room, and I'm grateful for the time alone. I need think of how I'm going to get Paisley to forgive me.

And how to get to her without her brothers finding me and then killing me.

Yep, should be a breeze.

NINE

PAISLEY

GRABBING THE DIRTY DISHES, I drop them into the sink, pointedly ignoring my brothers.

"Are you really going to ignore us for the rest of your life?" Jaxon asks.

I scrub furiously when I hear his voice. It's been four days of not speaking to them or going to work. Instead, I've put all my focus on finally getting the bed and breakfast ready. I just need to find someone to finish what is left. The rest I'll figure out how to do myself.

"This is getting old, Paisley," Wyatt calls out, and I slam the plate onto the rack.

"Sons, leave your sister be," Mum scolds, finishing her glass of wine.

"No, Mum. How long is she going to punish us? It should be her apologising to us for sleeping with the enemy," Reid snaps out.

I glare at my brother, slamming the plate back into the sink before facing Mum. "I'm tired. I'm going to head to bed."

Mum sighs, shaking her head in disappointment at Reid before giving me a tight smile. "Okay, baby. Don't forget to check your glucose levels. They've been really high lately."

I force a smile as I finish drying my hands. "Probably all the stress from living my life," I bite out sarcastically. I throw the tea towel onto the counter before storming out of the kitchen.

"Paisley," Jaxon calls, but I ignore him, holding back tears. I hate the distance that is now between me and my brothers, but they are the ones who put it there. I never dictate to them. Ever. I expect the same from them.

Mum walks up behind me as I reach the bottom of the stairs. "Paisley, they don't mean it."

I turn, fighting the urge to snap at her. She's stuck in the middle at the moment, and as hard as she's tried to be there for me, I don't need to hear her make excuses for their behaviour.

"No, Mum, they do. It's fine. If I'm one big disappointment to them, then I don't see why they care if I'm talking to them or not."

"I didn't mean it," Jaxon says, and I stiffen, hiding my surprise.

I face him, concealing the hurt I feel towards him. "You don't act like it."

His expression softens. "It was a shock, Paisley. You're my baby sister."

"Yes, your baby sister, not your daughter," I snap, feeling tears begin to threaten. "You treated me like some nobody, Jaxon. Nobody. I'm your goddamn sister. I do one thing you don't like and all of a sudden I'm the worst person in the world."

"Paisley, it's not like that," he says, taking a step forward, but I move a step back, away from him.

"It doesn't matter. I'm done. Until I'm ready to forgive you, I don't want to speak to you."

"At least come back to work. The new receptionist isn't the same," he says.

I shrug, and as much as it's killed me not to help out, I can't find it in me to care. "No. I need to stand on my own two feet without you guys hovering over me all the time."

"Wait," he calls out, but I shake my head, running up the rest of the stairs to my room.

After slamming the door shut and locking it, I head over to Midnight, who is sleeping on my chaise under the window. I pick her up and sit down, placing her in my lap. She begins to purr when I run my fingers through her fur.

"Everything will be fine," I tell her, but I'm telling myself more than anything. I have to believe it will because I've never gone this long without my brothers in my life, and for the past four days I've avoided them at all costs, except for dinner.

She lets out a meow in agreement.

Staring outside, I scan the front of our house. To the left, the outdoor lights from the bed and breakfast shine on the path to the front of the building. Soon, they'll turn off with the timer.

To the right, about a mile from the house, is where the Hayes Removals offices and factory are located. We have six vans in total, all parked out front by the box loading bay where we keep supplies.

The light flicks on, so I know Jaxon, who has a room, kitchen and bath in the back has returned home for the night.

I remember crying the first night he moved in there, even though it was only a short walk away. For some reason, it had felt like he left me. I understood his need for privacy, since we only lived in a six-bed house. With eight brothers, me and my mum, is was a tight squeeze.

How much has changed from then to now, I sigh wistfully.

A rustling sound diverts my attention, and I look around my room, wondering what the hell it was. Midnight sits up, rushing to the window and looking outside.

"What you seen, baby?" I ask her softly, kneeling on the chaise and looking through the window.

I scream when a hooded figure pops up behind the glass. "Landon?" I ask in a shaky voice, blinking to make sure I'm really seeing him. I push the window up, worried he'll fall. "What the hell are you doing?"

"The attic, really?" he whines, shuffling through the window.

How hasn't he broken his neck climbing up here? My muscles tense at seeing him, a heavy feeling in my stomach.

"Paisley, are you okay?" Wyatt yells.

"Paisley?" Mum calls, sounding worried as I hear her walking up my stairs. "Are you okay? Let me in."

Panicked, I move towards the door, checking it's locked. It is. I sag against it, resting my forehead on the cool wood.

"Yes, Mum."

"I heard you scream," he yells, and I hear his heavy footfalls on the stairs leading up to my door.

"We did," Mum agrees, just as the door handle begins to rattle. "Why have you locked the door?"

"Spider!" I yell, clearing my throat when it comes out high-pitched. All I need right now is for them to barge in here and have Wyatt see Landon.

With my focus still on the door, I flick my gaze a little to the left, and I know I'm not imagining him. The lunatic, who was mean not once, but twice, is standing in my bedroom. After climbing through my window, which couldn't have been an easy feat.

"I'm here," Wyatt yells, and I can hear the pout in his voice.

"A spider?" Mum asks doubtfully, knowing I've never been scared of them.

Landon chuckles behind me, and I glare at him. "Yes, a big, dumb spider."

"Um, want me to kill him?" Wyatt asks, sounding hopeful. But give the boy some string...

"Wyatt, go downstairs. I can handle this," Mum tells him when I don't answer.

Midnight begins to purr around my leg. "N-no. It's fine. You can both go. Midnight ate it." Which is believable because she's always bringing in some kind of kill she's captured.

"Are you sure?"

"Yes. Night, Mum."

"U-um, okay then, dear. If you're sure."

"I am."

"Night," Mum calls through the door, and I sag with relief.

"Night, Mum."

"Night," Wyatt yells.

When I don't answer, Mum steps in. "Come on, let's go get you some more cake."

"She's got to speak to us at some point," he whines, but I hear him following her down the stairs.

Once I know they won't hear me, I spin around and glare at Landon. "What the hell are you thinking?"

His eyes narrow into slits. "I could ask you the same thing."

I avert my eyes. "I was going to tell you," I whisper.

"The night I was attacked?" I nod, not speaking. "Why didn't you come see me at the hospital? Was I the reason you lost the baby? Did they hurt you?"

I sit down on my bed, my chest feeling tight at how torn up he sounds. "It was a high-risk pregnancy anyway. I have type one diabetes. The doctor said it could have been numerous things, but it was nothing I or you had done. I promise."

"And why didn't you come to see me after?"

I look up, meeting his gaze, and feel myself flinch. "I thought you were dead for weeks, Landon."

"What?" he asks, his eyebrows reaching his hairline.

I nod, grimacing. "I was there when your heart stopped," I explain, not telling him it was that moment I lost our baby. "By the time I woke up, I wasn't really with it. I had lost our baby and thought I lost you. It wasn't until a few weeks later when my friend came over that I heard you were alive. By then, I knew about your injuries and didn't want you to find out when you were so vulnerable."

His face crumbles as he drops onto the chaise. "I'm so sorry, Paisley."

"It doesn't matter. If that's what you came to hear, I'd like you to leave," I tell him, not meeting his gaze.

"What?"

Facing him, I straighten my spine. "I understand you wanting answers,

Landon, but what you did the other day in The Ginn Inn was uncalled for. You outed and embarrassed me in front of everyone,"

He runs a hand over the scruff on his jaw. "I fucked up big time, but I was just so angry at how aloof you were acting."

Now I'm over the shock of him being here, I want him gone. "Did you expect me to act any different after you left me on the side of the road with no underwear, or when the last time I saw you, you looked pissed off that I was there?" I ask him, trying to keep my voice low, but it's hard when I'm so god damn angry. "Just go!"

"No!"

His harsh voice has me looking up. "What do you mean, 'no'?"

"What I said—no. I'm not leaving," he declares, resting his elbows on his knees. "First off, I was pissed at the old gym because it isn't a place for someone like you, Paisley."

"Someone like me?" I ask, ignoring how much it hurts to hear.

He must hear it because he shakes his head. "I didn't mean anything bad about it," he says, scrubbing a hand down his face. "You're... Paisley. You're kind, sweet, generous, and you shouldn't be mixed up with people like that. I was shocked to see you." I watch him struggle for a moment on what to say next, probably choosing his next words wisely. What he says shocks me as I didn't expect it. "What happened that day I took you home; I... It—it did mean something to me."

"Please, just leave," I tell him, looking away.

"I got scared, okay?" he blurts out, wincing at how loud he gets.

"Scared of who? Me?" I ask doubtfully. "Have you looked in the mirror?"

He shakes his head, scrubbing a hand down his face. "Of you. Of us. Of what happened. I've loved one girl, Paisley. One girl, and she died because I cancelled. I don't get close to people, and being with you... it felt different," he admits. "Please, let me make it up to you. I shouldn't have treated you like that, and I certainly shouldn't have spoken to you the way I did in front of your brothers."

"I'm sorry I didn't tell you about the baby—you'll never know how much.

But you need to go. I can't do this—whatever this is," I tell him, gesturing between us.

"I can't."

"What do you mean you can't?" I practically screech, before watching the door in horror, hoping no one heard me. When I don't hear anyone after a few moments, I sigh a breath of relief.

"I'd never get down there without killing myself, so we have time to kill until I can leave through the front door. I think we should talk about me making it up to you."

My eyes widen with disbelief. "You can't be serious. I've already fallen out with my brothers because of your last run in with them. I don't fancy having to visit one—or all—of them in prison when they kill you."

I stand and begin to pace, wondering how I got myself into this position. I glance at him, then the window, then begin pacing again.

They'll hear him, investigate, then kill him. I know it.

"You're not speaking to your brothers?"

I snort. "Did you expect anything else when you put on that performance? Of course I'm not, and the only reason they're speaking to me is because I'm not talking to them."

"Huh."

"It's psychological. If I had begged for forgiveness, then they would have ignored me and treated me like shit."

"That's fucked up, but if it's any consolation, I am truly sorry, and I never say that to anyone but Charlotte or my mum."

"Look, can't you just make a rope out of bedsheets and shimmy down?"

His forehead creases. "No! Let's talk about the building you have outside."

I sit back down on the bed and shake my head from thoughts of how good that bedsheet rope ladder would be.

He'd probably make it… Or it could soften the fall. Somewhat.

"It's my new bed and breakfast."

"It's not finished?"

"This is so weird, Landon," I tell him. He doesn't do conversation and having one with him—in my bedroom—is just bizarre.

"What, having a conversation with me?" he asks and gets up. I stand with him, wondering what he's doing, fighting the urge to stop him from leaving.

Damn heart and brain. At war once more.

"What are you doing?" I ask incredulously when he gets on my bed, fluffing the pillows behind his back.

He grabs the remote from the side and flicks the television on before putting his hands behind his head, getting comfy. "Watching television until your brothers either leave to go to the pub or fall asleep."

"You can't be serious?"

"As a heart attack," he deadpans. "Now, when do they get finished?"

Sighing in defeat, I stomp my foot before dropping down on the bed next to him, making sure to leave enough room between us.

"They don't. The construction company slowly stopped coming until I fired them completely. Everyone else is booked."

"What needs doing?"

"Bathrooms and few other bits."

"I'll do it," he tells me, his gaze still focused on the television.

"That's not necessary," I tell him.

"It's fine. I'll come in the morning with Maddox and have a look at what needs doing."

"Don't you have other jobs?"

He shrugs. "I only went back to work last week so haven't been doing much."

Can I really be around him until the work is finished?

"I'll find someone else. I still don't forgive you. Plus, my brothers won't like it."

He switches his gaze from the television to me. "Are you really going to let them get their own way when it comes to you?"

I rear back. "No," I snap.

"Then I'll be here bright and early."

"Don't bother!" I snap. "Now go."

He jumps up from the bed, and I eye his attire. Why does he look like he's ready to rob a bank?

He reaches the window before turning back. "I am sorry, Paisley, and I promise to make this up to you. Any way I can."

When he pulls himself from the window, I jump up from the bed, panicking. "I thought you said you couldn't get back down."

He pops his head back through the window. "I'm a Carter; we've been doing shit like this since we could crawl," he says, then does something very un-Landon-like. He winks. He fucking winks, and it's so goddamn sexy I have to place my hand on the wall to stop myself from fainting.

"You lied?" I ask, open-mouthed when my brain registers what he said.

"Yep."

"You don't sound very apologetic," I say, silently cursing my damn heart for caring that he's leaving.

"Not even the slightest. See you in the morning. I'll have coffee, black."

"I don't want you to work on it."

"Night."

"Are you listening to me?" I hiss out, leaning out of the window as I watch him jump to the ledge below, which is the window to my mum's room. "Landon? Landon!"

Before I can blink, his feet are firmly on the ground. He scans the area once from his crouched position before running down the path, keeping to the side and out of the way of the lights.

"Damn him," I groan, sitting back down on the chaise. Midnight jumps up, purring. "Why does he care now? Does he think I'm a pushover? What is his game?" I ask her, sighing.

I look out, no longer seeing him, my heart feeling heavy. "Maybe he really does just want to show he's sorry before leaving me to mend my broken heart."

Meow.

"Yeah, you're right. Everything will be fine. It will be."

TEN

LANDON

Turning left into the road that leads up to Paisley's, I glance at the bed and breakfast. There are no lights on and no signs of Paisley being there. Which I was kind of prepared for. I knew last night she wouldn't take me seriously. She's in for a rude awakening.

The building looks huge, and it makes me wonder just how much money they were left for her to build something so extravagant. The only thing she needs is a sign at the road they've built in with the bed and breakfast's name.

"I can't believe I let you guilt trip me into coming," Maddox whines from the front seat, sucking on his caramel frappe. "You were in hospital months ago. You can't keep using the almost dying card."

"Will you stop complaining. You won't be doing anything; I will," I snap at him. "I told you, I just need you here for backup."

I feel his stare on the side of my face, and I know he's dying to ask me why I'm doing this. "You do realise we are going to be like two baby puppies walking into a lion's den. A lion's den with eight hungry lions."

I give him a dry look as I pull up outside the main house. "One, I told you I had a plan, and two, stop fucking comparing yourself to an animal. It's weird."

"Look, any other day, I'd call myself a bear. But, as it's just us two and you're still recovering, it's like there's one and a half of us. We're about to walk inside our sworn enemies' house with no backup."

"I should have brought Liam," I mutter, turning the engine off.

Maddox snorts. "Yeah, you would never have made it past the front gate, my friend. At least I can try to lighten the situation."

He has lost his ever-loving mind. But if anyone can get us through the front door, it's Maddox. He can charm a paper bag.

"Maddox, most of our fights are because you pissed someone off with your sense of humour and characteristics."

"Not my fault they've got sticks up their rear ends. I'm really fucking funny."

"Just come on. Nothing's gonna happen. If there's one thing I know, it's that the Hayes brothers hate upsetting their mum. And if she's anything like our mums, then she'll already be awake and fixing breakfast before her boys wake up."

Maddox's stomach grumbles at the mention of food. "I am hungry, now you mention it."

I roll my eyes when he licks his lips. "You ate a McDonalds on the way over here, and I'm pretty sure when I picked you up, you were eating cereal."

He shakes his head. "It was actually noodles. I ran out of Weetabix."

My mouth twists. "That's fucking disgusting."

He shrugs, uncaring. "You'd better be right about this," he mutters when I get out of the car. I slam the door shut, and before I can make it a step towards the house, a large figure steps out from the bushes.

"Not creepy at all, Jaxon," Maddox mutters, not even startled. Like me, he's aware of his surroundings, even if he does act like he can't tie his shoes laces. He just likes people to think he's stupid. That way, they underestimate him.

I agree with Maddox as I silently watch him glaring at Jaxon. Jaxon takes his gaze away from Maddox, aiming his anger at me. "I don't want you around my sister."

I shrug my shoulders lazily. "I don't care what you want."

He grunts. "Do you care what she wants?"

"Do you?" I fire back.

"Look, Carter; last night I let you leave without your legs being broken because I knew you needed to talk to Paisley, but I'm not letting you fuck with her. You've hurt her enough."

I step forward, hoping it doesn't come down to a fight because it won't help Paisley forgive me. I saw Jaxon last night when I jumped from the ledge of the window, and when he didn't step out and approach me, I kept going, not wanting a fight when I knew she was still watching from her bedroom window.

"And you've not hurt her? I don't need to explain myself to you. But out of respect that she's your sister, I will tell you I'm not going anywhere. Touch me, and I'll hit back harder. Fuck with me and Paisley, and I'll fuck with your life. This is between us, not you or her other brothers."

"You should have said that a little less intimidatingly," Maddox whispers loudly.

Jaxon's gaze cuts to him. "What are you doing here?"

Maddox grins, and I prepare myself for the stupid comment. It's just a given when it comes to a Maddox who isn't in work mode.

"I'm here for your mum," Maddox cheers with a wink, then when Jaxon angrily strides towards him, finishes it with, "Heard her cooking is the best."

The front door opens, revealing an older woman who looks much like Paisley, making Jaxon pause to look over his shoulder.

"Jaxon, you brought friends for breakfast?" she asks, astonished, but then a wide grin spreads across her face and she claps her hands once.

"She thinks he has friends; bless her heart," Maddox chuckles under his breath.

Jaxon glares his way, obviously having heard him. "No, Mum, they were just leaving."

"Nonsense. Come on in; I've got plenty of food for everyone."

I nudge Maddox in the back. This is why I had him come with me. He's better at charming people than me.

"I'd love some, Mrs Hayes. I didn't get chance to eat this morning, being busy and all. I would have come sooner had I known a beautiful woman would be cooking me food," Maddox says in a flirtatious voice.

Even her eyes smile when she beams brighter at him. "Well, you are a growing boy."

"I'm going to fucking kill you," Jaxon growls behind me as we follow his mum inside.

I turn back with a smirk. "Yeah, you and everyone else it seems. It hasn't worked out well for the last people who tried."

"Mum, where did you... Landon?" Paisley gasps in surprise, then trips over her own feet when she goes to place the eggs on the table.

I shoot forward, grabbing her around the hips, noting how good she feels as I steady her. Hair up in a messy bun, makeup free and in Tweety Pie pyjamas, she still looks fucking gorgeous. It's not even in a model beauty way, but a natural way. Her skin is flawless, not a blemish in sight, and she has these big, round, expressive eyes that pop out.

Over her initial shock, she takes a step back, and I miss the feel of her under my grasp.

Just friends.

I'm just trying to be her friend, I remind myself.

I have no idea what the fuck I'm doing. I just knew when I saw her again last night, something inside of me didn't want it to be the last time.

Hearing that she lost our baby made me realise I can't keep mourning and loving a dead girl. Freya meant everything to me, and she'll always be with me, but I need to move forward. Because if there's one thing I'm sure of, it's that I would have stood by Paisley if the baby had survived, and not just because she was pregnant with my kid. And having just a taste of what our future might be, I want it again.

First, I need to move on and to make sure Paisley doesn't do that while I sort my shit out. I want to make sure she is in my life, with no chance of leaving.

It honestly makes more sense in my head. At the moment, I just want to be her friend. She needs to trust me again, and to do that, I have to earn it.

"Landon?" her mum calls out, looking between us. Her eyes narrow unsurely on me for a moment, before she shakes her head, reminding me of my mum when she doesn't want to get involved in a sibling conflict.

"What are you doing here?" Paisley bites out, looking nervously over my shoulder where I know her brother will be.

"I told you I'd be here bright and early so we could go over to the bed and breakfast."

"You're working on the bed and breakfast?" her mum asks, looking happy now. "Oh, darling, isn't that great. You've been wanting it finished. Maybe if you had a date of completion, we could start taking bookings."

"I said I'd do it," Jaxon mutters, sitting down opposite Maddox, who has already dug into the food laid out by Mrs Hayes.

"You're busy with your own business," her mum says, waving him off. "Take a seat, Landon. I'm just getting the rest of the food off the stove."

I gesture for Paisley to sit down at the long mahogany table. With a huff, she sits down, crossing her arms over her chest.

"Why are you doing this?" she asks, looking utterly miserable.

I shift my chair closer to her and a growling noise grabs my attention. I look up, noticing Jaxon watching me with narrowed eyes.

Ignoring him, I lean down and whisper in her ear. "I told you why. Now, are you really going to turn down free labour?"

"Free?" Maddox chokes out, slamming his drink down. The glare I give him has him clearing his throat. "Of course, free. Of course."

"Look, if you're really going to do this then at least let me pay. I have savings in my bank to pay for it."

I shrug, uncaring. "I don't want your money. Just pay for the products you need and I'll do the rest. If you want to pay me, make me breakfast, lunch and dinner each day."

"What?" she gulps.

"Don't be rude, Paisley Hayes, and just thank him," her mum scolds.

"T-thank you," she forces out, looking down at the plate of food she has.

"Did you take your… u-um, thingy, Paisley?" Jaxon asks, looking like he just put his foot in it.

She turns her narrowed eyes on him. "Yes, I've taken my glucose levels and insulin," she snaps.

"Seriously? You're diabetic?" Maddox asks, curiosity in his eyes. "Can you check my levels? I always wanted to use one of those machines. Make me feel all medic-like."

I roll my eyes, wondering why I brought him along.

"Sure," Paisley shrugs, but a pink tinge flares to her cheeks.

"Something's cooking, good looking," I hear Reid yell.

Paisley tenses beside me as we hear footfalls coming towards the kitchen. Maddox, on the other hand, lounges back, gripping his cup of tea in his hand and watching the entrance with a grin on his face.

Reid, Wyatt, and one of the twins—Theo, I think, but there's a fifty-fifty chance it's Colton—walk in. I can never tell the identical twins apart. At least with me, Hayden and Liam, we all look completely different.

"What the fuck?" Wyatt yells, glaring at the both of us. He takes a step forward, and from the look in his eye, is ready to throw us out, but seeing Jaxon sitting in his seat has him pausing.

"Pinch me, because I think I'm having a fucking nightmare," Reid growls.

Theo or Colton leans over and pinches him; hard. Reid's face scrunches up as he howls in pain. "Seriously, that fucking hurt, Theo."

"Morning, sunshine," Maddox cheerfully calls out.

"Get the fuck out," Wyatt snaps.

Theo shrugs and sits down next to Jaxon, helping himself to some eggs.

"And let all of this go to waste?" Maddox answers, spooning some beans into his mouth.

"You gave him my food?" Reid asks him mum, looking pained about it.

Mrs Hayes rolls her eyes at her son. "Sit down and eat. We have plenty of food to go around."

"No, we don't. I didn't get to eat my midnight snack last night, so I'm starving. I come down here expecting a double breakfast to find out you gave it away to a Carter," he spits out, looking in disgust at Maddox. "And you have *him* sitting here."

When his gaze directs at me, I smirk. "Lovely to see you, too."

"Such good manners," Mrs Hayes swoons.

With slack jaws, three of four of the Hayes brothers glare at me from behind their mum's back.

"I'm going to get changed," Paisley whispers, having hardly eaten her food.

I place my hand on the edge of her chair. "Eat the rest because we might have to have a late lunch," I lie. After I was told about her diabetes, I read up online about it. There is no way that is enough food.

With a grumpy huff, she picks up a piece of toast and bites angrily into it with a crunch. I wince, glad those luscious lips aren't anywhere near my appendage.

"What are you doing here?" Wyatt reluctantly asks as he takes his seat, still looking murderous.

"Working on the bed and breakfast," Paisley answers, and his eyes widen.

"You spoke to me!" he states, looking around the room. Even his chest puffs out.

"And me," Jaxon adds, gloating.

Paisley narrows her eyes on them. "Don't make me start ignoring you again," she bites out, and both men shut up. "Now, I'm going to get changed. Do not start a fight because I'm tired, cranky, and will most likely kick you in the balls if you piss me off."

All three men swallow audibly as she gets up. Theo, however, puts his hand up. "So, this isn't the best time to tell you we borrowed one of the baths from the bed and breakfast and it accidently broke?"

Paisley turns slowly to face him, her expression tense. "Excuse me?"

He nods, ignoring the pissed off vibe coming from her. "Yeah, we kind of did you a favour. It broke after the fifth ride down the mud slope we made on the hill."

I can only assume they are talking about the massive hill four miles away at the back of their house, and I watch, wondering why I thought my family were crazy.

"I told you to stop making mud slides down there. I'm still confused as to how you got a hosepipe up there."

"A hosepipe?" Maddox asks, probably thinking the same as me. Where the fuck did they get a hose long enough to get it from the house to that hill?

Theo bites into his toast and waves her off. "If Mr Hall comes around, tell him we were in all night," he says, before standing up. "Got to go. Me and Colt want to see if we can go parasailing on the lake. Pretty windy today."

Mrs Hayes rushes off after him, screaming at him to stay indoors.

"I'll order a new one," Jaxon says, and I look away to see Paisley still standing there, her body tense and her hands clenched into fists.

"I am going to kill him," she screeches, before storming off out of the room.

Maddox leans across the table, reaching for the last of the sausages at the same time as Wyatt.

"Don't even think it," Wyatt bites out.

Maddox grins, snatching it up and taking a huge bite out of it before winking.

Wyatt shoves his chair back and leans over the table to grab Maddox.

Shit!

ELEVEN

PAISLEY

"**A**RE YOU SURE YOU'RE OKAY?" I ASK Maddox, who is holding an icepack on his eye. I was upstairs all of two minutes before I heard them yelling. Me and Mum ran into the kitchen at the same time to find Wyatt and Maddox literally on top of the table before they rolled off and onto the floor.

I will give it to one of the oldest Carter's, he really does know how to get out of a mess. One look to Mum with those eyes and a pout, telling her he was just hungry, had her reaching for him and cleaning him up. She glared at my brothers, which sent them packing.

All over a sausage. Had they looked further than their noses, they would have seen Mum had some keeping warm in the oven. Pesky boys.

He grins. "Yeah. Not had that much food in ages. I'm coming for breakfast more often."

I scrunch my nose up. "I was on about the black eye but, whatever floats ya boat."

He waves me off. "This is nothing. Your mum kissed it all better."

I roll my eyes, thankful my brothers aren't around to hear that remark. With that thought in mind, I glance around the field, hoping one of them isn't hiding somewhere.

Knowing Jaxon, he probably has binoculars and is watching Landon's every move through them.

"This place is great. Who designed it?" Landon asks as we reach the bed and breakfast. I scan the outside, noting it looks dull at the moment without any flowers to brighten it up. I'm hoping with a few potted shrubs it will look a little more inviting during the cold nights.

"I did," I answer, ducking my head when his gaze turns intense on me.

"Really?" he asks, and I can hear the surprise in his voice.

"Yep. I knew exactly what I wanted and how I wanted it. Want to see inside?"

He nods and I step up to the door and unlock it. The first room we step into is an open lobby with a small, intimate reception desk. At the back of the desk is a door to the office and the stairs leading up to what will be my new home.

The huge fireplace was the first thing I drew when I started designing the layout. I worked the rest of the bed and breakfast around that. I had it installed in the lobby and can't wait to light it on a cold night. I picture it lit and can't wait for that warm, cosy feeling. I've also ordered a reading chair, one I'll most likely get the most use out of. It will be perfect to sit in front of that fire with a cup of hot chocolate and a good book.

"Wow!" Landon breathes out. His jaw is slack as he scans the bare area, and I know, just like me, he's picturing what it will look like finished.

"This is fucking amazing," Maddox praises, walking over to the fireplace and sticking his head up the chimney.

Weird.

"This will be the main lobby and reception. That hallway next to the stairs leads to the back garden and the family bedrooms. To the left," I gesture to the wide-open entrance to the next room, "will be the dining room, and through those double swinging doors is a kitchen and another exit."

"You should put some patio doors on that wall," Landon says, pointing to the wall ahead of us. "It will bring light into the room and you could have some tables and chairs for outside in the summer."

"Can you do that? That sounds incredible," I ask, amazed and pretty giddy at the idea. I have a patio area at the back, but to get to it, you have to walk either around the entire house, or through the hallway near the reception area that leads to the backdoor.

"Yes—if you want one, that is."

"Of course. I didn't even think of doing that. I was only thinking of space when I designed it."

He waves me off, walking over to the wall and knocking his knuckles against it. "Did you want me to get started down here so it's finished and you can start doing it up? Then I can make my way upstairs to the rooms while you move everything in?"

"If you can, then yes. I need to get pictures taken of the property and rooms, so I can find someone to set up a webpage for me."

"You should ask Bailey, Aiden's girlfriend. She does that for a living, and from what I've seen of Charlotte's page, she's pretty damn good."

This is the most I've ever heard him speak. Wait! Charlotte has a webpage?

"She does?" I ask, feeling my heart lighten. It's really coming together. "How is Bailey doing after what happened at the park?"

"She's doing great. Better than expected after everything that went down."

"That's good to hear," I murmur, thinking back on that dreadful day. She'd been through a lot. Something he said hits me and I look up, titling my head to the side. "Wait, why does Charlotte have a webpage?"

A blank veil lifts over his expression. "It's a secret she doesn't want our family to know, so you can't say anything." When I nod, intrigued, he continues. "She's an author."

"Does she use her real name?"

"Nope, and you'll have to ask her for her pen name," he says with a smirk. "I'll ask Bailey to get in touch with you. What else needs doing down here?"

"The entire kitchen," I tell him with a resigned sigh, walking over to the kitchen. I push through the doors and try not to be affected as he follows. But it's hard not to when I know what those hands and that body can do. My traitorous body needs to get with the programme, because we aren't supposed to be attracted to the large, hot, muscled Carter. "He put all the electrics and piping in, but as you can see, none of the cupboards, units or anything else was fitted."

Landon rubs the back of his neck. "My uncle Maverick is good with kitchens. I'll ask him to come help me with the stuff I can't do by myself."

"Are you sure you don't want paying? This doesn't feel right," I admit, interrupting. No one does anything for free anymore.

His eyes soften when they land on me. "I promise, I don't want your money and neither will my uncle. He has more time on his hands than my cousins, so he will want to help out."

I suck in my bottom lip. "That's all that really needs doing down here. All the rest is décor I have in the storage units back at the removal factory."

"Your brother's?"

"Yeah. It used to be an old cattle barn, but Jaxon had it rebuilt so it was liveable and could be used for storage. We have fourteen containers that people rent, and then the rest of the space is for his removal business. He lets me use the fifteenth one that he kept open for one of us if we needed it. What I don't have yet to pay for, is in there."

"How did you afford this place; if you don't mind me asking?" he asks, and for some reason, I don't mind telling him.

"Money left to me. We don't have a big family, to be honest. My aunt and uncle never had kids before they died, and my mum didn't have any siblings growing up. I think it's why she kept saying one more kid to my dad. She hated being an only child. Mum grew up on this farm, so she was left this and my nan and granddad's money. She put half into savings and used the other half to build the farm up. We each had a share of the money when we turned eighteen. When my aunt and uncle died, we each got a share of that, and the same when my dad died, though sometimes I think I had more than the others."

"What do you mean?" he asks, leaning back against the wall.

I shrug, mimicking the same movement and resting against the wall. "I know Jaxon owns a majority of Hayes Removals, but the others—other than the twins—put shares into it. With the amount I had, they shouldn't have needed to put the money in together. Jaxon could have paid for it himself. And I hear them moaning they're skint until payday.

"We weren't allowed access to our money until we turned twenty-one or needed it to invest in a business. When I got mine, I passed out at the amount. I couldn't believe how much was there. When I questioned Mum and the others, they just shrugged and said my bank must have good interest rates," I tell him, and when he gets a crease along his forehead, I explain further, "Our accounts are with the same bank."

"Did you say anything else about it?"

I shake my head. "No. Because if they wanted me to have it, then there's no changing their minds. I'll thank them one day. I just hope their business doesn't go into a crisis before I can pay them back. Or, God forbid, mine doesn't pick up."

He looks at me in wonder. "You really are an incredible person. And I don't think you'll have problems getting bookings. The place isn't finished and it looks amazing already. Plus, you have the cricket club not far away, and that other hotel that does parties and stuff. No doubt people will book here so they don't have to pay their prices."

Blushing, I duck my head and step away from the wall. "Come on, I'll show you the rest of the house."

"Wait," he says. I inhale, not ready to face him. He's so goddamn good looking, I'm scared I'll give in and beg him to kiss me. "Please, just talk to me for a minute."

"We are talking," I state, slowly turning around to face him. He stares deeply into my eyes, watching, admiring, almost calculating.

He rubs the back of his neck before shoving his hands into his pockets. "Go out with me tonight," he blurts out. Completely taken off guard, I can do nothing but stare at him. "Please. I want to know how you're doing."

"Why?"

He looks over my shoulder and inhales deeply, before looking back at me with a determined expression. Nodding, he says, "I'll pick you up at seven."

"You will?" I ask, confused as to where all this is coming from. Trying to keep track of the conversation is also confusing. "Why now, Landon? Is it because of the baby? I've already told you it's not your fault. You don't need to do this."

"Do what?" he asks, looking genuinely confused.

I gesture between the two of us. "This. Whatever this is."

"Look, we're friends now. Friends go out for a meal with each other."

I roll my eyes. "We're not friends."

His lips twist wryly. "Yeah, we are. We even had breakfast together."

"You really need to start going out more, because you turning up at my house uninvited isn't us becoming friends."

"We're doing this, Paisley, whether you like it or not."

I throw my hands up in despair. "I don't even know what *this* is."

"I'm gonna go make a list of things that need doing and what supplies we need," he says, ignoring me and changing the subject abruptly once again.

"It's family movie night. Mum gets pissed if we miss it, so we never miss it," I tell him, half lying as I follow him out of the dining room. She does get pissed, but movie night isn't until tomorrow. Hopefully, he's over whatever he thinks is going to happen between us. If it's friendship, I can't give it to him. I loved him and fantasized about him for too long to become friends with him. If it's a relationship he wants, then he has no chance. I have more pride than to let someone treat me like something they trod on.

"Movie night?" he asks, pausing to face me. He nods mindlessly, deep in thought, before his gaze turns calculating. "Okay, okay. We can do dinner another time."

"Dude, you need to work on your game," Maddox says, chuckling.

I jump at the sound of his voice. He didn't even make a noise when he walked in.

"Fuck you," Landon snaps, glaring at Maddox behind me.

Maddox just continues to laugh. "Yeah, well, while you fucked up on epic proportions, I was making a list of shit you'll need. You'll have to add what you need for down here yourself."

"Already memorised it. I just need to take some measurements," he snaps, looking broody.

And this is the Landon I know. Not the overly talkative guy he has been recently.

Maddox begins to laugh, pulling out his phone. Landon steps forward. "Don't you dare!"

Not even blinking or afraid, Maddox continues to type on his phone. "Fuck that. The broody, moody, robot Landon Carter just got turned down. You couldn't even intimidate her into going out with you."

I smother the giggle that slips free at the murderous expression on Landon's face as he takes a step forward. His shoes squeak on the laminate flooring, gaining Maddox's attention.

His eyes widen when he sees Landon coming for him, and before I can blink, he's running out the front door, yelling over his shoulder. "No fun, Landon. No fun."

I giggle, heading out after them, watching as Landon sprints to catch up with him. He jumps on his back, sending them both flying to the floor. I hear a grunt as I lean against the doorframe.

"Are you going to do it again?" Landon demands harshly, shoving Maddox's face into the dirt.

Poor Maddox, I muse.

"If it gets me off this floor, I promise I won't do it again," he mutters, relaxing when Landon loosens his hold. Once he's off him, Maddox rushes to his feet. "That said, you know I'm totally going to do it again. It's just who I am."

He lets out a high-pitched squeal, jumps, then runs off when Landon begins to chase him again. I laugh, but soon lose it when I think of how I'm going to get out of tonight. For some reason, I have a feeling Landon isn't going to let it go, and I wouldn't put it past him to turn up at my house. Sometimes it scares me how well he can read me. It's the way he analyses people, like he's finding truths and lies in their eyes and movements. It was one of the things that drew me to him.

Yep, I'm totally not going to be here if there's a chance he will turn up. I'm not that strong.

Grabbing my phone out of my pocket, I send a text to Adam.

ME: SOS. Be at mine for six. We're going out.

ADAM: Sounds interesting.

———————————

I TUG MY BLACK dress over my slender body, glaring at my best friend through the mirror. "I don't see what was so wrong with what I was wearing," I mutter, then curse when I see my boobs spilling out of the dress.

Adam made me buy it for my eighteenth and dragged me out into town. He got pissed, made me dance in public, then threw me into a cab so he could take some random guy home.

It was a good but strange night.

And tonight, instead of letting me wear my yellow summer dress, he pulled this out of the back of my closet.

He gives me a disgusted look. "We're going to Paradise. You can't wear that there. It's too fancy."

I roll my eyes at him because Paradise isn't posh. Yes, people dressed up to go to the fanciest restaurant in town, but it was also known as a local hangout for men who have just finished work and fancy a pint. I was glad the two were slightly separated.

"I just don't feel comfortable."

"You never do in public," he shoots back. "I still can't believe you turned Landon Carter down. Landon fucking Carter. I think you're seriously off your trolley. Nobody turns down one of those boys."

I look at the watch on my wrist. "We need to go. And I told you, I'm not interested in him anymore."

He pats my arm when he gets up. "Yep, you keep telling yourself that, sweet cheeks."

"It's true!"

He smirks at me. "You really are delusional. No one gets over a Carter. What I wouldn't do if one of them batted for my team."

"Like they need to be gay," I snark.

He winks at me. "A man can admire."

"Let's just go, in case he turns up."

"Lead the way, chick-a-dee."

TWELVE

LANDON

"**W**ILL YOU STOP POUTING," DAD WHINES. "It's ruining my mood."

I grunt, not even bothering to glance at my dad. My plans for tonight with Paisley had been fucked up. She wasn't there. Her mum said she had gone to Paradise with her friend, Adam. The same friend she lost her virginity to. My hands clench into fists as I inhale deeply through my nose.

She would rather go out with him than with me? I don't get it. Did she lie about him being gay? Is she secretly in love with him? Are they more than just friends? The need to know eats away at me.

If she thinks I'll stand by and watch her with another man, then she doesn't know me at all. I'd kill him before she let him touch her.

I exhale, trying to slow down my heartrate. I want to punch someone, but I'm not ready for that and the gym is now closed. I don't like this feeling inside of me. It's foreign and unwanted. And I don't understand where all this anger is coming from.

Two good things did come from me turning up unexpectedly at the Hayes house tonight. One, her mum told me movie night was tomorrow night and said I was more than welcome to come. And secondly, she told me where Paisley is tonight.

I had hoped to bring Charlotte with me, but she was busy planning for the new cat I had talked Faith into letting her have earlier in the day. We're meant to go up tomorrow to have a look.

When she told me she couldn't come, I called around, but it seems everyone is busy except Maddox. I have enough to deal without having him here.

But as I look at my dad, I'm wondering if I made the right choice in asking him.

"Are you going to keep brooding?" he asks.

"I don't get girls," I admit, hoping he hears how serious I am.

"Girls are pretty easy, son."

I give him a dirty look. "Dad!"

He shakes his head as he pulls into the restaurant carpark. "Not like that," he replies quickly, chuckling. "Never say, 'okay', avoid answering questions on their wardrobe choices, always text back straight away, and most importantly, don't make eye contact in an argument."

"What?" I ask. That sounds completely ridiculous.

"Yep. Looked your mum in the eye once and it was the worst mistake of my life. I ended up saying yes to Hunter moving in to the new house with us. Fucking cat had it out for me, but did she see it? No! And the sly rat would wait until her back was turned to strike. Did she care? No. I felt so unloved, son," he rants out, and my lips quirk into a smirk. I think it's him who has it out for that cat. "Another time, we argued over what to go and see at the cinema. I wanted to see this action movie. Your mum, she wanted this sappy romance movie. I looked in her eyes for a split second and it was all over. I spent nearly two hours listening to her gush, cry, gush, and sob."

"I don't think Paisley is like that," I murmur.

His lip curls. "All women are like that. I've got a book somewhere. It will help you through a relationship. The most important one you need to remember—and run if it happens—is when they say they are fine," he explains. "Because, son, they aren't fucking fine. I'm telling you. If there's an exit, run!"

My eyes widen because he looks damn serious. But it's Dad. He can't be right. I'll message my uncle Malik later. As uncomfortable as I am talking about this shit, I know he won't bullshit me so I make a tit out of myself.

His lips twist wryly. "Actually, I take that back. The most important rule to remember is when a woman says, 'do what you want', never, and I mean *never*, do what you want. Don't blink—fuck, don't move. Just stand still and don't breathe. Hell, play dead; it worked for me every time."

I really do think my dad has gone crazy.

"I'll remember, Dad," I tell him, silently planning to text Malik the first chance I get. He nods, turns the car off, and gets out. When I meet him at the front of the car, I say, "Remember, act surprised when we see her."

Dad chuckles. "Not the first time I've done this, son. We've got this," he says, but then pauses just outside the door. "You really do like this girl, don't you? It's not about the baby, is it?"

I had told Mum and Dad the very next day, needing Mum to talk to. They both took it as well as expected, but Dad did look pale the entire time I was there, muttering about Hayden and tracking devices. I never did ask what he was up to before I left. He had that crazy look in his eyes.

"It's not about the baby. I just don't want to start something when I have so much baggage. I feel her slipping away though."

Dad looks at me with a serious expression. "Then don't let her. Embed yourself so far into her life she has no choice but to fall for you."

"I just hope I didn't fuck it up. I treated her pretty crappy."

Dad shrugs like it's no big deal. "You'll probably fuck up again. Just kidnap her for the weekend if all else fails," he says in all seriousness. Before I have chance to argue, he opens the door to the restaurant. "God, I'm starving."

Rolling my eyes, I follow him inside. Something inside of me senses her before I see her. She's sat at a table, her head thrown back and a tinkering laugh escaping her lips. I gulp, my gaze scanning her upper body, focusing on her cleavage long enough to be classed as creepy.

She looks beautiful, her hair curled and thrown up in a ponytail, some parts falling free and fanning her face. From here I can see the shine of gloss on her lips and a sparkle of eyeshadow on her eyelids.

I've never seen her dressed up before, and it takes me a minute to tear my gaze away and notice Dad is no longer with me. He's heading over to their table, favouring his good foot. I forgot he already knows her, having seen her at the bar with her brothers.

"Fuck!"

I rush up behind him, hoping she doesn't see me until the last second. He slows down when he nears their table. Either she senses me or sees movement from the corner of her eye, but when she looks up, her jaw slackens and she stares at me open-mouthed.

The fucker with her turns around, smirking when he notices me.

"Are you stalking me?" she blurts out, sounding shocked.

I shrug, ready to reply with the excuse I thought of on the way over here, but Dad beats me to it.

"Now, now. Stalking is such a strong allegation. This is more like being at the right place at the right time," he says, then scans the room. I do the same, noticing a few empty tables on the other side of the room. "You don't mind if we join you, though, right? I don't want to wait for a table to become available."

He takes a seat and Paisley continues to stare open-mouthed. I sit between her and her friend.

"More the merrier," her friend says, and she gives him a dirty look. I watch him smirk and wink at her and quickly shove my clenched hands under the table.

More for the fact I don't want her to hate me when I beat up her best friend. Or lover. Whatever they are.

"You on a date?" I ask, trying to soften my voice, but it comes out harshly.

"Um, he's gay," Dad comments, looking over his menu at me like I'm dumb.

I glance back at Paisley to see a light blush fill her cheeks. "No. This is my best friend, Adam."

"Adam," I repeat, narrowing my eyes on him.

Swallowing, Adam nods. "Yep, her very *gay* best friend."

"He won't touch you," Dad interrupts, making Adam shift nervously in his seat. "I think."

"Landon, what are you doing here?"

"Did you want us to move?" Dad asks, pouting. "I've not had anything to eat all day. The wife threw my dinner away 'cause I was late getting back from buying supplies with this one," he says, gesturing to me. It's a complete lie, but I'm grateful Dad has a great poker face.

Paisley blinks, looking up at him through her lashes. "No, you're perfectly fine. I'm sorry. I feel terrible now," she says, her gaze on me as her eyes narrow into slits.

Yeah, maybe I'll punch my dad instead. He's not supposed to get her to hate me.

He pats her hand. "It's fine, lovely."

"What did you do to your foot?" she asks. "You were walking with a limp. Are you okay?"

Dad gives her a suffering sigh. "A bloke named Butch pinched the wife's butt. Couldn't stand back and do nothing. Tried to use my moves on him, but he was just too big, and I was worried for my wife's safety, ya know?"

I glare at my dad.

"Oh my God. Is she okay? Are you okay? Did you report him? That's really heroic of you to stand up for your wife like that."

He places a hand over his heart. "He ran off before we could do anything really. I try to be. Landon's the same; will do anything for those he loves," he says, giving her a pointed look.

Okay, maybe he won't get punched.

I watch as he works his magic, because she ducks her head, her gaze flicking over to me, watching me intently.

"Maybe," she whispers, jumping slightly when a waitress walks over to take our order.

"I spoke to Bailey," I start, needing to fill the silence once the waitress walks off. "I gave her your number. She said she would text you tomorrow to book an appointment, so you can go over what you want and go from there."

"How do you have my number?" she asks slowly, scanning my face. I keep my expression neutral.

I shrug. "Got your phone after you showed me around upstairs and programmed it in. You have mine too."

"Upstairs?" Adam asks, his eyes lighting up with interest.

She glares at him before turning back to me. "Are you sure you're not a stalker?" she asks, her mouth agape.

"No," I drawl, and she watches me with scepticism.

"Would a stalker tell you he stole your phone whilst you weren't looking, or climb through your bedroom window?" Dad asks.

"What? You climbed through her bedroom window?" Adam asks, his voice high-pitched, amusement lacing in his tone.

She ignores him, turning to my dad with an arched eyebrow. "Um, yes, that's exactly what a stalker would do."

He tilts his head to the side. "Did he sniff any knickers?"

"Dad!"

"What? It's a legit question," he says, sniffing.

I'm caught off guard when Paisley begins to laugh. "No. But I'll remember to put a lock on my drawer."

Dad grins. "Probably for the best."

I should have just brought Maddox with me.

Paisley turns to me. "Next time, ask me."

Why would I do that?

"Why would he do that?" Dad asks, taking her off guard, thinking like me for the first time.

"U-um—"

"You don't want to talk to him?" Dad asks, staring at her with wide eyes.

I want to die. God, Sunday would have been a better choice at this point.

Sunday.

Next time, I'm bringing the cute baby that dribbles way too much. No one can resist her.

Now, if only Aiden would lend her to me for the day.

"N-no—I m-mean y-yes," she stutters, her cheeks flaming.

"Not much of a talker, though, is he? I can see why it could be a problem."

"Dad!" I warn.

She gives me a side glance. "I don't know. I've not been able to shut him up," she admits dryly.

Dad looks to me, his expression filled with humour, and before I can warn him, he has his phone out.

"Please, don't," I tell him, rubbing my temples where a headache is forming.

He scoffs. "Yeah, like please will work."

"What will it take?" I ask, and I relax slightly when he stops typing.

His expression turns calculating as he begins to tap his chin with his index finger. "Tell your mum that we lied, and it was a guy named Butch who hurt me."

"Butch, the guy who pinched your wife's arse?" Paisley asks, her nose twitching in an adorable way.

He waves her off. "Details. Details, Paisley."

I sigh, because there is no way Mum will believe it. The truth was more believable, as bizarre as it was.

"How about I get her to start making you dinner again?" I offer. If he sends a message to everyone saying I've been a chatty Cathy with Paisley, I'll never hear the end of it.

He gives me a long pause before finally nodding. "Deal. And get her to make a Sunday dinner for me."

Fuck's sake. He's asking for miracles now.

"Whatever. Just put the phone away."

I wait until he does before focusing back on the table. They're both staring at us, open-mouthed.

"I have a headache," Paisley moans.

"I stand corrected. Your family is sane compared to this one," Adam butts in. I glare at him, and he swallows, looking back down at the table.

Dad sits up straighter, puffing out his chest. "Thanks. That's the nicest thing anyone has ever said to me."

"I doubt that," Adam chuckles.

A sharp kick to my leg has me glancing at Paisley. "What was that for?"

Her cheeks flame bright red. "Sorry, my foot slipped."

"I bet it did," Adam says and begins to laugh at her horrified expression.

I hear a light thud, and when Adam curls over, his hands going under the table, I know she just kicked him. A small smirk pulls at my lips.

"Did you want to come and pick what patio door you want tomorrow?" I ask Paisley, changing the subject.

"Does it matter?" she asks, her nose doing that twitching thing again.

I nod. "Well, yeah. You might have a certain frame, colour or design you'd prefer. I could get a basic white one, but then it wouldn't go with the dark wood you have throughout."

"Since you know what wood it is, why don't you pick?"

"Because it's not my bed and breakfast," I fire back, my lips twisting. "Are you trying to avoid me?"

"Yes," she blurts out. "I mean, no."

I smirk. "Then you won't mind coming with me. I'll pick you up at eight tomorrow. I usually like to get to work earlier, but since the store doesn't open until nine, there's no point."

"Why pick me up so early, then?" she asks, watching me intently.

I lean in closer, close enough that I can smell her sweet perfume and want to run my nose along her neck and inhale. "One: because your mum invited me for breakfast, and two: because I want to spend more time with you," I tell her, watching her lips part with a small gasp. I lean in further. "And lastly, I don't want to give you a chance to run away from me again."

"Breakfast?" Dad asks, smacking his lips together. "Maybe work will give me the day off."

I watch Paisley for a few more moments. Her pupils dilate and her chest rises and falls with fast, hard pants. She licks her lips and my mind immediately goes to imagining them wrapped around my dick.

I groan, shifting back in my seat as I try to adjust myself discreetly in my jeans.

"So… breakfast with the Hayes family?" Dad asks, smirking at me.

I shake my head. "No, Dad."

"Why not?"

The waitress times it perfectly to show up with our food. Dad digs right in, not taking a breath. Everyone at the table watches as he inhales his food, acting like he's never been fed before.

He looks up, his cheeks puffed up with a mouthful of food. "What?"

"Just eat," I tell him on a sigh, squeezing the bridge of my nose.

My mind wanders to Paisley. I'm really hoping tonight hasn't made things worse for me—not that I'll give up. I'll never give up. Never have. She calls to me like a moth to a flame. There's no escaping the burn I'll feel if I do lose her. Being around her, I feel more alive, less dead, less like my soul was ripped out of me when Freya died. Sometimes I wonder if Paisley had me all along, because being around her feels like my heart is beating for the first time. My time with Freya is nothing compared to my time with Paisley.

Guilt tugs at me for thinking about Freya that way. But sometimes I hate her as much as I loved her. She only had to let me talk to my uncle Myles and she would have been safe. Her family would have been safe. When it comes to Freya, there's a lot of what ifs and maybes. With Paisley, I want the last 'what if' to be the last one.

I'll always ask myself, what if Blaze and his friends hadn't attacked me in that alley? Would our baby still be alive? Would we be together? Or was she there that night to tell me she didn't want me involved?

I never want to question myself with her again, which is why, until I've figured my shit out, I don't want to fuck it up by moving too fast. Another part of me—a part I won't ever admit aloud—is scared shitless that if I don't move fast, I could lose what I feel when I'm around her. Forever.

I glance at her, admiring the way she looks when she laughs.

Fuck, she's beautiful.

Her gaze meets mine, unmoving, even when I see a thousand questions flickering behind her eyes. They become heated, her cheeks flushing.

And I know, as strong as I am, I'm not strong enough to stay away.

Whether she knows it or likes it, Paisley Hayes is mine.

THIRTEEN

LANDON

PULLING UP OUTSIDE THE HAYES HOME, I resign myself for a morning full of arguments. Maddox was busy this morning, for which I was thankful. I can handle the Hayes brothers. The only challenge for me is Jaxon, and he's too worried about upsetting his sister again to step out of line. Hopefully, he'll keep the others in line so there won't be another fight to break up.

My phone vibrates, and I let out a small grunt. I've been ducking Dad's calls and text messages all morning. The greedy bastard will do anything for a free, home-cooked meal.

When it starts up again, I sigh, pulling it out of my back pocket. Fifteen missed calls from Dad and two from Benny. His name flashes across the screen once more, so I answer it. I've been putting this conversation off since the attack.

"'Ello?"

"Landon?"

"Yeah."

He exhales down the line. "Thank fuck you answered. Look, you've been avoiding my calls for months. It didn't bother me—I had fuck all to give you other than hope you would be okay."

"What's changed, then?" I ask, looking up at the house and hoping one of them doesn't come out. I scan the surrounding bushes and spaces where Jaxon could hide, but everything looks still and quiet.

"My boss wasn't too happy you were messed with, even if it took place outside of the fight. Any money made that night will be coming your way, just name a time and place and I'll be dropping it off. But that isn't why I called. Word on the street is you're back and fucking with Rocco's thugs."

"I don't know what you're talking about," I tell him, feigning boredom.

He snorts, like he knew that would be my answer. "If you say so. Anyway, we won't take any action against you. In fact, my boss has given strict instructions that either Rocco gets those four in the ring in two months with you, or he has to pay a hundred thousand fine."

I let my eyes widen at the amount and the fact they're willing to do this for me, yet keep my voice straight when I ask, "What will I owe in return?"

Benny chuckles. "Fuck all. He's charging entry for that fight and bets will start at no lower than a grand apiece. He just asks that you agree to the fight. There are a lot of people who are pissed off over what happened to you. He's lost business since no one feels it's safe."

"And me turning up will get them back," I finish for him.

'Yep, but you can't tell me you weren't planning on getting your own back," he states, sounding all too smug. When I don't say anything—because there's no use denying it—he chuckles. "I'll be in touch soon."

"Soon," I tell him, ending the call.

I don't know how I feel about the phone call. Getting even with them was something I wanted to do by myself. I want them to hurt the way I hurt. The only thing appealing about it is that it will be in a controlled environment.

Doesn't mean I'm not going to keep fucking with them in the meantime.

My phone vibrates once again, and I sigh, wishing people would leave me alone for five minutes. Guilt instantly hits me when I see it's Charlotte texting me.

CHARLOTTE: We still on for later? I'm going with the name Katnip. GTG (Got to go, in case you didn't know what it meant). Need to open up for coffee morning.

LANDON: Yeah, I'll pick you up after I've gone home and showered.

CHARLOTTE: I'm so excited. Did you want me to cook you some dinner?

Fuck no!

She and Lily are the only people I can't say what I think to. There's a vulnerability to both, though Lily has this fiery, survivor aura to her.

LANDON: I'm eating later with someone.

CHARLOTTE: Stop texting. Need to open up.

Is she for real?

LANDON: You're texting me.

CHARLOTTE: Yes, but it's rude not to text back. I feel bad, like you'll think I'm ignoring you.

I chuckle under my breath. Only she could think she'd hurt someone by not texting them back.

LANDON: Just go to work.

I shove phone into my back pocket, ignoring it when it begins to vibrate again.

Stepping up to the front door, I press down on the doorbell, hoping it isn't a Hayes brother who answers.

I'm surprised to see Paisley answering, already dressed for the day. I was kind of hoping I'd see her in her pyjamas again.

"Morning," she greets, ducking her head and not meeting my gaze.

"Morning," I greet back. I look around her when she steps inside. "No brothers?"

She walks into the kitchen and pulls out two plates filled with a full English breakfast. "No, Mum took them out to eat this morning to give us some time together to talk," she says, and she doesn't look happy about it.

"Talk about what?" I ask as I calculate how much fat is in this breakfast—now that I know I'll be back in the ring in two months. After today, I'll watch my diet better, because this food looks and smells too good to go to waste.

She sits down, grabbing her knife and fork. "The woman had nine kids; she's not exactly sane."

I chuckle. "Or she was onto something."

The fork pauses before reaching her mouth. "If we're going to talk, let me eat this first."

I nod and dig into my food, every so often taking a swig of orange juice she poured me.

It's only after five minutes of awkward silence—which is saying something coming from me, as I prefer it—I drop my glass of orange juice on the table with a thud. She jumps and stops playing around with the rest of her food.

"Since we have time to kill, there are some things I'd like to know. If you don't mind answering," I tell her, unsure if I should bring up something so painful.

She nods, frowning. "O-okay."

Resting my elbows on the table, I massage my temples. "Before... before you lost the baby, did you see it on one of those machines?"

Her lips turn down, her bottom lip trembling silently. She turns away before answering. "No. My ultrasound was due two weeks after I lost her. I did hear her heartbeat though."

I sit forward, feeling my throat tighten. "What was it like?"

Her eyes glisten. "A miracle. It sounded like a miracle. Describing it doesn't even come close to the actual experience. There's nothing more perfect than the sound of a life growing inside of you. It was fast, a constant *thump, thump, thump*. I didn't want the midwife to turn it off," she tells me wistfully.

And I missed it.

"You said she... Did you know the sex of the baby?"

She wipes the tears that manage to escape. "I didn't. It was too early into the pregnancy to tell. I just pictured a little girl every time I thought of her. I named her Avery in my head," she murmurs with a faraway look.

"Avery," I whisper, testing the name on my lips. "I like it."

She gives me a watery smile. "Me too," she says, before breaking down into tears. Not equipped for this kind of thing, I do what my mum would do and get up. I walk around the table, pull out the chair next to her and take a seat. She covers her face with her hands, her shoulders shaking with her cries.

I pull her out of her chair, lifting her into my lap. She protests at first, but settles down as I strengthen my hold and rock us back and forth gently. "Shh, I got you," I tell her, resting her head on my shoulder.

She clings to me, gripping my shirt. "I'm so sorry I didn't tell you sooner. You didn't even get to experience her heartbeat. I feel like I've taken everything from you."

"Not everything," I whisper, kissing the top of her head. "Your brothers let slip that you nearly died miscarrying. I didn't lose you, so you didn't take everything." I holder her tighter, remembering the confrontation I had with her brothers last night after leaving her mum.

She looks up at me through wet lashes, her nose bright red. She opens her mouth to say something, but nothing comes out. Instead, her hazel eyes lock on mine, and I feel like I'm drowning in them. Her lips part with a gasp of air as I draw closer, needing to taste her, feel her. Her hands linger on my chest, her fingers twitching before slowly moving upward. I inhale, closing my eyes at the rush of emotion just one touch can cause.

Only a mere breath away, my eyes flutter open. She's staring up at me, doe-eyed, and her tongue darts out to lick her bottom lip.

"Fuck," I groan, leaning in to take her mouth with mine.

She turns her head at the last minute, clearing her throat. Startled by what is happening, I don't fight her as she gets off my lap.

"We'd better get going if we want to get some work done," she says impassively.

"Paisley," I call out, reaching for her. She steps away before I can touch her.

"I just need to grab my bag," she evades.

"Paisley," I call out, louder and harsher.

She turns when she reaches the kitchen door. "I won't be long. It's just in my room."

I sigh when she walks out of the room. I've royally screwed up. I look at the watch on my wrist. I still have eight hours to turn this day around.

I WAS LYING when I told Paisley she needed to be here to choose her door. I knew exactly what door she was looking for after seeing her designs for the bed and breakfast. She wants it to be warm, inviting, and to go with the dark mahogany wood she has throughout the entire building.

I just wanted to spend time with her. Now, I'm regretting my decision. This is worse than going to strip club with my cousin/ best friend.

She bends down again to look at another price tag before snapping back up, causing a groan to rumble from my chest. Her arse in the air like that is giving me ideas, and if she's not careful, I'll be dragging her down a quiet aisle and pulling that skirt up around her hips before sinking slowly into her.

"I don't know," she mumbles.

"Can you just pick a door already," I demand dryly.

She looks over her shoulder at me, her eyes sparkling with mischief. "But there are so many. And it's like you said, I need to pick the right one."

She's playing with me. I see it in her eyes, hear it in her sweet tone.

"You are evil," I tell her, taking a step towards her.

"Whatever do you mean?" she says sweetly, batting those eyelashes innocently at me.

Another step closer.

"You know exactly what I mean."

She squeals when I narrow my gaze at her and goes to make a run for it. I grab her around the waist, pulling her back against my chest. I nuzzle her neck, breathing in her sweet perfume.

Giggling, she tries to wriggle free. "Put me down."

"No!"

"What do you mean, *no?*" She pauses when I start walking. "Wait, where are we going?"

"Back to the door you should have picked over an hour ago," I tell her, unable to keep the annoyance out of my tone.

She sniffs. "I don't know what you're talking about. I haven't liked any."

Lies. I watched the way her face lit up when we saw a double mahogany frame with the decorative glass on display.

When I drop her right in front of the display, she sighs. "Okay, I really did love this one. But how did *you* know?" she asks, turning to face me.

I roll my eyes. "Your expression kind of gives away your feelings."

A light blush fills her cheeks, making me inwardly grin.

"Hmm. I'll have to remember that," she says absentmindedly. "But you have you admit, you kind of deserved it for making me come with you."

"Or you really just wanted to spend some alone time with me," I state, giving her a pointed look.

She blushes, looking away. "Let's just order the door. I have a million things to do."

Hoping those *million things to do* will be inside the bed and breakfast, I nod and wave down an assistant.

My MIND IS back on Paisley as Charlotte and I walk through the building where Faith keeps her cats. Paisley was quiet on the drive home from the DIY store, and the second I pulled the truck into park outside of the bed and breakfast, she was out of the car in a flash. I thought we were making progress from that morning. She seemed to relax around me, even spoke up more.

"But, Faith," Charlotte whines, sounding devastated, which snaps me right out of it.

Blinking out of my fog, I notice Faith shift nervously on her feet, looking anywhere but at Charlotte.

"Isn't Katnip enough for the time being?" Faith softly asks, looking down at the beige and white kitten.

Charlotte lovingly strokes her, and the cat hisses, swiping her paw out. I step away from the thing, eyeing it carefully when it turns to look at me. Its big green eyes are all too knowing for my taste. It hisses at me.

"Maybe you should pick another one," I suggest, eyeing the thing with distain.

"No, I think she likes me," Charlotte says, rubbing her cheek against Katnip's head. It goes mental, clawing and hissing whilst trying to escape.

"Are you sure?" I ask dryly, clicking my tongue.

She beams at me, nodding before turning back to Faith, her eyes round and pleading. "Please let me have the last one. She'll be all alone if I don't."

Faith looks close to tears. "They don't get along, Charlotte." She's telling the truth, and as I look back down at the cat digging its nails into Charlotte's arm, it doesn't take much of a guess to know who the problem is.

"Why don't you have the other one?" I try again.

"I want this one. I walked right up to the cage and she came straight at me, lifting her paws," she gushes.

"Or trying to claw your face off," I mutter under my breath.

"What was that?"

"Nothing," I lie, eyeing the evil cat once again.

"Why can't I take her sister?"

I sigh, because there is no way I'm being partly responsible for two fucking cats. And if it means she goes home with the devil spawn, I can live with it—as long as she doesn't come back with two. Faith is two seconds away from giving in. "A little unfair on Katnip, isn't it?"

Charlotte watches me questioningly. "What do you mean?"

I shrug, like I'm not bothered. "I mean, she picked you, and you picked her, but then you go and pick another? She will probably think you don't love her."

I feel like a dick when her eyes glisten with tears as she looks lovingly down at Katnip. The cat hisses, digging her claws in further. I wince when I see it's drawn a little blood, wanting to grab it by the scruff of its neck and put it back.

"Oh, but I do love her," she tells us. "Maybe just having Katnip will be for the best. I don't want her to feel like that."

I don't think that cat gives a fuck, but I don't voice that out loud.

Faith claps her hands. "That's settled then. I just need to go check on one of the puppies before I hand over the paperwork for her. Is that okay?"

"Puppies?" Charlotte asks, her eyes glowing.

Faith winces. "Yes, it will probably be best if you put Katnip into her carrier."

Charlotte nods, hurrying to put her in. Katnip hisses, moving to the far end of the carrier. She walks around in a circle, hisses, then flops down, licking her paw.

Licking the blood from her latest victim.

We follow Faith into the second building, and I have to say, I'm impressed with what she has accomplished in such a short amount of time. Already, her practice can treat and house more animals. She's hired three more vets and run the shelter side here on the farm. Any strays that come here are treated and viewed until they are ready to be rehomed.

Beau, her fiancé, has been helping her get funding for the strays from all over the UK. It was his dedication to get it that cemented him into the family on my part. If some fucker can deal with them pompous arses for a woman, then he must love her. It doesn't hurt that we know he'd die for her. Faith deserves nothing less.

"What's wrong with him?" Charlotte asks, bringing me out of my thoughts. I hadn't even realised we'd stopped.

At the back of the cage is a black and gold German Shepherd, quivering in fear.

Faith sighs, bending down to empty the still full food bowl and replacing it with some fresh food. "He was found tied to a tree in a park by a couple walking their dog. We've tried to bring him into the house, but he's scared of Roxy, even though they're the same breed."

I don't know what compels me to do so, but I bend down, wanting a closer look. He lifts his muzzle, sniffing the air, and our eyes meet. A bond snaps into place, and an overwhelming feeling of being needed and wanted hits me. For some reason, I know this dog has had his fair share of loss and pain, but most of all, he knows what it's like to be abandoned. Which is exactly how I felt after Freya died.

His nose twitches as he warily gets up on all fours. "That's weird," Faith whispers.

"What is?" Charlotte asks, peering over my shoulder.

"He never moves… Oh my gosh, he's coming out of the cage," she says in astonishment.

I watch, feeling a piece of my heart mend as the dog walks up to me. His wet nose nudges my hand, and I let him sniff it before running my fingers through his dark, thick fur.

"Hey, buddy," I whisper, smirking when he begins to whine, standing up on his back legs. Chuckling, I lift him to my chest and stand up with him in my arms.

"Oh my gosh," Faith gushes, her hand to her chest.

"You got food for him that I can take with me?"

"You're taking him home?" she asks in bewilderment.

"Yeah," is all I tell her, reaching back down to stroke the little guy.

"He needs training, a *lot* of training," she says slowly, like that will change my mind.

I shrug. "I don't care. He's coming home with me."

She narrows her eyes. "If it weren't for the fact that this is the first time since he arrived two weeks ago that he has stopped shaking, I'd say no. But I can't bear to see him suffering any longer."

He licks my face when I stop paying him attention, and I chuckle. "Just bag up enough supplies for the night and I'll get the rest tomorrow."

"What are you going to call him? We've been calling him Shepherd."

I scrunch my nose up in disgust. "No wonder he's been fucking shaking in the back of the cage. I'll call him Rex."

"It took me days to name a cat, Landon. Maybe you should think about it. What about Brandy or Buttercup?" I slowly turn around to face Charlotte. She looks away, biting her lip at my expression. "It was just a suggestion," she sighs, her shoulders slumping.

"It's Rex," I state, then look down at my dog. "You like Rex, don't you?"

He yaps, licking my face, and I chuckle.

"Yep, he likes it," Faith says, giggling when he doesn't stop. "Charlotte, I don't have any supplies in at the moment for the cats. Our delivery doesn't come until the morning."

"It's okay, I already have everything. It's why I met Landon here. I forgot to get a scratch post from the pet shop, so I went to pick it up. Dad and Mum are coming over after to meet her."

More like check up on her. Little do they know it will be Charlotte who needs watching over. That cat is evil.

"Can you drop me off at Lily's? She wants me to look over Willa and it saves Beau dropping me off. Mum said she'll bring me back."

"Yes, of course I can. Is Willa okay?"

"Hopefully. Lily said she's bumping into stuff more than usual, so I might have to bring her to the vets for a check-up."

"I'll meet you out front to grab the stuff off you," I quickly tell Faith, who nods.

I rush to the front of the house, where I find Beau, this time out of his uniform and drinking a cup of coffee.

"Cute dog," he mutters as he watches me approach.

I don't say anything. Instead, I stare him dead in the eye. "You're coming to movie night with the Hayes family."

He chokes on his drink. "Are you fucking crazy?"

I tilt my head, then shrug. "Maybe."

FOURTEEN

PAISLEY

PUSHING MY HALF-EATEN FOOD AWAY, I begin to regret volunteering to help Mum on the farm today.

I want to blame Landon for the rash decision, but it would be unfair. It's me who has the problem controlling my hormones around him. Every touch, every twitch of his lips that threatens to pull into a smirk, get to me. They affect me so bad all I can picture is jumping him. And his eyes... My God. Those freaking eyes could cause women to walk into lampposts.

"Maybe you should come back to work until Carter has finished with the bed and breakfast," Jaxon suggests, his expression hopeful.

I narrow my gaze on him. "No."

"I don't want you around him," he grumbles.

"I don't want you sticking your nose in my business; we can't have everything."

Mum claps her hands to interrupt up. "Let's get the snacks for the movie ready."

Picking my plate up, I say, "Sounds good to me."

"Are you on your period?" Reid blurts out.

I slam my plate down on the table before slowly turning to him. "Are you being serious?" I ask, feeling my face heat.

He tries to act laid back as he lazily shrugs, but then his eyes dart around the room and he begins to rub the back of his neck. "You've been pissy since our argument. You were never bitchy or moody before then."

"Much," Wyatt adds.

I keep staring as Jaxon steps in, digging their graves deeper. "I think what he's trying to say is that you're snapping all the time. It's not like you. You're usually quiet—"

I hold my hand up, stopping him. "You mean obedient? Have you ever thought you might've pushed me to my breaking point? Before, I let you get away with your crap because it never hurt me. It never cut through my soul. Putting your nose in my business, saying those hurtful words to me… that broke me. Now, I'm not taking shit from you or anyone else again."

"So, you aren't staying away from Landon?" Reid asks, looking confused.

Give me strength.

"I'm going to say this once and once only, so do not mention it again. Landon only wants to be friends." I give each a pointed look as I take a deep breath. I don't tell them about the mixed signals. "I don't know what I want, and when I do, I won't be telling you," I tell them heatedly.

Jaxon goes to open his mouth—no doubt to argue—but Mum pushes her chair back, getting up. "Where the hell are the twins? They said they'd be back for dinner."

Shaking his head, he pulls his gaze from me to Mum. "They said they were doing a science project for school."

Isaac looks up from finishing his food, his eyebrows drawn together. "No, they 'ent. They were messing with the petrol for the mower in the barn."

Mum's eyes widen with horror. "If they are selling that again, I will ring their necks."

Luke chuckles. "Nope. I think they made something and need it for that."

Mum still looks doubtful, and Eli, third eldest, gets up from his chair. "I'll go get them. They can finish whatever it is tomorrow."

He heads out the backdoor, ducking his head as the rain begins to pour. It looks miserable out, and I'm kind of glad Landon managed to finish the doors today. I saw two people turn up to help, but I was too much of a chicken shit to walk over.

The bell to the front door rings. We all glance at each other, yet no one moves.

"Who is it?" Reid asks.

"The tooth fairy," I reply sarcastically, moving to go answer.

I walk down the hall, feeling a few of them follow me. Normally when someone comes around, they've messaged one of us beforehand to let us know.

Opening the door, I halt my next words when I find Landon standing on the doorstep, Beau, Faith's fiancé, standing behind him. They own the farm opposite ours. He looks anywhere but at me, not looking too pleased.

"What the fuck are you doing here?" Wyatt growls, and I feel his chest on my left shoulder.

I sigh, but look to Landon for answers. He grins.

"I was invited to family movie night."

"No, you weren't," I fume.

He tilts his head to the side. "Funny, my mum always said I had selective hearing, but I'm pretty sure I was invited."

"You were what?" Jaxon snaps, and I can hear the accusation in his tone but dare not look at him.

Landon grins wider, taunting my brothers. "Your mum invited me— pleaded really—said I was one of the family. She said I could bring Maddox, but Beau begged to come in his place."

Beau grunts. "Yep, that's *exactly* what happened," he states dryly, the lie rolling off his tongue.

"Mum!" Wyatt yells, storming off.

I cock my hip against the door. "What are you really doing here, Landon?" I'm too exhausted tonight to deal with him and my brothers.

His scrutinising gaze has me shifting on my feet. He's not at all bothered he's getting soaking wet. Sigh.

"I told you. I'm here to watch a movie," he confirms.

"And you brought a cop?" Jaxon voices.

Landon looks to my brother now, losing his smirk. "Got to have someone watching my back."

"Paisley, Jaxon," Mum gasps from behind. Moving to the side, she rushes to the door, her expression filled with disappointment. "Where are your manners? Come on in, Landon," she orders softly, then notices Beau with a pause. "Oh, hello again, Mr Johnson. How's that dog? You get the hole sorted?"

Beau chuckles. "Call me Beau, Mrs Hayes, and we did. They're all transferred into the new buildings now which all have concrete foundations. No more digging and escaping."

"I'm pleased."

I watch as he relaxes, following Mum down the hall and into the living room. Landon falls back to walk next to me. I glance over when I hear a yap and notice his zip up hoodie moving.

What the hell?

"U-um, Landon, why is your hoodie moving?" He unzips his jacket and the cutest black and golden muzzle pops out before a German Shepherd's head pokes through, yapping happily. "Oh my gosh, is he yours?" I ask, and before I can question myself, I pull him out the rest of the way and cuddle him into my arms. He licks my face, and I grin. I look up when Landon doesn't say anything, and my lips part at his expression, his eyes dilating with need.

Shaking the lust from my mind, I clear my throat. "Please tell me you didn't steal him."

"He was my plan B if you tried to shut the door in my face," he says, his face void of emotion.

Gawking, I choke out, "Are you kidding?"

He smirks. "Yes. Rex was a stray Faith took in. Someone found him tied to a tree."

My eyes pool with tears. "That's awful."

"Yeah."

"Is he yours now, then?" I ask.

He runs his fingers over Rex's head. "He is now."

"He's adorable," I tell him, before leaning down to kiss Rex's head.

Landon's nose scrunches in disgust. "He's fierce, not adorable." I giggle, ducking my face into Rex's fur. "And now I'm jealous of a damn dog," he mutters, taking a step closer. "Why can't you pay me the same attention?"

My heart rate picks up as his eyes skim over my body. I shiver at the intensity in his gaze as he surrounds my personal space, acting like he has every right to be there. He's so close I can breathe in his dark, spicy cologne, and it takes all my strength not to sway towards him.

Determined not to let him know how much he affects me, I shrug nonchalantly and clear my throat. "We should go into the living room before one of my brothers dares another to see if they can take down a cop."

"They'd really try to restrain a cop?" he asks in bewilderment.

I give him a 'duh' look. "It's on at least three of their bucket lists." I grimace. "You also brought him off duty."

"Ah, that explains it. My family has something like it," he explains, chuckling deep from his throat. "Better go save him before he or my cousin kill me for getting him into a fight with a Hayes. He only came so your brothers wouldn't kick off."

I giggle again. "They won't care. And what's on your bucket list?"

He takes a minute to decide whether to tell me. "I'm kind of boring. I've never really had one, just followed the others. Maddox wanted to see if he could rob an ambulance once, though."

"And did he?" I ask, intrigued. My brothers had never really thought of doing that. They wanted to steal a boat in Clearport, but Mum would never let them out of her sight long enough to run off and do it.

He sighs. "No. They have a kill switch or some shit."

I laugh as we come to a stop outside of the living room, forgetting about being annoyed with him turning up. "What did the paramedics do?"

"We were ten, so they told us to never do it again and drove us around the block with the sirens on. Maddox had the time of his life upfront, while I stayed in the back getting treated." Landon's lips thin as he begrudgingly admits the next part. "Maddox slammed my hand in the door when the paramedics saw what we were doing."

I burst out laughing when his cheeks turn pink.

"Are you coming in or what?" Jaxon grouches, glaring at Landon.

Landon rolls his eyes but gestures for me to go first. I smother a giggle when I see all my brothers have crowded up the seats. Beau is squished between Mum and Eli; Colton on the end. He looks none too happy when Eli accidently elbows him in the stomach.

Mum looks around the room and sighs. Jaxon has left me a seat next to him, and I know it's for me because he's put my favourite treats and mug on the side table. Theo and Isaac sprawl out on the other end, looking smug.

Landon's seat, on the other hand, is in the middle of Wyatt and Reid, Luke on the end of the huge sofa, leaving enough room for Landon to park his arse but be squashed the entire time. It's only a four-seater, like the other two in the room.

Mum, with a stern expression, stands up. "Eli, go sit next to Jaxon; Colton, go sit next to Reid." When she sees Rex in my arms, her eyes light up and she walks over to take him from me. "Puppy."

"Now, now, Mum," Jaxon starts, but one glare from Mum has him taking a seat, sulking.

Skipping over to my treats, I pick them all up, feeling his heated glare on the side of my face as I do.

I come to a sudden halt, though, when I go to take a seat. Mum is patting the seat next to her with one hand, while stroking Rex with the other. "You sit next to me, Beau."

He shuffles away from Landon, though not before giving him a look that promises retribution. I'd giggle if it weren't for the fact I'll be sitting between the two men.

"Why don't you sit here so you can put your snacks on the table?" Jaxon calls out, trying again.

"She's fine here, aren't you, Paisley?" Landon states, daring me with his eyes.

Under protest, I drop down into the seat, moving closer to Landon. If I wasn't so scared of the Carter females, I'd press up against Beau.

Feeling movement, I tense. Landon rests his arm along the back of the sofa. To anyone else it looks like he's just getting comfortable, but he does it so I have no choice but to move closer to avoid his hand being in my hair.

"Watch it, Carter," Wyatt warns, sitting up.

"Cop," Beau blurts out, sighing, not looking away from the television as Mum picks a film on Netflix.

Wyatt snorts. "One who's not on duty."

"Boys!" Mum warns slowly, and Wyatt sighs, sitting back down but keeping his narrowed gaze on us. "Paisley, your blanket is on the back of the sofa."

I groan. I hadn't picked it up because then I would have to cover both me and Landon. Or me and Beau. Not doing either and piling it all on me will just make me sweat. There is no way I'm smelling of BO when I'm this close to Landon.

"U-um, I'm okay, Mum."

She peers around Beau's large chest, giving me a curious look. "You never watch a movie without it, even if it's hot enough to cook bacon on the pavement."

She really had to use that expression?

"I said—" Before I have chance to finish, Landon has it thrown over the both of us, careful not to dip it into my mug of hot chocolate. With a grumbled, "Thanks," I pull the snacks out from underneath the blanket and settle them on my lap. He shifts as Mum presses play on a movie with Theo James in. I was excited to watch it when I heard he would be in it, but with Landon next to me, I'm too scared to breathe, let alone ogle the gorgeous man on the screen. I don't want to draw attention to myself.

"Here, let me have that," Landon rumbles, placing my drink on the side table next to the sofa.

As he gets comfortable once again, I end up even closer. I place the snacks between me and Beau, too tired and nervous to eat.

I shiver when our thighs rub against each other, and thinking it means I'm cold, he lifts the blanket higher.

"Hands where I can see them before I cut them fucking off," Jaxon growls.

Beau rubs his face, looking tired. "Fucking cop here."

Landon's chest begins to shake, but he complies with my brother and takes his hands out. I sigh with relief, but it's short lived when he leans over me, grabbing a bag of Doritos. And with another shift of his position, I end up dropping into the crook of his shoulder, my head resting on his chest when he lifts his arm to rest on the back of the sofa again.

Nope, this is going to cause trouble. When I go to move, his warm hand on my shoulder stops me.

"Stay," he says, his chest rumbling from the emotion in his voice.

I nod tightly, too tense to move.

"That's it," Jaxon snaps.

"Jaxon! Sit. Down. Right. Now. Or so help me God…" Mum yells, and I hear him dropping back down.

Chancing a flash of my brother's anger, I glance at him. His eyes narrow into slits, his lips pursing. "Friends?"

My cheeks heat, and without answering, I turn back to the television, my attention diverted when Theo James comes onto the screen in a suit. A suit.

He is so freaking good looking.

The day's activities catch up to me, and half way through the movie, I feel my eyes begin to drift shut. I'm too tired to fight my drowsiness, and in Landon's warm embrace, my fleece blanket covering me, darkness envelops me.

FIFTEEN

LANDON

Paisley had dozed off half way through the movie, her soft snores making me inwardly chuckle. I never knew holding someone while they slept could be so satisfying. Freya and I never had this level of intimacy. We were young and stole moments alone where and when we could, but it was never like this.

I don't want to move, afraid of waking her and losing my grasp on her. Even her brothers' glares don't stop me from snuggling the small woman against me.

The screen on the T.V. flickers, showing there is only ten minutes of the movie left.

My attention is drawn back to the woman who has been on my mind for months—if I'm honest with myself, years. I've always been attracted to her; however, her brothers weren't worth the effort. Then there was the fact I'd presumed she was a virgin, and I didn't do one-night stands with them. Even then I was lying to myself. Somewhere inside me, I must have known one time with her wouldn't be enough, that I'd crave to be around her more.

Her hair falls down over her face, tickling her cheek. Her nose twitches as her forehead creases, her lips forming an adorable pout.

Warmth spreads through me, my chest constricting at how beautiful she looks.

The credits begin to roll, and I sigh, disliking how our time has come to an end.

"Oh, she's asleep," Mrs Hayes whispers, then shakes her head at her daughter, a soft smile on her lips. "She run herself ragged today, helping me get caught up on the farm. She's worn herself out."

"Want me to take her to bed?" I ask, not looking away from Paisley.

"I'll do it," Jaxon bites out, but keeps his voice down.

Pissed he wants to come between us right now, I glare at him. "I'm capable."

"Let him do it, Jaxon. He's already got her in his arms," his mum tells him. When he goes to argue, she holds her palm up. "I'll follow them up. I need to take her levels and give her a shot of insulin. She should have done it before the movie."

"I can do it, if you'd like," I offer, not wanting to let her go. After reading up about it, I know pretty much all there is to know.

Her mum's eyes soften as she places Rex in her seat. "I've got it. Her room is—"

"The attic," I finish, getting up with her still in my arms.

"U-uh, okay then."

We're just walking out of the room when I hear Wyatt. "How the fuck does he know where her room is?" he bites out, his voice quiet and deadly.

"I swear to God, you touch me and I'll put you through that fucking window," Beau warns coldly. "And I'd rather not upset your mum."

Mrs Hayes chuckles. "Damn that bucket list. Come on, before they get arrested."

"You don't seem surprised," I state as we walk up the last flight of stairs. I notice a few photos of Paisley, taken when she was younger. One near the top catches my eye. It's of her and her dad. She's sat on a bike with a wide smile on her face, and he's standing next to her, looking down at her with pride and love. I can't even begin to imagine what it was like for her to lose her father. My dad might be full on sometimes—okay, most of the time—but I couldn't be without him. He makes life fuller. And he's my dad; I love him.

Knowing Paisley lost him at such a young age breaks my heart. You can see from the pictures that they shared a strong bond.

"She idolised him, and he was wrapped around her finger," Mrs Hayes says, startling me.

Walking up the rest of the stairs, I answer. "I can see. I'm sorry for your loss."

"Thank you. He was a good man—the best—and he loved his kids. I signed out when he died, and I'll always regret not being there for her. She was hurting, they all were, but Paisley took it harder than the boys. It didn't help that she felt she lost me, too."

"She's strong," I comment, uncomfortable with this heart to heart as I lay Paisley down on her bed. Her mum already has the covers tucked back and her bag with her insulin and stuff by the side of her bed.

"The strongest," she whispers, sitting down on the other side and sliding a piece of hair out of Paisley's face, before glancing at me with a determined expression. "But she also hurts like everyone else. When she lost the baby, I wanted to take her pain away. She broke in a way I don't think will ever be repaired. I watched my daughter mourn her loss, and the loss of you. She wouldn't eat, and her levels were getting dangerously high. In the end, Jaxon forced her to take her insulin, pinning her down while Wyatt or I injected her."

"I'm sorry," I choke out, feeling my throat tighten. I look down at Paisley, vowing to never cause her harm again.

I honestly had no idea just how bad it was for her, though I knew it hadn't been all rainbows and sunshine. Guilt and anger course through me. I wasn't there for her when she needed me. I was the cause of most of that pain.

A cold hand rests on top of mine. I hadn't realised I spaced out, but I glance from Paisley to Mrs Hayes. Her eyes glisten as she watches me.

"Please, don't hurt her. The boys have had their say on the matter, but I don't believe what they said about you. So, I'm putting blind faith in you, Landon. I'm trusting you with my daughter. I'm trusting you with her life. Because one more bad episode, and I don't think her organs will survive it."

Not even a second passes before I nod. "I promise to try. I can't promise I won't fuck up—I'm a Carter, so I'm bound to. It's why I want to be friends. I need her to trust me."

"And to trust yourself," she adds, reading my mind.

I nod, gulping. "I lost someone, too, someone I loved and pictured forever with. I've held onto a lot of guilt over her death, always asking myself, what if," I admit. I run a hand over my jaw. Clearing my mind, I glance at Mrs Hayes, wanting this heart-to-heart over with. "I'm not going to hurt her."

She nods. "That's all a mother can ask for."

"I'd better go." I stand, looking down at Paisley sleeping peacefully one more time, before heading for her door. "Oh, Mrs Hayes?"

She looks over her shoulder. "Yes?"

"Your sons, whatever they've said about me… There's a fifty-fifty chance it's true. I'm not a good person. I hurt people who threaten the people I love. I've done stuff I'm not proud of but would do again in a heartbeat if it protected my family."

Mrs Hayes smiles. "Then welcome to the family. I wouldn't want my daughter with anyone who didn't protect those he loves." She turns to read the machine she's holding. "Go home, get some rest, and we'll see you at breakfast."

Stunned, I can only nod, leaving the room speechless. I'd been prepared for her to kick me out, warn me to stay away from her daughter. Not welcome me with open arms.

She has eight Hayes'. What did you expect?

After jumping down the last of the stairs, I walk into the living room, finding Beau knelt on Reid's back, twisting his arm up in the air.

"Ready?" I ask, not even blinking at the destruction of the room as I walk over to pick up a sleeping Rex.

Beau shoves Reid's arm away and gets up, dusting his clothes off. "Yes!"

We walk out into the rain. "Where was Jaxon?"

"Followed you and his mum," Beau states dryly.

Fuck! How much did that wanker hear?

I snort. "Dickhead."

Beau rounds on me as we get to my car. "Next time you need a fucking bodyguard, call Maddox."

I grimace. "It wasn't that bad." It's a lie, but I won't admit that.

"Not that bad? *Not that bad?* I'm dying of fucking thirst because there was no way I was drinking anything a Hayes brother gave me. And if that isn't bad enough, all three triplets thought they could take me on. Now, take me back to my fiancé before I change my mind and punch you in the face."

We get in the car and I shake the rain out of my hair. "Just think, Faith is going to be super grateful you spent time with me. You know how worried she's been."

Beau's glare heats the side of my face. "Don't make me hate you, Landon. You're one of the few I can tolerate for more than twenty minutes."

I chuckle. "We 'ent that bad."

He lifts his head off the headrest. "After spending two hours with the Hayes', I'm beginning to think you're right. It still doesn't mean I'll be doing it again."

"Got ya."

I pull up outside Faith and Beau's. She must have heard the car because she's standing under the porch roof, waiting. Beau opens the door but pauses with one leg out, turning back.

"Just so you know, to win that girl over you're going to have to make friends with those brothers. They dote on her."

I look at him like he's got a screw loose. "Are you mad?"

He chuckles. "No, but you are. They will never accept you."

I shrug, not caring. "They don't have to. She does. And if they want her in their lives, they will do what makes her happy."

"What makes you so certain she'll choose you?"

I smirk. "Because after tonight, I'm fed up of playing 'let's be friends'.

I'm going to make that girl fall so deeply in love with me she will never see the surface again."

Beau gets out of the car before ducking down to peer through the window. "You really are screwed," he warns, shaking his head before parting ways.

I watch as he takes Faith into his arms, lifting her up to kiss her.

He has no idea what he's talking about. When a Carter wants something, they get it. He'll see. They all will. And just like with every aspect of my life, I'm willing to fight to the death to win her over.

"YOU'RE LATE," LIAM tells me from the brown leather chair in my living room. My body tenses as I put Rex down, letting him roam around his new home. "Cute dog."

The one-bed flat is small, but it was the only thing I could find on such short notice, wanting to get out of Mum and Dad's hair. I'd also been ready to kill Liam and all his one-night stands. However, at the rate my new neighbour is going, I'd rather put up with Liam living with me or my parents all over each other.

The couple are either yelling at each other or trying to break in the bed.

The last Liam and I spoke, he was ready to move out himself, Hayden agreeing, saying Mum and Dad were becoming too much. But both didn't want to move until they found their forever home, like the rest of our family. Me? I just wanted to get out of there and have some privacy.

"Remind me to get them keys off you later," I state dryly.

He grins, glancing over at Maddox. "Hear that? He's cute when he thinks he can scare me into giving him what he wants."

I glare at his smug look. "I didn't give you permission."

He shrugs, his attention going back to Maddox, who is typing away on his phone. "Earth to Maddox!"

Maddox jumps then flashes us his white teeth with a wide grin. "Sorry, meeting up with a chick named Nat later."

I roll my eyes. "The way you go through chicks, I'm surprised you haven't caught an STD."

"No glove, no love, my friend. Didn't your dad ever teach you that?"

Repeatedly. In a million different ways.

It was always an uncomfortable time when we left to meet a chick, but the worst was when he sat us down, telling us how to please a woman. It took us five minutes to realise what he was yapping on about before we made a run for it.

"Is Mark coming?" I ask, looking at Liam now, since the two mostly work together.

"Yeah, he just had to drop some food off to Aunt Teagan. She's feeling under the weather."

"What about Aiden?" I ask Maddox, annoyed he's glued back to his phone. "Will you pay attention."

He pushes his phone into his coat pocket. "No, Aiden isn't coming. He's swapped his culinary classes to nights so someone can watch Sunday once they've finished work."

"So, it's just us four?"

Maddox looks around like he's waiting for someone else to pop out. "Yeah."

"Unless you want me to ring Dad?"

I narrow my gaze at Liam. "Do not get the old man involved. He nearly got himself killed the last time."

"All right. Sheesh. Let's get this done."

RAIN PELTS DOWN on my windshield as we watch the bar where Blaze and Rocket are. Both, in my opinion, are the weakest links.

Thanks to Liam, Dad's friend, we were able to intercept all their messages. Last night, Blaze and Rocket both got a message from Rocco, their boss, saying they had a massive order to deliver later tonight.

We are going to make sure the buyer doesn't get the package. What better way to get revenge than make each and every one of them feel alone. I want them to have no one to turn to when I come for them.

Maddox chuckles from the back. "Keeley said we owe her. Apparently, getting them drunk has been harder than we thought."

Keeley is a girl Maddox met when he went to Ireland last year. She was an aspiring actress who was down on her luck. Maddox helped her out, introducing her to the girl he was fucking at the time, who owned a bar. She got a job straight away, and he gave her money for a place to stay.

She messaged him a few days ago, saying she was visiting with a friend and did they want to meet up.

When the text messages came in last night, we were planning on spiking their drinks, so they wouldn't remember us. But a text from Keeley came in, and well… here we are. Keeley and her friend are doing Maddox a favour by getting the two wankers shitfaced.

Liam turns around in his seat. "What do you mean? They aren't drunk?"

"I didn't say that, did I?" he tells us amusedly. "Her friend, Sophia, had to offer body shots."

"Eww," Liam groans, wincing.

"Tell them we'll pay them extra," I mutter, eyes still on the bar. We've searched the car, and it's not in there, so it has to be on them. For my plan to work, we can't let them know it was me. "Where the fuck is Mark?"

I'm getting impatient, needing this done. Tonight. One by one, I will destroy them. Then, once I'm finished with them, I'm going to make Rocco wish he never crossed me.

Liam checks his phone. "Fuck if I know. He hasn't answered my messages."

I sit forward, squinting through the rain, and spot two bodies swaying out of the bar. Both Sophia and Keeley, who I met before, try to hold the two up, looking around the empty carpark for help. I'm about to head over, but out of nowhere, two large figures step out from the side of the building.

"Is that…" Liam starts, gulping.

"Dad?" I mutter dryly, watching Dad sneak up behind the girls and pull them out of the way. "Yes, yes it fucking is."

"He just knocked them out." Maddox chuckles, leaning forward, his face between the two headrests.

"Let's go," I say, but as I go to open the door, Liam stops me.

"Wait, what is he doing? Why is Mark standing there with his hands on his head?"

I turn away from Liam to watch the show, wincing when Rocket's head bounces off the side of the taillight as Dad shoves him in the boot of Blaze's car—a car he's clearly bought on the cheap if the rust is anything to go by. Dad shrugs before bending down and grabbing Blaze, dumping him in the same way.

He's seriously lost his goddamn mind.

And he wonders why we never invite him anywhere.

Mark begins throwing his hands up, yelling at Dad. But Dad just shrugs, pushing the boot door down until the car begins to bounce with the force. I wince when he jumps, slamming the boot down with all his weight.

"Fuck, I'd hate to be those two in that boot right now," Liam mutters.

"What do you think Mark is yelling?" Maddox asks, his voice filled with amusement.

"I swear he just begged to go to hell. Or he doesn't want to go to hell. It's hard to read his lips through the rain. Bailey's been teaching me to lipread, but I'm not that good," Liam says absentmindedly.

I watch him like he's grown two heads. Dad shouldn't even be here. "Who the fuck cares? We have to stop Dad before he gets himself arrested."

"Wouldn't be the first time," Maddox replies.

I shoot him a glare and get ready to sort this shit out, when Liam stops me again. "I swear to God, Liam, brother or not, I'm ready to lay you out."

He raises an eyebrow. "So, you wanted to waste your time standing in the rain when Dad just pulled out?"

"What?" I ask, snapping my head in the direction I last saw Dad. Sure enough, the taillights to Blaze's car are half way down the street. I start the engine and follow them. "Ring him and ask him what he's playing at," I demand.

"You really want me to ring Dad while he's in a stolen car with two unconscious bodies in the back?" Liam asks.

"Ring Mark, then," I snap, putting my foot on the accelerator.

"I've been trying, but by the looks of it, he's trying to talk your dad out of whatever he has planned," Maddox informs us.

Liam leans forward in his seat. "Huh, you're right," he replies, chuckling. "He's still flapping his arms around like a scared chicken."

I groan, wondering why I bothered bringing them along. Instead of engaging in conversation, I concentrate on not speeding yet remaining as close to Dad as possible.

Twenty minutes later, we pull into a secluded part of Deacon Forest and follow the dirt road further in. If I'm remembering correctly, there's a lagoon nearby where kids used to hang out. It wasn't until a group of teenagers died that people stopped coming, not wanting to risk a riptide pulling them out into deeper waters. Every so often, though, we do read how someone got hurt jumping from the cliff into the lagoon.

"Please tell me he's not here to bury a body," I plead, speaking more to myself than anyone else. Why? Because I'd never get a serious answer.

Maddox's phone beeps. He begins to laugh as I stop a short distance away from Blaze's car. "Mark just texted me asking if Uncle Max told us to bring shovels."

Liam starts laughing as he jumps out of the car. I get out, leaving the car running in order to light up the space between the two cars.

"Dad?" I growl through the rain.

"Get back in your car. I've got this," he says, slipping in some mud.

I snort. "Dad, I have a fucking plan."

Opening the boot, he turns his back to me. "I've got this."

"And what is it you think you've got?"

He throws Blaze to the floor, sighing. "This. Just go home. I've got them.

My plan is probably a little better than what you came up with. I'm more mature; have a lot more experience."

"In what? Getting yourself injured?" I ask dryly. "What is your plan?"

He grins. "I'm going to tie them to a tree, cover them in honey, and hope to fuck some bears eat them."

I roll my eyes. "We don't fucking have bears."

"Mountain lions?"

"Them neither," Liam chuckles, kicking Blaze with the tip of his boot. "They gonna wake up?"

"Don't know. Max got those two girls to slip them a strong sleeping pill," Mark admits, not looking at me.

"And how did Dad know about this?"

"I'm right here," Dad snaps. "And I've got friends, too, ya know. They tell me shit."

"How the fuck do you know Keeley?" Maddox asks, stepping closer.

Dad runs his fingers through his wet hair. "Why do you guys chat like old ladies? I'm gonna catch the flu if you keep flapping ya gums," he grouches. "And to answer your question, I read your messages when you met your dad at the pub. You were in the loo."

"You weren't at the pub," Maddox growls. "And who gave you permission to read my phone?"

He looks at Maddox like he has two heads. "I don't need permission."

"Shut up!" I yell when Maddox goes to argue. I glance at Dad, pleading with him. "Dad, they have a lot of fucking heroin on them right now—thousands worth—and we're stealing it."

Dad's eyes light up. "Ah, separating the pack before you slaughter them."

I wouldn't put it quite like that.

"That means you can't touch them," I reason.

"Stand back. I got this," he says, struggling to move Blaze. "Mads, come help."

Maddox shrugs before helping Dad drag Blaze to the front of the car.

"I'm surrounded by dickheads," I growl.

"I'm kind of scared of your dad," Mark admits.

"Liam, don't just stand there," Dad yells, and I squint through the dim light to see shoes being removed.

"Oh God. I should have stayed in the car," Liam mutters, before heading over to them.

I step over to Rocket, who is still in the boot of the car, and pat down his jacket. I inwardly grin when I find the large brown package and tuck it into my own jacket pocket.

Dad shoves me gently out of the way before I have chance to step back. "Mark, write a letter from those girls saying, 'Don't call, arseholes'."

"Huh?" Mark asks, shaking his head as Dad drops Rocket on the ground.

"Just do it," Dad wheezes. "God, what the fuck does this shithead eat."

Maddox starts laughing, leaning against the back of the car. I walk over, nearly losing my shit when I see what he's doing. "Are you seriously texting some fucking chick right now?" With a smug smirk, he waves the phone at me, and I grimace, then gag. "Why the fuck are you showing me your dick pics?"

Losing his smile, he narrows his eyes at me. "One, my dick is six times bigger—*soft*. Two, do I look like an insecure twat who needs to send dick pics to get attention?"

"What the fuck is it, then?" I ask, throwing my hands up. Tonight isn't going as planned. Nothing is.

"Good ol' Blaze's dick. I'm sending it to his boss with a few dirty messages."

A laugh slips free. "You didn't?"

He chuckles, nodding. "And his entire Facebook and Twitter contacts now have the unfortunate pleasure of seeing what he's been shamefully hiding."

"Dad, what the fuck are you doing?" Liam screeches, staring into the front of Blaze's car.

I rush over and duck my head in, my eyes widening in horror. Stripped down to their boxers, both sit with their seatbelts on and their heads tilted to the side. But that isn't what has my eyes widening. No. It's Dad, gingerly pulling Rocket's boxers open and squirting honey inside them.

He looks up, shaking his head at me. "Did I teach you nothing?"

Does he want me to answer that?

When he leans over, I lean back, worried about his next move. Light dawns when he squirts honey all over Blaze's mouth, using a tissue to rub it in.

I inwardly gag.

"Ew, that's fucking gross, but utterly genius," Maddox mutters from over my shoulder.

"Yep," Dad utters, concentrating. "Wonder who will cry the worst; Rocket, thinking he got a blow job from a guy, or Blaze, who thinks he's badass, giving one."

"Probably both," Liam mutters.

"Did one of you get the heroin?" Dad asks.

I open my coat, showing him, but then Mark, who is on the other side of the car, next to Dad, leans forward, showing us another package the same size before handing it over to Dad.

Shit. Just how much is this worth?

Dad opens the corner with a pocket knife, tipping some on the dashboard and floor, along with a burnt spoon and some foil. "Dad? Did you have this planned all along?" I ask suspiciously.

He looks up with drawn eyebrows. "No. My brilliance comes spare of the moment. I have some rolled-up fivers and a mirror in my pocket, just in case it was coke."

I shake my head doubtfully but pull out the counterfeit money I had Liam get from a friend, shoving it in Blaze's jacket.

Dad finishes up. "All done," he says, wiping his hands on his jeans.

In silence we walk back to my car, all of us getting inside.

Dad sits up front, a wide smile on his face. "And that, my friends, is how you get revenge. It's just a shame we couldn't have given them a few bruises— besides the ones I accidently gave them on their heads. But where would the fun be with them unconscious?"

"Uncle Max," Maddox calls from the back. I look into the rear-view mirror as I drive back to the main road, watching as he visibly gulps.

"Yes, nephew of mine."

"Remind me never to piss you off," Maddox mutters.

SIXTEEN

PAISLEY

MONDAY COMES AROUND FAR TOO slowly. All day yesterday, I found myself missing Landon. *Missing him.* How bizarre is that? But there was no mistaking the heavy feeling in my chest when I woke up in bed and found he was no longer there. All day I kept peeking out of the window, hoping to get a view of him working on the house. There was no such luck. He was like a ghost the whole day.

I've just gotten so used to having him around. And Saturday, I know he was the one who carried me to bed. Mum had the pleasure of telling me how sweet we looked and how protective and gentle he was with me.

Gentle isn't a word I would associate with Landon. Protective, yes, but only with family. Mum wouldn't have lied though, and I could see the truth in her expression and on the frowns creasing my brothers' foreheads—all of whom took great measures to try and talk me out of seeing him again. Wyatt even went as far as to say he'll take leave from the company and work on the bed and breakfast.

I want space from my brothers, not to begin a new adventure with them hovering over me.

The kitchen goes quiet when I walk in, and everyone begins to stare. "What?" I ask, looking down at my dungarees. I wear them when I'm working in the barn, so they're a little dirty.

"Do you have makeup on?" Reid asks.

Glaring, I storm over to the hotplate and grab some food. "No!"

"Yes, you do," Jaxon argues.

I sit down opposite him, pouting. "It's just a bit of mascara and blusher," I whisper.

"Take it off. You look weird," Wyatt says.

My throat tightens. I duck my head, feeling stupid.

"No, she doesn't," Mum snaps. "She looks beautiful, as ever. Now say you're sorry. Each of you."

"Sorry," Wyatt mumbles, pouting like a scolded boy.

"Soz," Reid says, shoving more food into his mouth.

"I just don't get why you're wearing it," Jaxon states. "You're pretty without it."

"Jaxon," Mum warns, dropping her fork on her finished plate.

"Sorry. I didn't mean anything bad by it. I was just saying she doesn't need it."

I blush, refusing to explain to them that I wanted to look good for Landon. Not that he'd notice; he's a boy. Last night I watched hours of YouTube makeup tutorials, but in the end, I decided a little mascara and blush would do. I ended up looking like a clown when I tried to go for more.

"You excited to paint your kitchen today, sweetheart?"

My shoulders relax at Mum's change of conversation. "Yes. I'm still shocked at how quickly he got the kitchen fitted yesterday. I've still not seen it yet. He didn't text me until late last night that it was ready to be painted."

She pats my hand. "I'm so happy for you. Your dad would be proud of what you've achieved."

I nod, feeling tears clog my throat. "Thank you."

"What will you be doing next?" Jaxon asks through a mouthful of food.

I roll my eyes at his lack of manners. "After I've finished painting, we'll lay the flooring in the kitchen, then I'll start unpacking for downstairs, get it all set up. Landon said he'll finish the bathrooms, then start painting the rooms."

"Do you have your website up yet? When are you hoping to open?"

"Hopefully in seven weeks' time. I need to double check with Landon first," I explain. "And I'm meeting Bailey tomorrow for lunch at her house."

"Want me to come with you?" Jaxon asks.

Raising my eyebrow, I give him a pointed look. "No. Aiden has moved in with her and I'm not having you pick a fight when he has a baby to look after."

Snorting, he shrugs. "I still can't believe he's got a kid. Out of all of them, he'd be the last I expected."

I finish the last bite of toast before dusting my hands off. "I'd better get a start on the painting," I tell them, before looking at Jaxon. "If you're free later, can you help bring some stuff over for me to unpack tomorrow?"

His eyes soften. "Of course I will. If there's anything I can help with, just let me know."

"Yeah, we'll all help," Wyatt says.

"I will if you make a Swedish chocolate cake," Reid bargains.

And this is why I love my brothers. They might be pains in my arse, but each one would drop whatever they're doing to help me.

My voice softens when I answer. "I'll make it for you anyway. Thank you, all of you."

"We'd do anything for you," Jaxon declares, and the rest nod in agreement.

"I'll text later," I inform them, getting up. Reaching the kitchen door, Mum calls me back.

"Wait, I've packed you and Landon a lunch and some drinks."

"Mum, you didn't need to do that," I say, feeling my cheeks heat.

"You'll be busy all day. It's the least I can do. It's in the basket by the front door."

"Thanks, Mum." I walk over, bending down to kiss her cheek. "Love you."

MY SPIRITS DROP when Landon's car isn't outside the bed and breakfast when I arrive. With a resigned sigh, I move towards the door, letting myself in with my key.

Heading straight for the kitchen, butterflies begin to flutter in my stomach. I'm so excited to see it.

I drop the picnic basket Mum made up and attentively open the door. A small gasp of surprise escapes my parted lips.

It's beautiful.

Tears gather in my eyes as I stand stock-still, taking every little detail in. White, rounded cupboards with dark brown tops line the wall underneath the window, where the sink sits with its huge, curved tap. Two more rounded cupboards are above, on either side of the window, white wood framing the glass set into their doors. I can already picture the flowers I'll put on the windowsill and the brown, beige, and pale green blind that will fit the window perfectly.

In the centre of the room is a large island with loads of different cabinets, one side dedicated to holding bottles of wine.

On the right side are more cupboards on either side of a huge double oven with a wall fan above it. I walk over, opening the biggest cupboard and finding the dishwasher already inside.

I skim my fingers down the work surface towards the other window. It has a bench fitted underneath it that wasn't in the plan before; however, I know the perfect pillows to put there.

I turn back to the room, my eyes never leaving the worksurfaces, until I reach the American style, double fridge freezer. It is huge, bigger than I remember it being when I ordered it.

"Do you like it?" a hoarse voice asks.

I startled scream escapes me, and I spin to face Landon with a hand on my chest. "You scared me."

His lips twitch as he lazily leans against the doorframe. "What do you think?"

I look around the room once more, feeling so at home I don't ever want to leave. Landon's still watching me when I turn back around.

"Landon, I love it. I can't… I don't have any words right now. This is more than I could have hoped for."

"I just fitted it," he says, looking around the room.

I shake my head, walking up to him. "No. You made a bare, cold room into a warm kitchen, a place everyone will want to hang out. Thank you," I tell him, leaning up to kiss his cheek.

His eyes heat as I slowly pull away, feeling electric zap my lips from the small contact.

"You're welcome," he replies, so softly I barely hear him. His eyebrows draw together as he takes in my face. "Are you wearing makeup?"

I should have wiped it off when Wyatt said to.

I shrug, trying to act aloof. "A little. Why?"

He studies me further, his pupils dilating. "I'm trying to figure out which I prefer. But in all fairness, you're beautiful with or without it. Although, it does make your eye colour pop. They kind of remind me of autumn."

My chest flutters at his words. I didn't think he'd notice, no matter how much I hoped he would. "T-thank you?"

He shakes his head a little before focusing. "Are you ready to paint?"

I bite my bottom lip. "I'm kind of worried about painting in here now. I don't want to ruin anything."

He chuckles, rubbing my arm. "I didn't put the sheeting over anything last night because I wanted you to see it first. The fridge freezer might take some time to shift though. Could you get one any bigger?"

I nod absentmindedly. "Yeah, but I thought it might be a bit much for the room."

A laugh passes through his lips. "I was being sarcastic, but good to know you weren't trying to kill me."

Heat fills my cheeks. "Sorry. You should have said you needed help. I would have come," I tell him, trying to hide the hurt I feel for not seeing him yesterday.

"Jaxon helped me."

My eyes widen. "He did?"

"Yep, fucker looked constipated the entire time," he admits, making me giggle.

"Sounds about right." I pause, taking in the room once more. I really can't believe this is mine. "I'm so grateful, Landon. I really do love it."

His expression softens, something I rarely see when it comes to Landon. "My pleasure. Now, what colour are we painting the walls? I was going to start it yesterday, but Mum called me home for Sunday dinner."

Remembering the conversation he had with his dad in the restaurant, I laugh. "Did you really talk her into it?"

He frowns, not looking happy about it. "I rarely ask for anything, so when I do, I think they find it hard to say no," he tells me, before pausing, seeming to think something over. "I think that's why my family ask me to talk their latest victims into something. Because they know they won't say no."

"Kind of genius, if you ask me."

"Unless you make your mum think you miss her Sunday dinners," he mutters.

"She a bad cook?" I ask, wincing a little. The boys can't cook at all. The one time me and Mum were down with the flu and we ended up with food poisoning too.

"No, she's a great cook. But she made me eat four plates before she let me leave. I'm supposed to be gaining back muscle, not fat."

"There's no fat on you. You're hard as rock," I blurt out, scanning his body. When I realise what just vomited out of my mouth, I blush further.

His chuckle is deep, caressing my skin. "Been looking?"

"U-um, n-no," I stammer out, then when he pouts, I shake my head. "Y-yes. No." I groan, covering my face with my hands. "Oh my God, just kill me now."

"I'm okay with you checking me out. Feel free to anytime," he offers in a sexual tone.

"W-what?"

"I can take my top off while we paint, if you want?" he says, nodding like it's a good idea.

"N-no," I rush out, my face on fire when he goes to lift his shirt. Good God, if he lifts that, I will be on the floor. "Don't. You're fine. I'm fine. I mean, your body's fine. Oh God," I groan.

He wraps his large hands around my forearms. "Calm down. I'm playing."

I open my eyes, and he winks. "You're a terrible person."

He chuckles, shrugging. "Are you going to tell me the colour?"

"Egg blue," I whisper, too afraid to speak any louder and make a bigger fool of myself.

"Egg blue?" he asks, looking doubtful.

"I know, weird name, but I love the colour."

"All right then. The paint is in the hallway, but I need to get Rex out of the car."

"You left him in the car?" I accuse, walking ahead of him.

He sighs behind me. "I saw the door open and wanted to check it out first, in case someone was in here. I didn't want him to get hurt."

I come to a sudden halt at the front door, slowly turning to face him. "You didn't want him to get hurt?"

He looks at me like I've lost my mind. "Well, yeah. He's not trained that well, even though he's listened to everything I've said so far. I didn't want him to rush up to someone breaking in and then have them lash out, thinking he was gonna bite them."

My mouth gapes open as I stare at him in disbelief. He truly meant what he said. My shoulders drop, and I give him a bright smile. "You really are a sweet man, Landon."

He winces like I've punched him in the balls. "I am not sweet."

"You totally are. You aren't as mean as you pretend to be."

"I fucking am," he yells. "I'm not sweet at all."

I shrug, skipping down the steps to his car. "Whatever you say, buddy. Whatever you say."

"Paisley, you're wrong. You can't say things like that. People will believe you," he calls out, sounding close to panicking.

I giggle louder. "Don't worry, your secret is safe with me."

He opens his mouth to say something, but Rex barks, gaining his attention. "It's all right, you can come out now."

I grin wider at how gentle he is in getting him out of the car. Rex yelps, licking Landon's face, his tail wagging like crazy.

"You really are a big softie," I murmur.

He scans my face, sighs, and his shoulders drop. "You look too fucking beautiful to argue with."

With flaming cheeks, I stare at him a moment longer before saying, "We should start the painting."

I walk off, nearly tripping over my own feet to get away.

Damn Landon Carter and his sexy eyes, sexy voice—sexy everything.

His chuckle echoes behind me as I storm up the steps, embarrassment filling my cheeks.

SEVENTEEN

PAISLEY

THE RAIN PATTERS AGAINST THE KITCHEN windows by the time lunch rolls around. My stomach grumbles, reminding me to eat and take my glucose levels.

We've managed to get the painting done, having finished the second coat an hour ago. I watch as Landon fits the last wooden flooring panel, sweat beading his forehead. I'm just glad he didn't follow his words and take his shirt off. I'd never have gotten anything done. It was bad enough just being in his presence. A half-naked Landon and I'd have the intellect of a one-year-old.

Landon brushes past me once again, and a shiver runs up my spine. I close my eyes, not sure how much more of his innocent touches I can take. I feel like I'm on fire, burning from within. Being this close to him… He's just too much. His size, his scent, his intensity. It's making me dizzy.

I clear my throat, drawing his attention. "I'm just popping to the bathroom, then we should take a break and eat something."

A pained look crosses his expression as he glances at his phone. "Shit."

Does he have somewhere to be?

My stomach sinks at the thought and starts to cramp. I hate feeling this way, but somehow, he's wormed his way back into my heart. I've not forgiven him—not by a long shot—but today, he seems different. He's been more open with me, chatting freely, like we've been best friends our whole lives. And the heated looks… they've driven me insane all day. However, that isn't why I've felt closer to him. I can't quite put my finger on it, but it's there, on the tip of my tongue. It could be a mixture of things really. Like the softness around his eyes when he watches me, or the darkness I usually see lurking in them now barely noticeable, no longer shining like a beacon.

"Do you have to be somewhere else? I mean, it's okay if you do. You don't need permission," I ramble.

He fists his hair. "What? No. We can go somewhere. Do you think there's a place that will let Rex in?"

I forgot to tell him about the picnic Mum made up. I'm ready to mysteriously forget about it, but looking outside, it's miserable. I like it here with Landon, where we're alone with no interruptions.

"U-um, Mum made us a picnic for lunch. It's just outside the kitchen door."

His gaze goes to the door. "She did?"

"She did. But if you'd rather go out, I can give it to my brothers."

For a minute, I think his head is gonna spin off he turns that quickly. "No! We can stay here. I don't think there's a place we'd be able to take Rex in with us."

I smile. "Okay. I just need to go to the bathroom first. I think she packed us a blanket too. Do you have anything for Rex?" I ask, knowing the dog is in the lobby, sleeping in front of the fire.

"I do. I left it in the car. Be right back," he says. I nod, grabbing my bag from the door and heading to the bathroom.

It doesn't take me long to inject my insulin and wash up. I chuckle to myself when I see specs of paint on my face. It has nothing on the amount I have on my clothes though. Even with all the work we've done, I still look pale. I pinch my cheeks to give them some colour before heading back to the kitchen. I pass the laundry room and step into the lobby, where I stop.

Landon is sitting down on the blanket, gently pulling out the cartons of food. He and Rex both look up when I walk in, making me smile.

"Your mum made a lot," he comments.

"I think she went by what you ate for breakfast when you came over," I tell him, chuckling.

He grins, patting his hard abs. "I can't wait to dig in. I didn't realise how hungry I was until I pulled this out. She made turkey sandwiches and everything."

I roll my eyes as I sit down cross-legged on the blanket. Rex stirs, shuffles over, and rests his muzzle on my leg. I smile down at him, stroking him. "I think running around the bed and breakfast has tired him out."

Landon chuckles. "Would you believe me if I told you he was a scared dog when I met him?"

That's hard to believe. "Really?"

He nods. "Yeah, he was shaking and everything."

I look down at a sleeping Rex, surprised. "He must be happy with his new owner."

"You think?"

I catch Landon's gaze. "Of course. He clearly adores you already."

"And you, it seems."

"Who wouldn't?" I tease.

His pupils dilate. "An idiot with no brain."

I glance away, grabbing the tub of potato salad and the plates and forks from inside the basket. I hand a plate and some cutlery to Landon, then try to open the tub of potato salad. It doesn't budge. "Bloody thing is glued on," I mutter.

"Here, let me," Landon orders, reaching out for it.

I pull it away. "I got it." I take the knife from the floor and wedge it under the seal. The knife slips, slicing my thumb. I wince, sucking in a breath when blood begins to pour down my hand and into the potato salad.

"Fuck!" Landon hisses, and before I know it, he's gently taking my hand in his and pressing a paper towel onto the cut. "Are you okay?"

I watch in amazement as he gently pulls the tissue away, frowning when blood still seeps out of the wound. He looks into the basket, pulling a dish towel out, before pressing it down on the cut, eyeing me with concern.

"Are you okay?"

Shaking myself out of how quickly he moved and how carefully he's treating me, I nod. "The knife slipped."

"I know." He grimaces. "You should have let me do it."

"I'm not defenceless, you know."

He looks up at me, his eyebrows drawn together. "I know you're not. I know you can take care of yourself. But I could have opened it."

"I don't like blood," I whisper, the coppery smell overwhelming me.

"It doesn't look deep, so it should stop in a minute," he tells me soothingly.

I bite my lip to keep the tears at bay as our eyes lock. "Thank you."

"Go out with me," he whispers. Not what I expected to come out of his mouth at all.

Mouth agape, I study him, trying to gauge whether he's being earnest or not. There's no denying something has shifted between us today, like he's finally letting his guard down in front of me, but it doesn't change the fact he hurt me.

"I can't," I whisper, looking down at our joined hands for a brief second.

His eyebrow lifts and his chocolate-coloured eyes begin to study me. "I really am so fucking sorry I hurt you, Paisley," he rumbles, his voice low and pained.

Questions that have had me crying into my pillow every night burn to the surface. "Why did you leave me on the side of the road like that? I know you said you were scared, but why not take me home? Why treat me like you do the other girls in your life? And why... God, why has everything suddenly changed now?"

For years I wanted to matter to him, to be noticed. But not like this, not out of pity. He didn't promise me forever, he didn't promise me tomorrow, but somewhere deep down, I feel like that's what he's asking for now.

He brushes a piece of hair away from my face, sending my body into overdrive once again.

"Honestly?"

My breath hitches, and I wonder if I really want to know the answer or not. I don't know how, but I know whatever he's going to say is going to cut deep. It will hurt, there's no doubt about it, but do I want honesty from him? Yes. Yes, I do.

"Honesty is all I ever want," I tell him, keeping the doubt out of my voice.

He sighs, switching the hand holding the towel over my cut. "I wasn't lying when I said I got scared. I knew being with you was different from how I used other girls to drown out the grief of losing Freya." He takes a breath, rubbing the stubble on his jaw. "All my life I've felt different from everyone else. I never understood why, because I have amazing parents, a great family, and have had the best upbringing. I love each and every one of them. But other people?" he says, his gaze distant. "It was like ice would run through me. I just didn't care. I couldn't stand people talking to me, being near me, or even looking at me. I hated any and all social interactions. It got better during high school. Most people knew to leave me alone. After that, I started hanging out with my family more when they went out places.

"Then I met Freya, and she sat down next to me," he says, chuckling. His expression cuts deep, and jealousy hits me over how much he loves her. "One look at her and I didn't feel that coldness inside me, that void. For the first time in my life, I wanted someone to talk my ear off, to touch me. Then she died and everything felt cold and dark. An anger like nothing I've ever felt before grew inside of me. I lived for years holding onto that anger, onto Freya and what happened. I needed it."

Seeing the anguish on his face doesn't sit well with me. Pushing away the jealously, I place my hand on top of his. He looks up at me, and what I see has me taking in a breath.

"Then you happened."

"Me?" I ask, terrified of what he will say next.

"Yeah," he croaks out. "You always intrigued me, even when I was with Freya. I would watch you, you know?"

"You did?" I squeak out, cheeks filling with heat. I seriously hope it wasn't one of the times I daydreamed whilst watching him across the dinner hall.

He chuckles, rubbing his eyes. "Yeah. More than I cared to admit."

"Why didn't you speak to me?" I blurt out, then look away when I realise Freya was the reason why. He had a stunning girlfriend, and I didn't compare. Not even close.

"Your brothers," he admits.

"My brothers?" I ask doubtfully. He wasn't scared of them, that much I knew, with the amount of times they fought at school. Thinking back, however, none of those fights were started by Landon. It was always one of his cousins or his brother.

"Yeah. I didn't think it was worth the hassle of having them breathing down my neck. I liked being alone, remember?"

Ouch. Double fucking ouch. That hurt more than I realised it would. Being told you're not worth the effort… Yeah, it fucking sucked.

"And now?"

"Now I know what it's like to be with you. That day in the car, I felt like I betrayed Freya. I got angry at her. Angry at you. I hated that I felt something again. Just one touch and I felt warm, Paisley. I was a dickhead for making you walk back home. A part of me wanted to turn back, but I knew I wouldn't let you go, and it wasn't fair to you when I was still mourning a dead girl. For weeks I fought to stop myself from seeking you out—to hell with your brothers. I just wanted you. Again, and again. I knew I'd never get enough of you, Paisley. The night I was attacked, I had already come to the conclusion I couldn't stay away. I was fighting more often than not, and then I realised in the ring that I wasn't really fighting my demons but fighting my feelings for you."

Wow. Just wow.

"I'm scared you'll hurt me again," I admit through a lump in my throat.

His knuckles bump my chin, lifting my head to meet his gaze. "Then let me prove I won't."

"I don't get it. Why me?"

He shakes his head, his lips twitching. "You really don't see how special you are, do you?" I shake my head, my nose twitching. He chuckles. "In school, you used to sit next to a girl in the dinner hall. You would slyly give her stuff from your lunchbox because she never had lunch."

I scrunch my nose up. How did he remember Hannah? She had a shit upbringing, always getting picked on for wearing worn and torn clothes far too small for her. She was skinny and pale, and she never had money for food.

"I made extra sandwiches and would pretend my mum had overpacked so she would take it," I admit.

He nods. "Daniel Morgan found the courage to ask Louise Billings to the end of school dance. She embarrassed him in front of everyone outside of school, and you walked right up to him and asked him if he wanted to take you. It wasn't even your year to have a dance."

I blush, remembering David. He had a tick, a nervous stutter, and a bad case of acne. I had watched him walk up to her outside of school, in front of all her friends, and ask her to go to the end of year dance.

"She was a mean person."

"Last year, I watched you try to correct the disaster Charlotte made of her cake."

My lips twitch. "She picked up salt, not sugar."

He shrugs. "You crawled out from behind that bin to protect me, knowing you would be in danger."

My heart sinks and tears gather in my eyes. "They were going to kill you."

He cups my cheek. "I know, but you still stepped in front of me like a shield. You're special, Paisley. You're kind and giving. When you laugh, your entire face fills with happiness. And you don't see it, but people stop to take notice. They watch you, and they smile."

I shake my head, denying it, too lost for words. He leans in closer, and I no longer care he's invading my space.

"You asked me, why you. That isn't even close to why. You're beautiful, Paisley, inside and out. And that's rare. So fucking rare."

"Landon," I whisper, pleading with him to stop as the walls I built around my heart come crumbling down.

"I've never, not once, laid myself bare to someone. I don't let people in, but I'm taking a chance. You're worth the chance. So, I'll ask you one more time. Will you go out with me?"

I meet his gaze, the intensity making me squirm. "What if I say no?" I ask teasingly, wanting to lighten the atmosphere.

His lips twitch, and he shrugs. "I'll just keep on asking, because I'm not giving up. I'm not giving up on you. On us. We have something worth fighting for," he declares, his gaze heated and determined. "What's it going to be, Paisley? Are you going to fight with me or against me? Because, baby, I'm ruthless, and I won't give up."

The air rushes from my lungs when his lips hover over mine. My eyelids droop, and I begin to sway towards him.

"Say yes," he whispers, his lips brushing against mine.

"Yes," I whisper hazily.

The feel of his soft lips has me swallowing down a gasp, my heart beating wildly against my chest. His fingers glide across my jaw, over my ear, and into my hair, where he grips on like he's afraid I'll pull away.

I moan into his mouth at the feel of his tongue swirling against mine. I forget about my cut hand and grip his biceps, needing an anchor to keep me steady before I fall.

His kiss has my entire system on fire, my senses focused on him and only him. His touch, his scent; it's all too much.

"Oh dear, I'm sorry," a voice squeaks out.

We break apart, and I run my fingers over my swollen lips. Landon's eyes are hooded, his breathing heavy as he watches me.

I clear my throat. "Hi, Mum," I croak out, glancing over to the door where she's standing, her hand shielding her eyes. I grimace, glad it's her and not one of my brothers.

"I just thought I'd come give you a heads-up; your brothers have a few hours to spare and are outside, ready to unload."

My eyes widen at the thought of what they could have walked in on. I look at Landon, who tries to hide his smug grin.

I roll my eyes, ready to get up and help unload the car, but Landon's hand on my arm stops me.

"Paisley's cut herself on a knife. Do you have any plasters?"

Mum's eyes are round when she glances down at my hand. "Oh Lord. Were you sick?"

My cheeks heat with embarrassment. "No," I grumble.

Landon chuckles. "And she hasn't eaten yet."

I look down at the food, grimacing. "I got blood on everything."

Mum rushes over, packing everything up. "Not to worry. I'll go throw something together. There's plenty more in the fridge."

"Mum, you don't need to do that," I tell her.

Mum sighs, shaking her head at me as she finishes throwing everything back into the basket, Landon helping her. "It's no trouble. Maybe you two should come up to the house. We'll get that hand cleaned and put a plaster on it while your brothers unload."

I look to the door, hearing them arguing outside, and nod. "Maybe it's for the best. Is that okay?" I ask, looking at Landon.

His eyes soften. "I'll go wherever you go."

"That's settled then. You coming, big boy?" Mum asks, and I choke, horrified. "I meant the dog, Paisley."

Landon chuckles, but I don't find it funny. At all. Rex perks up, following Mum.

Standing, I dust off my dungarees, feeling a little uncomfortable now Mum has left the room. I don't know how to act, what to do.

Grabbing my bag, I go to wait for Landon by the door, but he blocks my way. I tilt my head to look up at him, butterflies fluttering in my stomach.

"Something wrong?"

I want to get out of here before my brothers come in and ruin what we just shared.

"Yes."

My lips twist. "What? What's wrong?"

His lips pull into a small smile. "I need to know you meant it when you said yes, that you'd go out with me."

There's a vulnerability in his gaze that makes me soften against him. "Yes. But please, don't hurt me."

"I won't," he declares.

I nod. "Then it's a date." I begin to head for the door, ignoring what the relief on his face does to me. Halfway to the door, I glance over my shoulder. "If you hurt me, I'm going to use the moves Jaxon taught me when I was five and twist your balls so tight you'll be pissing red for a week." I wouldn't, but he doesn't know that. I'm not even sure if a guy would piss red if someone twisted his balls, but going by how visibly pale Landon turns, I'm guessing he doesn't know either.

I head out of the door and into the rain, whistling a tune. "You're joking, right?" he yells after me. "Paisley?"

My brothers stop what they're doing in the back of the van when they hear him, eyeing me with suspicion. I roll my eyes. "Do you want those goodies I'm baking later or not?"

At once, they move, tripping over themselves to get the boxes out of the van.

Brothers. They're so freaking easy sometimes.

EIGHTEEN

LANDON

NERVOUS ENERGY RUNS THROUGH MY system as I drive up to Hayes Farm. I've never been on a date before. Freya and I hung out, yes, but I wouldn't class what we did during those times as a date. And I certainly never had to dress up.

Charlotte texted me earlier to pop by with some cat food. She hadn't had chance to go to the shop with working all day at the library.

When I walked in, I had expected to be in and out, but nope. The girl was a mess. You'd think she had a new born baby, not a kitten. Her hair was a knotted mess, she had scratches all over her arms and legs and looked like she hadn't slept for a week. However, she beamed like I hung the moon when I walked in, always so fucking happy.

After staring at me for an uncomfortably long time, she frowned and demanded I take her back to mine so she could pick out something for me to wear. I hadn't understood what was wrong with the jeans and T-shirt I wore, but not wanting to argue, I let her pick out a navy-blue shirt and black trousers, paired with my black shoes she polished before allowing me to wear them. I put a stop to any more when she went looking for fucking hair gel. Fucking hair gel. I think the lack of sleep was getting to her because it's Liam who wears that shit.

"She's special, she's different, she's mine," I chant to myself as I pull up out outside. Cutting the engine, I get out of the car, grateful the rain has finally let up. When I grab the flowers from the backseat, I silently curse Mum.

Charlotte had texted her on our way back to mine. Just as we were leaving, Mum shoved flowers into my hand and told me to give them to Paisley. Apparently, girls loved receiving flowers. I'd presumed only dorks in movies did that shit.

My gaze shifts over the top of the car, finding all eight Hayes brothers blocking the doorway, arms crossed, glares on their faces. The only ones who seem disinterested are the twins. They look bored, like they've been forced to stand with the others.

Now I feel a bigger dick; not only dressed up but holding a bouquet of flowers.

I walk around the car, relaxing my stance. "Guys, I know you love me, but the welcome committee? It's flattering and all, but it really isn't necessary," I drawl.

"Funny," Reid bites out.

I sigh. I don't have time for this. "Move," I demand.

"No," Jaxon barks, stepping closer to me.

I spread my legs a little, ready for the fight. "If you're going to threaten me, get it over with, but I'm telling you now, it won't work."

"What makes you think that?" he asks, studying me.

"Because I'm not going to let you come between us. She won't let you, either. But more importantly, I don't give a fuck what you have to say."

"Give this up, Landon."

Pissed, and late, I step forward, getting in his space. "No!"

His jaw hardens. "I'm not going to sit by and watch you hurt my sister. She isn't some slag you can fuck around with."

Just hearing him compare her to the girls I usually fuck has the hairs on the back of my neck rising.

"I'm not going to fucking hurt her," I bark out.

His eyes narrow into slits. "Yes, you fucking will. You're a fucking Carter. None of you can keep it in your pants."

I snort. "You're one to talk."

"I won't let you do this," he warns me. "She doesn't deserve to be treated like shit. You're going to fucking break her."

My free hand clenches into a fist. "Yeah? And how are you going to stop me?" I demand. "I'll tell you one last time. Move. Before I fucking move you myself. And I'd rather not piss her off before the date has started."

He grabs me by my shirt, and I growl.

"One petal breaks and I'll break your fingers."

He shakes me again, but movement by the door catches my eye, so I don't move, keeping my hands by my side as I smile smugly at him.

"Jaxon Hayes, please tell me you don't have that lovely young man's shirt in your grip," his mother states in a reprimanding tone.

Jaxon's lids close, and he groans. He lets me go, patting down my shirt. "No, Mum. Never," he lies, looking at me dead on. "This isn't over."

"It never fucking started, because I'm not giving her up," I whisper in a menacing tone.

"She deserves better than you," he bites out.

Yeah, she fucking does.

"That might be true, but us Carter's are known to be selfish bastards when it comes to what we want."

"Jax?" a tentative voice calls out.

My breath escapes my lungs when Paisley steps out from behind her mum, looking between Jaxon and I, biting her lip worriedly. She looks fucking stunning. Her hair is down, falling past her shoulders. Her makeup is minimal, but I can see the faint glow to her cheeks and how her eyes pop with eyeliner on.

She's wearing a red velvet dress, scrunched up over her full breasts before falling down to her knees in waves. A black cardigan or jacket hangs over her arms—I can't be sure which, not wanting to take my eyes off her.

I'm utterly speechless as I take her in. When she shifts on her feet, I glance back up to her face, noticing how uncomfortable she looks. I push past Jaxon, not even revelling in his pained grunt.

Standing in front of Paisley, our gazes meet. "You look fucking beautiful, baby."

Her mouth parts. "T-thank you." She looks down at the flowers in my hands. "You brought me flowers?"

"Yeah," I tell her, grinning. Guess Mum knows her shit, if the expression on Paisley's face is anything to go by.

"Probably cost a fiver from the petrol station," someone mutters behind me.

"Let me go put them in water," Mrs Hayes says with a wide smile. She takes the flowers from Paisley's grip.

Paisley looks around the front of the house, her nose twitching. "Why are you all out here in the cold?"

I help her down the steps before turning to her brothers. My lips slip into a smug smile.

Wyatt clears his throat. "Just checking the drainpipes."

"Watering the plants," Reid squeaks out.

"It's been raining for a week straight," Paisley points out, sounding pissed. "Get inside and leave us alone. You promised," she whines, but her eyes look accusingly to Jaxon. "You *promised*."

He holds his hands up. "I don't know why these fuckers are out here. I was just leaving when Landon pulled up."

Her hand clenches in mine. She knows he's lying. "I'm going," she sighs out before turning to her mum. "Can you tell Adam thank you again for cleaning up?"

"I will, dear. You go have fun tonight."

"I will," she answers, blushing.

I chuckle. "Come on, it's cold out. The car should still be warm."

She nods, letting me lead her to the car.

"Don't be late getting back," Jaxon warns.

Paisley stops, pulling on my arm to face her brother. "I'm a grown adult. I'll be back when I'm ready."

His jaw hardens, and he looks at me. "She only has her emergency bag, so don't get any fucking ideas by taking her back to yours."

"Jax," Paisley hisses.

He winces but recovers quickly. "Sorry."

"Bye, Jaxon," I call out, steering Paisley back towards the car. Maybe I can salvage this date before the night is over.

"Oh, and Jaxon?" Paisley calls out, one leg in the car.

"Yeah?"

"I've hid all your keys. I heard you were planning on following us. I'll text you where they are on my way back."

His face reddens and he looks ready to argue. I chuckle, shutting the door behind Paisley as she takes her seat before flipping the angry beaver off.

Maybe I really don't have to worry about them after all. Paisley has it covered.

———————————————

PAISLEY FIDGETS WITH her napkin when the waitress comes to take our drink order. Once alone in the car, she went shy and quiet. I didn't help matters. My mind went blank, and I couldn't come up with a conversation starter.

"What would you like?" I ask Paisley.

"U-um, I—I can't drink alcohol," she blurts out, her cheeks turning pink.

My lips tug up at the corners. "That's okay. I can't either. I'm driving. I'll have a J20."

Paisley lets her lip fall from between her teeth. "I'll have one too."

"Are you okay?" I ask when she looks nervously around.

Her shoulders sag. "I'm sorry. I'm just so nervous."

I smile now, glad I'm not the only one. "Me too."

She scoffs. "I doubt that." She pauses, looking around once again but this time with a smile on her face. "How did you know I love Indian?"

"You eat all the free samples at Family of the Year, so I doubled checked with your Mum. She said it was, so I looked up the best restaurant I could find," I tell her, shrugging like it doesn't matter. But looking around, I'm glad I let Charlotte change my clothes. I would have stuck out like a sore thumb in this place.

Mini chandeliers hang from the ceiling above all the tables, which are set out like the queen is visiting, and classical music plays through the speakers. It's unlike any Indian I've been to.

"You noticed?" she asks in awe. "Then did this for me?"

I look up from the four forks precisely set to my left and nod. "Yeah, why?"

She shakes her head, giving me an adorable little smile. The waitress comes back over with our drinks, both poured into wine flutes.

Why the fuck didn't she just hand us the bottle? Save on washing up? I don't get it.

Awkward silence fills the air until Paisley clears her throat. "I'm just going to pop to the ladies' room."

I nod stiffly. "Okay."

Once she's gone, I grab my phone out of my pocket and quickly send a text to Dad.

LANDON: What can I talk to Paisley about? We're on our first date.

The second it goes through, I regret it, wishing I had just Googled, *what to talk about on your first date.*

DAD: Let me just Google it. I only had to smile at your mum and she talked my ear off.

Fuck's sake.

I pull up Google and type in, *best conversation starters,* flicking through ones I think will interest Paisley. Most of them I already know, and Charlotte told me to stay clear of work talk.

My phone vibrates in my hand, and I quickly look down at the text Dad sent through.

DAD: Fucking boring conversation starters. Ask her what colour underwear she has on. She'll laugh and relax, and then lead the conversation because you're too stupid to.

Yep, should have just stuck with Google.

LIAM: Dad said you need help. Ask her what she does in her free time.

MADDOX: Ask her what her favourite position is, then go from there.

HAYDEN: Ignore Dad, Liam and Maddox. They don't have a clue. Lightly bring up something you've watched and ask her if she's watched it. Or ask what her favourite food is. You should only need to bring up one thing and it will flow from there. If not, ask how she feels about us getting payback on her brothers. One of them let down Maddox's truck tyres, thinking the car was yours.

My eyes are drawn to the other side of the room, and I watch as Paisley sashays towards me, the sexy swing of her hips hypnotising. I shift in my seat when my dick stirs. Fuck, she couldn't look any sexier if she tried.

I slide my phone back into my pocket, waiting for her to approach. Do I get out and pull her chair in again? I felt like an idiot the first time, nearly taking her out by the knees.

"Hey," she says, her voice like a whisper as she takes a seat.

Thinking back on Hayden's text, I open my mouth and ask, "Is Indian your only favourite food?"

"Have you always wanted to work for Maddox?" she asks over me, blushing.

I chuckle.

She sighs, her shoulders slumping back in the chair. "Did you Google conversation starters too?"

Not wanting her to know I text my family, I nod. "Yeah," I admit sheepishly. "You answer first."

"I love all food, but Indian is my favourite. When they give it away at

Family of the Year, I can't help myself. I indulge," she tells me, letting out a small giggle. "Now you. I didn't picture you working for Maddox."

"What did you picture me working as?" I find myself leaning forward, interested in her answer.

She shrugs. "I don't know. Maybe owning a gym or something? But to be fair, when Maddox opened his business up a few years ago, I didn't think he'd do something like that. I saw his drawings once when we went to school for this thing Eli had done. I thought he'd become a tattooist or something."

I don't like that she's thought of Maddox that deeply. Even so, I chuckle at her apt description of me. "I would like to own a gym one day."

"Why not now?" she asks, adorably confused. "Sorry, that's nosey."

"It's fine," I chuckle out, then take a sip of my drink. "I like working construction. It keeps me busy. Drew, the guy who owns the gym I go to now, has asked me a few times to buy into his business. He wants someone to run the martial arts side of things."

"That sounds amazing. Why haven't you done it?"

I shrug. "A few reasons really. I hate talking to people for one, and a job like that will entail me to talk a lot. Another reason is because I really do love my job with Maddox. He's a fair boss, even if he does act like he can't tie his shoe laces half the time."

She nods like she understands. "I heard he takes his work seriously."

"He does," I say slowly, studying her carefully. "But how do you know?"

She blushes. "My brothers were talking about him one day. I only listened because they were saying how good you all were."

"I always thought you would make those giftsets you used to sell at the market with your mum."

She groans, and then laughs, embarrassed. "Oh God. I still get asked about those."

"They were really good. Mum still has one of the picture frames you made."

She blushes. "Your mum still has it? I made those years ago."

She did, and the one my mum bought still hangs proudly in her living room. The white wooden frame holds Scrabble tiles, spelling out each of our names, and has rose petals scattered across the background.

"She does," I tell her, then feel the words slipping out of my mouth before I can stop them. "And I have your hand."

"My hand?" she asks, startled.

I rub my jaw. *Shit.* "I mean, the clay, varnished hand you made in school. I won it in a raffle Charlotte bought me a ticket for. I later found out it was your hand."

The pale, shocked look on her face has me wishing I kept my mouth shut. She probably thinks I'm a creeper.

I was going to throw it away or give it to Charlotte, but when I saw her name scrawled in her handwriting on the bottom, I kept it. I didn't know why back then. I didn't give myself a reason or an explanation. I just kept it.

"You have that?"

I nod slowly. "Yeah."

"You've still got it?"

"I do—somewhere," I lie, knowing exactly where it is. It's in an old shoe box under my bed.

"Hmm," she mutters with a smile. "So, what else did Google tell you to ask?"

I chuckle, relaxing when she drops the clay hand. "I don't know; I only looked at a few. You tell me," I tease back.

She laughs, and with that, the atmosphere relaxes and we fall into easy conversation. First dates aren't as bad as people make them out to be.

NINETEEN

PAISLEY

AS FIRST DATES GO, THIS ONE HAS TO have been a success. I can't wipe the smile from my face as we drive back down the lane to the farm. I've never had so much fun in my life. I've laughed so much my cheeks hurt.

I've envisioned what a date with Landon would be like a thousand times since I was twelve years old. But nothing, not one of those images, comes close to what it really feels like.

He made me feel special, like no one ever has. When he spoke to me, he looked directly at me, never once fading out and losing interest or gazing off and focusing on something else. When I spoke, he really listened. His phone had gone off at one point, and instead of looking to see who it was, he turned it off, never taking his eyes away from me.

I also found the fact he didn't have a drink kind of romantic. He knew he could have at least one, but he chose not to, and I think that was because of me. It was incredibly sweet of him.

I loved how he ordered for me first. Whenever the waitress asked us if we needed anything, she never once looked at me. She had only asked him, but immediately, his gaze had come to me and he asked *me* what *I* wanted.

As we near the house, I begin to stress over what to do next. Do I invite him in, even though there is no doubt in my mind my brothers will be waiting up for me? Do I kiss him? I'm sure I read somewhere you aren't supposed to kiss on the first date. Or is it invite them in? I don't really remember. What has me frazzled is the fact my mind is debating whether to kiss him or just call it quits.

My mind might not have completely forgiven Landon for the way he treated me, but I guess, somewhere in my heart, I have, because I desperately want to kiss him. There have been a few moments during the evening when I've wanted to lean in and steal a kiss. He'd say something funny, or the lines on his forehead would crease in an adorable way when he got confused over something I said, and my entire body would sway towards him.

He pulls to a stop outside the house, and my stomach sinks when he doesn't turn the car off.

He doesn't plan on staying.

I don't know why I thought he would. It's not like we'd get any privacy here, and I sympathise enough to understand why he can only take my brothers in small doses.

"I had a really good time tonight," I tell him quietly.

Unzipping his belt, he turns to me, his face blank. "Enough to go out with me again?"

I bite my lip to stop myself from smiling. "I don't know about that."

"And why's that?" he asks, amusement in his voice.

I bat my lashes at him and shrug. "I don't think you could top tonight."

A smirk lifts at the corner of his lips, making him look dangerously sexy. "And if I promise to top it?"

I pretend to think it over, then shrug. "Then I guess we can talk."

He chuckles, the sound sending goose bumps all over my body. "It's a deal, then." He sighs, looking up at the house, the lights still blaring brightly downstairs. It's late, and Mum will be in bed by now, so I know my brothers are waiting up. I'll be surprised if they aren't acting like creepers and stalking the windows. "I really don't want tonight to end just yet."

His honesty astounds me. I didn't think he'd lay himself out there like that. "Me neither," I admit, then look around the buildings. "Want to go see the piglets? Pug, our mummy pig, had them last week."

At first, he shows no emotion, giving me no indication of what he is thinking. I mean, I just asked him to visit piglets, for Christ sake. Not exactly how most men want to finish a date.

"Go on then," he says, his expressive eyes shining.

I meet him around his side of the car, my eyebrows drawing together when he opens the back door, pulling out a zip-up fleece jacket.

"It's a bit dusty but it will keep you warm," he says, looking sheepish.

A big, stupid smile spreads across my face at the sweet gesture. I take the jacket from him, but not before leaning up and kissing his cheek.

His smouldering eyes lock on mine, holding a promise.

"Thank you," I whisper, my voice breathless as he moves closer. Sexual tension swirls around us, making sweat bead at the back of my neck. As much as I don't want the date to end, I also don't want to go *there* with him. Not yet. "Piglets."

"Piglets?" he asks, his forehead creasing, his movements towards me pausing.

I clear my throat. "We were going to look at the piglets."

He takes a step back, jerking his head in a nod. "Yeah, piglets."

I chuckle under my breath and lean in close to him, walking towards the back of the house where the pig hut is. We've got them inside at the moment, what with the cold weather.

"I never realised how big your property is," he murmurs when the floodlights turn on.

"Your cousin's is just as big," I tell him, switching the light on inside the barn.

"No shit?" he asks, turning his head sharply to me, his eyes wide.

I nod. "Yep."

He leans against the wooden beams, looking into the hut where the piglets snuggle up to their mum. I watch his expression, noticing how his lips twitch into a small smile.

He might come across as dangerous and broody, but deep down, Landon Carter has a soft spot. I don't believe the rumours about him being soulless. He may be brutal when it comes to fighting, but it's not who is at his core.

He has more layers than an onion. And I don't think I've begun to peel off the first.

Speaking of fighting, my mind goes back to the night he was attacked. My heart skips a beat when I picture that knife plunging into his stomach, and I have to swallow, fighting back tears.

I still get nightmares, the night replaying over and over until I wake up screaming, gasping for breath. I cried non-stop those first two weeks, not only for my baby, but for Landon. Mum would tell me she heard me calling out his name in my sleep.

But what kept me up after I found out he was awake, was that those thugs were still out there. I feared for my safety, but worse, I feared they'd want to finish the job. Because there is no doubt in mind that those four men wanted him dead.

"Landon," I call quietly.

He loses his smile when he sees my expression. I know I must have gone pale after thinking about that night. "Yeah?" he rumbles, his face a mask of concern.

"Can I ask you something about the night you were attacked?"

A guarded expression veils his face. "What?" he asks, slowly, reluctantly.

I take in a deep breath, bracing myself for his reaction. "Those guys that night…" I start, gulping when his jaw hardens. I hate that I'm bringing up bad memories for him, that I might be hurting him somehow.

"What about them?"

"You knew them, didn't you?"

He jerks his head sharply in a nod, his teeth clenched together as he looks away. "Yeah."

"Why haven't you told the police who they are? When they came to take another statement from me a few weeks after you woke up, they said you didn't remember anything." I pause, taking a lungful of air before continuing. "It didn't register at first, but when you climbed through my bedroom window, you spoke about that night, and you did again the other week. You remember everything, don't you? I know you do."

I feel the pain rolling off him when he answers. "Every. Single. Blow. I felt everything, but it was the fear they'd see you that keeps me up at night."

My lips part in surprise, but I gain my composure, asking what I really want to know.

"You're getting revenge, aren't you?"

He nods tightly. "Are you going to change your mind about me now? Because I won't lie to you, Paisley. I am going to get revenge. I'm getting it, and nothing—no one—will stop me. I need to know if you can handle that."

Taking a step closer, I place my hands on his chest. "I didn't mean to sound judgemental, Landon. I just wanted to understand why you wouldn't tell the police who they are."

He relaxes slightly, but not completely. "You don't care that I'll hurt them?"

"Are you going to kill them?" I ask dryly. That is something I don't think I could live with. As badly as I want those men to pay for what they did, I don't believe they should be killed for it. There are laws in place to handle this.

He arches his eyebrow. "I won't be killing them, no, but they will wish I had," he says, and I relax, pressing my chest against his as he grips my waist. "I can't say their boss won't kill them though."

I shake my head. "Probably best not to tell me any more."

He chuckles, but then sobers, a serious expression crossing his face. "You really won't use this to not see me anymore?"

"No. I don't see what this has to do with us. I know you'd never get me involved or let anyone hurt me. And even if someone did try to use me to hurt you, they'd have to be crazy enough to go through my brothers."

He tucks the strand of hair that keeps falling into my eyes behind my ear. "You keep on surprising me."

I grin at the husky sound of his voice, pressing myself against his hard, ripped chest. His hands immediately seek me out, gripping my hips. I visibly shiver at the feel of his warm hands.

"I do, do I?" I ask, my own voice quiet and breathless.

Being this close, I watch as his pupils dilate, and his eyes darken. My breath catches in my throat. "Please tell me I can kiss you, because I'm holding on by a thread. A thin fucking thread."

My lips twitch. "And if I say no?"

Like hell I will. I'm struggling to gain control of my own emotions, wanting to kiss him so goddamn bad.

His eyes narrow into slits. "You don't want to me to lose control right now," he warns, his voice deep and raspy.

"Why is that?" I ask, titling my head to the side, studying him.

"If I lose control, I'm likely to perch your arse on that beam, push your dress up to your waist, and slide inside you."

"Oh yeah?" I ask, my voice silky and smooth. I try to hide my lust, my need for him, but it's no use. I sway towards him, feeling my eyes droop a little.

"Then I'm going to fuck you so hard you'll be screaming my name."

"We'll wake the piglets," I blurt out, making him chuckle.

He ducks his head a little, and when his head comes back up, my lips part on a gasp. His look is one of pure desire and lust.

"Paisley," he warns, and I don't know if it's the tone of his voice or the predatory look in his eye, but I lean forward, stepping up on my tip-toes, and press my lips against his.

Idly, I run my hands up his chest, and then use my fingers to grip his broad shoulders, steadying myself.

One second, I'm in control, the kiss smooth and soft, and the next, he's crashing his lips against mine, devouring me in one breath. It's the most carnal, soul-searing kiss we've ever shared. His grip tightens almost punishingly, pressing me against him until my chest is brushing his.

A growl vibrates through his chest as he lifts me off the ground, my back pressing against the wooden beam.

Every nerve ending in my system is on fire, drawn to him like a moth to a flame. I moan into his mouth, frustration hitting me when I can't get any closer. It doesn't feel like enough. Not nearly enough.

He drags his hand down my chest to the valley between my breasts, and a moan escapes me, my hips rolling against his. My skirt has long ridden up, leaving me exposed, and I feel the cool wind on my bare thighs.

With a groan, he pulls away, kissing along my jaw to my neck. My lips part as I tilt my head to give him better access.

"Please," I moan, begging for more.

He forces his mouth away, staring at me intently. "You're not ready," he rasps out.

I grip him tighter, afraid he'll pull away. "Trust me, I'm ready," I tell him, rolling my hips to drive my point home.

He chuckles, his fingers tangling in my hair as he presses his cheek to mine. "You aren't ready."

Frustrated, I blow out a breath. "Landon, trust me. I'm ready."

Why won't he take me? Why won't he give us both what we desperately want?

"Because I won't take you like I did last time," he answers, and I groan when I realise I said that out loud.

"Landon—" I start, but he silences me with a kiss, his lips almost bruising.

"Paisley, it's late and you need to check your glucose levels," Jaxon orders, startling a small squeal from me.

Landon tenses, pulling back until his eyes are fixed on me. "And how long has it taken you to walk in here and interrupt?"

My gaze is drawn to Jaxon when he begins to fidget, looking nervous. I groan, dropping my forehead against Landon's, embarrassment washing over me.

My brother just heard me practically begging Landon to fuck me in the barn.

"Come on, Paisley. I'll walk back to the house with you."

"I'll be there in a minute," I tell him, finding my voice.

"I'll wait," he bites out.

I groan and push Landon away a little. He steps back, allowing me the privacy to straighten my dress before my brother sees.

I step around him, glaring at my brother. "I'm not a child," I snap.

His jaw ticks. "Paisley, do not argue with me right now."

Walking past him, I look back to make sure Landon is following. Jaxon's hand snaps out, pushing on Landon's chest.

Landon pauses, staring blankly at my brother.

"Go ahead, Paisley. I need to have a chat with Landon here."

"Jaxon, let him pass. Right now," I warn, stomping my foot. My heel sinks into the soggy ground, and I inwardly groan. I completely missed the path and stepped onto the grass. The mud will be a bitch to wash off later.

"It's fine, Paisley," Landon soothes.

I study his face to see if it's really okay. He nods, not moving. A tiny growl of frustration escapes me, making him smirk.

"I'll see you in the morning?" I ask hopefully.

His smirk morphs into a grin. "Bright and early."

I give him a tight nod before stomping over to my brother and poking him in the chest. "He'd better show up in pristine condition, Jaxon, or so help me God, I will get you back."

Jaxon doesn't even blink when he looks down at me. "It's just a friendly chat."

Friendly, my arse.

My lips tip up into a smirk, and I step past him, leaning up and giving Landon one last kiss for the night. A sound erupts from Jaxon's chest, and I grin against Landon's mouth.

When I pull back, his eyes are smiling back at me. "Sleep tight."

"Goodnight, Landon," I whisper, my body heating all over again.

"Goodnight, Paisley," Jaxon bites out.

I glare his way before stomping off, nearly tripping over in these goddamn heels. A chuckle sounds behind me, and my face flames.

Great exit strategy, Paisley.

TWENTY

LANDON

Aᴄᴛᴇʀ ɢʀᴀʙʙɪɴɢ Rᴇx ꜰʀᴏᴍ ᴍʏ ꜰʟᴀᴛ, I pack him into the passenger side of my car, slamming the door shut behind me. I run around, ducking my head against the rain that started pouring the second I left Hayes Farm.

I grit my teeth just thinking about the sanctimonious prick. Where the fuck does he get off telling me what I can and can't do? He tried so fucking hard to scare me off, was even willing to pay me, the fucking wanker. If he thinks cheap shots and threats will work with a Carter, then he really doesn't know us. The only reason I promised him I wouldn't tell Paisley about how our conversation really went was because it would hurt her more than him. I don't want her hurting. And not over that wanker. I also don't want to put that rift between two siblings. I don't know what I would do without Hayden and Liam, even if they do annoy me sometimes.

We left after Wyatt came outside, splitting the two of us apart when we got into it. Luckily, he didn't aim for the face, only punching me in the ribs, though not hard enough to do any damage.

Maybe Hayden was right earlier and I should check with Paisley first if she's okay with me getting her brothers back. I wouldn't do anything that would affect her or her mum.

I sigh, wishing I wasn't such a prick in the beginning. I wouldn't be second guessing myself constantly, afraid I'm going to scare her off.

Although, she surprised me tonight. She truly meant it when she said she wouldn't let my plans for revenge come between us. It's just another reason why she's special, different from all the other girls.

A smile tugs at my lips as I pull out into the deserted road. Who knew dating could be fun. Whenever someone mentioned it, it sounded dull and boring as fuck. I always wondered why someone would waste so much time on talking when they could just go back home and fuck each other silly.

Yet, tonight I had laughed more than I have in my entire life. I keep hearing her laugh and seeing her smile. I keep going over everything we talked about, dissecting everything she said in case I need to remember it later on.

Rex yaps when we pull up to a red light around the corner from the gym. I'm grateful to Drew for letting me use it during the night, after I leave Paisley. What with getting to the bed and breakfast early in the mornings, then talking Paisley into spending time with me after, I haven't had time to train during the day. And I can't miss training, not when I need to make my body stronger, harder and faster, so I can take down Blaze, Terry, Rocket and Flash.

My ringtone cuts through the silence in the car, and I use the handsfree on my steering wheel to answer when I see it's Liam calling. I've been waiting to hear from him all night, since he and the others risked the next part in my plan. If I hadn't forgotten about it before I planned my date with Paisley, I would have carried it out myself.

"Did it work?"

Liam chuckles. "Yes, fucking demolished."

A grin tugs at my lips as I think of Terry's home being bulldozed down. It's amazing what you can do with a bit of money, Maddox's company, and a location.

It seems Terry inherited a house not too long ago, has hidden it from his baby mama, and plans to sell it and keep the money. And from the information we've gathered, he keeps a lot of things from his girlfriend.

With a foolproof plan, we made sure he didn't have insurance before bulldozing the house down tonight.

"He wasn't there?"

"No, we double checked the entire house in case any homeless were squatting in there. It's gone. Mark stayed behind to record the whole thing. Terry should be arriving any minute."

"I can't believe it worked," I murmur as I pull up in front of the gym. I notice a few of the streetlamps are still out, and I scan my surroundings warily.

"Believe it. They really fucked with the wrong family," he says, his voice deadly now. "Are you still going the gym? I'm nearly there, thought I'd hang out for a bit."

"I'm here——"

My door suddenly opens and rain immediately soaks me. Rex begins to growl viciously.

"Get out of the fucking car," Blaze growls, his hard eyes boiling with anger.

I smirk, undo my seatbelt, and step out of the car. I scan both of the men in front of me, smirking at all the bruises covering their body. It seems their boss punished them, enough so they were hurt yet not injured to the point they couldn't move.

I knew he wouldn't kill them over the missing drugs. If there's one thing I've learned in my research, it's that Rocco makes sure people pay. Killing these two low-lifes wouldn't get him his money back.

"Landon?" Liam calls, sounding panicked.

I tower over Blaze and his good friend Rocket. "What do I owe the pleasure?" I ask, fighting the urge to flinch when I see they both hold bats. "Still need weapons?" I arch my eyebrow, mocking them.

"Shut the door on that dog before I make it feel the force of my bat," Rocket snarls.

I slam the door shut with force, drowning out Liam's yelling and Rex's barks. "Touch my fucking dog, and I will rip you apart."

He smirks, thinking he has the upper hand because he's holding a bat. That night I was outnumbered, and fucking scared for Paisley. This time, it's just me and them. I fight the urge to reach for Blaze, remembering it was him who kicked me in the head before everything got blurry.

"Yeah? There's no chick here to save you tonight." Blaze's nostrils flare as he starts towards me, bouncing the bat in his hand. "But don't think I'm not looking for her."

Any emotion at hearing he's been looking for Paisley quickly dissipates. If I throw the guy a bone, he'll sniff harder to look for it. Instead, I eye the bat in his hand, smirking as I think of the one I took pleasure in burning. "New bat?" I ask calmly.

His eyes narrow, and he takes a step forward. "I knew it was you. I fucking knew it!"

"What was me?"

"You were in our homes. You stole from me, Carter," Blaze states in a menacing tone.

"And you made us—"

Blaze shoots Rocket a glare. "Shut it!"

I smirk, leaning back against the car. "Lovers' tiff?"

Rocket pales, stepping away from Blaze like he's a disease. I see Dad's plan worked like a charm. Blaze turns green, but his eyes darken, hatred blazing in them.

"It was you?" he hisses out slowly, lifting his bat. "You had a hand in what happened that night."

I spread my feet apart, ready to fight, my eyes never leaving the two. His foot lifts, ready to come at me, to strike.

"Take one step closer to my buddy there and I'll show you how this pole beats your wooden fucking bat," Drew snarls out, walking up behind them. His hair is down, wet, and curling around his shoulders.

Rocket visibly startles, stepping back when he sees the size of Drew and the tattoos and piercings covering his body.

A car comes skidding to a stop, and from the corner of my eye, I see Liam and Maddox fly out of it, coming to stand beside me.

"Shall we see how it feels to have four against one?" Liam bites out, taking a step forward.

I grab his shoulder, pulling him back. We've got plans for these four, and I want to make them sweat before I finish them. I want to destroy them before I show them how wrong they were for ganging up on me.

"He's going to get us killed," Rocket snaps at Liam, his eyes filled with fury. I see a flash of fear as he takes a step back. "We know it was you who stole them drugs."

"I have no idea what you're talking about," I say clearly, in case they're recording this.

"Drugs are really bad. Seems to me, someone did you a favour," Maddox tells them solemnly.

"You're going to fucking pay for this, Carter."

I push off the car, stepping closer to Blaze. "No, you're going to fucking pay for what you did to me."

"We had orders," Rocket blurts out, looking around for any more of my family. He should be wary. We're all out for his blood. And there's no doubt in my mind my family have been following them, letting them see we're watching, waiting.

I arch an eyebrow. "And you think I give a fuck because…?"

Blaze's seething gaze doesn't leave me, so I look to him questioningly. "This isn't over."

"No, it really isn't," I deadpan.

Without another word, they slink off into the rain before disappearing. "Did they touch you?" Liam asks, scanning my body.

"No," I tell him, turning to let a growling Rex out of the car. He sniffs around, and once he's happy the threat is gone, he nudges my leg with his nose. I pat his head, before clipping his leash to his collar.

"Fuck, you're one scary motherfucker with your hair down," Maddox blurts out, eyes round as he stares at Drew, who kind of looks like a dark angel.

Drew turns to him, rolling his eyes. "Still as charming as ever, Maddox." He shakes his head before turning to me. "I'm glad I stayed tonight. I wanted to talk to you."

"Thanks for stepping in like that," I tell him, avoiding the subject he wants to talk about. I already know he's going to offer me partnership with his gym.

"No biggie." He shrugs, swinging the weight bar over his shoulder. "Gutted I never got to use this though."

He turns around to head back inside, and we follow to get out of the rain.

Breath at my ear startles me.

"Dude be, like, crazy."

Arching my eyebrow, I give Maddox a dry look. "Seriously?"

He shrugs, grinning. "Dude is fucking scary. Like Jason Momoa scary."

"You're really fucking weird," Liam mutters, swinging the door open. We step inside, and I lock it behind us.

"Trust me, watch Game of Thrones. Shit be all up in the air on that show. Great tits and arse, too."

"Shut the fuck up," Liam tells him, shaking his head.

Maddox groans. "Don't hate me because I'm cooler than you. It makes you look like a twat."

"Who's next on your plan?" Liam asks, facing me so suddenly I nearly trip over my feet.

Great, I'm turning into my dad.

Maddox pouts at being ignored but obediently follows us further into the gym.

"What do you mean?"

He rolls his eyes. "Don't play dumb, Landon. You've done Blaze, Rocket, and now Terry. We know that Flash dude is next. What do you have planned?"

I sigh, sitting down on a weight bench and resting my elbows on my thighs. "Honestly? I don't know. He lives with his sister, who has Down syndrome. He's her main caregiver."

"Fuck," Maddox hisses, sitting down on a mat. "There has to be something that doesn't affect her too."

I shrug. "I don't know. It would have worked out better if he had been the one to do the drug run. I was going to take her away from him, but watching them together, she really does love and care for him. I don't think she knows just how bad he is."

"He should have thought about that before fucking with you," Liam snaps out.

I look to my brother with concern. It's usually me who doesn't give a fuck, not him. "I know you're hurting still, but Liam, we can't fuck with her. She's only fifteen. Their parents left her with Flash once he turned eighteen."

"There has to be something we can do. Does he have a job?"

I glare at him. "Yes, with fucking Rocco. It's how he affords her care."

Running a hand through his hair, Liam looks around the room. "I'm going to go punch something. Maybe something will fucking come to me. Because that fucker isn't going to get away with this."

He walks off, and Maddox clucks his tongue. "He's really riled up. He wouldn't even let me drive the bulldozer. He wanted to be the one to tear that house down."

I turn my head sharply to Maddox. "He didn't say that on the phone."

"I think he's still adjusting. You didn't see him outside your hospital room. He and Hayden… they knew before those machines declared your heart had stopped that you were going to die."

"What the fuck are you on about?" I growl, my chest tightening at the image he just painted.

He holds his hands up. "I don't fucking know. It must be that weird twin/triplet thing people rave on about. Me and Maddy don't have it, but then, we've never been in that situation. But I watched as Hayden looked sharply at Liam. Their eyes widened in horror and they gasped for air, and then everything went fucking crazy. Your machines were blaring, doctors and nurses were rushing around you, and you died. They fucking felt it."

I gulp, feeling a lump in my throat. No one had told me that. Not even Hayden or Liam. "What do I do?"

He shrugs. "If it were me, I'd let them have some of their own revenge. A part of them died with you, because the light was gone from them. It was rough as fuck."

"I'll let him fuck with Flash, as long as it doesn't affect the sister," I declare hoarsely.

"They'll be fine. We're fucking built to be strong," Maddox says as he lifts off the floor. He smacks me on the shoulder. "Just don't push us away next time. That part didn't help."

"I didn't mean to," I say, tilting my head to the side to watch him. He looks down at me, unblinking.

"Yes, you did. And I fucking get it," he says, and I duck my head, ashamed for lying. "I'm gonna go let Liam think he can land a punch or two."

I chuckle under my breath but wisely warn him, "I wouldn't. He's been training with Drew every other night, and he's gotten good."

Maddox scoffs. "Yeah, we'll see."

"Don't say I didn't warn you," I call out, listening to his laughter.

Locking my hands together, I gaze down at the floor. I've been so fucking selfish with my revenge. I honestly didn't know how bad Hayden and Liam had been. I was prick for not even asking myself what they went through. If it were reversed, and it was one of them, it would have killed me inside.

And it's not just them. I've neglected everyone around me. I've forgotten my family values, exactly what we mean to each other. None of us are ever alone.

I need to make things right, to show them I'm not broken, that I'm okay. What Maddox said has hit a nerve. I've pushed them all away, and Hayden, Liam, Charlotte and my parents have taken it the hardest.

Clenching my eyelids shut, I suck in a breath while pressing my fists to my temples. I have so much to make up for.

My dad's actions since I went into phase two with my revenge plan come to light, and I groan. He's been hurting, and I didn't even fucking see it. Under that carefree exterior, he's held it all back

I pull my phone out, bringing up my dad's number, needing him to know I love him and that I'm fine.

"You all right, son?" he answers on the first ring.

Clearing my throat, I look over my shoulder, making sure Liam and Maddox are out of earshot. Both are in the far corner, sparring, so I feel it's safe to talk to him. If they got wind of this conversation, they'd lay into me and make fun. And I'm one person who hates being made fun of, even if it is light banter.

"Yeah, I just wanted to say I'm sorry."

"So you should be. You knew bulldozing a house was on my bucket list. I feel like I was cheated out of a life experience. Mark sent me a video to rub it in my face that Liam got all the fun."

Hearing him mention bucket lists reminds me of the conversation I had with Paisley not so long ago.

I chuckle down the phone. "Dad, that wasn't why I was calling to say sorry."

He pauses a beat before letting out a long sigh. "I've got nothing. I don't understand what you're sorry for. Help an old man out here."

"For everything. For putting you and Mum through the wringer. I just wanted you to know I never meant for things to get out of hand. Dealing with the grief from losing Freya clouded my judgement. Fighting gave me the release I needed. It nearly killed me, and in part, killed you guys, too. But you need to know I didn't intentionally put myself in danger, and I won't be doing it again. You can stop worrying about me."

"Son," he whispers hoarsely down the phone. "You don't need to be sorry. We love you and care for you."

"I know, Dad. But I've been selfish. It's only just come to my attention that you guys were hurting too. I was too blind to see it."

He snorts. "You're my son. Give yourself some credit. We're naturally selfish and want to have all the fun."

"I just need this, Dad. I need this revenge," I tell him, feeling my throat tighten.

"I know you do, and I hate it. I hate you're going through this, and I fucking hate someone tried to take my son away from me. But *I* need this too."

"Dad—" I start, but he continues, cutting me off.

"No! No, son. I was young when I had you three. So fucking young. And I shit you not, when I found out we were expecting, I fainted and knocked my head on the kitchen counter. Had to stay in overnight at the hospital and everything. Then, six weeks later, I found out you were triplets, and let me tell you—"

"Dad," I let out with amusement. "I know this. You got drunk as fuck and had to get your stomach pumped."

"I did, yeah," he says, before going on and acting like he nearly died. "It was a terrible time, let me tell you. It was over a year before I had a drop of alcohol again, and weeks before your mum forgave me for freaking out."

"You're going off topic," I tell him.

"Then you were born. I swear to you, son, I sat down, holding Hayden in my arms while your mum held you boys, and vowed that I wouldn't regret a moment with you. Not one. I swore an oath to protect you and to be by your side when you got into shit. I vowed to be your father, to be everything mine wasn't, and never what he was. You were all so fucking tiny I was scared you'd crumble in my hands, but I knew you'd grow up to be strong. I knew there'd be a day when my three kids wouldn't need me anymore, and guess what?"

"What?" I ask, feeling my eyes sting. My dad never gets serious or emotional. Ever.

"I told your mum I didn't care, that I'd be there anyway, backing you, loving you, protecting you. When you died in that bed, I failed you. I failed as the person Maverick and Grandpa brought me up to be, but mostly, I fucking failed as a father. I failed not only you, but my wife and my other two children. I prayed to God that day—I don't believe in all that crap, but I prayed. I prayed God would take me and not you. To not break my heart, my wife's, my children's, and to take me. And that, son, is why I need revenge. I need those little bastards to pay. I need to do something. Anything. Don't take that away from me, kid."

"I won't," I promise, rubbing at my eyes. "I'm sorry, Dad. I really am."

"You don't need to be. Just promise me you'll stop fighting after we've made those fuckers pay. Just promise me, son."

"I promise, Dad."

"Good," he says softly.

"Who are you talking to, sweetheart?" Mum says in the background.

"Landon. He won't shut the fuck up, yapping away like he's one again and talking for the first time," he yells back.

Fucking wanker. Yet, I find myself smiling.

"Landon?" Mum asks, sounding closer.

"Baby, we're having a man to man chat."

I hear the phone rustle, and I chuckle as I listen to Dad squeal in pain. "Give me that phone," she demands.

"No. He called me. If he wanted to talk to you, he would have called you."

"Max, I will make you sleep on this couch," she snaps. "Don't you forget it was me who pushed them out."

I hear Dad chuckle. "I pushed them out my ball sack first," he banters back.

"What the fuck, Dad?" I growl, moving the phone away from my ear, grossed out.

"Not the nipples," he squeals, just as the phone thuds, as if dropped on something hard.

I wait a few minutes, hearing Mum's heavy breathing down the phone before she says, "Landon, you still there?"

"I'm here," I chuckle, closing my eyes.

"Good, good. I just wanted to ask you to invite Paisley to dinner on Friday at the restaurant. Your uncle Cowen and uncle Evan can't make it, but the rest will be there. We've not had one in a while. Please."

Under any other circumstances, I'd say no, but I know my mum needs this. I think seeing how happy I am with Paisley will also ease her mind. It's the only reason I'm agreeing. That and I've already upset her enough.

"I'll message her. If she says yes, we'll be there," I promise.

I can hear her relief when she says, "Really?"

"Really," I repeat, chuckling.

"Oh good," she squeals excitedly. "I can't wait for everyone to meet her. I'd better go; I want to tell your aunts."

"Hey, Mum," I say before she ends the call.

"Yes?"

"I love you. You know that, right?"

I can hear the smile in her voice when she says, "I do. I love you too; so much."

"Night, Mum."

"Night, son."

I end the call before sending a message to Paisley.

LANDON: You awake? x

A few minutes later, my phone beeps.

PAISLEY: Miss me already ;) x

LANDON: ALWAYS. x

PAILSEY: Thank you again for tonight. I had such a good time. xx

LANDON: Me too. Um, I just spoke to Mum, and she wants to know if you're okay to come to a family dinner on Friday. Nearly all my family will be there, but if you can make it, I would love it. x

PAISLEY: I'd love to. x

LANDON: I'll let her know. Sweet dreams, sweet Paisley. x

PAISLEY: Night, Landon. X

I place my phone back into my pocket with a grin on my face. She doesn't know it yet, but once my mum finds out we're dating, she'll be inviting her everywhere, wanting to get to know her better.

"Are you going to train or smile into space like a creeper?" Liam yells.

With a bolt of energy, I jump up from the weight bench, more energised than I felt before coming in.

I'm ready to get this fight over with, because for the first time since Freya died, I don't feel like I've been robbed of the future I lived for.

Paisley Hayes is mine. Now I just need to make her believe it too.

"What the fuck, dude? I think you broke my nose," Maddox yells, clutching his bloody nose.

Maybe I'll make her believe it away from my family first.

TWENTY-ONE

PAISLEY

"You're giving me motion sickness," Adam says, sprawled out on top of my bed, Midnight on his stomach, purring away at the attention he's showing her.

I roll my eyes at his lack of humour. What a best friend he is. My stomach is in knots as I sift through racks of clothing. I've got nothing to fucking wear. Out of all the clothes I own, not one single item is calling out to me.

Why is it that any other day of the week I can walk blindly to my wardrobe, grab the first thing my hand connects with and feel happy about my choice? Now that I need something special to wear, I can't find anything. Nothing is good enough; either it's too dressy or too casual and I end up looking like I'm ready to work on the farm.

I even tried re-enacting what I do most mornings and closed my eyes and randomly grabbed something. I pulled out the Chucky Bride costume I wore last year.

I growl, roughly shoving more clothes to the side. Landon will be here in half an hour to take me to the meal his mum invited me to. A meal with his entire family. I didn't realise just how big of a deal it was when he asked me. Then I had one of those moments where you wake up from a dream after falling from a cliff, and I was gasping for air. The importance of it all was like a horrible wake up call. I'm going to meet his parents.

And his entire family.

And yes, I've met them before, but that was under different circumstances. Me and Landon are... I don't even know what we are because we've never spoken about it. What if his parents ask me? What if his other family members ask what we are to each other? What do I say? How do I answer a question I don't even know the answer to?

My stomach sinks with dread, and I clutch it, feeling the blood drain from my face when I think of other questions they'll most likely ask me.

What if they mention the baby or why I kept it a secret?

Sweat beads on my forehead, and I feel like I'm going to pass out. My breathing is heavy as I faintly hear the bed creak.

A hand lands on my shoulder, another on my back, both guiding me over to my bed. "Lie down for five minutes, then take your levels again. You're stressing out over nothing."

I lie down in the bed, shivering as I snuggle up to my pillow, breathing in nice and slow.

"I'm not stressing out," I snap through clenched teeth after I get my bearings together.

He chuckles, ruffling my hair. "Yeah, you are. I've never seen you this nervous. You've met most of his family before, so I don't understand why you look ready to spend the night getting close to your toilet."

"Yeah, but that was before. This is now. And I'm not going to be sick," I tell him, though I'm not sure how true that last part is.

"You mean now you're fucking Landon?"

I feel my cheeks heat. "We're not actually—you know... doing that."

He laughs when sees my expression before getting up and looking through my wardrobe. "You really do need to relax. And if someone asks something you aren't comfortable answering, just let Landon do the talking. That boy might not be known for using his words, but I doubt he'd let them put you in a difficult situation or make you feel awkward. He seems kind of possessive, ya know?" he states, and I nod, because I one-hundred percent agree. I actually kind of like Landon's possessive nature. "Now, get that panicked, scared look off your face, take your levels, and get ready."

"I've got nothing to wear," I mumble, watching as he turns back to the wardrobe. "All my clothes are stupid."

"Stop being a baby," he chuckles. "And you do now. Wear this. I've seen the Carter's heading inside for a family dinner before. They tend to keep it casual. And as you live in these almost all year round, they'll expect you to wear it," he says, holding out a flowery dress in one hand and a denim jacket in the other. Leaning back in, he kicks over a pair of black ankle boots.

"What if they're all dressed up?" I whisper, feeling my trembling subside. Now that I've got something to wear, something that doesn't suck, I feel a little better.

"Then you'll still fucking rock because you're hot as fuck."

I roll my eyes as I sit up. "You're only saying that because I'm your best friend."

"No, I'm saying it because it's true. If anyone could have turned me straight, it would have been you, you know?"

I scoff at that. "We would never have worked out. Eventually you would have tried it on with one of my brothers or fallen in love with them."

His eyes light up. "Already in love with the eldest ones," he says, then winks at me.

I chuckle, grabbing my kit. I take my levels, sighing when it comes up higher than earlier, but not enough for me to take another dose.

"I'll let them know."

He nods, pursing his lips. "Just make sure you big me up. Put in a good word and all that."

My brothers have nothing against men who are gay, but there is no way any of them would give up women for him. Reid might feel smug that men love him too, but that's because his ego is that big. The rest will shift uncomfortably and find a reason to escape.

Weirdos.

"I'll do that. Right after you turn around so I can get dressed."

He sighs, turning around so I can drop my dressing gown and pull the dress over my head.

I'm just finishing tying up my ankle boots when there's a tap on my door.

"Yeah?" I call out.

"Mum wants us downstairs. Family meeting," Colton calls through the door.

I scrunch my eyebrows together. Mum knows I'm going out tonight, so whatever it is must be important. I begin to bite my bottom lip, worrying over what it could be.

"Okay," I call back.

"I guess that's my cue to leave. Call me, bitch, and don't leave it so fucking long this time. We've not hung out in weeks. Well, not for longer than it takes for me to get you ready," he whines, walking over to me to fluff my hair up.

I slip on my jacket, smiling apologetically at him. "I'm sorry. I've been so busy with the bed and breakfast. I'm exhausted."

"And because you have Landon Carter sniffing around you." He pouts, sounding a little jealous.

"And you never ditch me the first chance you get, when some good-looking guy walks past?" I snidely ask, not happy where he's going with this.

He grins. "Touché," he teases, but I'm a little annoyed and hurt he thinks I would do that to him. "Relax, I was playing. I'd ditch me too if I had Landon Carter warming my bed."

"I'm not ditching you," I tell him sharply. "I really do have a lot going on."

His shoulders slump, guilt marring his expression. "I know you do. I'm sorry. I just miss you."

My expression softens and I wrap my arms around him, pulling him in for a hug. He wraps his arms around my shoulders, bending down to kiss my head.

"I'll make some time before the grand opening," I promise him.

"Good, because I can't watch *Grey's Anatomy* without you."

I giggle, pushing him away. He's watched every episode more than once, but I agree, it's not the same if we're not together. "Let's go. I promise to text you soon. We'll do something."

"Good. And you looking smoking, by the way."

I beam up at him. "Thank you."

He shakes his head whilst chuckling and leads the way downstairs, his movements hurried. I scoff, and he turns back at the sound, a smirk lifting his lips.

"What? I'm hoping to catch a glimpse of one of your brothers partially undressed."

"Eww," I moan, following more slowly behind, because my brothers do tend to walk around half naked, and watching Adam turn dumb in front of them isn't something I want to see.

AFTER SAYING GOODBYE to Adam, I head into the kitchen, wondering what Mum needs to talk to us about that warrants a family meeting.

Landon will be arriving in the next ten minutes or so, and I don't want to keep him waiting. However, I also know what Mum has to say must be important, and something urgent for her to call it without much notice.

As I step into the kitchen, my eyes scan the huge table. My brothers all look tense, no doubt the anticipation killing them.

"Hey, sweetie. You look beautiful," Mum says, eyeing my attire.

I run the palms of my hands down my dress, blushing slightly. All my brothers are glaring at me. You'd think after weeks of me hanging out with Landon they would have relaxed around him. Somehow, it's made them all worse, more determined than ever to split us up.

Jaxon is still pouting after my date with Landon last week. Whatever happened between the two outside of the barn, neither will tell me the truth, but whatever it was, it seems Landon won and Jaxon is licking his wounds.

I just hope they didn't get into a fight. I'm still holding out hope the two will push their hard feelings aside and start to get along. I won't give up Landon, but I don't want to lose my brothers either. They mean everything to me, even if they can be annoying.

"Thanks, Mum. Colton said you wanted to talk. Is everything okay?"

She pats the table where I usually sit, so I take my place, watching the others warily. None seem to know what's going on either, all looking at Mum questioningly.

"Has something happened? Are you okay?" I ask, feeling my stomach tighten.

She glances over at me, shaking her head in confusion. "What? Oh, this is good news, Paisley. Very good news."

I sit up straighter, as do my brothers. Mum normally only calls a family meeting if one of us have gotten into trouble or something is happening with the farm.

I'm glad it's neither. Although, if I had to put money on someone being in trouble, it would be the twins. They've been getting bored far too quickly lately, which can only mean one thing: they're upping their game and getting into trouble.

"Your grandpa, Barry, has finally agreed to move to town."

"What?" I ask excitedly. "Really?"

I love my grandpa and miss him so much. I hate that he lives so far away from us. If I could, I'd see him every day.

"Yep," she beams, looking at the others for their reactions.

They groan, all ducking their heads. It's only Jaxon who chuckles. "What made him finally agree?" he asks Mum, not hiding his amusement.

Grandpa has lived in Wales, in the middle of nowhere, alone, since my nan died eight years ago. He's at the age where he shouldn't be alone, but the stubborn old fool wouldn't come and stay with us. And he wouldn't take my mum's invitation to live with us, even when we said we needed help around the farm. He saw through it and refused our offer.

A part of me knows he didn't want to leave the house he and Nan moved into after Dad moved out. They have fond memories there, and from what Nan always told me, it was going to be their forever home, one where they would spend their last days together.

Mum huffs angrily. "The stubborn man had to have a hip replacement a few months ago. He had a fall cleaning the gutters out and didn't bother to call any of us."

"Why the fuck didn't he tell us?" Jaxon snaps, banging the table. I jump, startled.

"Language," Mum scolds, and we all roll our eyes. She swears like a sailor, so she's one to talk. "And I don't know. Maybe because he knew we'd go up there. His carer told him he will go in a home if he doesn't either have someone move in with him or if he doesn't move closer to family. He's bought a bungalow near town so he's close but not close enough he feels like a burden."

"He'd never be a burden," I say, biting my bottom lip. I only spoke to him the other day, and although he sounded tired, I thought he was okay.

I feel guilt for how much we've neglected him, and though distance is an issue, it isn't impossible for me to get on a train and a few buses to spend the weekend with him.

"Speak for yourself," Reid snaps. "He *hates* us."

Isaac and Luke both nod in agreement, looking grumpy and defeated. I roll my eyes at their dramatics. Grandpa is a big ol' teddy bear.

"You drank the bottle of whiskey that had been passed down through his family," I remind them, remembering that week like it was yesterday. I'd never seen Mum yell like that before.

"I didn't know whether I was yelling because I was scared I'd lose you to alcohol poisoning or because you did something so stupid and reckless," Mum sighs.

"We thought it was shandy," Luke defends, crossing his arms over his chest.

"The fact it was in a posh-looking box and locked in a cabinet didn't give you any suspicion it wasn't meant to be touched?" I ask dryly.

"We paid for our mistakes," Reid yells. "We thought it was a treasure hunt and that was our prize."

"You weren't doing a treasure hunt," I sass back.

"We could have been," Luke growls, crossing his arms over his chest.

"Whatever," I mutter.

"I'm sure he's forgiven you by now," Mum says sceptically, looking away from the boys.

I chuckle under my breath, earning glare from each of the triplets. I look to Mum, unable to stop myself from smiling.

"When is he coming? I can't wait for him to get here," I tell her, feeling giddy.

"At the end of the month. He wants Jaxon and the boys to go and pack up his belongings. Will you be able to do it?"

Jaxon nods. "Yeah, of course. I'll get someone to cover the jobs we have on that day."

"Good," she says, relaxing. "I can't wait for him to be closer. I miss him."

"We know, Mum," I say, placing my hand on hers.

Grandpa Barry is from my dad's side of the family. They moved to Wales once Dad flew the nest, wanting to get away from socialisation. Nan still worked at the hospital until she died, but Grandpa retired when he damaged his knee. He was no longer able to drive lorries across the country.

"We'll make sure he's settled. And it will be nice to have him back for Christmas," I tell her, lifting her spirits.

The doorbell rings, and all my brothers growl like animals. I roll my eyes, snorting. "You all sound like a pack of wolves."

"Guess what wolves do when they think one of their own are being hurt?"

I glare at my stupid brother. "They can also travel up to twenty-two kilometres a day, Reid. You couldn't run that in a week," I snap, grabbing my emergency bag from the side.

"They're protective of their young too," Jaxon calls out.

"Well then they're stupid. They raise them to be as fast, as strong, and as determined as they are, so they don't need to baby them for the rest of their life," I tell him, pausing at the door.

His expression softens a touch.

"Are we really talking about wolves?" Luke asks, watching me like I've grown two heads.

"Oh God," Reid groans, slapping him upside the head. "No, we're actually on about Landon and Paisley."

"How does what you just said have anything to do with Paisley and that idiot?"

Reid looks like he's seconds away from punching him. "Nothing. Nothing at all."

"Have a good time, sweetie. I need to go check on the pigs, but make sure you tell Landon I said hi."

"I will, Mum."

"You do know we will kill him if he hurts you again?" Wyatt states before I can leave. The doorbell rings again, and I huff in frustration at my brothers.

"I don't have time for your dramatics," I snap out, leaving them behind as I head to the front door.

My heart melts at the sight of Landon when I open the door. He looks as sexy as ever with his jacket zipped up to his chest, leaving a glimpse of a silver chain and white T-shirt.

His eyes sparkle, which they've doing a lot lately, as he takes my hand. "You look beautiful," he whispers against my lips.

TWENTY-TWO

LANDON

PAISLEY SEEMS JITTERY AS WE PULL up outside the back of the restaurant. She seemed fine when we left, albeit a bit pissed at her brothers, but other than that, she seemed like her normal ray of sunshine self.

If I wasn't so fucking nervous myself, I might have been able to relax her, but a part of me is scared she'll plead for me to turn back and take her home.

I have plans for tonight, plans I've been putting into action since our date last week. I just hope everything is perfect.

I want her to meet my family. I want my family to meet her. I just don't want them scaring her off or making her feel unwelcome. Though I don't see that being a problem when it comes to my family.

I look out the windshield, staring at the door leading into the downstairs part of the restaurant. I watch as Maddison walks in with Trent, both chatting away.

"Are we not going in?" Paisley asks, her voice shaky.

My gaze meets hers, and I shake my head, swallowing down the nerves fluttering around my system. "No. Not until you tell me what's wrong. Do you not want to be here?"

"What?" she asks, taken aback.

"You seem uncomfortable, like you'd rather be anywhere else. Did I do something to upset you?"

Her expression softens as she leans over to take my hand. "No, silly, you didn't. I'm just one big ball of nervous energy right now."

"Why?" I ask, my eyebrows drawing together. "You've met most of my family before now."

She exhales and rests her head back against the headrest. "Yes, but that was before, you know, we… I don't even know what we are. What are we doing, Landon?" she asks, her voice low, sad.

I squeeze her hand, hating how vulnerable and unsure she looks. "You mean because we're going out?"

I watch as a slow smile spreads across her face, her eyes seeming to come to life. "Like boyfriend and girlfriend?"

I chuckle at her terminology. It makes us sound like we're twelve. "If that's what you want to call it, yes. But we are a couple. You won't look, flirt, or fantasize about another male." It's not a request or a demand, just me simply stating a fact. I will knock some fucker out for even thinking of looking at her, let alone touching her. It makes me murderous just thinking about it.

She tilts her head to the side, her lips twitching. "If I wasn't so happy right now, I'd be a little pissed about you barking commands at me like I'm a dog."

I wince a little at that. "Sorry. I'm warning you more than anything."

She sighs dreamily, her attention on my mouth. My eyes are immediately drawn to hers, but if I kiss her tempting, delicious mouth, we'll never leave the car.

And someone will come looking for me. My eyes flicker briefly to the door of the restaurant, my suspicions correct.

"Sorry, baby, but if you keep looking at me like that, I'm going to be forced to kiss you. And I'm pretty sure Liam just went back inside, no doubt to tell everyone we're in the car."

She startles, her gaze snapping to meet mine. I groan at the fire in her eyes, wishing we had time to finish this.

"I don't want us to be late," she yells, wide-eyed. "Get out." I watch in amusement as she tries to scramble out of the car. With her seatbelt still on. "Damn seatbelt." She curses when the wind slams her door shut.

Leisurely, I lean over and unclip her belt, making sure to run my nose along her ear. She shivers, her body tensing for a split second before she's pushing me away. I chuckle at the glare she gives me.

"You need to turn that off," she says, gesturing to all of me.

I arch an eyebrow. "Turn what off?"

She waves up and down at me. "Sexual tension."

A tap on her window has a startled scream coming out of her. I growl low in my throat when Dad shoves his face up against the window.

"You coming in?"

Paisley squeaks but nods. "We were just unclipping my belt."

He grins, winking over her shoulder at me. "Hurry up, son. Your mum is on her second glass of wine."

Paisley grabs her bag from the floor and I wait until she's safely out before shutting the car off and getting out myself.

"What did you do to piss her off?" I ask as I meet them at the front of the car. As soon as Paisley is close, I wrap my arm around her shoulders, pulling her against me.

He rolls his eyes. "What makes you think I did something?"

"Because Mum only drinks when you've pissed her off."

"She loves me," he scoffs, but then sighs. "Okay, I tried to fix the leak in the bathroom. You know plumbing isn't one of my strong suits. Anyway, a pipe must have been seriously weak or something. I didn't break it or anything. It just burst, everywhere. Of its own accord. Nothing to do with me at all. She's just a tad upset over the flooring being ruined."

I snort. "Not because she asked you to either ask Maverick to look at it or hire someone, then?"

He glares at me. "For once, take my side. I was trying to do something good. I was going to run her a hot bath with candles and seduce her."

I inwardly groan, my body shivering. "Didn't need to know that."

"I was just being a good husband. She should be baking me cakes."

"Ah, I get it. You broke something else and wanted to fix the leak so she wouldn't be mad about the other thing," I say, nodding now it's all coming together.

His narrows his eyes at me. "I hate that you know me so well."

"What did you break?" Paisley asks, speaking up for the first time. We stop just outside the door to the room we'll all be eating in.

"Her favourite perfume," he admits, exhaling as he warily eyes everyone inside through the window.

"So why not buy her a new one?" Paisley asks, sounding confused. Me, too, if I'm honest. It would have been easier.

He snorts, glaring softly at us. "Because the bloody perfume was discontinued. They don't do it anymore. I looked everywhere, even overseas. It was either tell her or fix something else she's upset about and hope she forgives me when she finds out."

The look in his eyes tells me something different. "What was you really going to do if she found it missing?"

If looks could kill, I'd be dead. My lips twitch at his frustration. "I was going to blame Maverick, tell her he did it when he failed to fix the bath."

Uncle Maverick's deep voice sounds from behind us. "You were, were you."

Dad squeaks, his eyes wide as he turns around to face his brother. "Nope. Not at all," he rushes out, before his eyes land on Paisley. "Need to introduce Paisley to everyone. Can't stop."

The air rushes from Paisley as she's pulled away, looking helplessly back at me. I chuckle, shrugging.

Dad won't hurt her, but he might annoy her to death. I'll save her in a minute.

"I swear, he will never grow up," Maverick mutters, sounding resigned as we slowly follow them inside.

I chuckle. "But how fun will it be when Mum finds out he broke her perfume, too?"

An evil grin spreads across his face as he walks over to Mum. Dad, who has taken Paisley to the other side of the room, where Myles is, looks pale when Maverick starts talking to Mum.

Aunt Teagan whistles, gaining everyone's attention. "Food will be ready soon. Take your seats."

Heading over to Paisley, I pull her away from Dad. Dad looks confused, pulling her back towards him. "She's sitting next to me."

Gently, I try to pull her closer to me, but he doesn't let go, glaring at me. "Dad, she's sitting next to me."

Paisley's wide-eyed, biting her bottom lip worriedly. "Um, I'll just——" she starts, but Dad cuts her off.

"You don't have to give into him, darlin'. He won't be hurt because you chose me."

"Dad," I snap.

Mum walks up beside us, and I'm grateful as she looks at Dad's hand on Paisley's arm. He lets it go so fast it's almost funny. Taking the moment, I pull her against my chest.

"Your dad has no boundary issues," she whispers.

I look down at her, amused. "You have no idea."

"What are you doing, Max?"

He rubs the back of his neck. "I want to get to know my future daughter-in-law. He's hogging her."

Paisley begins to choke, so I pull her away before Dad scares her away completely. Hayden and Charlotte are stood talking to the side, and when Charlotte sees me, her face lights up.

"Landon, you made it," she gushes, rushing over.

I let go of Paisley, pulling Charlotte into my arms with a smile on my face. I've barely seen her since the incident and working on Paisley's bed and breakfast. I've missed her more than I realised.

"How are you?" I ask, pulling her away an inch so I can take a look at her. I arch an eyebrow at the fresh claw marks on her arms and neck.

She covers the one on her neck, blushing sheepishly. "I think she just needs to settle in."

I nod as I pull Paisley against me, contemplating the pros and cons of kidnapping Charlotte's cat when she isn't there and then making her believe it ran away. Wouldn't be the first time a pet has done it to her. I just don't want her to cry and think she's done something wrong.

"And don't go kidnapping her," she mutters grumpily. "She really is just settling in."

"What do you have, a lion?" Paisley blurts out, ducking her head when she realises she said it out loud.

Hayden laughs. "You'd think so, but no, it's a kitten."

"She's so adorable," Charlotte exclaims excitedly. "You'll have to come and meet her."

"I'd love to," Paisley agrees, her tone wary.

"Oh, I know. Why don't you two come over for dinner. I've not seen you in forever, Landon," she says, her eyes turning sad.

"Can I bring a friend?" Paisley asks before I can speak.

Charlottes eyes light up, and I can see her mentally planning what to cook, what to watch, and what to talk about.

"Yes, more the merrier. This is going to be so much fun," she squeals, clinging onto Hayden.

Mum walks up and steps into our little group, her eyes alight with happiness. "Lovely to see you, Paisley."

"You too, Mrs Carter."

Mum giggles, shaking her head. "Please, just call me Lake. Now, you guys sit down. I'm going to get a glass of wine or two. Would you like anything?"

"I've got ours, Mum," I tell her, leaning down to kiss her cheek.

She pats my cheek affectionally. "Such a good boy," she murmurs. "You take after me, not your dad."

I chuckle when she glares in Dad's direction and he gulps, looking away fearfully.

"Come on, why don't you sit next to me," Hayden says, pulling out two chairs.

Paisley looks to me and I nod, letting her go so I can get our drinks. Mum keeps pace beside me, a small smile on her face.

"She's so pretty, Landon."

I glance over my shoulder, watching as she throws her head back, laughing at something Hayden has said.

"She's beautiful, Mum, inside and out."

A small squeak has me looking down at Mum. She dabs under her eyes. "I'm so happy for you."

I roll my eyes as I wrap my arm around her shoulder. Trust Mum to get emotional over nothing. Before I have chance to answer, Dawn, the bartender, walks over and takes our orders.

"Promise me something, Landon," Mum whispers hoarsely when Dawn walks away to grab our drinks.

At the seriousness in her voice, I look down in concern. "What, Mum?"

"Promise me you'll give this a real try. Promise you won't let the past define your future. Just promise me you'll let yourself be happy."

I swallow past a lump in my throat as I nod, feeling my chest tighten. "I will try, Mum. I promise to try."

"I love you so much. I just want you to be happy."

I think back over the past few weeks I've spent with Paisley and look down at Mum, rubbing her arm. "I am, Mum. I am happy."

She gives me a watery smile. "Good," she whispers, before gaining her composure. Her focus turns back to the table, her eyes alight once again with happiness. "She fits in well."

She does. She's laughing with Hayden, Maddox and Trent, talking to them like she's always been here.

"Let's go sit down. Your dad is gonna give himself an aneurism if he stresses over what I might do much longer," she says, and begins cackling when Dad's gaze focusses on us, fear lurking behind his eyes.

"He looks seconds away from shitting himself," I tell her, my lips twitching.

She picks up their drinks while I pick up mine and Paisley's. "You not drinking?" she asks in surprise. I always have a beer when we're at these things. It helps a lot when we're all together.

"Paisley doesn't drink. I don't want her to feel uncomfortable that she isn't, and we are," I explain as we walk over.

"You really are a good boy," she sighs, before wandering off towards Dad, who crouches low in his seat.

I shake my head, amused, and take a seat next to Paisley, sliding her drink over. I put my arm around the back of her chair, smiling when she shifts closer but doesn't pull away from her conversation.

"She's not having bridesmaids," Lily says when I tune into what they're saying.

Faith, who sits not that far down the table, clears her throat. "Actually, Lily, there's something we wanted to ask you."

Lily leans around Charlotte, eyeing her sister with confusion. "Is everything okay? You are still getting married, aren't you?"

Everyone eyes Beau murderously. He holds his hands up, glaring back. "We're getting fucking married, dickheads. Lay off with the killer looks."

Faith giggles, looking back at Lily. "I already spoke to Nina and she is fine with not being a bridesmaid or anything. She knows she means a lot to me, and I'll still want her help."

"Okay," Lily says slowly, looking like she has no idea where this conversation is going.

Faith turns on her megawatt smile, clapping her hands together. "Would you be my maid of honour?"

Lily's jaw drops, tears gathering in her eyes. "Me?" she whispers.

Faith rolls her eyes. "Of course, you, silly. I'd love to have you all standing beside me but I don't think the front of the church is big enough. But I can't get married without my sister and best friend beside me."

Lily gets up, silent tears streaming down her face. She bends down to Faith, wrapping her arms around her neck. "I'd love to," we hear her answer, sounding choked up. When she pulls back, she's smiling, wiping under her eyes. "I thought for sure you'd pick Nina."

Faith squeezes Lily's hand, smiling up at her. "Nope. It will always be you."

"Thank you. I'll be honoured."

"You know what this means, don't you?" Teagan says.

"What?" Lily asks softly, taking her seat. She hasn't stopped smiling.

"We get to go bridal shopping," Teagan answers, earning groans from the men and excited squeals from the girls.

"Wait," Aiden calls out. Normally, I'd ignore anything he'd have to say, but since he had Sunday, he's kind of made sense. Sometimes.

"What?" Beau asks with the expression I normally reserve only for Aiden and Maddox.

"Which one of us is going to be best man? I mean, I'm her brother, so it's only right I get first dibs."

Beau groans, and I inwardly chuckle, tuning them out as they all argue over who should be picked. I hear Dad mutter something, pushing his drink away with a sour expression.

"What did your drink do to you?" I ask him.

He quickly checks to make sure Mum is still talking to Teagan about weddings before leaning in to whisper, "She winked at me when she handed me the drink."

I arch an eyebrow at him. "And?"

"I've never been so scared of a drink in all my life," he says, eyeing it like its poison.

"Not thirsty?" Mum asks, smiling at Dad.

Okay, even I think she looks creepy.

Dad whimpers, pushing the glass away. "I fancy a pint, not a Bud tonight, babe."

I chuckle when Dad gets up, taking the drink with him.

"You okay?" I ask Paisley when her body tenses beside me.

"Will they really snort chilli powder? I heard that's dangerous."

I look up to find Mark, Aiden, and Maddox arguing over who will be best man, firing out ways to prove to Beau who will be his best choice.

I scrub my jaw. "Um, probably. It sounds better than the drink they put together once."

Her wide eyes meet mine. "They're kind of crazy."

I chuckle, leaning down to nuzzle her neck. Her intake of breath proves my plans for later were right.

"Not as crazy as you make me," I whisper, feeling her shudder.

TWENTY-THREE

PAISLEY

I'M DRUNK ON LIFE AND LAUGHTER as I walk out of the restaurant hand in hand with Landon. Tonight has been so much fun. And my brothers are completely wrong about them. They're just like us, yet friendlier. My brothers wouldn't go out of their way to make someone feel welcome.

Landon's dad walks beside us, a drunk Lake swaying beside him, clinging to his arms for balance. I guess she doesn't handle her wine very well, I muse. She's been a hoot, and it's so entertaining to watch her bicker with her husband.

"I'll order the Tay-Tay T-shirts when I get back," Max exclaims excitedly as the door shuts behind us. Half of the family left not too long ago, but some are still downstairs drinking.

"Looking forward to it," I tell him. I can't wipe the smile from my face. Who knew someone like Max Carter—someone his age—would be obsessed with Taylor Swift. Once we got talking, I found we had a lot in common.

"We home?" Lake slurs, making me giggle. "I think my bed has a lump in it."

"Shake it off, babe, shake it off," Max tells her, grinning. Then he starts shaking his arse as he lifts her into his arms.

Landon arches his eyebrow. "Want me to take you home?"

Max snorts. "She promised me dirty, drunken sex. I stayed sober, so I could remember it."

"Dad!" Landon groans loudly.

Max doesn't even look embarrassed. "I'm good. I didn't even drink my pint, son. Do you need me to take *you* home?" he asks, wiggling his eyebrows. I giggle.

"I didn't drink, Dad, but thanks," Landon states dryly. "Oh, and thanks for hogging my girlfriend all night."

"It's the charm." Max grins, winking at me. I giggle, resting my head against Landon's arm.

"Get Mum home," Landon says tiredly. Lake snorts in her sleep, making me laugh hard.

Max grins down at her. I become envious at the love shining in his eyes. He really does love his wife. It reminds me so much of Mum and Dad it makes me a little sad. I miss him so much, and I know my mum does too. She hasn't dated once since he died. It must be lonely for her, even with a house filled with kids.

"She's so adorable," he whispers, shaking his head. He looks up at Landon. "I'll speak to you tomorrow, son."

"Night, Dad."

"Night, son."

Landon takes my hand, and together we walk over to the car. When we reach the passenger side, I step in front of him before he can open the door and beam up at him.

"I had such a good time tonight. Thank you for inviting me. Your family is amazing."

"How would you know? You spent most of the time talking to my dad," he pouts.

I giggle, rising to my toes so I can wrap my arms around his neck. "Are you still annoyed he wouldn't give you your seat back?"

He rolls his eyes, but his lips twitch. "I went to get drinks. I was only gone a few minutes!"

Laughter spills out of me. "You really don't like to share, do you?" I ask, remembering Hayden said he hated sharing certain things as a kid.

"Only the things that are *mine.*"

I melt against him, feeling the meaning behind those words. He doesn't share those things that are special to him.

It's kind of sweet.

Instead of answering, I give in to the overwhelming urge to kiss him. I devour him, pushing my breasts against his chest.

He shoves his hand into my hair, the other grabbing my hip to pull me impossibly closer as he takes over, the kiss hungry and feral. The warmth of his tongue causes me to whimper, my core heating.

He breaks the kiss, the scruff on his jaw rubbing against my cheek. I go limp in his arms, staring up at him in a daze.

Why does he have to be so good looking?

The weight of his gaze has me flushing, sucking in my bottom lip. He blinks, seeming to focus, and smirks down at me.

"I want to show you something," he rasps.

Please let it be what's hard and tenting his trousers.

"What?"

His eyes spark. "It's a surprise."

I sigh, now gripping his biceps for balance. "Okay," I whisper, still high on desire.

I'VE NEVER BEEN one to be ungrateful. Ever. My nan used to knit us jumpers for Christmas, and I say jumpers, but they were a work in progress. She'd never get the sleeves the same size and there would always be holes where she dropped a stitch. Yet, she took time to knit those jumpers, so I took the time to make sure I wore one when she was around.

Wyatt, for my thirteenth birthday, got me a box of tampons and a leaflet on STD's. I thanked him and went on my way.

However, Landon has brought me to the bed and breakfast, and this wasn't what I had in mind when we left the restaurant. When he said he wanted to show me something, I was kind of hoping he'd take me back to his place.

I guess Drew, his friend who is looking after Rex, would kill the mood.

"Um, the bed and breakfast?" I ask, trying to keep the disappointment out of my voice.

He grins over at me after shutting the car off. "Come on, you'll like it. I promise," he says.

I raise an eyebrow but undo my belt and get out of the car. The first thing I notice is the porch and lobby lights are on.

Weird, they've not had to be turned on yet since most of the work has been done in the day.

"Landon, I think we should call the police," I whisper, my voice trembling.

He chuckles, and I narrow my gaze up at him. "God, you are hard to surprise," he says, taking my hand in his.

Smiling, I follow him up, intrigued by what he wants to show me. I'm a little confused when he locks the door behind us. At my look, he grins.

"Your brothers," he explains. "I changed the locks so they wouldn't have a key. I only gave one to your mum, and I've already swapped the old key for the new key on your key chain."

"Okay," I say slowly, still not understanding what is going on. He pulls me past the reception and opens the door that leads to my empty apartment. We've still not brought up the furnishings.

"What?" I gasp out, surveying the stairs that have battery lit candles on.

"Come on," he whispers, leading me up by my hand.

I look down at the candles, then back up at his tall, lean body as he walks up the narrow staircase. He pushes open the door and dim lighting spills through.

The place is still bare, except for the few boxes that were brought up last week. He doesn't stop walking though, dragging me towards my bedroom.

I raise an eyebrow as he pushes open the door. A puff of air passes through my lips when I see a gigantic mattress on the floor, soft purple sheets and big, fluffy pillows covering it.

Landon shuffles closer to me, looking nervous. "The bed didn't come in time. I'm sorry."

Candles flicker around the room, some battery lit, some real, their scent filling the space with a relaxing aroma. The warm glow has me relaxing.

There are even a few bottles of Sprite next to the bed, which makes me giggle.

"You did all of this?" I ask on a surprised whisper, feeling my eyes begin to water.

"I had a little help," he says sheepishly, looking uncomfortable.

I shake my head. This can't be real. "This is beautiful, Landon. You didn't need to do all of this though."

He pulls me into his arms, his strong body holding me close. "You're shaking," he says with a frown. "We don't have to do anything you're not ready for."

I give him a rueful smile. "I never said I wasn't ready. I'm shaking because I do want this. I want you. I always have. But you didn't need to do all of this."

"Yes, I did. I wanted our next time to be more special, not some quickie," he says huskily, running his fingers through my hair.

I sigh, closing my eyes as I lean in to his touch. My pulse quickens with anticipation, and when I open my eyes, all I see is him.

I want him. *Need* him.

"No more talking," I whisper, running my fingers up his hard chest. I push under his jacket, pulling it off his shoulders and down his arms. It falls to the floor, the sound of his keys falling echoing around the room.

He groans, lifting me off my feet and walking over to the bed. I wind my legs around his waist before slamming my lips against his.

He bends, lowering me down on the soft mattress and coming down on top of me. A low moan sounding from the back of his throat sends shivers down my spine.

He pulls back a little, bringing me with him as he grips the back of my head. I follow, not wanting to lose the feel of his lips. It's too good. His fingers on my jacket have my pulse racing. He pulls it down my arms, freeing me, and I help, flinging it across the room. Needing to be naked quicker, I kick off my boots, thanking God they slip off easily. He kisses me like he's in no hurry, like he isn't as affected as I am. It makes me want to make him insane with desire too.

He looms over me, pressing his hard front against me. I can't help but rock against him, gasping at the sensations powering through me.

Idly, I run my fingers down his chest, gripping the edge of his T-shirt before pulling it up. He breaks the kiss to pull it over his head, but is back on me the second it's off, his lips trailing kisses down my jaw to my neck, nibbling lightly on my collarbone.

I moan, rubbing against him. He pulls away, holding my gaze as he breathes heavily. "Are you sure?" he rasps.

"Never been so sure about anything," I tell him, running my fingers through his hair.

His gaze loses focus for a second, before he shakes out of it, his touch soft when he reaches for the thin strap of my dress. I shudder, not looking away from him as he does the same thing to the other.

"So beautiful," he whispers, leaning down to kiss my collarbone.

He expertly slides my dress down my body, leaving me in my purple lace underwear. The dress had a built-in bra, and I'm kind of grateful for that fact, needing to feel his skin on mine. And it's one less item to take off.

I grab the back of his head, pulling him down before fastening my lips to his. He pushes against me, causing me to cry out.

"Take them off," I demand, and he releases a husky laugh.

I watch his body, in all its glory, stand up, mesmerised as he unbuttons his jeans, letting them fall open. He pulls something from out his back pocket, then grips it between his teeth.

The condom only heightens my need, knowing this is really happening.

He joins me back on the bed, coming down on top of me and sucking a nipple into his mouth. I arch my back, a small gasp escaping at the sensation. His silky hair brushes against my skin, heightening the experience.

I need him.

I feel like I'm going to combust if I don't have him inside of me now.

"Landon," I whisper hoarsely, but his fingers running smoothly up my leg cut off what else I was going to say. I shiver, feeling him tug my knickers aside before his fingers rub through my wetness. "Oh God," I cry out, arching my back when he plunges two fingers inside of me.

"Fuck, you're so fucking wet," he groans, adding another finger. I tighten around him, too far gone in the thrones of passion.

"Please," I beg. "I can't take it anymore." I rock against his fingers, no longer able to form any words.

"You're killing me," he whispers, before leaning back on his knees. He tears open the foil packet with his teeth, spitting out the bit he tore before taking the condom. He throws the packet to the side before slipping the condom down his raging hard-on. My lips part, our eyes meeting as he shuffles forward, using his hands to part my thighs.

"You're mine," he rasps out fiercely, moving closer. I can feel him pressing against me, and I arch my back, ready for him.

He kisses me at the same moment he plunges inside of me. I cry out against him, and he swallows down my cries. He pulls out, before driving back inside.

"Say you're mine," he demands against my lips.

He feels bigger than I remember, filling me to the point it's almost painful. Almost. Pleasure overrides the little pinch of pain.

"Say it," he demands, harsher.

I glance up to meet his gaze, digging my fingers into his sides as he plunges in once more. "Yours!"

He thrusts again, lowering his large chest and wide shoulders until they're against me. I cry out, raking my nails up his ribs before gripping his shoulders.

"More," I cry out, feeling braver than I have ever felt before.

"So fucking beautiful," he groans out, thrusting harder.

I dig my heels into his arse, meeting him thrust for thrust. "Mine!" I whisper, claiming him like he claimed me.

His eyes darken as he leans down, rubbing his nose against the tip of mine. "Yours."

I believe him too. It's in every touch, every look, every breath.

My eyes roll as my core begins to tighten, gripping him harder and tighter. He leans down, releasing one of my legs so he can push it up against my chest. He reaches further inside of me, hitting the back of my core and causing me to yell out his name.

He keeps hitting the same spot, over and over, until I can't take it anymore. My eyes close, my back arches, and my mouth opens to cry out in ecstasy, but no sound comes out. Not one word.

I feel his dick twitch inside of me, and I open my eyes in time to see he's close, a look of pure pleasure across his face as he chants my name.

I cling to him, still feeling the aftershocks of my powerful orgasm. I know if he keeps going, I'll orgasm again. I can feel it in the pit of my stomach. And just as I feel him begin to finish, another orgasm washes over me. My entire body tenses as I cling to him, riding it out and feeling like I'm on cloud nine.

"Landon," I whisper, holding him against me when he drops his head to my shoulder. A part of me tenses, scared of what will happen now. Though I know he is mine as much as I am his, a part of me is scared he will run off like last time.

When I look up, all I see is love. He might not know what that emotion is, and it could be the effects of great sex, but it's there, shining in his eyes like a beacon.

He opens his mouth to speak, but no words come out. He sighs, rolling off me, and I feel the wetness from my orgasm between my legs.

He pulls me against his hard chest, and my body immediately relaxes.

"No one else," he declares, running his fingers through my hair until I'm boneless. My entire body is limp, my eyes drooping as I vaguely hear him whisper something.

"I love you, Landon," I whisper, just before I fall into the sea of darkness.

TWENTY-FOUR

LANDON

I T'S STILL EARLY WHEN I FIND myself pulling up into the graveyard. The air is thick with fog and the ground covered in frost.

I shiver and pull my hoodie closer around me. I didn't go home, planning on doing this on the way back, after I got a change of clothes. Paisley promised me she'd stay in bed until I got back, not even questioning where I was going this early in the morning.

It's another thing that draws me to her. She never pries.

Leaving her naked in bed killed me, but I knew when I woke up with her snoring lightly in my arms that I needed to do this today. Not just for me, but for her too. She has all of me, and she doesn't even know it yet.

She will though.

I get out of the car and shut the door behind me, the sound echoing through the entire cemetery.

Briefly, I close my eyes before following the path to where her grave is.

The day Freya died, my life changed. I was supposed to meet her that day but cancelled, and a part of me has lived with the guilt of that decision ever since. If I had been with her, her dad would never have gotten them in that car. She would still be alive. Whether we would have still been together, I don't know. We were young, stupid. We didn't really understand life back then. I understand it now. I know I was wrong turning a blind eye over her dad. She told me he was abusive, mostly to her mum, but I listened to her when she said she could handle it. I should have seen that she couldn't.

It cost Freya her life.

My feet drag as I walk up to Freya's grave, where she's buried next to her mum and sister. I kneel on the damp grass, feeling it seep into my jeans.

"Freya," I croak out, rubbing my eyes. This is harder than I thought. How do you tell a girl you promised to love forever, goodbye?

Although I don't believe in God, I do believe our spirits go somewhere peaceful; maybe not heaven but something close to it. I'm hoping if Freya is still out there, she's listening. I hope she grants me forgiveness and understands why I need to do this, say this. "This is harder than I thought."

I swipe some dry leaves off her grave before running my fingers over the lettering of her name. I swallow past the lump in my throat.

"You know I was never one for words, so forgive me if I fuck this up completely," I tell her, chuckling dryly. "I've come to say goodbye. Not just for today, but for good. I have to let you go," I choke out, feeling my throat burn. Saying it out loud is harder than I thought it would be. "I've met someone. I don't know if you remember her, but her name is Paisley Hayes. She was the one you asked me about once because I kept watching her. I didn't mean to fall for her, but I did. She makes me feel, Freya, like really feel. It's not like you and me. It's different. I'm so fucking sorry, Freya. I never meant for this to happen, I swear," I declare in a scratchy voice.

I don't tell her that what I feel with Paisley is more. I don't want her to think I love her any less. Because I do—did—love her. She was my world, but now Paisley is my everything. I can't go a minute without thinking of her.

My eyes burn with unshed tears. It's like I'm tarnishing her memory by thinking these things, but I always promised to be honest with Freya.

I scrub a hand down my face, exhaling. "I've spent years loving you and hating you. I hated you so much that sometimes it trumped my love for you. I wanted to ask you why you wouldn't let me help you. Why you didn't tell me things were so bad.

"Why did you leave me? I would have dropped everything to come and get you. I wouldn't have lost you. I've carried the guilt of your death around with me, and I felt I deserved it after losing you. I shouldn't have shouldered the blame, and that's on me, not you. I've been too scared to say how I really feel, worried you were still there somehow, listening. I thought you would hate me, blame me I guess, for cancelling that day. Deep down, I knew you wouldn't, but that guilt inside of me wouldn't let me hear that. All I felt was anger, Freya. I didn't feel love, and for months, maybe even a year after you died, I couldn't even stomach to love my family. All of it built up inside of me until I was no longer living, just existing. Until her."

I sit back on my arse, ignoring the cold and wet seeping through my jeans. I grip my hair, resting my elbows on my knees.

The first tear falls, disappearing into the damp grass. "I'm so fucking sorry I couldn't save you. I'm so sorry that I get to live, and you had to die. I would have taken your place in a heartbeat. But I need her, Freya. I need her so goddamn bad I feel like I'm dying when I'm not with her."

I dry laugh escapes me. "I really hope I'm not fucking this up," I rasp out, tugging my hair tighter. "I really need you to understand why I'm moving on. You may have owned a piece of my heart, but she owns all of me; mind, body and soul. Please forgive me," I plead as I stand up, looking down at her grave. "I hope you, your mum and sister are together and happy. I hope for a lot of things, but mostly, I hope you are free of *him*, and that you've found peace."

I kiss the tip of my index finger and press it to the top of the gravestone. Freya would always do it through her bedroom window, kissing her two fingers before pressing them to the glass. She would do it anywhere she couldn't reach me to kiss me, like in class or from within a car after being picked up. Doing it back feels like the best final goodbye.

I step away, glancing at the grave one more time before leaving.

Though I'll always remember her, always feel the guilt, I can finally move forward. My gait feels lighter which each step.

My phone rings in my pocket as I walk through the graveyard gates. "'Ello?"

"Bro, you are never going to believe what happened last night," Liam sighs, sounding frustrated. "I didn't find out until I got back this morning."

"Wait, you've only just got back home?"

"Duh, we went out on a bender after you lightweights left for the night," he says, like that should be obvious.

"What the fuck happened?" I ask, ignoring his sarcasm.

"Well, we had this brilliant idea of kidnapping Flash and taking him out to the woods, scare him a little, maybe get him to spill secrets about his boss. The weakest link is always easiest to break."

"So," I drawl out slowly. "What happened?" I growl when I hear him taking a gulp of something.

He clears his throat, before belching. I grimace, holding the phone away for a second. "He wasn't there, so we went to this cool pool bar."

I pinch the bridge of my nose. "Just get to the point, please."

"Craig, who heard about your attack and knew who the culprits were, messaged me. He said there was a raid at Flash's house last night and his sister was taken away by social services."

"Why?"

"Well, I called Dad's friend, Liam, to see if he could hack into the police database, and he said Flash was using her as a drug mule to bring drugs over from abroad."

"No fucking way?" I hiss out, my fists clenching. He used a young, vulnerable girl, who doesn't know right from wrong and who trusted him. When I did my checks, nothing in their relationship came up as suspicious. I didn't even see they'd been away, so they must have been using fake passports.

"Did they arrest him?" I ask slowly, wishing I took him out when I had the chance.

"No. The fucker saw all the police cars outside his flat and fucking ran by the sounds of it. No one has been able to find him. And that's not all. I don't know which one, but one of Rocco's goons have done a runner. We need to find out which one, something I'll do when I'm more fucking sober."

"What do you mean, *done a runner?*" I yell, feeling walls closing in around me. I slam my fist down on the top of my roof, denting the metal. They can't get away, not now, not when my revenge is almost complete. I need it to finish them all together, so they don't know what is happening around them.

"Fuck knows. I've got a feeling it's either Blaze or Rocket. Word on the street is Rocco was making them get his money back, and I don't think they could hack it. Rocco's pissed and out for blood."

"We have to find them," I growl.

"If Rocco doesn't find them first," he points out.

"I shouldn't have fucking waited," I snap.

"You did the right thing, bro. They might have swung those bats, but Rocco is the one who ordered it. They'll all get what's coming to them. They're no longer free men. We've got this, Landon. You just have to relax."

I scrub a hand down my face, leaning back against my car. "I need this revenge, Liam."

"I know. Just give me a few hours to sleep. I'm so fucking drunk still, and we had our last drink hours ago."

"All right. I need to go collect Rex and a bag of clothes. I'll be at the bed and breakfast if you need me."

He chuckles down the line. "Ahh, getting all domesticated. Is that where you are now?" he teases.

I clear my throat, looking around the eerie cemetery. "No, I'm at the cemetery."

"Bro," Liam whispers painfully. "You can't keep doing this to yourself."

"Liam—" I start, but he continues.

"You've got something good with Paisley. She's fuck all like her brothers— she's actually pretty fucking cool. She gave us permission to fuck with her brothers as long as it doesn't sabotage any of their businesses."

"Liam," I snap.

"And she's fucking hot for a nerdy chick. Just saying."

"Liam!" I yell.

He inhales. "Jesus, shut the fuck up. I've got a hangover."

"If you let me get a word in, you'd know I've come to say goodbye. For good."

"For reals?"

I groan. "I wish you wouldn't speak like that. It reminds me too much of Dad."

"Don't hate on me because I take after him," he chuckles. "And you're just pissed you can't pull it off."

"I'm going. I need to get my dog and a change of clothes."

"Talk later," he says through a yawn, before he cuts off the call.

I shake my head down at the phone. I want to go search for the fuckers, but I'm not leaving Paisley.

Last night, just before she passed out, she whispered she loved me. There's no way I'm going to play around with her feelings, not after getting her to forgive me a second time. I'm doing this right. Which is why I had to come this morning. I couldn't put it off any longer.

And going to collect Rex and my clothes, then getting back to her, is the right thing.

She needs to know she has me, all of me, and that I'm not going anywhere.

REX GROWLS AS I open the car door. I chuckle at him before grabbing my bag from the passenger side floor.

"You have to be the only dog who hates the cold," I mutter, locking the doors.

He moves slowly up to the door. He looks pitiful with the expressions he's been giving me since I grabbed his lead off the side. I went to take him for a walk before coming, but he was having none of it. He just sat there, whining.

I don't think he's a morning dog. He seemed grouchy and moody.

I let myself inside, and without being told, Rex begins to sniff his way to the stairs leading up to Paisley. I roll my eyes. Figures he'd get excited for her.

When we step inside the flat, I notice a few more boxes have been added and see a few empty ones.

My stomach sinks at the idea of her being gone. She promised to stay in bed, but by the looks of it, she didn't.

My steps are quick as I head up to the bedroom. My eyes widen when the door swings open, revealing a damp Paisley wrapped in a white, fluffy towel.

Holy fucking shit. My eyes must bug out because she begins to giggle, tucking the towel around her tighter. She bends down to pat Rex, who licks her for a few seconds before heading off into the corner where a rug is now placed.

"You're back." I nod, unable to find my words as I watch her rise from her knees, giving Rex an amused look. She turns back to me, tilting her head to the side, but all I can see are the globes of her breasts, water dripping down her pale, silky skin. "Are you just going to stand there and stare?"

I nod again, but then her giggle shakes me out of it. "I thought I told you to stay in bed," I say hoarsely, but when my eyes go to the bed, I find the mattress is no longer on the floor but on a frame.

"Mum came with the twins and put it up for me. She also brought me some essentials and clean clothes."

"I can see," I whisper, taking a step forward.

She doesn't move, gazing at me intently, like she's searching for something. "You seem different," she whispers, bending her neck right back to look up at me.

I run my fingers through her damp hair. "Yeah?"

"You look different too," she tells me, watching me harder, like she can't figure it out. "Has something happened?"

My fingers dig into her hip as I pull her to me. "Something will in about twenty seconds."

Her eyes spark as she presses against me. "Oh yeah, and what would that be?"

My lips pull up into a smirk as I quickly lift her. She squeals, laughing lightly when I walk her back to the bed.

"I'll show you," I declare huskily, coming down on top of her.

"Maybe we should do something productive, like eat. Mum said she'd bring us some food when you got back."

I arch an eyebrow at her. "You really want to eat right now?"

She bites her bottom lip. "Maybe not right now."

"Later," I promise her, kissing the corner of her mouth.

She exhales, her lips parting, making me inwardly smile. "Definitely later," she whispers back, sounding excited.

With those words still in the air, I undo the towel, letting it fall open as I lean down and take her lips in heated kiss, showing her, without words, just who she belongs to.

TWENTY-FIVE

PAISLEY

EVER SINCE LAST SATURDAY, LANDON has been different. There's been a change in him that transcends his behaviour or the way he dresses. It's something he's done within himself. He smiles more, laughs more, and I swear to God, he made a joke the other day in front of my brothers.

It's not a bad different, it's a good different. I guess I'm just waiting for the other shoe to drop. I've let myself hope for weeks now, but I'm worried that somewhere along the line, we'll lose what we have.

And I love him. I thought I loved him before, but my feelings back then are nothing compared to how I feel about him now. I know him now, more than I ever thought someone could, besides his family. I love the things he does for me, like how he makes me a cup of tea in the morning, or does a chore before I can, so I don't need to. And the way he listens, holds me… it's all overwhelming. The best kind.

And the sex… The sex is phenomenal, mind-blowing to be exact. But it isn't just that either, it's the way he can't keep his hands off me, even if it's a light touch or a kiss. It's like he can't get enough. There have been so many times the words, 'I love you', have wanted to spill out of my mouth. I want to say them desperately, but fear of rejection holds me back. I gave him all of me before; he knew how I felt. This time I promised I'd follow his lead, not expecting too much, so I wouldn't get hurt. A lot of good that did me.

"You okay?" Landon asks, squeezing my hand.

"She's probably daydreaming about you. She did it a lot in high school," Adam so unhelpfully confides.

I turn my narrowed gaze at him. "Remind me why I brought you again?"

He smirks. "Because you two have been fucking like rabbits and have been shitty best friends. This is your way of making it up to us," he reminds me.

My gaze softens, instantly feeling terrible. He ruffles my hair and moves forward. "She lives here?" he asks, looking around the cute cottage.

"Yeah," Landon says, frowning at Adam.

He admitted this morning that it's gonna take him time to get used to Adam. He finds it hard to be around him when he knows we've been intimate. Doesn't matter to him that Adam is gay. He even got annoyed when Rex fussed over him when he arrived, yet it's okay when Rex listened to Mum, who is watching him for the night.

Adam steps aside when we get to the front door. Instead of knocking, Landon pushes the handle down and walks in.

I hear him take in a breath, ready to call out, but a voice from down the hallway stops him.

"Yes, it was like, four inches. It didn't even touch the sides," Charlotte says softly.

I look up at Landon, feeling a little uncomfortable. His jaw hardens and his gaze narrows. He lets go of my hand, moving down the hall.

Adam meets my gaze, his eyes lit up with excitement. He takes my hand, pulling me down the hall when I try to refuse.

"Got to see this," he whispers.

We make it to the kitchen as Landon rips the phone from Charlotte's hand. She looks startled for a second, before she sees Landon.

"You made it," she gushes.

"Who the fuck is this?" he growls down the phone, his tone deadly. Even I shiver, but Charlotte just arches her eyebrow, looking adorably confused.

When his shoulders relax, I do. When he glances at us, he looks a little embarrassed. But when I hear him order pizzas, I begin to laugh, and a few seconds later, so does Adam. Landon glares at us, and it just makes us laugh harder.

He sheepishly hands the phone back to Charlotte.

"You were really rude at the start, Landon. Are you that hungry?"

"Think he just wanted to make sure you got a bigger pizza," Adam says, causing me to choke.

"Shut it!" Landon warns him, before his expression softens. "Sorry, thought it was someone else."

Her nose scrunches up. "Who else gives four inches?"

"My ex," Adam mutters. I chuckle at the glare Landon gives him, promising the next time he says something, he'll go for him.

"Hey, Charlotte," I say, interrupting the moment.

She smiles as she walks over to give me a hug. "Landon said you don't drink alcohol, and I know he won't drink whilst driving, so I got some fizzy pop. I tried to make some homemade lemonade, but Hayden accidently spilt it everywhere. I'm sorry. I didn't have time to get some more lemons."

"I'm sure whatever you've got is fine," I tell her, leaning back into Landon when he steps up behind me, wrapping his arms around my waist. I'll have to remember to thank Hayden later. I've tasted Charlotte's cooking and it's terrible. Though I'd never tell her that. She's just too damn kind, so I've never wanted to hurt her feelings.

She looks to where Landon's arms are around me, and her eyes take on a different light, glistening with tears that don't fall.

"I'm so happy you two are together," she says.

"Thank you."

"What movie did you pick?" Adam asks. "And please tell me you have snacks."

Charlotte, having never met Adam, steps over to hug him. "Hi, Adam, it's nice to meet you. I'd say I've heard so much about you—it's what people normally say when they meet someone—but I've not heard much about you at all. Only that you're Paisley's best friend, who she neglected," she rambles.

He grins, wrapping his arm around her shoulders. "She's fucking adorable. Me and you are totally gonna get along."

"No, you won't," Landon snaps out before facing Charlotte. "Did you buy or make the snacks?"

She bites her bottom lip, guilt spreading all over her face. "I had to buy them. Katnip has been taking up so much of my time, I didn't have chance to make anything. And I don't think she likes me cooking. She must feel left out, 'cause I made her some pork as a treat, and ever since, she gets a little upset when I start cooking."

"I'm sure it's not your cooking," Adam soothes. He doesn't know how terrible it is, but I don't correct him.

I bite my lip to stop myself from smiling. Landon grunts under his breath before letting me go to walk over to the fridge. He grabs a bunch of drinks, then picks up a Bud.

"Heads-up," he yells, just before he throws the unopened bottle to Adam.

I yell, "Adam," but it's too late. Adam's eyes widen as he reaches out, palms upwards. The bottle bounces off his hands and onto the floor.

I groan, closing my eyes before turning to Landon. "Never throw him anything. Ever. He has the worst coordination."

"Really?" Landon mutters, looking down at the mess.

Charlotte steps away, grabbing a dustpan and brush from the cupboard. "I've got it. I don't want Katnip to cut her paws."

"Here, let me. I made the mess; I'll clean it," Adam tells her, reaching for the dustpan and brush.

"I've got it," she tells him, moving it out of his way. He sighs, giving up.

"At least tell me there's something I can pick up and carry to the living room."

She smiles up at him. "There are some Doritos and a box of Roses on the top shelf," she says, gesturing to the cupboards on the opposite side of the kitchen.

He nods, heading over, and I turn my attention back to Landon as he steps up to me, handing me a bottle of Ribena.

"Thank you."

He grins down at me, pressing a kiss to my lips. "You're welcome," he whispers when he pulls back.

"They do that a lot according to Mama Hayes," Adam tells Charlotte, his arms weighed down with junk food.

"I like it. It's nice to see him so happy," Charlotte says, swooning. "I can't wait to have what they have."

"You can wait until you're about thirty," Landon mutters dryly.

She laughs. "You even make jokes now."

When she heads off into what I presume is the living room, Landon looks down at me, his forehead creased in confusion. "Did that seem like I was joking?"

I shrug. "I dunno anymore."

He looks back down the hallway. "I was being dead serious."

I giggle, taking his hand in mine and leading us out of the kitchen. "She's going to find someone eventually."

He grunts. "Not on my watch. People take advantage of her already. Imagine what some dickhead with no morals would do. I don't ever want to see her spirit broken."

Hearing him being so serious, I pause before the door Charlotte and Adam walked through. I place my hand on his chest, looking warmly up at him. "She wouldn't pick someone like that. It's Charlotte. And she has so many Carter's surrounding her, the poor schmuck wouldn't last five minutes."

"I just don't want her to get hurt," he grumbles.

I soften against him. "You really are just a big ol' teddy bear."

His eyes narrow into slits. "I am not!"

I grin bigger. "Yes, you really are. You have a big heart, Landon." The words *I love you* nearly spill out of me, and a look of disappointment flashes across his face. Before I can question it, he masks it, his eyes drooping when he looks down at me.

Leaning in, he takes my lips in another kiss, this time deepening it, and the taste of his tongue has me squeezing my thighs together.

"Are you two going to do this all night? It's a little uncomfortable," I vaguely hear Charlotte whisper loudly.

Adam begins to laugh, and I pull away, sighing. I was close to dragging him into another room, just so I could have him again. I'll never get enough of him.

Landon grins over my shoulder as he squeezes my hip. "We're coming."

"I thought we could watch Transformers," Charlotte tells us as we follow her into the living room.

"Sounds good," Landon replies. He halts me from sitting down on the two-seater sofa and unzips my coat. "Mum always said to take your coat off inside, otherwise you'll be cold when you go out."

I grin up at him and mouth, "Softy."

I watch as he walks around the sofa to the table and chairs, draping our coats over the back.

The second he's back, he pulls me into his arms and we take a seat. I snuggle up to him, and the sensation of being overwhelmingly happy consumes me. No one should be this happy, but I am. Life can't get better than this.

Every moment we share feels like a new experience.

"Do you have a girlfriend?" I hear Charlotte ask when my foggy brain begins to clear.

Landon tenses beneath me. "Why do you want to know that?"

Her smile is blinding. "I was going to ask him out, so we could double date. Maybe then we could spend more time together."

"No, you aren't," he growls, but Charlotte just rolls her eyes, not even the least bit affected.

Adam, however, looks a tad uncomfortable, which makes me kind of happy. "U-um, under any other circumstances, I'd take you up on it, Charlie, but I'm gay."

"Her name's Charlotte," Landon bites out.

Charlotte practically bounces in her seat, a look of excitement and wonder all over her expression. "Are you really?"

Looking worried at the turn of events, Adam slowly nods. I know why he's sceptical of her reaction. Most girls, at this point, go into the reasons why they think they can change his mind and make him turn straight. It's kind of hilarious to watch, but not so much fun for Adam, who has to rebuff their advances.

She pauses the movie that hasn't even started. "I have so many questions. I'm—I mean, a friend is thinking about writing a male, male romance novel, but she doesn't have any gay friends. She doesn't want to upset the LGBT community by writing something offensive."

"Charlotte," Landon groans.

Adam, relaxing back into the sofa, smiles at her. "What kind of questions?"

I didn't think it was possible, but she gets even more excited. When her face begins to flush, I worry she's going to faint.

"When did you know you were gay? How long did it take you to tell your parents? Have you ever had sex with a girl? And did it hurt the first time you were with a man? During research, I was told by a lot of women that the bum sex hurts a lot. Most stay away from it," she rushes to explain. Adam opens his mouth, believing the line of questioning is over, but it seems that Charlotte has only just begun. "And how did you know what to do? I mean, I read a lot so I kind of know, but put a male in front of me and I'll probably forget. I am excited for sex, though. A lot of women said it's pleasurable, but a majority said they take care of themselves. Whatever that means, right? Do you have a boyfriend?"

Adam chuckles. "Take a breath."

Her shoulders relax a little. "Sorry, I just don't want to leave anything out. Wait a minute, let me just get a pen and paper."

She rushes out of the room and Adam turns to us with wide eyes. "Who gave that midget speed?"

I laugh so hard my entire body shakes.

"You tell her you had sex with Paisley, and I'll fucking rip your dick off," Landon warns as we hear Charlotte rummaging somewhere close by.

Adam's gaze turns horrified, and he gives me an accusing look. "Would it make you feel better if you've touched my dick too? There's no need to get jealous," he says, trying to lighten the mood.

When Landon goes to stand, I push him back down, tilting his head to face me. "Kiss me."

His body softens, and he leans down, capturing my lips in a kiss. I moan quietly, flicking my tongue against his.

"It really is awkward," Charlotte mutters dryly. I chuckle against Landon's lips before pulling back.

Our attention turns to Charlotte, who sits cross-legged, notepad and pen in hand. "Okay, start from the beginning. I want to know when you knew you were gay, and how."

"I guess as a teenager. All my friends were obsessed with girls, pointing out body parts they thought were banging."

Charlotte's nose twitches. "Why would a body part bang?"

Landon chuckles under his breath.

"It means hot, sexy, or something that turned them on," Adam answers.

She shakes her head in bewilderment. "Why don't they just say that?" she murmurs, before taking a deep breath. "Never mind. So, you knew young. Did you ever fancy another boy?"

"I did, yeah. I always found myself attracted to them."

She nods. "I can understand that. I'm attracted to them too." Adam chuckles at her abruptness. "Were you ever with a girl—you know, to check? At that age, it can be confusing."

"Charlotte, stop interrogating him," Landon tells her softly.

Her eyes meet Landon's before she turns back to Adam. "Am I being rude? I can't really tell."

Warily, Adam looks over his shoulder at Landon, looking torn on what to do or say. "U-um, no, you're good. And yes, I did."

"Did you lose your virginity to a boy or a girl?" she asks, the light back in her eyes.

Landon's body goes rigid, and his grip on my waist tightens.

Adam gulps, shifting in his seat. I have to admit, even I'm a little uncomfortable. Aside from Landon and Mum, no one knows what happened between me and Adam. I'd like to keep it that way.

"I lost it to a girl, but let's not talk about that."

Charlotte, not feeling the tension in the room, just continues to smile. "That's okay, we can get to the bum sex now."

"Can you please stop calling it that," he says, chuckling.

She tilts her head to the side. "What else can I call it?"

"Sex?" he answers through a choked laugh.

"Seems a little plain, but what do I know; I'm a virgin," she tells him, clapping her hands together. "Did you put your penis inside his bum hole, or did he put his penis in yours?"

Adam, being in the middle of taking a sip of his drink, begins to choke. I laugh from the horror, and Landon mutters curses under his breath.

"Where's the damn food?" he yells, making us all jump.

"Quiet, I want to know," she tells Landon, scanning his expression. "You've got the same look you get when we go to the strip club."

It's my turn to tense. "You go to a strip club?" I ask slowly, facing him. A dull ache takes up residence in my chest.

Why would he go there?

"No. Yes. No," he says, looking panicked. "It was before, and it isn't what you think."

"He's right. He didn't get a dance either, and I offered to pay. It was quite arousing," Charlotte explains.

Landon turns bright red, groaning loudly. "I didn't need to know that."

Charlotte bites her lip. "Too much information again?"

"Yes," he nods tightly.

"You went to a strip club with your cousin?" Adam asks, his eyes round. "Dude, what were you thinking?"

"It was for research," Charlotte blurts out. "For a friend."

"For a friend?" Adam repeats, looking doubtful.

"A strip club?" I ask Landon, still upset. None of what she has said has made me feel better. Does he still go? I look nothing like those kinds of girls. I pull on my T-shirt self-consciously.

"It really isn't what you think. And I've not been since we—you know, the first time," he whispers quietly. I relax, but the thought of him being around them leaves something sour in my mouth.

"He found out what I was doing and got really mad. He wouldn't let me go on my own, even though I told him I'd be fine. The only strip club we have is in the bad side of town. The place was quite posh, but outside it was kind of rough-looking. And he looked pained the entire time we were there."

Hearing Charlotte's explanation has me melting into Landon's side. "You really are the biggest softy ever. You look out for so many people, protect them. I don't get how you think you have a darkness inside of you, Landon Carter. All I see is light," I tell him, not caring who hears.

His gaze heats with desire, his mouth opening but no words come out. Without glancing away, he says, "Charlotte, I'm really sorry, but we have to go. I promise to make it up to you."

I hear a sniffle and turn to investigate, afraid we've upset Charlotte. She waves us off, wiping her nose with the sleeve of her top.

"You two go. Me and Adam are fine," she says, before her glistening eyes turn to me. "Thank you."

A lump forms in my throat at her words and the intensity behind them. All I can do is nod.

When Landon doesn't say anything as he grabs our coats, I begin to worry I've upset him somehow.

TWENTY-SIX

LANDON

THE DRIVE BACK TO THE BED AND BREAKFAST is quiet. I'm tense, but it's only because I'm about to lay myself bare. I'm scared I'll fuck it up, or she'll say she hasn't forgiven me.

For a while now, I've kept thinking she's about to tell me she loves me again. The words never come, but I can see them in the air, waiting to be said.

The outdoor lights are on as we pull up outside. The place has come along nicely, and with only a few small things left to do and the sign above the door to be delivered and fitted, she's ready to launch her website. Bailey is coming tomorrow to help her.

I shut the car off, taking a deep breath as I find my bearings.

"Landon, I didn't mean to upset you," she tells me quietly. She sounds unsure, and it breaks my heart. What she said to me hit me in a place I never thought I had. The heart. It meant more to me than she'll ever realise, but I'm hoping I can show her enough, so she gets an inkling.

"You didn't upset me, Paisley," I tell her roughly.

"Then why did we leave?"

"How can you see me like that, after everything I've done? I cancelled on Freya and it got her killed. I kicked you out of my car, got you pregnant, then most likely was the reason you lost our baby."

She sighs, undoing her seatbelt so she can turn to face me. "Because I look beyond the surface, Landon. I see you—the real you. You might be ruthless when it comes to your family, but it is done with love. You went to a strip club with your female cousin, just so she could do some research. I can't even get into the list of stuff you have done for me, and I don't just mean with the bed and breakfast either. And you didn't cause me to miscarry, Landon. For ages I blamed myself for my body being defective, but I realised it happens every day, to thousands of women, and there's nothing you can do to prevent it. You have a heart of gold, Landon. Please see it," she stresses. "I love you for who you are. I love you so much that it kills me to think of losing you."

My lips part, and I feel the back of my eyes begin to burn. "How? How can you love me?"

She takes my hand in hers, her eyes glistening with tears. "Because maybe all the best love stories begin with second chances. I love you, Landon. All of you. I love you in spite of your quirks and faults. You were my dream as a teenager, but you're my everything as a woman."

I wipe the lone tear that falls down her cheek. "I love you, too, Paisley. So goddamn much."

Her surprised gasp has me holding her closer. "You do?"

"More than I've ever loved anybody. I can't live without you."

She leans over the parking break, pulling my head down for a kiss, before a sob tears through her throat.

"You really love me?" she chokes out.

I chuckle, running my fingers through her hair. "I do; so much."

She looks up, her lashes wet from tears. Before I have chance to reach for her, she's kneeling on her seat before moving to straddle me. She kisses me, and I taste her tears on her lips.

I grip her hair, tilting my lips and taking the kiss deeper. My mind is whirling with sensations, passion taking over, making me ache for more. Her hips rolling has me moaning deep in my throat. I'm hard as a fucking rock and likely to blow my load if I don't get inside her soon.

I push my hands inside her coat, reaching under her T-shirt. I slide them up her delicate ribs before cupping her breasts. She arches into me, moving closer as her breaths come in shallow pants.

I pull away, pressing light kisses to the corner of her mouth and along her jaw, before trailing my tongue down her neck. She makes a mewling sound in the back of her throat.

"Let's take this inside before one of my brothers turn up," she pants out.

I tense at the thought of anyone seeing her like this, even her arsehole brothers.

My eyes inch open, finding her watching me. "Let's go," I say roughly, opening the car door. She giggles, lifting herself off my lap, causing me to groan painfully at the loss. As soon as I'm out, I press the lock for the car and grab her around the waist. She laughs, throwing her head back, and it's the best sound in the world.

With her legs wrapped tightly around me, I head up to the front door, kissing her soundly on the lips.

"Keys are in my back pocket," she tells me breathlessly.

I slide my hand into her back pocket, feeling the keys with the tips of my fingers. Instead of grabbing them, I squeeze her tight arse. She moans, rocking against me.

Sliding the keys out, I open the front door before kicking it shut behind me.

She begins to trail kisses down my neck, her tongue sneaking out to lick a path up to my ear, and it's driving me fucking wild. When I reach the bottom of the stairs, I can't take it anymore and slam her back against the door.

I kiss her hard, swallowing her gasp of surprise. She lets her coat fall off her shoulders, giving me a sexy grin.

I grin back, pressing my hard-on into her. She loses her smile, a low moan erupting.

When I lean back, I grip the bottom of her T-shirt and pull it off in one swift motion. Her face fills with heat as I lean down, kissing the globes of her breasts.

"Landon," she moans, gripping my hair enough to pull it.

I groan, lifting my head up to look at her. "I'm kind of at a disadvantage from here. I want you naked," she says huskily.

Smirking, I nod, and begin carrying her up the stairs, my gaze straying to the sway of her breasts.

The second we're in her bedroom, I rip my coat off my body, never taking my lips away from hers as I walk her backwards to the bed. She falls backwards when the back of her knees hit the mattress. I look down at her, smiling.

"I love you."

Her gaze softens. "I love you too."

I reach down, taking her foot and pulling off her boot. I do the same with the other, never taking my eyes off her.

A shiver runs through me when I pull off my shirt. She sits up, undoing the button on my jeans, her eyes round with excitement. I've never seen a more beautiful sight.

She grabs the sides of my jeans, pulling both my jeans and boxers down in one swift motion.

I arch an eyebrow, and she shrugs. "I want you."

Kicking off my shoes, I don't waste time removing my jeans and boxers. I lean over her, kissing her deeply, and she moans.

Thankful she's wearing leggings, I pull them down and throw them across the room. Her bra is the last to go, and then she's naked before me.

I'll never get over how magnificent her body is. She's beautifully sculptured.

"So beautiful," I croak, taking her nipple into my mouth. She falls back down onto the mattress, and I follow, flicking her nipple with my tongue.

Wrapping my arm around her back, I lift her a touch before pulling her up the bed. I settle myself on top of her as she loops her arms around my neck.

"Inside of me, now," she whispers.

"I need to get a condom," I tell her.

"I'm on the pill. I have been since…" she trails off, her expression clouded. She means since she lost the baby.

I sit up, running my hands down her body. She lavishes in the attention.

"So, I can be inside you, nothing between us?" I ask to clarify, my voice deeper.

She nods, still looking a little lost. I'm about to get her back on track, and I do when my fingers run through her wet heat.

She moans, her hips arching towards me. *Always so responsive.*

"Don't play with me. I need you," she cries out.

"So demanding," I whisper, leaning down to kiss her.

"Landon," she groans when I rub myself against her.

The blood rushes into my ears as I thrust inside her without warning. She cries out, her nails digging into my back. I throw my head back, letting out a moan. Nothing has ever felt so good. My passion and need for her is all consuming.

Her legs cling tightly around me, her heels digging into my arse as she pushes up to meet my thrusts, her hips rolling. I grunt, feeling out of my depth. There are too many sensations running through me, too many thoughts, too many feelings. It all comes out in one burst as I thrust back into her harder.

I grip her hair before capturing her lips in a heated kiss. She pants against me as I thrust harder, pleasure rippling through me. I build up a steady rhythm, feeling her walls close around me. My entire body tingles, and my dick throbs inside her.

"Landon," she cries out, and I feel her tighten around me once again. I thrust faster, needing her more than I've ever needed anyone. I cup her cheek as sweat runs down my back and temples.

This is going to be over before it started. Thinking quickly, I switch positions. She squeals at the sudden change, now looking down at me in shock. I smirk up at her, gripping her hips to keep her moving. Lifting her arse, she comes back down on me hard, throwing her head back as a cry escapes her lips.

I reach up with one hand, rolling her nipple between my fingers. She moves faster, coming down on me and rolling her hips like she can't get enough.

The new angle doesn't do anything to ward off my upcoming orgasm. Instead, it's allowing me to go deeper, more pleasure rippling through me every time her tight pussy clenches around me.

"Fuck, you feel too fucking good," I croak out, thrusting up hard. She moans loudly, her fingers digging into my pecs. "I'm not going to last."

"I'm so close," she rasps, moving faster and harder as her eyes squeeze shut.

Every nerve in my system begins to spark and flicker, and I tighten my fingers on her hips. I reach between her legs, rubbing my thumb through her wetness before circling her clit.

"Landon," she cries out, tightening around me. I sit up, grabbing her hips and moving her up and down my dick.

Her pussy spasms around me, and when she opens her eyes, her gaze is hooded with lust.

"Another," I grit out, trying to hold off my own.

"I don't think I can," she moans as she keeps on moving.

I take her lips in a kiss, moving her up and down as I force another orgasm out of her. I can feel her pussy clenching around me, so I know she's close.

She takes me by surprise when she bites my bottom lip before sucking it into her mouth. The action undoes me, and I thrust harder, feeling her pussy convulse around me. My orgasm hits me like a train, more powerful than ever before. Clenching my eyes shut, I speed up her movements, drawing out our orgasms until she's milked all of me.

I slump down when I feel her finish. She comes down on top of me, exhausted and breathing hard. She moves to roll off, but I hold her tighter against my chest, needing the closeness.

A small smile graces my lips as I kiss the top of her head. I'm completely done. My muscles feel like jelly as I try to catch my breath.

She sighs contently above me. "That was amazing," she breathes out, kissing my chest.

I run my fingers up and down her back, keeping my eyes closed. "That's what heaven feels like."

I feel her lift her head, and opening one eye, I find her watching me. "Please don't ever leave me," she whispers.

I pull her higher, moaning when I slip out of her and her breasts brush against my chest. I kiss her briefly before staring into her eyes.

"I'll *never* leave you. I might be strong, but I'll never be strong enough to walk away," I tell her fiercely.

She melts against me. "You say the sweetest things," she whispers, her eyes glistening again.

"Hey, don't cry," I tell her, running my fingers along the side of her face.

She laughs through her sniffles. "I don't mean to be such a baby, but sometimes it's hard to believe this is real. I never thought you'd love someone like me."

Her honesty is like a knife through the chest. And I should know, since I've had a knife sliced through me.

"You're the only person who could have made me love again, Paisley. It's everything you do, everything you are," I tell her, then to lighten the mood, add, "And you're seriously fucking hot."

She giggles against my chest. "You're such a goof," she tells me, before she loses some of her smile. "Where do we go from here?"

"What do you mean?" I ask, genuinely confused.

She runs her finger through the crease between my eyes. "Don't go getting broody. I guess I'm asking if, um—if you'd… God, this is stupid. Forget I said anything."

"No, go on, tell me."

"No, it doesn't matter."

I groan because I hate it when Charlotte and Hayden do this to me. "Paisley," I warn.

She moans into my chest before meeting my gaze again. "I just… I mean, you stay here a lot. Practically live here with Rex," she starts, her cheeks flushing.

Wait. Does she want me to leave, to not stay over again?

"You don't want me here?" I ask, a foreign feeling of hurt hitting me.

She groans. "No. Yes. I mean… Oh God. You've finished my house, and all my stuff is moved in here now. I was just wondering if you'd share it with me. I mean, for good. Like you and Rex permanently. Permanently, meaning you'd have to get rid of your flat."

I'm monumentally stunned. When her face falls, I can see where her thoughts have taken her and cup her cheek.

"I'd love to move in with you. I thought I already had," I tell her, shrugging. "I just haven't gotten around to getting all of my stuff.

"Really?" she asks, hope blossoming in her eyes. "Wait! You already moved in? When?"

I chuckle under my breath at her expression. "The morning after we first stayed over. I went home to grab a bag. I knew then I wasn't leaving. I let Drew have my flat."

"You did?"

I nod, grinning. "Yeah. He's been boxing my stuff up for me. I thought we could keep your stuff and let him keep mine. I'll just need my clothes and shit."

"You do?"

She looks kind of spaced out, but it could be because she's overwhelmed with excitement. I can never tell. "Or I could walk around naked."

Snapping out of it, she glares up at me. "When were you going to tell me?"

I rear back in shock. "Uh, tell you what?"

"That you moved in," she yells.

"Baby, I thought you already knew."

"Well, I didn't," she snaps, before softening her gaze. "I'm sorry. I've been worried sick about how to ask you, and all along you had moved in."

"Why don't we go get cleaned up and I'll make it up to you in the shower?" I offer, running my fingers through her hair.

Her gaze turns hooded. "Promise?"

Grabbing her around the waist, I lift us. She squeals, clinging to me as she begins to laugh. "You need to stop doing that," she demands through laughter.

"Never." I grin, throwing her over my shoulder. I slap her arse as I walk us over to the shower.

TWENTY-SEVEN

PAISLEY

I**T FEELS LIKE MY FEET ARE** barely touching the floor I'm bursting with so much joy. The bed and breakfast is pretty much complete. All that's left is putting up the signs Landon ordered. The place looks freaking fantastic. More than fantastic. It looks like something out of the movies. Everywhere I look, something new will catch my eye and I'll be awed. My vision of the place has become a reality, and it's a dream. A dream I never want to wake up from.

Everything in my life is bliss.

All the bits and bobs I bought to add more character to the place… they've worked out perfectly. Everything has a place, and they own it; nothing else would have gone as nicely.

Yesterday, I hired four maids, a receptionist, and two waitresses until business really kicks off. The cook I hired a while back even came in with more breakfast foods for us to taste. Landon had already eaten half of it when my brothers conveniently popped in and finished the rest. It means a lot that he's trying with them and didn't get *too* baited by their little digs.

Today, though, is the day Bailey's arriving to take the final pictures and launch my website. She'll also sit down with me and show me how everything works for bookings and stuff.

It's all a whirlwind. I'm ready to have guests—desperate for them, even.

I finish making up the last room, the red and brown sheets bringing more warmth to the space. The rooms all have a television, a phone to call reception, and a kettle with sachets of tea, coffee and hot chocolate next to it. On the dressing tables are some little business cards, postcards with pictures from the farm, and a pen for guests to keep. We have mini soaps, shampoos and conditioners in the bathrooms, along with thick, fluffy white towels. The dressing robes I ordered with a bargain discount should be arriving in the morning, along with matching slippers. All in all, everything is prefect.

I beam as I look around the room. I never thought this dream would become a reality. And tomorrow night, I will get to show my family, along with Landon's, just how perfect this place is. It's also the perfect opportunity for our families to meet officially.

Hearing a car, I race to the window, seeing a taxi pull into the drive. I squeal escapes my lips as I rush away from the window, giving the room one last glance before I leave.

The wide stairs with dark wooden banisters come into view, and I run down them, excited for the magic to happen.

The car door is slamming shut when I open the front door. Bailey walks around to the other side of the taxi, and my eyebrows scrunch up in confusion as the taxi driver goes to the back of the car.

When I see her holding a little girl—who I'm presuming is Sunday—and struggling to pull a car seat out of the car, I rush down to help.

"Here, let me," I say, taking the changing bags from her arms.

"Thank you," she sighs with relief. "Aiden thinks it's a necessity to pack pretty much everything this little one owns."

I laugh because the bags are even weighed down. There must be loads in these bags.

"Here you go, love," the taxi driver calls, pushing the pushchair towards us.

"Thank you," she tells him, quickly strapping Sunday in. When she's done, she reaches out for one of the bags. "I'll shove that one under the pram. It only has spares and more spares inside." I hand her the other two bags when she reaches for them, my mind blown by how efficiently she moves. She's a natural, setting everything in place like she's done this her whole life. A pang of jealously hits me, and I try to tamper it down, looking away from her.

She stands up, exhaling. "Right, I'm ready," she says, then looks up for the first time. Her eyes go round as she takes in the bed and breakfast behind me. "Wow! It looks like something out of a magazine. You know, the places you want to go but can never find in real life?"

I laugh, nodding. "Thank you. Would you like to come inside?"

"God yes! If it's as good as the outside, I can't wait to see. I swear, I'm coming back if it snows this year and taking more photos. Make sure no one ruins it before I get here," she gushes, still looking around with excitement. "Just think of how this will look at Christmas."

Finally, someone who has the same vision as me. My brothers don't see what I see. Only a handful of people do, and it makes me happy Bailey is one of them.

"I've already ordered loads of decorations. My brother has them in storage for me. And I can't wait to put in a real Christmas tree. I want it to be huge," I tell her as we walk inside. I hear her inhale, and I smile to myself.

"This place is beautiful, Paisley. Your family must be so proud of you."

I blush a little under her praise. "They are."

She shakes her head in wonder. "I can't get over this."

"Did you want me to show you around?" I ask, then look down at the pushchair.

She grimaces. "Sorry. Aiden had to go into work today. His uncle Mason is short staffed. I didn't think about getting the pushchair around."

"It's fine," I tell her, waving off her concerns. "You go look around, do what you've got to do, and me and Sunday will wait here. I'm gonna make a hot chocolate first though. Would you like one?"

She licks her lips. "I'd love a coffee if you have some."

"I do." I flick my head towards the dining room. She follows behind me as I head to the kitchen.

"I've got the website all set up. The only thing I have left is to drag the pictures from today into the boxes and hit launch. Are you excited?"

I glance over my shoulder, beaming at her. "Like you wouldn't believe. It's like I'm constantly walking on air. I keep picturing guests sitting by the fireplace, kids running down the hallway to get to breakfast," I tell her wistfully. "Another part of me is scared shitless it's going to turn to shit."

She rubs her palm up and down my arm. "Don't think like that. I'm telling you, if I had to choose between this place and some hotel, it would be this every single time. What you've built here is going to be amazing, and something you can pass down."

I look away at her last comment, not wanting her to know how much her words have affected me, and concentrate on making the drinks.

"Thank you, Bailey."

I offer her the mug of coffee. She takes it from my hand, glancing around the kitchen. "This place really is beautiful."

I snort. "You live in a mansion."

Her lips twitch in amusement. "It's not a mansion. It's just a really big house."

"How are you and Aiden now you're living together?"

"He's loving my gran and granddad being there. I think he gets a kick out of all the fuss he gets from Gran and the lady who lives next door."

"I thought they moved out?"

She nods after finishing her sip of coffee. "They have. We've been swamped with work, and Sunday has been having a rough time with teething. They saw the toll it was taking on us and showed up a few days ago to help out for a few weeks."

"That's so sweet of them. My granddad is moving to town. Finally," I stress out. "I've not been able to see the new house he bought yet, but Mum said it was suitable for him. Grandparents are the best."

"That they are, Paisley, that they are," she says. "Right, I'm going to get this done before little miss wakes up."

"We'll wait in the foyer for you," I tell her as I finish my hot chocolate by adding a few marshmallows.

My eyes close, feeling in heaven when I take a sip. It's been so long since I had one.

With my cup in one hand, I grab the handle of the pushchair in the other and exit the kitchen, manoeuvring Sunday past the table and chairs and into the foyer.

I take a seat in the reading chair, tucking my legs under me. Sunday sleeps peacefully, her lips shaped into a pout. I smile. She's so beautiful, so innocent. I can't look away from her.

My throat burns with emotion as I continue to stare at her. I'm jealous of both Aiden and Bailey for having this, for having her. I rub the ache that has started to form in my stomach.

Sunday stirring has me straightening in my chair. She twitches, and I watch as her beautiful face scrunches up seconds before she begins to cry.

Fuck!

I look towards the stairs, hoping Bailey has heard her cries, but no such luck. She's probably on the top floor taking photos.

I stand, looking down into the pram, nerves fluttering in my stomach. "Shh, baby girl. It's okay," I soothe. She cries louder, and automatically I reach for her clip to get her out.

My entire body tenses when I hold her, and I feel the ground give out beneath me. I drop down into the chair, feeling my breath freeze in my lungs. She quietens, sucking her thumb into her mouth.

I blink back tears, feeling the world spinning around me as I hold the most precious little girl in the world.

I don't look up when the door to the bed and breakfast opens. It's probably Mum coming in to see how the pictures are going.

Sunday's hand reaches up to cup my jaw, and a tear falls down my cheek.

"I've finished work for the day, so I went and got us some lunch," Landon's voice rumbles. I'm startled to hear it's him and suck my bottom lip into my mouth to stop the sob rising up my throat. "Baby, what's wrong?"

When I don't say anything, he kneels in front of me. He glances down at Sunday, his expression softening as he reaches out to stroke her cheek. "Why do you have Sunday?"

"Aiden has to work. Bailey's upstairs taking photos," I whisper, my throat feeling raw.

"Do you want me to have her?" he asks, always so attentive.

I pull her a little closer. "No, I'm fine."

He reaches up, cupping my jaw. I lean into his touch as I taste the salt on my lips.

"No, you're not."

I open my eyes and glance at him, feeling my lower lip tremble. "I'm never going to be able to do this. I'll never hold our baby. I shouldn't still be grieving, should I? I thought I had made peace with it, come to terms with the fact that I no longer carry the life we made inside of me. But there are moments when I forget," I explain.

"You forget?" he rumbles, his own voice filled with emotion.

"I forget I lost her. I'll wake up in the morning, and for a few short moments I forget and reach out to rub my stomach, wanting to be close to our baby. Then reality slaps me in the face and I remember it all. I remember what it was like to wake up and be told the baby didn't make it," I choke out, feeling more tears run down my face. "But it wasn't until now, until this moment, that I truly realised what I lost. I didn't just miss out on the big things like our baby's first Christmas, Halloween or birthday. I've missed out on a lifetime of happy moments. I'll always wonder what my life would have been like had I not lost our baby. What I would be like as a mum."

"Hey," he says, wiping under my eyes. "You can still be a mum, Paisley."

I shake my head sadly. "How? My diabetes might not prevent me from getting pregnant, but I don't think I could go through losing another baby. And the chances are high with diabetes," I tell him, then look down at Sunday. "I'll never get to do this with our child, Landon."

He clears his throat. "Yeah, we will."

I look up, tilting my head in confusion. "Do you not understand what I'm telling you? I can't lose another baby. I can't. There's this gaping hole in my heart that can never be filled."

He sighs, leaning up to kiss my forehead. "Yes, I did. But there are plenty of ways to have children. Paisley, I ask this in the most sensitive way I can; is this something you want *right now*?"

Do I want children now? After losing the baby, no. Somehow it would feel like I was replacing them. I loved my child, loved them before I even met them, and I was excited. Becoming a mum wasn't something I planned, but when I found out I was pregnant, it was all I wanted to be. It was bizarre. I went from wanting kids when I was older, to being pregnant and unable to stop planning. I planned for everything but names. It didn't feel right when Landon hadn't even been told.

"In the future, yes."

He relaxes slightly. "Good, because I'm not ready to share you. Between Midnight and Rex, I feel kind of left out."

Laughing, I wipe my cheeks with the sleeve of my cardigan. A thought occurs to me, and it's something I should have asked him already. "Landon, if I were still pregnant, what would you do?"

He loses some of his colour. "Do you want the truth?"

I can feel my blood pressure rising, my heart shuddering in my chest. "Always," I tell him. Sunday fusses a little, so I start to sway slightly, with her in my arms.

Landon scrubs a hand over his face. "Back then I was messed up. I don't know if I would have been a good dad, but I would have been there for you every step of the way. I'd have done everything asked of me. Never forget that," he tells me, almost demanding I don't. I nod, lifting Sunday a little higher. "When it came out you lost the baby, it hurt, and I felt the loss. But I don't think I'm feeling that loss the same way you are. I'm sorry, so fu—" he looks down at Sunday, grimacing. "I'm sorry."

I reach up to run my fingers through his hair. "Don't be. Grief can't be measured; it's not a competition. I love you, Landon."

"I love you too," he whispers, leaning up to capture my lips. I kiss him back, flicking my tongue against his.

He pulls back, his expression pained. "I can't get turned on right now."

I raise an eyebrow. "Huh? Why?"

He eyes flick down, a smirk pulling at his lips. I follow his gaze, laughing lightly when I see Sunday looking up at him with big doe-eyes.

Landon wipes the tears from my cheeks, giving me an attentive smile. "Feeling better?"

I nod. "Some. I guess I'll always have moments where I feel the loss stronger than other times. It just really hit me, holding her."

"We'll have kids, Paisley, but there's no rush. We're young. You've just built a bed and breakfast, and I'm thinking of going into business with Drew."

Excitement strums through my body. "Are you really?"

He chuckles at my expression. "If he still lets me work part-time with Maddox, then yes, I will. I think I need the balance of the two. Plus, I will get to spend more time with you. Maddox tends to send me and Mark for the out of town jobs. Now I won't have to."

"Oh, Landon, that is awesome," I gush, happy things are coming along. Then something hits me. Something he said. "Wait, you actually picture us together that long?"

He arches an eyebrow at me. "Don't you? I thought all girls did that shit."

I smack his bicep lightly, giggling. "Not all girls. And yes, I have, but I'm surprised you think that far ahead."

"I'm not finding a compliment in that comment," he teases, then leans in closer. "I'll let you in on secret."

"What's the secret?" I ask, feeling lighter as I brush my lips against his.

"Our parents—mine and my cousins'—they started a curse."

"A curse?" I ask sceptically, trying to gauge whether he's being serious or not.

"Yep, curse. Let me finish," he scolds playfully. "Malik started it, from what I remember. It could be Mason, we're not sure." He shakes his head before getting back on track. "All of them have loved one woman. And they're still married to those women. Sickeningly so. But as soon as Malik confessed his love for my aunt Harlow, the domino effect went into play. Everyone began to slowly pair off, finding women they loved. They had children, got married, and the rest is history. But then Faith had to go and fall in love with the copper, and now those two are getting married."

Realisation dawns on me. "The domino effect," I muse.

He nods, a grin pulling at his lips. "The domino effect," he repeats. "Aiden was next to fall, then it was me."

"And this has to do with you planning a future?" I ask, a little confused.

He grins now, flashing his white teeth at me. God, when he smiles like that, butterflies flutter in my stomach. "It has everything to do with it. Because you, Paisley Hayes… I plan to spend the rest of my life with you."

My heart stutters for a second, before beating wildly against my chest. "I'm your domino," I whisper, overwhelmed.

"You're *my forever*," he declares as his gaze darkens with need.

It's hard to tear my gaze away from his, but I manage, looking down at Sunday with a sigh. "Do you think Bailey would mind if we gave her back, so we can sneak off?"

Landon laughs, and my eyes widen when I find Bailey standing at the bottom of the staircase, an amused grin on her face.

"Don't mind me," she tells us with amusement. "I'll come back later. Aiden wants us to pop in for a bit while it's quiet. I'll sort the pictures out and come back later when Aiden finishes work. That sound good?"

Landon's gaze doesn't draw away from mine. "Sounds perfect."

TWENTY-EIGHT

LANDON

I SHAKE OUT MY HANDS, HOPING IT WILL somehow get rid of my fucking nerves. Mum and Dad will be arriving any minute. They got stuck in traffic while picking up Charlotte.

Paisley tucks her arm under my shoulder, wrapping her other arm around my waist to shield herself from the cold night air. I pull her close, kissing the top of her head.

"My brothers and Hayden are arguing again," she tells me.

I chuckle. "She can handle herself."

Noises from behind us catch my attention. "All I'm saying is how do you know I have a small dick if you've never seen it," Reid snaps, pouting.

I groan. Why do men constantly ask her that question? It makes me feel sick every time she answers.

I turn to find her cocking her hip to the side, and I wish she'd worn something different. She's wearing leather trousers, so tight they must be fucking hurting her, and a black tank top that I'm pretty sure she picked up in the wrong size. It's showing too much fucking flesh, and she refused to take the jackets me and Liam offered, saying her jacket was warm enough.

She blinks up at him as she runs her finger down his chest. "Because, dickhead, your jeans are as tight as mine, and I thought that to be impossible. There's no bulge. Trust me, it's small. I've probably swallowed bigger pills."

"Hayden," I groan, just as headlights coming down the path hit us.

She looks innocently at me. "What?"

I shake my head but keep a wary eye on Reid as he grits his teeth. "My dick is a fucking monster. It would rock your world."

Hayden rolls her eyes. "Puh-lease, you talk about your dick like it's your best friend. The only thing you can probably do is toss yourself off."

"Can you stop talking about your dick?" I snap.

He turns his hateful gaze towards me. "I didn't bring it up. She was staring."

Hayden is walking towards us but stops to look over her shoulder at him. "It's not nice to be objectified, is it? You shouldn't have been staring at my fucking tits."

"Reid Hayes, I taught you better than that," Liza, Paisley's mum, scolds.

Hayden's smirking when she turns back around, and Reid is bright red, looking anywhere but at his Mum.

"Mum, Dad," Hayden calls out, grinning.

"My princess," Dad calls back, making Hayden snort as she passes us.

"Hey, thank you so much for coming," Paisley greets, leaning in to hug Mum and Charlotte.

I'm about to pull her back, but Dad gives me a smirk over her head, and before I can warn him, he picks her up into a bear hug, swinging her around. "How's my Tay-Tay loving bestie?"

She giggles. "Still rocking the tunes, Mr Carter."

He puts her down, rubbing the top of her head. "Call me Max, sweetheart. Mr Carter makes me feel like some old, rich dickhead who can't wipe his own arse."

She laughs again and wisely steps back into my embrace. I quickly kiss Mum and Charlotte on the cheek.

"You two good?"

They both share a soft smile and nod. "Glad to be here," Mum says.

"I'll introduce you to Mrs Hayes in a minute, Mum. We just need to do something first."

"We do?" Paisley asks, looking up at me.

I grin down at her. "We do," I say, before yelling, "Is everyone here?"

Jaxon looks around and gives me a quick nod. I face Paisley towards me, and her forehead creases as she looks around nervously.

"Paisley, before we do the big reveal, I just wanted you to know how proud we are of you. How proud I am of you. The place is amazing, and I have no doubt in my mind that it will thrive. Before we show you the sign, though, we have other surprises for you," I tell her, then pull out a box from my back pocket. I don't know whether this is the best time to give it to her, but I wanted her to have something, so she felt like the baby was with us.

Her mouth falls when she opens the box, her fingers running lightly over the delicate chain. She looks up through misty eyes.

"Landon," she whispers.

"I wanted you to wear it, so you had her with you when this happened," I tell her, taking the silver chain out of the box. The heart pendant has the inscription, 'Always in my heart', and inside the love heart is another pendant, this one a circle. On it is a printed picture of a mother's hand and a baby hand, making a pinky promise. On the other side it reads, 'Always loved'.

"I love it," she tells me, lifting her hair so I can put it on for her. When it's done, a few tears have fallen, and I can hear a few sobs behind me. She leans up, kissing me for all to see, and I take pleasure in hearing her brothers groan.

"Don't fucking look if you don't like it," Hayden snaps.

"Hayden," Mum groans, but Dad laughs, muttering something under his breath.

I pull away from Paisley and grin. "I'm glad you like it."

"I love it. I'm never taking it off."

"My turn," Liza chuckles, stepping beside us. She looks at her daughter with so much love shining in her eyes. "I'm so, so, so proud of you. And I know your dad, looking down on us, would be too. You've surpassed any dreams I had for you, my darlin' girl. You've gone through so much and still accomplished everything you've dreamed of," she tells her, wiping under her eyes as a few tears begin to fall. "This is so you can start your dream for the land on the side. I know you want to build a play area for the summer, and to start building a spa."

Liza hands her a cheque, and Paisley staggers backwards when she reads it. She looks up, her expression horrified. She looks around before leaning in closer to her mum. "Where the hell did you get this kind of money?"

"I think you're meant to say thank you," Dad whispers loudly.

I want to slap him, but Paisley seems to be struggling. I look down at the cheque in her hands and nearly fall over my feet. Eight thousand pounds.

Liza chuckles, waving her off. "Your dad owned some of the land your grandpa lives on. I've never felt comfortable about selling it with your granddad still there, even though your dad was going to sell it before he passed. But your granddad said it was fine. I'd like you to have it."

"What about the others? This can't be my share," she says hoarsely, staring back down at the cheque.

"We're okay with you having it. We've each had some, so you don't need to worry," Jaxon says, stepping forward.

"Jaxon—" she starts, but he holds his hands up to her.

"No, we all agreed. No one was pushed into it. I promise," he declares, and that act alone makes me waver a little towards the brothers. "I've watched you grow up, Paisley. I've seen how you've struggled with your illness and Dad's death. We saw how many days of school you missed and how hard you worked to catch up. This is the one thing we can make easy for you, Paisley. We want to. If anyone deserves it, it's you."

Sniffling, Paisley wipes her nose with the sleeve of her cardigan. "Thank you," she rushes out, before throwing herself into his arms. "Thank you so much for being the best big brother a little girl could wish for. Thank you."

"Um, you have us too, ya know," Reid groans, pouting.

She giggles, staring at her other brothers. "Thank you, all of you. I love you all so much."

Their gazes soften a touch, and I notice Reid and Wyatt look away, misty-eyed.

"Aw, you just gained points for crying," Hayden says, slapping Reid on the chest.

His attention snaps to her, and he looks at her, wide-eyed. "I am not crying. I've got gravel in my eye."

Hayden's shoulders slump, looking disappointed. "So close."

Jaxon clears his throat, and me and Paisley turn our attention back to him. "I have something I'd like to give to you. The only thing I ask is that I have it back if I'm ever fortunate enough to have children."

"What?" Paisley asks, her nose twitching. Even I'm confused, as I didn't know about this. I knew her mum was giving her money, albeit not that much, but I knew nothing about this.

He pulls out an old pocket watch, and Paisley gasps, her hands covering her mouth. "Jaxon, I can't take that," she chokes out.

Jaxon clears his throat, still holding the old pocket watch out. "It's been passed down for generations, Paisley. I remember Dad showing it to me as a kid. He said when I started my first job, he'd give it to me. He wasn't there to give it to me," he tells her, looking pained.

I feel like a jerk for giving him shit earlier. My dad might be a complete goof sometimes, but I wouldn't be able to live without him.

"I want to give it to you. For you to have it until I give it to my firstborn. He would want that for you," he tells her. He places it gently into her hand, closing her fingers around it.

I watch, feeling helpless as she begins to cry quietly. "Thank you. This... this means a lot to me," she whispers.

"I'm so proud of you, Paisley. So fucking proud." She steps forward, hugging him once again. I have to fight the urge to pull her away. My mind knows he's her brother and they're sharing a moment, but the primal need inside of me doesn't read the fact.

"I'm not feeling the love," Wyatt calls out teasingly. Paisley laughs against Jaxon's chest before rushing over to hug each of her brothers, thanking each of them personally.

"That was a beautiful thing you did," Mum says, standing by my side.

"Yeah?"

I'm comforted by her hand rubbing down my back. "Yes," she replies softly.

"Tonight was beautiful. Thank you for inviting me," Charlotte says, and for the first time, she seems unsure, looking around at the others nervously.

I don't like that look on her face. She never feels out of place, even when she says something random and makes a situation awkward. She pastes on a smile and carries on. It's the one thing that makes me stick close to her.

I pull her to me, kissing her temple. "Wouldn't be able to do this without you here. You're my bestie. And this is where I'm living now."

She tears up, blinking furiously so they don't fall. "I needed to hear that."

"Is everything—"

"You do not fucking live here," Jaxon growls.

Paisley pulls away from her twin brothers, who are sandwiching her in a hug. She bites her bottom lip as she walks towards me.

"Jaxon," she speaks slowly.

He pulls at the strands of his hair. "This can't be happening."

Paisley fits perfectly against me. I forgot we hadn't announced it to her brothers yet. Everyone pretty much knows except them.

Guess they're really happy about it.

"We can't have a Carter living on our land, P," Reid growls. "It's bad enough you're with him *romantically*." He says the last part with a sneer.

"Reid," she tries, but he turns away, cursing.

"Paisley, you have to agree. This is never gonna work. He's a Carter," Wyatt snaps.

"And we're fucking awesome, thank you fucking very much," Dad growls. "We got a problem?"

Liza sends her sons a disapproving look. "Don't ruin tonight with your nasty comments. I thought you were over her being with Landon."

"We are. But moving here... We're Hayes'; we have a reputation," Jaxon growls.

"What reputation?" Hayden snarks.

With an angry snarl, he faces her. "People are gonna think we're a push over."

"You kind of are," Hayden says patronisingly.

Paisley relaxes against me. "What if we don't tell anyone outside of the family?"

"You'd do that, for us?" Reid asks, looking hopeful.

Her shoulders shake. "Yes, I would."

He shrugs. "Then I guess it's okay. But no sex until he puts a ring on it."

Coughing, Paisley tenses beneath me. I see her head turn slightly away from Reid, so I know she's about to lie her pretty little arse off. "Of course."

"Right, now that's settled, shall we see the sign?" Liza asks, clapping her hands.

Jaxon grins. "Two seconds," he warns us, before jogging up the path.

"It's a shame he's a Hayes. He has a great arse," Hayden mutters.

"My boys are all single, Hayden. They'd be lucky to have a girl like you," Liza tells her. All the Hayes brothers step away, looking at their mum, horrified.

Hayden chuckles evilly. "Thank you, Liza, but I'm good. They couldn't handle me."

Their mum sighs. "Probably not." Then her eyes meet Charlotte, and they begin to sparkle. "What about you, dear. Are you single?"

"God no," Wyatt moans, and I turn my narrowed gaze to him.

"I am." Charlotte beams. "I've tried to set dates up, but it doesn't go any further than texting. I'm still getting used to it. I'll get there."

I groan, scrubbing a hand down my face.

"My boys are single," Liza says, looking hopeful. "You could have your pick."

Charlotte bites her lip. "As handsome as they are, I don't think they're ready for marriage."

"Marriage?" Wyatt chokes out. "You want to get married?"

Charlotte looks at him with pity. "I'm sorry, but not to you, no. You're handsome, but you aren't what I'm looking for."

He clears his throat, scrubbing the back of his neck. "Um, yeah. Cool."

"Are you ready?" Jaxon yells, and I rub my hands up and down Paisley's arms.

"You ready, baby?"

"My stomach hurts I'm that excited," she tells me, making me chuckle.

Rex comes barrelling out of the bed and breakfast, knocking into Jaxon. Losing his footing, he pulls on the rope, and the sheet covering the sign falls to the ground.

Paisley gasps, her hand covering her mouth. "Oh my God!"

On the wall above the door sits an old, rustic wooden plank that artistically looks to have been snapped in half. On it, in gold writing, reads, 'Meadow Inn', with Ivory carved into it.

"You have similar boards on the road that leads onto the property, and another one at the end of this lane. Bailey helped design those ones."

She turns in my arms, her bright eyes staring up at me. "I love it. Seriously, I love it. Thank you."

The air leaves my lungs in one rush when she throws herself into my arms. I chuckle, lifting her off her feet and swinging her around. She giggles, leaning back and kissing my cheek.

"Thank you, thank you, thank you," she says between peppering kisses all over my face.

"It's beautiful," Liza gushes, but my gaze never leaves Paisley's as I gently lower her to the floor.

"I'm glad you like it," I tell her, tucking her hair behind her ears.

"Landon, what you've done for me, for this place…" she starts, then shakes her head when her eyes become glassy. "I can never thank you enough. I can never repay you for this. It should be me giving you something, not the other way around."

I pull her closer towards me. "I didn't do anything, baby. This… All of this," I start, looking around the building. "It was all you. You would have done this with or without me, and I'm so fucking proud of you."

"I love you so much," she whispers. Her lips press against mine before I have chance to tell her back. I wrap my arms around her back, pressing her harder against me.

Fuck, I love her. I love her so goddamn much it's consuming me.

When we pull apart, the front of the bed and breakfast is empty.

"I love you, Paisley Hayes."

She gives me a dopey smile. "I love you, too, Landon Carter."

THE MATTRESS DIPS as Paisley gets into to bed wearing nothing but one of my T-shirts. My dick stirs at the sight of her. She's fucking sexy when she wears my clothes.

I wait for her to get in before leaning over and flicking the light off. Immediately, she seeks out my warmth, and I grin against her head.

"Tonight was incredible. It doesn't feel real," she whispers tiredly.

"The big reveal or the fact me and Liam didn't fight with your brothers?" I ask, almost teasingly.

For real, her brothers were close to getting laid out, gloating and dropping hints that they were the ones who vandalised Maddox's truck. I don't think they realise yet that it was his and not mine. Our work trucks are all the same.

She giggles lightly against my chest before pressing a kiss above my heart. "Both. Everything. Our families get on so well."

I begin to run my fingers along her shoulder and arm. "Yeah," I sigh. "Mum is looking forward to spending the day helping your mum on the farm. I think she's bored. She lost her job during my recovery."

Her warm hand runs up my chest. "Hey, you sound like you think it's your fault."

I shrug. "She didn't love the job. She prefers helping my aunt at the flower shop with Madison, but I still feel like they lost that bit of extra income because of me. I just feel bad she lost something because of me. Then I acted like a wanker when I woke up."

"But you're not acting like one now. Your parents love you."

"They're the best," I tell her.

I shuffle down the bed so we're facing each other, my feet accidently kicking Rex. Paisley is determined to let him sleep where he wants. Give it a week or two, and I'll have the little fucker on the floor in his own bed. The cat hisses when he moves to get comfy again.

Paisley giggles. "Midnight is still getting used to sharing my space."

I grin into the dark. "Yeah, she'll get used to it. Are you happy?" I ask.

Her fingers tighten into my side. "Deliriously so."

"Really?" I ask huskily when her fingers run further down.

"Yeah, but I could be happier," she rasps.

"Is that so?" I ask, running my hand up her top.

Her breath hitches. "I know so."

I grin, and with a swift move, I'm above her, pinning her down into the mattress. A smirk tugs at my lips when I see the desire all over her face.

My girl wants me. And I'm going to show her how much I want her.

"Then let's make that happen."

TWENTY-NINE

LANDON

THE COLD NIGHT AIR BITES AGAINST MY FACE as we walk through a maze of people rushing towards the rides.

Tonight is bonfire night, and we're just a few short days away from the bed and breakfast opening. Already, Meadows Inn is fully booked for a month straight, and Paisley has hired some overnight staff, something she thought she could handle on her own. After explaining she will be needed in the day more than through the night, she put out an ad in the paper, and within a day, her phone was ringing off the hook.

I knew she was going to be busy for a few weeks, getting used to running her business, so tonight I planned for us to come to a firework display. In the day the park was kind of like a safari. People are allowed to drive around the animal enclosures before parking and heading into the actual park. A few animals still remain tonight, including the bats I was forced to endure not five minutes ago. The rest of the animals, I guess, were sedated and locked away for the night.

As nights out go, I'm enjoying myself. Seeing everything through her eyes makes a difference, and I find myself enjoying it.

There's just one problem.

Jaxon fucking Hayes decided to tag along with his new fuck buddy for the night. No fucking clue who the bitch is, but she's grating on my last nerve. And if she insults my girlfriend one more time, I'm punching Jaxon in the face.

"I still don't get it," she snidely bites out.

I sigh, my hand tensing around Paisley's. She squeezes my hand when I open my mouth, ready to bark something at the cheeky little cow.

"You don't have to," Paisley tells her, sounding calmer than I am right now.

"But he's—"

"So not into you," Paisley snaps out. "Jaxon, control your date."

Jaxon, his eyes on another girl's arse, blinks and turns his attention to his sister. "What?"

Paisley sighs, pinching the bridge of her nose. "Can't you go off and do your own thing?"

The girl next to him squeals. "You can win me a unicorn teddy."

"Yes, you can do that," Paisley mimics in the girl's voice.

"That sounds nothing like me," she drawls out, before turning to me. "I still don't know what you're doing with her."

My gaze hardens on her, and I'm ready to lay into the bitch.

"At least he knows my name," Paisley mutters dryly, leaning against me. A tug of her hand has us walking again, and unfortunately, Jaxon follows, unable to get the hint. I guess he doesn't want to be alone with his 'date' until the actual main event later.

"You know my name, right, babe," she calls, sounding so sure.

She only introduced herself to us an hour ago, and even I've forgotten her fucking name.

Jaxon clears his throat as he catches up to us. "Yeah, course I do."

From the corner of my eye, the girl visibly relaxes, but I feel Paisley's shoulders begin to shake as she leans away from me.

"Ask him what it is," she whispers loudly.

Jaxon narrows his eyes on his sister, and a grin tugs at my lips. The fucker doesn't know her name either.

"I know it."

"Then say it," the bimbo demands, stopping. I would carry on walking, but seeing Jaxon light a fire under his own arse is an opportunity I don't want to miss.

"It's, um… it's…" he trails off, staring up at the night sky before looking down at her and clicking his fingers. "It's Clare."

"It's Louise," she snaps, glaring at him. "Clare was my friend."

Uh-oh. I grin. "Something wrong in paradise already?" I drawl, earning a glare from him.

He turns with what he must think is his charming smile and grabs hold of her hips. "I know why I remembered the name. She's the one I had no interest in."

Smooth.

She melts against him. "Yeah?"

"Yeah, babe. Why don't we win you that unicorn teddy?"

She squeals, jumping up and down. "I'd love that."

Paisley squeals, but it's forced, and I chuckle down at her when she starts tugging on my jacket. "Can you please, please, please win me that big monkey teddy?"

I'm grinning like a fool as I reach down and kiss her. "Anything for you, babe."

Louise huffs and takes Jaxon's hand. We follow them to the booth next to the unicorns, and I look at the barrel game, watching as another person plays. The ball flies back out and he loses.

"You want a go?" I ask Paisley.

She pulls away from cuddling my arm, tucking her hat down further. She looks fucking beautiful all covered up in her winter gear.

"I was only joking," she mutters, but a pink tinge to her cheeks tells me she wants me to win the teddy.

"How about we both have a go?"

She tilts her head, considering it. "All right. If I win, I'll get the brown monkey."

"I'll get you the pink one," I tell her, grinning at her enthusiasm.

"My hero," she sighs, resting her hand over her heart.

"You havin' a go, mate?" I look at the kid behind the counter and grunt. "Put three quid in the pot."

I grab change out of my back pocket, slotting the money into both mine and Paisley's machines. He hands us two balls each before stepping back.

"Aim of the game is to get the two balls into the barrel and make 'em stay there. If they come out, you don't win."

I grunt, wanting to grab the prick around the neck when he begins to eye Paisley with appreciation. If it weren't for the fact I know she secretly wants the damn monkey, I'd lob them at his head.

Paisley steps forward, holding out a ball in her right hand. I chuckle when she closes one eye, squinting through the other as she lines up her shot.

Her ball lands inside too hard and bounces back out. She makes a cute growling sound in the back of her throat as she throws the other. It misses completely, and I laugh.

She turns to me, arching an eyebrow. "You think you can do better? It's harder than it looks."

I rub the ball across my shoulder and wink. "I know I can."

She rolls her eyes but steps closer. "Let's see, then."

Holding the two balls, I stand closer and a little to the side. I lightly throw the ball and it lands inside, staying there.

A gasp escapes her lips, right before she starts jumping up and down. "You did it!"

I laugh, kissing her briefly. "Not yet. Still got one more, babe."

She claps excitedly before turning back to the game, her eyes on the barrel.

This had better go fucking in now. I couldn't stand to see the disappointment in her eyes if it didn't. Fuck, I'll get some more cash out and play all night until I win if it means I can give her that damn monkey.

Taking a deep breath, I get into position and throw the ball the same way I did the first time. I hold my breath as it flies through the air and into the barrel. When it doesn't come out, I sigh with relief.

Paisley slams into me, knocking the breath out of me as she wraps her limbs around me. I laugh, grabbing her by her arse.

"You won!"

She pulls back to cup my face, her smile blinding.

"Are you gonna pick a prize. I've got other customers," the kid snaps rudely.

Turning away from Paisley is hard, but I do, glaring at the son of a bitch cruising for a slap in the head.

"We'll take the pink one," I snap.

Placing Paisley down, she grabs the monkey from the kid and hugs it to her chest. "I love it."

I grin down at her, pulling her back into my arms. "I love you."

Her smile turns goofy as she melts against me. "I love you, too."

"Get a room," Jaxon growls, coming to stand beside us.

"We would, but you'd probably invade that too," I snap.

He rolls his eyes while his date looks dejected, eyeing Paisley's teddy. I chuckle when Paisley sees where Louise is looking, hugging the monkey tighter. You'd think she was holding a crown jewel, not something that probably cost a few quid.

"Landon!" is yelled from the crowd.

I look around for the source of the voice when it's yelled again.

Liam.

I take Paisley's hand, pushing her away from the crowd forming in front of the game booth and towards my brother, who is running towards me.

"What's wrong?" I ask when he reaches us, looking pale.

"A body was found earlier this morning," he gasps out. He bends over, placing his hands on his knees. "Fuck! I think I'm dying. I think I've run around the park three times looking for you. I'm so unfit."

Paisley's hand tenses in mine, and I pull her close. "There was a body?" she asks, fear filling her voice, the joy from earlier now gone. I'd punch Liam for putting that look on her face, but I can see this is important. My stomach sinks with dread.

"Who?"

"Rocket!" he breathes out, standing straighter.

"The lad that done Landon over?" Jaxon asks, eyeing me warily.

"Shall we try another booth?" Louise says, but we ignore her.

I narrow my eyes at Jaxon. "I didn't fucking kill him."

He holds his hands up to me. "Didn't even ask."

"Didn't fucking need to," I snap.

"Why are you here?" Liam asks him.

Jaxon huffs out a breath. "For fuck's sake. Just get on with telling him what happened already."

Liam eyes him for a few more moments before turning his attention to me. "It was bad. Liam has an alert on his computer for any details regarding, um, everyone," he says, looking at Louise like he wishes she would disappear. I wish she would too. "He was tortured—bad. The report said he must have been beaten for a week or so. Some of the broken bones and bruises were old."

"Rocco?" I ask.

He grimaces and nods. "Yeah. It looks like Rocket was used to, um, make his money differently to Blaze."

He looks away from us, and Paisley hugs my arm tighter, her body shivering. I wrap my arm around her. "What did he have Blaze do?" I ask, not wanting to think of the sick shit Rocco had Rocket do. I don't even feel bad. He made his bed; he can lie in it. He's only got himself to blame.

"Fighting."

I'm about to question him more, but my phone begins to buzz in my pocket. I pull it out, finding a message from Benny.

BENNY: Get to Larkhill in twenty minutes. Fight is tonight. Rocco's time is up since Rocket was found dead this morning. Get here.

I gulp, my stomach tightening. I've been training for this, waiting for it, and now that it's here, I can feel the blood burning through my veins.

"I need to go," I say cautiously, not looking at Paisley.

"Go?" she squeaks out. "Go where?"

Clearing my throat, I pull my gaze away from Liam, who takes the phone from me. Paisley's eyebrows are pinched together as she waits for me to answer. Her gaze moves from me to my phone, then back again, biting her bottom lip.

"I have to go, um, somewhere. You can stay here with Jaxon, go on some rides. I'll be a few hours."

Her hand reaches out, squeezing my bicep. "No, wait! Where are you going? Tell me!"

Seeing her tears gathering is my undoing. I reach out, giving her a quick hug before pulling back and resting my forehead against hers. "It's time. Can you remember a while back, when I told you I was getting revenge?"

She nods, her eyes closing. "You can't go. Someone died, Landon. They died. I can't lose you, not again. I won't survive it this time."

"Mate, maybe she's right," Jaxon says.

I glare up at him. "If four people beat the living shit out of you, would you stand back and let them get away with it?"

He scrubs the back of his neck. "Nah, I wouldn't."

Paisley looks between us before focusing on me, her tears falling now. "Please. Please, don't go."

"I'm not going to die, baby. I promise."

She looks to the ground as she clings to me, shaking her head. "You can't. You can't go. I won't let you."

I kiss the top of her head. "I love you."

"I love you, too, but you can't leave me. Please."

"I'm sorry," I say on a pained whisper.

Looking at Jaxon over her head, I give him a chin lift. He steps forward, pulling Paisley away. Her fingers dig deep into my jacket, and my chest begins to burn.

"No! No! Jaxon, don't! Landon, please don't do this," she begs, her eyes pleading with me now.

I pry her fingers from my jacket and take a step back. It pains me, the heartbreak in her eyes.

"I have to do this," I tell her, then tap my brother on the shoulder, taking my phone back from him.

"Landon," she screams.

"Bro, are you sure about this?" Liam asks.

My voice is raspy when I answer. "Yeah."

When we can no longer hear her screams, I relax somewhat. Liam looks to me, seeming distant.

"You not coming?"

He shakes his head, still seeming faraway. "I'll catch up with you."

I feel like I've been sucker punched as I stare down at my brother. "You'll catch up?"

He nods. "There's something I need to do. I'll be there before your fight, I promise," he tells me. "Go. Maddox is waiting by your car. You won't be alone."

I snort. "I'm not bothered about being alone, Liam. I want to know why you're not coming."

"I'll explain everything later. Look, I don't have time. Just go," he tells me, before running off in the other direction.

I shake my head, but glancing down at my phone, I see I've got fifteen minutes to get to Larkhill. I run through the crowd, making my way to the car. Maddox is leaning casually against it.

"About damn time. Liam text me to get here and said it's happening tonight. I'm guessing he meant the fight and not you losing your virginity."

I roll my eyes. "Yeah, but he's fucked off somewhere."

He shrugs. "Must be important then."

"Hmm," I mumble, opening the car.

"You ready?" he asks over the hood.

I grin. "Been ready for weeks."

"Let's go show everyone why they shouldn't fuck with a Carter, then."

And that's what I plan to do tonight. I've finally put on muscle, after having lost so much after the accident. I was skin and bones, but gradually, I've built it back up. I've never felt stronger.

I'll never get my revenge on Rocket, but Blaze, Flash, Terry and Rocco don't know what's coming. They're going to wish they never laid fucking eyes on me by the time I'm done.

THIRTY

PAISLEY

I WATCH THROUGH BLURRED VISION AS Landon disappears into the crowd. My heart tears in two. Once the back of his head disappears, I round on Jaxon, pushing against his chest, hard. He doesn't budge, and I growl low in my throat.

"How could you!" I scream furiously, gaining attention from others around us. I push him again, angrily. "How could you let him leave like that? Did you hear what they said? Someone died, Jaxon. They died! I'll never forgive you for this."

My feet slide in the mud when I turn to leave, ruining my epic exit. Tears cloud my vision as they stream down my face, but I still see the patch of mud I'm about to become closely acquainted with. Jaxon grabs me before I faceplant on the floor, and for a split second, I forget I'm mad at him.

"Paisley, stop!"

I shove him away from me, then slap his hands when he goes to reach for me again. "No, *you* stop. I'm going after him. I have to stop him." I can't breathe. It feels like someone's pressing down hard on my chest, and the pressure is becoming too much.

My heart races as I picture Landon leaving me. I understand his reasons, I really do, but he left me. I need to stop him before something bad happens. I can feel it in the pit of my stomach.

My body shivers and my hands clench into fists at my sides as I bite my lip to keep the sob from tearing up my throat.

I can't lose him. He's my forever.

My domino.

Jaxon grabs my arm again, stopping me, and a frustrated scream bubbles up my throat. "It's too fucking dangerous, Paisley. You aren't going. Do you know the kind of people that go there, huh? Do you?"

My fists clench together. "And that's meant to make me feel better? You didn't even try to stop him. Do you want him to die, is that it? You hate him that much you're willing to destroy me?"

His face falls like I've punched him in the stomach. A moment of guilt hits me, but it's gone in a split second when I think of what Landon could be walking in to. It could be a trap for all he knows, one he might not walk out of this time.

"Of course not," he yells, taken aback. "I'm doing this for you. Come on, I'm taking you home. All this stress is going to cause you to have an episode."

"Fuck you," I snap out, shocking myself. "Don't use my diabetes as an excuse to get me to do your bidding."

"Hey, what about the fireworks?" Louise asks, stepping closer to us.

"Do you think I care about the goddamn fireworks," I scream at her.

She snuffs her nose up at me. "I wasn't talking to you."

"Go away," Jaxon snaps.

She gives me a smug smile, but when I tilt my head at her, her gaze goes to Jaxon, confused. "You can't seriously mean me?" she asks in sheer disbelief.

With a sneer, he turns to her. "Yes, I fucking do. Now go!"

He takes my arm, pulling me through the crowd. "It's for your own good, Paisley. There are too many dangerous people there."

"I hate you," I snap bitchily.

"Don't hate me," he says, sounding pained. I ignore him, pushing through anyone who gets in my way. Because whether Jaxon knows it or not, I'm not giving up. One way or another, I'm going to stop Landon from fighting.

Or be there to help somehow.

"Paisley, talk to me," he pleads when we get to the car.

Talk to him? I snort, looking away in disgust. It's scary how unlike myself I'm being, but I'm just so fucking angry at him. And he has the nerve to ask me to talk to him. Like he talked to me when he held me back from going after Landon. Did he ask me what I wanted? No!

I puff out a breath, throwing the door open and getting in. He bends down into the car, and I keep staring ahead, focusing on a group smoking under a heater.

"Paisley, don't do this. I'm trying to protect you."

I face him, tears still gathered in my eyes, but I feel more determined, stronger than I did before. "No, you aren't. If you were, you wouldn't have let him leave, Jaxon. I—" I shake my head, pulling my hat off. "*I love him*, Jaxon. I love him so much I feel like I'm suffocating when he's not around. I get an empty feeling in the pit of my stomach every time he walks out of the door. I need him. And you might have just let him walk to his death. So yes, I will do this. I'll never forgive you for this. Ever," I sob out, looking away again.

He doesn't say anything for a few moments. I stiffen when he leans further into the car, kissing my temple. "Fucking hell," he curses. "I am sorry, Paisley. I really am. But I'd do it again in a heartbeat, even knowing you'll react like this. Those thugs won't think twice about hurting you or worse just to get to him. You being there could distract him. I'd do it all over again because I love you. You're my baby sister, and I'll never let anything happen to you. Family comes before all else, remember," he tells me, using the quote my dad used to tell us daily.

What he fails to mention is that Landon is family. He's my family now, whether he likes it or not.

Clearly not expecting me to answer, he straightens and shuts the car door.

He doesn't say anything when he gets in the driver's side, or on the drive home.

Ten minutes away from the house, I send a text to Adam.

PAISLEY: I need you to find out where the fight is tonight and get to mine ASAP. Don't try to stop me or ask questions, but we need to get to Landon. I'll explain everything when you get to mine. Don't let my brother see you.

PAISLEY: Don't let any of them see you.

A few minutes later, Adam has texted back.

ADAM: Give me fifteen. Need to get rid of my date. X

I fall back against the seat, closing my eyes when all the lights whizzing by begin to give me a headache. Landon's face comes to my mind, and a lone tear slips free. I've never believed in God, but if there's any time to start praying, it's now. I'll do anything to make sure he's okay and unharmed.

Images of him bleeding out in the alley play in my mind, and my lips part on a gasp as my lids fly open. I swallow down bile as I look around the familiar surroundings. We're home.

"Paisley, please talk to me," Jaxon pleads as he takes the lane turning into the bed and breakfast.

"Why?" I ask hoarsely. "I can't lose him."

He slams his fist against the steering wheel. "Fuck!" I jump, startled at the outburst. "I'll go see if he's okay, alright. Just please, stay here and don't do anything stupid."

"How do you know where it is?" I ask warily.

He pinches the bridge of his nose. "Because I got the alert message to say a fight was happening tonight. I've been to them before."

I make a sound in my throat. I'd been too busy looking at Landon and Liam. I hadn't really noticed what Jaxon or his date were doing.

"I'm going inside to try and ring him."

"Paisley, I am sorry," he says, reaching for my arm.

I turn to him, feeling like an idiot as more tears gather in my eyes. "I know."

He sighs, letting me go. I get out, shutting the door quietly before making my way up the steps. He waits in the car until I open the front door. And it isn't until I'm inside that I realise I'm still clutching the monkey Landon won for me. A sob tears from my throat as I slide down the door, clutching it to my chest.

"Please be okay. Please," I beg.

———————————————

IT'S NOT LONG before I hear another car pulling up outside the bed and breakfast. I get up from the floor, wiping my wet cheeks with the sleeve of my coat.

Hearing a door slam, I quickly place the monkey onto the side table by the door and lock up behind me.

The skies have opened up, the rain falling heavily. I pull my hood up, but the heavy wind just blows it back down.

"Come on, we need to go. It's starting any minute," Adam yells.

"Where is it?" I yell as I race to the car.

He waits to answer me, getting us in the car and out of the rain. "He's fighting in Larkhill tonight. I thought they stopped fighting outside when the weather was shit. I guess everywhere else is being watched or something."

I face Adam, noticing the seriousness in his expression. "What aren't you telling me?"

"I was near one of the factories that they normally fight in. I saw three police cars, the coppers obviously thinking they were out of sight. Something's going down tonight. Something big."

Anxiety fills my chest. "He can't get into trouble."

He reaches out as we pull out of the farm, placing his hand on my knee and squeezing. "I can't speed there in case a cop pulls us over, but fingers crossed we get there in time."

"Someone died, Adam," I tell him.

Horror flashes across his expression when he shoots a quick glance to me. "You can't be serious."

I nod, then proceed to fill him in on everything Liam had told us earlier tonight. He exhales, rubbing a hand across his jaw.

"Fuck, this shit is messed up. We're nearly there. Can you see the lights up ahead?"

I squint through the windshield, finding it hard to see with the rain falling so heavily. It takes a few seconds for me to see it, but when I do, my lips part in surprise. There are tons of cars parked in a circle, more cars behind them, parked the same way. All their lights shining into the middle.

Larkhill used to be a place where people walked their dogs. But ten years ago, the ground began to sink in places. The papers reported old tunnels were underground, causing the ground to sink. The council never had the money to restore it, and instead put a restricted sign on the gates around the property. Now it was overgrown grass, a few trees and lots of rubble where people have been fly-tipping. It's a shame because I remember it from when I was a child, and it was beautiful.

"Do you think there's a code or pattern to the parking?" Adam asks, gulping.

"Just leave it here," I snap out, then grimace. "Sorry. Here is fine."

I don't wait for him to get nervous about anything else. I can't deal with his problems right now, not when Landon is out there. I step forward through the roaring crowd, my heart beating wildly against my chest.

Men and women curse as I shove my way through the crowd. I ignore them, scanning the area for my target.

I jump when a loud voice booms through the speakers. I'm nearing the front, and when I see a man step out between two cars with a mic in his hand that is connected to a speaker in the back of a car, I begin to shake.

It's happening.

"You guys know why we're here," he yells, and everyone begins to scream. I almost cover my ears but refrain myself.

"Don't rush off like that," Adam hisses in my ear, bumping into me when someone knocks him.

I don't take my eyes off the guy in the middle. He's rough-looking, a lot older than I expected, and I wonder how Landon got mixed up with someone like him. I follow the guy's line of sight, and my gaze narrows on a man in a black trench coat, glowering under his umbrella. Everything about him screams money. And I don't mean because he has someone holding the umbrella above him while they get soaked, or that he has three men in suits surrounding him. It's the way he stands; his back straight, his jaw clenched, and his gaze unwavering, uncaring and dead.

I shiver, moving closer to Adam.

"Who is that?" he whispers, but I ignore him, unable to tear my eyes away from the intimidating man off to the side.

"Tonight, we are going to make money," he screams, raring up the crowd. They go wild, screaming things I can't hear over the loud buzzing in my ears. "Tonight, we right a fucking wrong."

He scans the crowd, and an unknown feeling runs up my spine. It's like he's looking everyone in the eye, making sure they understand that he means what he's about to say next.

"No one fucks with us. No one. You try, and these are the consequences. Remember that," he tells them, his gaze once again reaching the man in the trench coat, hardening on him. The man glowers back, but other than that, seems unaffected.

"New rules for tonight and tonight only," he screams to the crowd, wiping rain from his face. "Anything goes."

"What does that mean?" I whisper, feeling hysteria rising in my throat.

"First up, we have Rocco's thugs," he yells.

I'm compelled to move forward, my feet having a mind of their own. My heart stops when three men I recognise from that night step out from between the cars near the man in the trench coat. The one I remember as Blaze leans down to listen to something the guy says, a smug smirk lifting at his lips as he nods. He turns back to the others, but my attention is pulled away when women begin to scream.

"Fighting the three thugs who are left, I introduce you to… Demolition Man," he screams.

My breath catches in my throat as Landon steps out, his physique ripped and perfectly toned.

Wearing only a pair of gym shorts, showcasing his obliques, and his trainers, he looks like a force to be reckoned with. His powerful build screams strength as he smacks his taped hands together.

I take another step forward, my mouth opening to call out to him, but nothing comes out. I freeze, watching as the man I love becomes somebody else. It's like he's flicked a switch, and in his place is this dangerous machine, one that looks ready to snap his opponent's neck. Just watching his movements as he nods to something Drew, his friend from the gym, whispers to him has me relaxing somewhat. One on one, he can do this. Everything about him right now suggests he could take them on.

My eyebrows scrunch together when three of the four men from that night step further into the circle.

"No," I whisper when I realise what this means.

"No fucking the cars up, dickheads," the man with the mic yells. He steps back, looking between Landon and the group of men, shaking his head. "May the best man win."

"Wait! No!" I scream, horrified he's going to fight all three at the same time.

He must hear my voice, because for a split second, his eyes catch mine. Mine widen in horror when I notice one of them pick up a stick from the ground, swinging it around before going for Landon.

I scream at the top of my lungs, and without a thought, I step further into the circle, ready to run to his rescue.

"No!" I cry out, when strong arms wrap around my waist, pulling me back. The last thing I see before being pulled into the crowd is Landon taking a hit to the side with the stick. Tears run down my face as struggle to get free. "Adam, put me down."

When I look up, blowing the hair out of my face, I notice Adam is in front of me, not behind me.

"Adam?" I call out, tensing.

Jaxon.

When I'm suddenly spun around, I'm surprised to find Max standing in front of me.

"You can't distract him," he tells me forcefully.

"You're going to let him fight?" I snap, glaring at him.

He grins down at me, patting my head like I'm a little girl. "Little one, my boy has this. If he didn't, I'd be next to him."

"He's right. Landon isn't alone," Maverick says, coming to stand next to Max.

I shake my head at them, blinking like I'm seeing things. "You could stop this!"

Malik, his reserved uncle, steps up next, his lips twisting. "No, we can't. He needs to do this whether you understand it or not. That night…they took something from him. Tonight, he is getting it back. You need to get yourself together, because one wrong move could get that boy killed."

I sigh, looking away. "Does he know you're here?"

Max looks at me like I've lost my mind. "You, cray-cray, lady. No, he doesn't."

I look over my shoulder where I can hear the fight continuing, and anxiety bubbles in my stomach.

"Come on, we need to get back on the other side. I don't trust this side. I keep seeing his little minions running around," Maverick says, warily scanning the crowd. I'm confused as to what he means.

"Why am I picturing little yellow Minions running around?" Max asks.

Maverick pinches the bridge of his nose. "Let's go watch the kid knock these fuckers out."

I growl under my breath. "You really can't be serious?" I ask, my voice shrill. "There are three of them. One of them is already dead. And it's three against one." I'm becoming angry, and Adam touching me is making things worse. He's trying to be soothing, rubbing my shoulders, but all it's doing is making me irritable.

"I'll tell you what, after Landon has won, I'll buy you a cape. How does that sound?" Max asks softly. Again, speaking to me like a child. I guess I'm acting like one, but I have every right when the man I love is fighting right now.

"A cape?" When I tilt my head in confusion, he places a hand on my shoulder, intentionally knocking Adam's hand away with a gleam in his eye.

"Yes, a cape. That way, you can be super mad at him."

A few groans echo around me, but for some reason, a laugh mixed with a sob bubbles up my throat.

"Come on," Max says, pulling me against his chest. "Let's go watch the boy kick arse."

Too exhausted to argue, I cry silently into his chest, letting him half carry me to wherever they are taking me.

When we stop, I look up, my eyes widening when I see Jaxon with Landon's uncles, Mason and Myles. I gulp when he steps forward.

"What did I fucking tell you?" he roars.

"Jesus, quiet the fuck down," Max snaps.

Jaxon glares at him for a split second before moving away to stand next to Liam.

"I think he's mad at me," I whisper.

Max looks down on me with pity. "Yeah. Wait till Landon's finished. He's going to be so pissed."

My gaze turns to the fight, and my breath hitches. "He can be as mad at me as he likes as long as he walks out of that circle," I tell him, feeling a coldness seep into my bones.

I close my eyes when blood splatters out his mouth, his body unmoving. I cross my fingers, praying he makes it out of there.

THIRTY-ONE

LANDON

I'M BEGINNING TO THINK LIAM ISN'T going to show. Then I see him pushing through the crowd towards me, and he's not on his own. Mark is with him, looking worried as fuck as he scans the people around us. Even pissing it down with rain, this fight has still drawn out a huge crowd. There has to be hundreds of people here.

"You do what you needed to do?" I ask, watching him closely. I have no idea what was so important, but right now isn't the time to question it. The fight is about to start.

I tune out Benny has he begins to give me a run-down on what's happening and focus on Liam.

"Yeah. Are you ready?"

I nod, shaking out my arms and legs. "I am."

"You know this isn't going to be the same as before? I've heard they've been training. Nowhere near your level, but it still might be a challenge with all three fighting you."

I shrug, not caring. I've got this, and when they see me out there, they'll get that too. "I'm not worried. I want this over and done with. It's all three or nothing, Liam. I don't want to risk something happening and then have to go through all of this again."

He nods in understanding. "All right but be careful."

"Fighting the three thugs who are left, I introduce you to… Demolition Man," Benny screams.

I roll my shoulders, giving Liam and Mark one last look before facing the circle. I walk down the path lined between cars and feel my blood pumping through my body. The day of reckoning is finally here. Today, they get to meet their judge, jury and executioner. Me.

Drew blocks my path, surprising me. I didn't know he was here.

"They have something planned, mate. Take them at the knees. Don't let them get back up."

I don't say anything and instead nod in acknowledgement.

Stepping into the ring, I raise my chin at Benny in greeting. We spoke when I arrived, and although he wants the money that tonight will bring in, he did warn me something didn't feel right. I shrugged it off, ready for anything.

My resolve hardens when I step into the circle. I ignore the screaming men and women and concentrate on the three motherfuckers with a death wish walking towards me. Blaze's stance is cocky, knowing, like he has something up his sleeve. I don't take my eyes off him, but in my peripheral vision, I see the other two get ready. My gaze quickly flashes over them, and I notice when Flash's hands begin to shake.

A small smirk tugs at my lips.

"No fucking the cars up, dickheads," Benny spits into the mic. He steps back, looking between me and those dickheads, shaking his head. His gaze reaches mine briefly, and a look that says, 'They're so dead', is shared between us. "May the best man win."

Lifting my leg, I get ready to attack, but a voice echoes over the crowd and rain. I'd know that voice anywhere.

Paisley.

Our eyes meet through the rain, and hers widen in horror. What the fuck was her brother thinking in bringing her here? And why the fuck is that twat with her?

I watch as she steps forward, screaming. I'm about to change course, go to her, but then I see my dad step up behind her, holding her back.

She's safe. He won't let anything happen to her.

I sigh in relief just as I see movement in front of me. It happens in seconds, enough time for me to jump back and miss Terry's hit. I look down at the thick sticks his hand and growl under my breath. There is no way they were randomly found on the floor. They were left purposely.

I grunt when something sharp whacks me in my side. I grunt, and look down at the piece of wood imbedded in my side, the rusty nails attached to it ripping through my skin.

A guttural growl erupts from my lips as I look up, staring dead into Blaze's eyes. His grin is smug, like he's won, but I smile, tilting my head. In a flash, the stick is my hand, and with a spin, I smack it around his head. He goes down, falling to the ground, clutching his bleeding wound.

Terry and Flash take that moment to come at me from both sides. I grab the stick Terry is holding whilst kicking my leg out, hitting Flash in the centre of his chest, winding him and hopefully breaking a rib or two. He goes down, sliding onto the ground. I pull hard on the stick for a few moments. It catches Terry off guard when I push it forward suddenly, smacking him in the chin and knocking his teeth together.

He grunts, staggering backwards, and drops the stick to the floor.

"You think you can win this?" Blaze growls.

I bare my teeth as I clench my fists together. "I know I can, you silly fucking cunt. Not so big without ya bat, are you."

"You think tonight will be the end?" he asks, circling me. I know he's trying to get me to turn away from the other two, who are getting back to their feet.

A smirk tugs at my lips as I spread my legs a part, ready for the assault. "I know it fucking is."

All three fly at me, and the crowd begins to scream. I grab Flash first, swinging him into Blaze and knocking them both to the ground.

I spit on the both of them, feeling an out of body experience. I don't feel like me right now. I want blood, puddles of it, and it has to be theirs.

"Stay down," I bark patronizingly.

Terry's eyes bug out of his head when he sees his two friends on the floor with little effort from me. I grab him, hearing a faint squeak leave his lips before my head comes down on his nose. He roars in pain, pushing me away.

And in a blur of movements, someone grabs me from behind, and Terry smirks, like the playing field is even.

It's not. I'm ready for them this time.

Punches to my chest and abdomen burn through me, but I harden myself and punch back. At the same time, I swerve around, lifting my leg out and kicking Blaze in the head. He grunts but this time stays standing.

His murderous expression makes me inwardly smile. He moves, tackling me, and before we reach the ground, I turn us, so I land on him. With quick movements, I get up to my knees, practically straddling the dirty scumbag, and begin to rain down punches. My knuckles split from their onslaught. I don't feel it, hitting him harder each time. His face is torn open, the blood washing away with the rain. He blinks, still trying to fight back, but I don't feel any of his hits. I don't feel anything.

Satisfaction swirls through my body with each blow, until someone hits me around the head.

I groan, feeling dizzy from the surprise attack. Pain throbs through my head, but I ignore it.

An anger I've never felt before takes root in my body. I get up slowly, and both Terry and Flash watch me warily, turning to each other with worry written on their faces.

They have just woken the beast within me, and now it's time for them to meet him. I grin, and Flash looks ready to piss himself.

He can wait.

Ducking down, I shove forward, ramming my shoulder into Terry. He grunts, but I take hold of his arm, twisting it in an unnatural way until I hear bone cracking. He roars in pain, pleading with me to stop. I don't, pulling that much harder, until I feel his shoulder come out of its socket.

Time seems to skip. I don't see what's in front of me now. I'm not in control. I'm not in my body. I'm standing to the side, watching on. I see a savage animal attacking its prey, tearing through them. I can feel the injuries my body has endured, but not *really* feel it. The sound of knuckles hitting bare flesh echoes through the air.

Flash sways as he gets back up, blood pooling from his mouth. I lick my bottom lip, tasting my own blood. I wipe it away with the side of my hand as I take step forward, my fist aching from clenching it so hard.

He holds his hand up, warning me away, but I slap it away, just like I've done all his other attempts to hurt me. Again.

Movement to the left has me turning, and although my body moves towards Blaze, it's Flash I want to finish off, so bending down low, I swipe my feet out, knocking his out from under him. He slams down on the wet ground, grunting in pain.

Getting up, flashes from the night they attacked me assault me. The memories are vivid, and when I close my eyes, I can see Flash standing above me, his boot rising in the air before hitting me. I lift his leg, yanking hard until he's facing me. The fear in his gaze as he stares at me appeases the beast somewhat.

It's not enough.

I watch him, feeling no pity or remorse as I lift my own foot, smacking it down on his face. The crunch I hear is like music to my ears.

A scream of warning from the crowd has me spinning around. I almost forgot about Blaze behind me. I jump back when I see the silver blade coming at me. The sting and spray of blood shock me, giving him time to swipe at me again.

I lift my arm to block the attack and end up hissing through my teeth when the knife slices my arm. I fall to my knees, stones and dirt rubbing against my bare skin. I blink through a red haze, staring up at him.

Blinking again, I notice his foot coming towards me, but before his foot connects with the side of my face, I reach out and grab his leg, stopping him. His feet come out from under him when I yank his leg up, and he lands on his back with a grunt.

I get up, stepping on his hand that still wields the knife.

More memories of him plunging it into me that night surface, and subconsciously, my fingers smoothly run across the jagged scars he left on my stomach.

My foot presses down harder, and his fingers open, letting go of the knife. I kick it away.

Suddenly, air is rushing around me, and my head smacks against the ground. My ears ring, and I struggle to think straight. It takes me a few seconds to realise Blaze used the same maneuverer I did and knocked me to the ground.

Fucking dickhead.

Slowly, I try to sit up, but every muscle in my body aches. I blink up at the night sky, and as my eyes open, he's looking down at me, sneering.

He manages to get a punch or two in before the ringing in my ears gets louder, and I shove him off. I roll over, feeling dirt and rain caking my skin. I kick out, hitting him in the jaw, and blood sprays from his mouth.

Everything begins to darken, and time moves faster. When everything comes into focus, I've got more pain in my side, more blood dripping down my head, and Blaze is crawling over to his knife like the wimp he is.

I step over him, grabbing his hair in a fist and pulling his head back.

"Can you not fight like a man?" I growl, picking the knife up and throwing it under the nearest car.

He spits blood on the ground. "Fuck you!"

I shove his face into the ground, but the earth is so soft, it doesn't do anything. I stand up, feeling worn out and tired. The adrenaline has begun to wear off.

He turns in surprise, thinking it's over. Before he can question it or beg for mercy like the other two, I lift my foot down on his face, knocking him out cold.

The crowd is silent for a few seconds before everyone begins to scream, jumping around and celebrating. I don't feel like celebrating.

I stagger towards where I last saw Paisley. I need her. Her hand is covering her mouth, and her eyes are red from the tears running down her cheeks.

I watch as they all begin to move forward, my eyes catching my dad as he sags with relief. But then the look of horror, the one I've only seen once before, when Hayden nearly got run over as a kid, spreads across his features.

I close my eyes, knowing something bad is coming.

I can sense it.

Almost see it.

Everything moves in slow motion when I open my eyes. Paisley's running towards me, the same horror-struck expression on her face. Dad snaps out of it, running right behind her.

I turn around, the rain splattering against my face as I see Blaze coming towards me, a large metal pole in his hand. My gaze flicks to Rocco, who stands behind him with a smug, calculating look.

I stagger forward, ready, when a soft body knocks into me. I'm so stunned, I fall to the floor.

I blink through the rain, but what I see has the hair on the back of my neck standing on end. Paisley is above me, screaming and crying as she clings to me, almost like she's trying to cover my body. When I look over her shoulder, I roar in agony, and utter panic sets in.

Blaze is standing above her, the metal pole high above his head, ready to come down. I duck my head in to her shoulder, and mustering all the strength I have left, I roll us.

I can't lose her.

Life without Paisley Hayes in it would be a dark and miserable place. If I die to save her life, it will be worth it. *She's* worth dying for.

When I don't feel anything after a few seconds, I chance a look over my shoulder, my eyes widening when I see my dad stomping the fuck out of Blaze. He picks up the pole, and I look away when I hear the distinct sound of Dad shattering Blaze's kneecap.

I'm breathing heavily when I finally lock eyes on Paisley. Her eyes are shut tight, so I lean down, kissing her soft lips. She blinks, looking adorably confused for a second before one huge breath escapes her lungs. She grabs hold of me, pulling me down on top of her. She squeezes the life out of me, and I chuckle.

"Thank you, thank you, thank you. I thought we were dead," she cries out, clinging to me. When she pulls back, I lift my weight off her. She begins to scan every inch of my body, but all I can do is stare at her.

She's okay. She's not harmed. I tell myself that over and over, but all I can see is Blaze standing over her with that pole. One hit and he would have killed her. She's too small and delicate to survive such brutality.

"Are you okay? How badly are you hurt?" she asks, her voice high. I nod, feeling my throat tighten.

Then she shocks the shit out of me when she starts slapping and shoving at my chest. I wince inwardly at the pain.

"Paisley," I whisper.

"Don't ever, *ever*, fucking leave me again. Ever. No more fighting. I don't care if it's a cute little puppy that nipped your ankle. You. Do. Not. Fight."

"Paisley, calm down. I'm fine."

Her eyes widen in disbelief. "You are not fucking fine. You're bleeding all over my new coat, your eye is nearly swollen shut, and I'm pretty sure the number one question you'll be asked is if you're storing food in your cheek like a hamster. You are not fine. None of this is fine," she continues to yell. "And you've reduced me to swearing at you. *Swearing.*"

Someone drops down next to us. Maddox shakes his head at us, pouting. "I hate it when Mum and Dad fight."

I groan as Dad kneels, his face dripping with rain or sweat—likely both. He grins at us.

"Is this a private party or can anyone join?"

I glare at him, but then Maddox starts chuckling. "Slowly repeat that question in your head, Uncle Max."

My dad closes his eyes, and after a few moments, they snap open. He grimaces. "Yeah, it did sound pervy when I said it. Sorry."

Paisley reaches for me, worry creasing her features. "We need to get you to the hospital. And what were you thinking taking on all three?"

"It would have been four," I rasp out. "They shouldn't have underestimated me."

"Please don't do anything like this again. I can't bear the thought of losing you."

"I promise," I whisper, briefly kissing her. She sighs against my lips, not caring she's getting covered in sweat, rain and mud. "I love you."

"Aww, Mummy and Daddy made up," Maddox cheers. I glare up at him, noticing everyone else around me. Shit! With a pain-filled groan, I lift myself off Paisley, swaying slightly on my knees.

"Cops!" is yelled, and I look around as Dad and Maddox quickly reach under my arms to help lift me. Liam steps out of the crowd with Uncle Maverick, and together, they help pull Paisley from the ground. I wince when I take her in because she not only has blood on her, but dirt too.

"Come on, we need to watch this," Dad mutters.

"Dad, I can't be here," I hiss out. If the cops see me like this, then I'll definitely get taken in.

"They don't want you," Dad scoffs. "Not when they've got bigger fish to fry."

I pause mid-step and look at him. "Please don't tell me they're here for Rocco?"

He nods, grinning. "Yep. Although, I don't know whether I'm more relaxed now that I know he's going to jail or whether it's because I took out that dickhead's kneecaps."

I place my hand on his shoulder, panicking. "Dad, I wasn't ready. I haven't got all the information I need."

I might not be able to touch Rocco physically, not with his bodyguards and connections, but it doesn't mean he's untouchable. There's more than one way to skin a cat.

"No, but I do. Just watch," he tells me, resting me against a tree. Most of the cars have gone already. I look around for Benny, not seeing him, and I know it's because he doesn't want the cops seeing his face. So far, he's been able to stay under their radar. I'm grateful, because even though he isn't a law-abiding citizen, he's a good guy.

The police begin to read Rocco his rights. When charges of murder and other shit come up, my eyes widen in disbelief.

"He really killed Rocket?" I ask.

"Yeah, and he wasn't smart about it either. We managed to find footage of him torturing Rocket and then killing him."

Suddenly, Rocco's attention snaps to me. I stand up straighter, even though it kills me to do so.

"You're going to fucking pay for this. Watch your back, Landon. Watch it. Because I'm coming for all of you," he yells, before he begins to laugh, looking crazy as fuck. "You think they have anything to hold me on?"

The officer holding his handcuffs shakes his head. "You do realise we're cops and everything you do say will be given in evidence?"

Rocco starts to shout threats at me as they pull him away to a car.

Dad turns to me, frowning. "He always so fucking cheerful?"

"Dad," I say, my expression softening. He did something I was unable to finish. I shake my head, speechless.

"You're my son. I'd do anything for you," he tells me, then pulls me into a hug. I hiss through my teeth, feeling everything. Paisley moves in closer when Dad pulls back, looking away when his eyes begin to shine with tears.

"Sir, we're going to have to take you in," an officer says, stepping into our little group.

Uncle Maverick gives the cop a murderous look. The cop shrinks back, looking at all of us before looking at me.

"We need you to come with us."

I jump when Dad begins to wail, flapping his arms around. "They kidnapped my son, and you're telling me he's being arrested?"

"Kidnapped?" the cop says, looking at me warily.

Dad begins to cry louder, clutching his chest. "We've been looking for him… for ages. A long time. And we've got him back."

"That isn't what the gentlemen we've arrested are saying. They say that you are the ring leader."

I don't say anything, letting Dad deal with it. He has a knack for talking his way out of shit. Times like this, it's best to keep quiet.

Dad gasps in outrage. "How dare they! They stripped him of his clothes," he yells, pointing at my half naked body. "The shirt off his back, sir. He was made to fight for his life. His life!"

Another cop steps up, catching the last bit of what Dad is spouting off. "Sir, we won't be arresting your…"

Dad sniffles. "My son. My only son."

The cop's gaze turns to Liam, then to me, his lips twitching. "Well, uh, your son won't be arrested, but we do need him to come down and answer a few of our questions. My boss called and said you helped get these men off the streets tonight. We've been trying to get something on Rocco for years."

Dad's chest puffs out. "My wife said I should have become a cop, ya know. Or was it she wanted me to dress up as a cop?" he asks, tapping his chin. He sighs, shaking his head. "I don't know. I've dressed up from Tarzan to that Grey dude in a suit."

"Dad," Liam and I groan.

The cop chuckles, stroking a hand over his beard. "Why don't you take your son to the hospital. We can meet you there to get a statement. But you will need to come down and sign them tomorrow."

I nod. "Yes, sir."

He gives me one parting glance before walking off. Paisley steps away and begins to shiver. Her bottom lip starts quivering when she takes in my injuries. I go to reach for her, but she puts her hand up, stopping me.

"I feel sick," she says, right before her eyes roll.

I move, catching her, and cry out when I feel my injuries being pulled.

I quickly scan everyone to find Jaxon already rushing towards me. He chuckles when he checks her pulse.

"She's passed out. I think the excitement got too much for her."

"She doesn't do that in the bedroom, right?" Maddox asks. Both me and Jaxon growl at him, and he wisely backs away with his palms facing us. "Joke. It was a joke."

"You sure?" I ask Jaxon.

He nods. "Yeah, but I'll check her glucose in the car."

I push the loose strands that have fallen over her face away. "I don't want to leave her, but she needs to go home and rest. Will you tell her I'll be there as soon as I can?"

Jaxon snorts, taking Paisley gently from my arms. "Not a chance, buddy. I'm bringing her to the hospital. I'm hoping when I tell her you wanted to send her home, she'll forgive me for not listening."

My vision begins to blur when I try to stand back up. "Here, let me help," Dad and Uncle Maverick say.

"I'm fine," I tell them, but it's not true. My legs feel like jelly and my head is throbbing.

Malik stands in front of me, smirking. "One, two..."

His voice fades into nothing when everything goes dark.

EPILOGUE

PAISLEY

A WEEK HAS PASSED SINCE THE FIGHT, but it still plays on my mind constantly. For a few moments, I thought I would lose Landon. I thought I was going to die myself. Thankfully, he promised it would be his last organised fight, but he couldn't promise to never fight again. He was a Carter, after all.

I still can't believe we both passed out. I eventually woke up in the hospital. My glucose levels were high when Jaxon took my readings, but other than that, I was fine. They just put me in a bed until I woke up.

Landon managed to come away with only a few bruised ribs and superficial wounds. He only needed stiches for the gash on his arm. He was lucky that was all he had. From my point of view, some of those hits he took looked life threatening.

Once I found out the extent of his injuries, I forgave Jaxon for taking me away. It also helped that he sat in Landon's room with him while Max went out to meet Landon's mum downstairs.

Still, I never wanted to witness anything so brutal ever again. I still break out in a cold sweat anytime I hear something that sounds close to a bone breaking. Even the rain makes me want to puke now.

My focus is switched from last week to now as people bustle about the foyer. A smile lights up my face when two kids run away from their parents and head outside.

The place is full, booked to capacity, and I couldn't be happier. Even with the long, busy hours, I wouldn't change a thing. It's been great, and everyone who's stayed so far have been lovely and made the place feel homey.

A figure steps aside from the door when someone comes barging inside. I'm surprised to see Charlotte.

"Charlotte?" I call out, worried when she looks close to tears. "What's wrong?"

She clutches her jacket tighter around her, looking around the space with a wary expression as she rushes towards me.

"Hayden said to get out more. I've been missing Landon a lot. I was so used to spending all my time with him. And I'm not trying to make you feel bad. Please don't feel bad," she rushes out, and I can hear her struggling not to cry.

"Charlotte, it's fine. Calm down and tell me what happened."

She goes on like I didn't speak. "So, me and Madison went out for a drink. We don't normally drink, but she was stressed, and I was missing Landon. We got drunk, and as we were walking past the park, I wanted to see the ducks that attacked Aiden. It seemed like a good idea at the time."

She trails off, biting her bottom lip. "That sounds really nice. Did you do anything else?"

She looks up at me, her eyes watering, before she bursts into tears. I go to reach for her, worried something terrible happened to them, but when I move forward, she relaxes her hold on her jacket, and a head pops out.

What the fuck?

"I stole a duck! I don't remember much from last night, but I remember it getting picked on. I kept thinking it looked sad. Really sad. And I didn't want it to be sad. So I brought him home. And now the police are going to find out and arrest me. I don't want to be arrested," she cries hysterically. "I was going to see if your mum could look after him, maybe hide him out on the farm. I can't ask Faith. She can't find out. Beau's a police officer. He might turn me in."

I have to bite the insides of my cheeks to stop myself from laughing. No wonder she looks rough. Her kindness is something else. I've never met anyone, other than Lily, with a heart like hers.

I reach over to her, rubbing my hand up and down her arm. "Hey, it's okay. Everything is going to be okay," I tell her soothingly. "Mum can keep her on the farm, it's no problem. And no one needs to find out."

"I don't want to get your mum arrested," she sniffles.

"No one will get into trouble with the police. They would have rescued him themselves if they saw him being bullied. It's what they do," I tell her, trying not to laugh at how ridiculous I sound.

When her shoulders relax, I relax. She beams up at me like I've given her the world, and it melts my heart. I can see the tension and stress were becoming too much for her.

"You're so right. They would. Thank you, Paisley. I knew I could come to you for help."

I smile back at her. "Let's go and see my mum."

"Aren't you busy?" she asks, biting her lip worriedly.

I gesture outside. "The staff have everything covered, I promise."

"Okay," she agrees in a small voice.

We step outside to find Landon parking up.

"Oh no," Charlotte whispers.

He looks up at us, confused for a minute, his gaze going from Charlotte and back to me. I notice Charlotte discreetly step behind me a little, pulling the jacket tighter around her body.

"What are you hiding in your coat?" Landon asks, his voice rough and sexy. Even with all his bruises, he still looks hot as ever. They look a lot better than they did a week ago.

I shake my head subtly, warning him not to push when Charlotte squeaks behind me. Ignoring me, he gives her that stare. The one that means, 'don't lie to me'.

She inhales, then without taking a breath, her words rush out, confessing what she's done. He just stands stock-still, his hands shoved into his coat pockets, his expression blank.

When she's finished, she takes in a deep breath and watches him closely. "So now you know what I've done," she whispers, sounding so ashamed. I have to reach out to her, giving her a side hug.

His eyes widen for a split second, before he bursts out laughing. He doesn't laugh often, but when he does, everything around me disappears and I file away the image in my mind, so I can cherish it. He takes my breath away when he laughs.

"And now what are you going to do with it?" he asks when he sobers. She bites her bottom lip, her eyes flicking to me. "You? Where are we gonna put a duck?"

I laugh at his expression. "No, we're going to take it to Mum. She'll love him."

He grins, looking over at Mum's place. "Let's go."

I step into his arms, watching him curiously. I know he loves my mum, but he's never been eager to go there when he knows my brothers are always hanging around at this time.

"What are you up to?" I ask as we begin the walk down the lane.

"Nothing," he tells me, kissing my temple. I sigh, walking with him. Charlotte walks ahead, talking quietly down at the duck. "I can't believe she stole a duck."

Chuckling, I silently agree. "She looked ready to hand herself in to the police."

He sighs, shaking his head. "She's special. People think she's dumb, but she's really fucking clever. What she lacks is social cues. She doesn't get them.

She's kept a secret about herself for so long, and I know it's killing her inside. She acts guilty around the others. I've told her what she does in her spare time has fuck all to do with them, but she doesn't see it like that."

What secret does Charlotte have that she wouldn't want the others knowing? It's going to bug me, but I know better than anyone not to pry.

"She's incredible. When she told you what happened, she missed out the fact she did it because she's missing you."

"She stole a duck for me?" he asks in a low voice.

I look up at him and shake my head. "No. She's been missing you. I think she felt lonely, so your sister told her to get out more."

His jaw clenches when I mention his sister, but I also see a flash of guilt. "I need to spend some time with her.

"Oh my gosh," Charlotte squeaks.

I glance up, seeing her looking over at Hayes Removals. Following her line of sight, my eyes widen.

"What on earth?" I whisper in horror.

Landon begins to chuckle, pulling out his phone to hit record. "I didn't know they went this far."

I watch him, my mouth still gaping open. "You knew?"

His attention briefly flicks to me. He nods, then turns back to the clusterfuck of a van.

One of the removal vans has a massive light pole sticking out of it. How did they get the light from ground? Or did they put the van over the light?

I squint my eyes, but nope, the light at the top of the pole isn't damaged. How in the world…

"Why does it say, 'we take it, big or small,'" Charlotte asks, tilting her head to the side.

I look again, and she's right. Instead of the usual slogan, 'We pack it all, big or small,' it says that.

"How?" I ask, to no one in particular.

Landon's hand squeezes my hip. "Don't ask questions you don't want the answers to."

"But—"

"Nope," he chuckles.

"Here we go," Charlotte sings, jumping on the balls of her feet. The duck begins to fuss, and she starts cooing soft words at it.

My mind is on Jaxon and the others as they pile out of the building. Landon chuckles, holding his phone up and recording the whole thing.

Jaxon starts yelling, his hands gripped behind his head. The others, at first, looked shell-shocked, but slowly, one by one, they all begin to curse up a storm.

Mum must hear the commotion, because from the corner of my eye, I see her walking towards us.

"Did Maddox do this?" I ask Landon.

He nods, grinning at me. "He just wanted to welcome them to the family. And payback. Since me and your brothers have been getting along, I stayed out of it."

"But Jaxon needs that van," I tell him nervously, not wanting to let our family come between us. But this is their livelihood.

His expression softens, and he reaches out to cup my cheek. I love it when he holds me like this. It makes me feel small, delicate and cared for.

"Baby," he whispers, and I can feel his body press up against me. I open my eyes, looking up into his dark brown ones. "When they've calmed down enough, they'll probably figure out it's the van from around the back."

"The one that's broke?" I ask, relaxing against him.

"Yes. We swapped them over," he tells me. "I promised we wouldn't fuck with their business and I meant it."

"I'm sorry."

He grins. "Don't be. You can make it up to me."

I bite my bottom lip, but there's no denying the heat swirling between my legs. "I can't. I've got guests."

He glances at me, then looks over my head. "Mrs Hayes, Paisley isn't feeling well. She's going to take the rest of the day off. Can you watch the bed and breakfast?"

"Of course. Hope you feel better soon," she calls out in amusement.

"You okay?" he asks, and I know he's talking to Charlotte.

I hear the laughter in her voice when she says, "Yes, but you might not be. The Hayes brothers are on their way over. Jaxon looks seriously angry—or constipated. It's hard to tell from here," she rambles on.

I groan into Landon's chest and it vibrates under me. "Best be off then," he calls, and in one swift movement, I'm up over his shoulder.

"Landon," I squeal, but begin to laugh when he starts running, with me still over his shoulder. My brothers are yelling at him to stop, but he doesn't.

Gripping the belt on his jeans, I glance up. My brothers all stop when they reach Mum, their hands flying around as they talk.

My lips spread into a wide smile because life can't get any better than this. If someone had told me a few months back that I'd be this happy, I would have grunted and carried on with my boring old life.

Now, it's filled to the brim with happiness and joy. Every night, I fall asleep wrapped up in the man of my dreams, and when I wake, he's right there beside me, making every day perfect.

Life is bliss.

Life is good.

Our love is epic.

AUTHOR'S NOTE

I'd like to say a few things, but first, I can't thank you enough for being patient with me when it came to Landon. The responses to his character were just overwhelming, and at times, hilariously funny.

If you're wondering who is next, then I'm sorry, it's top secret once again. Okay, I lie. I know who is going to be next, but then another story for another Carter called out to me. I'm debating what to do. LOL

I really hope Landon's book was worth the wait, and that you've fallen in love with his character as much as I have.

Thank you, from the bottom of my heart, to all my readers; old and new.

I also have to give a massive shout out to my kids, Paige, Ellie and Mckenzie. This year has been really tough for me, but they've kept me going. They've given me time to complete the last four books, which were all released closer together than any of my other books. There's been a lot of sleepless nights.

Stephanie, thank you once again for editing another book. You're one busy lady, so I'm grateful when you take the time to answer questions, read something over, or listen to my rantings when I can't figure something out. You go above and beyond, for which I'm thankful.

PS, I'm still freaked out over you crushing on Jason Voorhees.

Readers, as always, you ROCK!

If you loved Landon, please leave a review on Amazon, Goodreads, Nook, or Kobo. Every little review helps.

OTHER TITLES BY LISA HELEN GRAY

ABOUT THE AUTHOR

Lisa Helen Gray is Amazon's best-selling author of the Forgotten Series and the Carter Brothers series.

She loves hanging out, but most of all, curling up with a good book or watching movies. When she's not being a mum, she's a writer and a blogger.

She loves writing romance novels with a HEA and has a thing for alpha males.

I mean, who doesn't!

Just an ordinary girl surrounded by extraordinary books.

Printed in Great Britain
by Amazon

45191385R00175